HER EVIL WAYS

ALYSON LARRABEE

WHISKEY CREEK PRESS
www.whiskeycreekpress.com

Anne,
For a fellow author and
literature enthusiast,

Alyson Larrabee ♡

Published by
WHISKEY CREEK PRESS
Whiskey Creek Press
PO Box 51052
Casper, WY 82605-1052
www.whiskeycreekpress.com

eISBN: 978-1-63355-684-3
Print ISBN: 978-1-63355-757-4

Cover Artist: Nancy Donahue
Editor: Dave Field
Printed in the United States of America

Dedication

For my support team: Kathleen, Lois, Nicole, Mary,
Amy, Kelli and Maura
Thanks for "getting me" and putting up with me.

Chapter 1

Losing Sucks

Eastfield High's soccer team lost today. Hence, we're out of the playoffs and the season's over. My best friend Meg and I watched it all happen from the opposing team's bleachers. My boyfriend, Wyatt Silver, missed a key goal. He's gonna be pissed at himself for a long time.

As usual, when the right wing passed him the ball, Wyatt charged toward the goal like a heat-seeking missile. The ball hit his left foot and he shot, sky-rocketing it over the goal, somewhere into outer space. That thing's still zooming around in the stratosphere. No one's ever gonna find it.

With ten seconds left on the clock, the other team's center-forward scored the only point in the game. Meg's boyfriend, Ryan Snyder, was in goal when it happened. He dove for the ball and missed.

After Ryan failed to stop the shot, Meg glanced at me and shook her head. "Ryan looks pretty pissed off."

"Bollocks." My brother Clem is planning to spend a semester abroad next fall, in Australia. He's started saying "bollocks" a lot.

"What the hell does that mean, Annabelle?"

"It means balls. In Australian."

"Disgusting. Speak English, please."

"There'll be no joy in Mudville tonight."

"Now what the hell are you talking about?"

"The mighty *Casey at the Bat*. It's a line from a famous poem about a baseball player who strikes out in a clutch moment during an important game."

"What did the mighty Casey's girlfriend do when that happened?"

"She probably stayed out of his way for a couple of days until he started acting human again. Wyatt and Ryan are gonna be pissed off for a while."

"So we should keep out of their way."

"Right. Who wants to hang out with a couple of Debbie downers?"

"Not me. Come over to my house. We can watch a couple of rom coms. Eat some Lean Cuisines. Maybe I'll bake some cookies."

Meg's mom is always on a diet so she never cooks. That's why Meg wants to be a pastry chef when she grows up. Her only hope for decent desserts at home has always been to make them herself. She's already been accepted early action to the best culinary school in New England: Johnson and Wales.

"Sounds good. I'll be over later." Suddenly, I feel my phone vibrate and whip it out of my pocket. A text from Wyatt.

"F*** my life☹." I show it to Meg.

She pulls out her phone, slides the screen open and tilts it so I can read the message. "Life sucks☹."

Unnecessarily, she explains, "From Ryan."

"Looks like it's Lean Cuisines, chocolate chunk macadamia nut cookies and Jennifer Aniston movies for you and me tonight." I put my arm around Meg's shoulders.

"Yup. See you around seven."

When I get to Meg's, our friend Jen's there too and we pop one Lean Cuisine at a time into the microwave; heating up eight of them altogether. Meg and I eat three each and Jen calls it a meal at two. She's trying to drop five pounds. We save the incredible smelling, just-out-of-the-oven cookies for during the movie.

"Any word from the self-loathing-slash-pity party?" I haven't heard from Wyatt since his postgame text.

"Nope they're out drowning in a sea of misery together; I'm sure."

"Whenever Wyatt's depressed he watches *Saving Private Ryan*."

"I hate war movies." Jen says what we're all thinking.

"I'll drink to that." Raising my diet soda, I clink cans with my two best buddies and then take in a big gulp. "Ew! Don't you have anything besides this stuff? It tastes like alligator pee."

"And what exactly does alligator pee taste like, Annabelle?"

"Thankfully, I have no idea. It's just something my dad says."

"Your dad's hilarious."

"Angela Curran thinks he's hot."

"That's gross. He's my dad."

"He built the Curran's house."

"Duh! I know that. It doesn't give her permission to say weird awkward things about him."

"I'll drink to that." Jen laughs.

"Here we go again with the alligator pee." Meg clinks her can with mine.

"I'm putting the movie on, chicas. It's one I've seen before, but never get tired of."

We grab some cookies, head down to Jen's finished basement and slide the first feature of our Jennifer Aniston film festival into the DVD player. For about a half hour, the three of us sit there, laughing our asses off. But soon we're all hungry again. The Lean Cuisines were pretty good, but not nearly enough. So we pause the movie, run into the kitchen, grab another plateful of cookies and then return to the cinematic trials and tribulations of our fave celeb.

Meg announces, "If Jennifer went to our school she'd be part of our group."

"Duh. She's like forty."

"If she went to our school and she was our age." Meg rolls her eyes.

Around midnight, right before heading home, I check my phone. No word from Wyatt. He must be unbelievably depressed. Usually he texts me about five hundred times a day when we're not actually hanging out together in person.

I start to feel anxious.

Chapter 2

WTF

Wyatt must be really upset about the soccer game because he's still not answering his phone and the whole disaster went down yesterday. How much time will he need to get over it? After ten unanswered calls, I give up trying to reach him because his stupid voicemail message makes me wanna gag.

"Hey, this is Wyatt. Say something if you feel like it."

I leave him the lamest sounding message ever. "I feel like it. Call me."

Ten calls in twenty-four hours and he still hasn't picked up; I switch to texting. Again and again. Starting to panic, I resort to stalking him.

When I drive by his house, his car's in the driveway. Why the hell isn't he answering his phone? Wyatt!

* * * *

After two days of trying to contact him, I stop. Maybe we're breaking up and I'm clueless about it. I have no way of knowing how he feels, though, because he won't talk to me.

I decide to take a week off. Stop calling him. Stop texting him. Start playing hard to get. Except I don't think it's going to work because Wyatt isn't trying to "get" me.

* * * *

Finally, my week of not calling Wyatt, but merely thinking about him twenty-four/seven, is over. If I were a nail biter, I would have completely devoured my nails off of my fingertips by now. My wretched fingers would end in bloody naked nubs. But I'm not a nail biter, so only my feelings are painful and wretched. My nails are fine. I examine my normal-looking nails and promise myself I'll try one more text. If he doesn't answer, I'm giving up for good.

One more attempt. Pathetic and emotionally needy. "Call me so we can talk, please. We've both been thru a lot together. I miss U."

Still no response.

Now what? Legit real life/real time stalking didn't work too well for me, so I decide to try cyber-stalking: anything to relieve the stress. Wyatt has a Facebook page, a Twitter and an Instagram. Maybe he posted something online. Grabbing my laptop, I flip it open and start with FB. His profile pic is still one of him and me together, goofing around in my basement. I'd just beaten him in ping pong for the millionth time and he's holding up my hand, with the paddle still in it, as if I were the winner of a championship boxing match. He hasn't posted a new status in months, which doesn't surprise me. Wyatt's not much of a social networker. When I click "About", on his timeline, it still says, "In a relationship with Annabelle Blake."

Okay, so that's good. After sucking in a deep breath and then exhaling slowly, I switch back to my own FB page and think about changing my profile pic to one of Wyatt and me together. Maybe he'll see it and start thinking about the good old days when we were a couple. Right now it's a photograph my brother Clement took of me when I was heading toward the finish line in a race. Full speed ahead. Nah. I'm keeping it. I'm proud of that moment. Even I have my limits when it comes to emotional neediness.

In real life I have about seven friends. On Facebook I have eight hundred and fifty-nine. Who are these people? I start scrolling through my news feed, reading the statuses of eight hundred and fifty-two people I don't care about. It's too boring so I start obsessing about Wyatt again. When I check his Twitter and his Instagram, I find out that they've also been sitting idle for a long time. At least there are no bad surprises. I switch to FML, which always makes me laugh, plus it could also be the title of my autobiography.

An hour later Wyatt still hasn't texted me back. Doesn't he miss me too? Doesn't he at least owe me a break-up text? Every morning, first period, we have History class together, but he's moved from the desk next to mine to a seat across the room. I think he did it just to avoid me but I haven't called him out face to face on it. The only place we see each other is in school and I don't want to cause a scene. That would only make everything worse. He has to answer his phone soon. I can't take it much longer.

Maybe food will help. The odors wafting up from the kitchen smell incredible. Roasting meat, garlic, butter. If I were a dog, I'd start drooling. Hanging my head, I wander downstairs to see what my mother's making for dinner.

Standing silently on the bottom step, I watch my parents for about a minute. They're sitting at the kitchen table with their heads together; the candlelight softens my mother's profile and reflects off what's left of my father's silver hair. As she leans closer to him, one of my mother's tangled curls slips loose and brushes against his cheek. He tucks it back behind her left ear and smiles. If she wants to talk quietly, she has to sit really close to him. He's old and getting kinda deaf.

The delicate scent of lavender mixed with orange peel drifts out from the candles' aura; even the powerful smells of garlic and roast chicken can't obliterate it. I know what my Mom's up to. She makes her own candles and teas from herbs and flowers she grows herself. With the right combinations, she can change your mood. Lavender and orange peel are supposed to calm people down but the candles aren't working for me. As I walk closer, Mom stops talking to Dad and looks up.

"Hi, honey, I roasted a chicken and made garlic mashed potatoes, too. Are you hungry?"

I want to answer her, but no words come out when I open my mouth because my lungs have filled up with sadness and I'm drowning. A flood rises up from my chest and begins dribbling out of my eyes. Squeezing them closed, I try to stop the deluge but fail. The first sob escapes before I can gulp it back down. Then my self-control bursts open and a monsoon of misery explodes out of my body, blows across our kitchen and washes away everyone's hope for a normal, peaceful Sunday night. Mom leaps out of her chair and pulls me into her arms. I can't see the look she's sending Dad over my shoulder, but it gets rid of him fast, even though there's a giant serving bowl of potatoes and a roast chicken sitting on the counter. Dad loves Sunday supper and I'm screwing it up. Thinking about this makes me feel even worse. So I don't look up from the growing wet spot on Mom's shoulder. I just keep on soaking her sweater with my tears.

"Wyatt won't answer my calls. He won't text me back. He hates me and I miss him."

"He doesn't hate you."

"He hates me. I know it and you know it."

"This isn't like you, honey. Stay positive. He's only a boy."

She knows damn well that Wyatt Silver isn't only a boy. She knows there will never be anyone else like him ever. Just in case she hasn't figured it out yet, I croak through my hysteria, "There will never be anyone else like him ever!"

"I know, Annabelle. I know. Maybe he'll get over whatever it is."

"How will I know what it is if he doesn't tell me?"

"Maybe it has something to do with Anthony leaving."

"Do you think it's because I kissed Anthony?"

She puts her hands on my shoulders and nudges me away from her, just a few inches, so she can look at my face. "You kissed Anthony?"

"Only once, right before he left. Do you think that's why Wyatt broke up with me?"

"Wyatt's the only person who can answer that question. I'm not going to make any wild guesses."

"He seemed okay the day we said goodbye to Anthony. Then the next day they lost their soccer game. He can't blame me for that, though. It wasn't my fault."

"So maybe it does have something to do with Anthony."

"What if later on, you know, after the game, he was in a really bad mood because they lost and then he kept thinking about Anthony kissing me and decided he was really pissed off?"

"I'm not going to play the 'What if?' game with you. Try to calm down."

"If Wyatt kissed someone else, I wouldn't forgive him."

"Maybe you would if the person he kissed was dead."

I stop crying for a second to laugh at how ridiculous that sounds.

Then Mom tilts my chin up and looks into my eyes. "There are no rules in the relationship handbook for love triangles where one of the boys is a ghost and the other one is a medium and they both inhabit the same body."

I dig a tissue out of the pocket of my mother's jeans, blow my nose into it and then put it back in her pocket. She laughs. "Thanks."

"Hey, my snot is your snot."

My mother has been wiping my nose since I was born so it doesn't gross her out. Dabbing at my tears with a clean tissue, she says. "Maybe after he thinks about it for a while, he'll forgive you."

My sobs finally die down to a quiet sniffle or two. "Yeah, he can't keep up this level of jealousy indefinitely. Wyatt has to realize that I'll never see Anthony again. Ever." Thinking about Anthony makes me feel like exploding into tears all over again, but I try to control myself.

"Annabelle, you're going to feel sad for a while. It's going to hurt a lot at first, but then you'll feel the pain ease up; a little at a time. Life's hard and you have to be strong and get through it. People die. Sometimes you lose someone you love."

"He was already dead when I met him."

"You know what I mean. He was dead but not gone. Now he's gone."

"Do I look like I need to be reminded that Anthony's gone?"

"No, you look like you need some chicken and potatoes." She hands me yet another tissue. "Blow your nose and then go into the den and tell your father it's safe to come out here now. He won't drown in a flood of tears."

"Not funny." I smile anyway and leave to get my dad. Then we sit down to eat and talk about stupid stuff. Like the weather and which of my friends has applied to which college and a house my dad's trying to finish building before the really cold winter weather sets in and the first snow falls. I feel okay for a while. I'm still sad, but I'm not weeping uncontrollably anymore.

* * * *

Monday morning Wyatt comes in late and misses History class. The school day drags on until it feels like a year has passed by, but it's really only seven of the most boring hours of my life because I don't get to see him at all. Finally the dismissal bell rings. Cross country season's over and I don't play a winter sport, so I have plenty of free time until tennis starts in the early spring. Not good. I need to keep busy so I don't sit around feeling sorry for myself because of "The Big Breakup."

Toward the middle of February, and into March, I usually take a few indoor tennis lessons to get ready for the spring when I'll play first doubles with my friend Steph on the varsity tennis team. But it's only December, so I don't even have that release. I'm not scheduled to take out my frustration by whacking tennis balls as hard as I can for at least another couple of months.

Toward the end of the fall, I was worried about a situation involving a ghost named Anthony. He was obsessed with me. Wyatt, who was my boyfriend at the time, is a medium. He channeled Anthony's ghost and then couldn't get rid of him. Anthony kept taking possession of Wyatt's body because he wanted to be with me. At first it was pretty horrifying but once Wyatt and I got used to Anthony, the three of us became inseparable.

Together we solved the mystery of Anthony's death so he could leave. Our ghost finally found the answers to the questions he needed to ask here on Earth and headed out of our lives for good; back where he belongs. Wyatt and I should've felt relieved, but we both had grown to love

Anthony and we both still miss him. At least I think Wyatt misses him, but I don't know because he won't talk to me. At all. Ever.

Wyatt broke up with me, without a word: no phone call, no text. I miss him horribly. Maybe I need to get out there and pound through the woods with the wind in my hair, at the mercy of the New England weather. Nothing better than freezing, pelting rain in your face. I love feeling like there's something infinitely more powerful and inevitable than my will. But I can run through it. Tackle the forces of nature head-on. If you complain about the weather in New England, you'll spend the whole winter complaining and whining about something you can't do anything to change. You may as well admire it for its craziness and the way it makes you stronger just to deal with it. But all this is beside the point now. My life stinks because Wyatt broke up with me, not because cross country season is over.

Along with this horrifying problem, I have another one. The whole school knows I'm the girl with the broken heart.

Poor Annabelle, she looks so lonely and sad. Next to "humiliation" in the dictionary, my senior year book picture should be displayed. That picture was taken last summer, right after Matt Riley dumped me. I managed a believably happy smile for the photographer and then I got over Matt. He's a douche bag. Wyatt isn't. I'll always love him. I'll never get over him.

On top of my pile of hurt lies a ton of embarrassment, too. I know what people are saying. Even some of the jealous girls who were mean to me when Wyatt and I were together feel pity for me now. I miss the nastiness, the evil sideways glances, the whispers, the occasional hurtful insult delivered in the hall on the way to class. I prefer their hatred to their pity. Everyone knows I'm pathetic.

Two nights after the episode of Sunday evening pre-dinner hysteria, my dad arrives home from work and announces that he has a surprise. Looking up from the plate of lasagna I'm picking at, I ask, "What?"

Dad bends over and puts one arm around me and one arm around Mom, who's sitting beside me at the kitchen table. He smells like sawdust and the cold, clean night air. With one strong forearm, he scrunches my head up against his face and kisses my cheek. Turning his head the other way, he kisses my mother on the lips which is awkward, so I pretend I didn't see. Then he straightens up, runs over to the door and goes back outside. Mom and I look at each other and shrug.

A few seconds later, he stumbles back in, lugging a huge box. I rush over to help him.

Grinning at Mom, he announces, "An elliptical, for my girls. I'll set it up in front of the TV in the den and we can all use it. Low impact exercise, good for cross training and the elderly who are fighting off osteoporosis, arthritis and cardio vascular disease."

"Speak for yourself, Gramps." My mother sounds sarcastic but I can tell by the glimmer in her eyes that she loves the surprise. "Grab your coat, Annabelle. We're going shopping."

"For what?"

"We're going to buy things we don't need with money we don't have, the best kind of shopping. Your dad can assemble the elliptical while we're gone and we'll take turns using it when we get back."

I pull my brother Joe's huge sweatshirt off the peg by the back door and yank it over my head and Mom and I run out to the car, giggling like high school girls, which is normal for me because I am one. We skip over to the mom-mobile, known as "the Soob", short for Subaru. She loves that car because it has heated front seats.

People's cars can tell you a lot about them. Because he's a builder and he needs it for his business, my dad drives a truck. I drive my brother Clement's old 1998 Chevy Prizm which sends the message that I'm broke and should be grateful I have anything at all to drive. I am grateful, too. It beats walking or riding a bike. And my mom's car says *I like to be safe and comfortable* because that's what she's all about.

She laughs and turns to me. "Why don't you drive, Annabelle? The Burkes look like they could use a new mailbox anyway. Their old one's all rusty and dented."

"Very funny." When I first learned how to drive, I hugged the right too much and once, I damaged the passenger side mirror when I sideswiped our neighbor's mailbox. But only once. Dad made me buy them a new mailbox and pay for the mirror, too. That was over a year ago, though, and I'm a good driver now, so we head for the nearest mall together with me at the wheel of the Forester, and her riding shot gun; our butts nice and cozy in the heated seats.

When we get there, Mom takes out the credit card and we load up on DVDs to watch while we're on the elliptical, about five movies altogether, plus two seasons of television shows. Most of our purchases come from the bargain display, but we choose a couple of new releases, too.

Then we go into another store and I pick out some already ripped jeans that look really sexy on me. Mom makes not one comment about them, either, but I can tell she's bursting to say something about the holes or the tight fit. She allows herself one understated eye roll. My mother is an excellent role model for self-control. Grinning into the triple full-length mirrors, I check out my rear view which looks awesome. Nothing can mend the rip in my heart, but the holes in the jeans cheer me up tremendously. As I walk down the hall at school tomorrow, strategic glimpses of knee and thigh will peep through, but nothing important will be on display. I know how to walk that fine line between sexy and desperate. I have never crossed over it and I never will. I may be pathetic, but I'm not skanky.

When we arrive home, I get the first turn on our new exercise machine. And according to the digital display, I run five miles while watching back-to-back hilarious episodes from *The Office, Season Two*. Afterward I take a long, steamy shower, and then run back downstairs to kiss my dad's cheek. "Best dad ever!" I announce. He laughs and wishes me pleasant dreams. I sleep pretty well. Plus, for the next few nights, I also manage to sleep well. I'm actually starting to believe that Wyatt and I will get back together.

I hope it's soon because the weekends are particularly tough. My best friends are all in relationships. The six of us used to hang out together on

Friday and Saturday nights when I was dating Wyatt, but not anymore. My friend Meg is in a long term relationship with Wyatt's friend Ryan Snyder, the goalie on the soccer team. And my other two closest friends, Jen and Connor, have moved from the friend zone into the relationship zone. So I call Steph, my tennis partner, to see if she's doing anything and she comes over to slay me at ping pong. I start to feel even more depressed because I could always kill Wyatt at ping pong and he didn't care. He thought it was funny. What a guy, not self-centered or egotistical at all! Anyway, I barely survive another weekend without him.

Monday morning, Meg meets me in the school parking lot wearing a serious expression on her wind-reddened face. Her eyes are watering from the cold and her long blond hair's all tangled around her head. "Annabelle."

She looks horrifically serious which can't be good. "I have to tell you now, before you go into History class. It's hard for me to say this, but you need to hear it from me, not from someone who's just spreading around gossip."

Suddenly, I feel like my heart is attached to a bungee cord. Plunging off a tall bridge, it falls into the pit of my stomach and springs back up again, like it wants to jump out of my mouth. Because my uncontrollable heart is now stuck in my throat, I'm unable to speak, so I use my eyes to ask Meg about the bad news. I know it will involve Wyatt.

"This might be just a rumor, but a lot of people are saying that Wyatt and Colleen Foley are together now."

Hanging my hopes on the phrase, "might be just a rumor", I assure Meg that I'll be okay.

Like always, she has my back. "If it's true, he's an idiot. She's ridiculous. She's so fake. He'll hate her in a week if he's the person we thought we knew."

That's a pretty big "if". Maybe Wyatt isn't the person I thought I knew. Maybe he has fallen in love with somebody else, somebody who's a good-looking phony, someone who's superficial. Colleen Foley's been coming on to him since the beginning of September on the first day of school. I don't know her very well, but you can't go to Eastfield High and not know who she is. She's the president of multiple organizations; always running around the school squealing and hugging people. No one would ever vote for me for anything, because I'm too weird. I really wanted to be tennis captain, but someone else got it. Colleen Foley wins every election she ever runs in, and she runs for president of everything.

Colleen must be smart, because she's president of the honor society, but she's always screaming and laughing really loud, which seems stupid to me. I've never hung out with her, nor would I want to. But I always see her in the hallways and a lot of other places around the school. Her group of friends all behave the same way. They're the hottest girls in the school, and last year, when we were juniors, Colleen started the rumor that she only dated college boys.

However, this past spring, she took a quick break from older boys to flirt with my friend Connor. He couldn't believe his good luck and asked her to prom, where she ignored him the whole night. After that she continued to ignore him. She only needed him for one night and he looked good in the prom photos, so she achieved her goal. Obviously, in hindsight, we all figured out that whatever college boy she'd been hooking up with didn't want to go to a high school prom with her. Connor hates her now, but he still thinks she's hot. Everyone does. At the beginning of senior year she made sure everyone knew that she still only dated college boys but she was willing to make an exception for Wyatt Silver if he was interested in her.

Colleen's tall, with a year-round tan and a big white smile. She has shiny, shoulder-length blond hair which hardly ever shows its dark roots. And the very day I find out she might be dating the boy I love, she's everywhere. Whenever I leave a class, there she is, talking to one of her friends in that high, loud voice, flashing those big, white teeth like a sleek, fast-swimming shark.

I ask for a bathroom pass in English class, and when I come out of the stall, she's brushing her hair and putting on lip gloss in the mirror. Her roots need a touch-up. About a half inch of dark hair is showing, but I'm not going to tell her. Let her figure it out for herself. I'm not going to do Colleen Foley any favors. After washing my hands quickly, I flee without ever looking over to acknowledge her.

Finally, one of the worse days of my life is almost over and I head out to my car, my little old 1998 metallic beige Chevy Prizm. Colleen drives a brand new Lexus SUV. What does her car say about her? *My parents are rich enough to buy me this car. I feel entitled to stuff like this and I'm president of every effing organization in this whole effing school.*

Putting my head down, so I won't have to make eye contact with her if she's in the parking lot, I take my car keys out and move fast. Also, it's freezing and windy. Crouching down with my back to the wind, I struggle to fit my key into the lock on the passenger side. The Prizm is so old and so cheap that it doesn't have keyless entry.

"Annabelle," a familiar voice shouts out my name. It sounds so good the way he says it.

Before I can straighten up from my bent-over position, a huge rough tongue licks my face. "Jeff!" I kiss the big, handsome dog back, on the top of his furry head. I've never been so glad to see anyone before in my whole life. Pocketing my keys, I race Jeff over to the van, a few parking spaces past my car. Nathaniel Flyte is sitting there in his electric wheelchair. Grabbing both my freezing cold hands in his big warm ones, he tries to rub away the chill. As I stare into his heavenly eyes, I catch a glimpse of hell in my peripheral vision.

There they are. It wasn't just a rumor, as I had hoped. Wyatt and Colleen Foley are standing outside his car and she's looking into his face and flipping her hair around, laughing. The sight of them together rolls me over like a rogue wave and drags me out to sea on a riptide of misery. Nathaniel turns his head to see what's changed my happy-to-see-you expression into a horrified mask of despair.

Reaching up, he hooks one hand around my neck and pulls my face down to his, so my hair falls all around us, forming a dark, silky tent. With my forehead pressed against Nathaniel's and my hands resting on his powerful shoulders, I manage to steady myself for a second. Then an emotional tsunami knocks me over and threatens to pull me so far under I'll never find the surface again. Nathaniel moves his hands to my freezing cold cheeks. Inside the shelter formed by my long hair, his breath smells like peppermints and his face like spring flowers.

"Stay strong, Annabelle. No matter what happens you have me to lean on, but don't waste any tears on that immature idiot. If he is who we thought he was, then he'll come to his senses soon. If he is who he's acting like right now, then you're better off without him."

"Thank you." I feel like I can breathe again. Nathaniel and Wyatt are both mediums. Nathaniel acted as Wyatt's mentor throughout our whole drama with Anthony's ghost. No one knows Wyatt better than Nathaniel does, except maybe me and his Uncle Oliver, who he lives with. Wyatt's mother kicked him out last summer because she doesn't believe in ghosts and he's a medium. So he moved here, to live with Oliver.

"Self pity is a really destructive force; the worst. Don't give in to it, Annabelle. Self pity will cripple you. Don't waste one second on it. You're better than that."

I sniff, struggling to fight off tears. "I'm so pathetic."

"He's the pathetic one. Don't spend another minute thinking about him until he morphs back into the old Wyatt again. C'mon I'll buy you a cocoa. Leave your car here. I can drive you back later."

Straightening up, I answer, "Sure. I'd love a cocoa, with marshmallows, mmmmm."

"That's my girl. Can I have one small kiss, for saving your ass during a crucial moment in your big emotional crisis?" He taps his cheek with his forefinger, pointing to the spot where he wants to be kissed. Laughing, I bend over to peck him on the cheek, but he pulls a fast switch and presses his mouth against mine for a second.

"Hey, Flyte! What the hell?"

"Don't flatter yourself, Annabelle. That was a strategic move. He was watching."

"Wyatt?"

"Yup, none other. And we're not going to look over there, but I bet if we did we'd see his handsome face turn ugly and green with jealousy.

Chapter 3

Nathaniel and I Fight Fire with Fire

"Damn it, Nathaniel! That's what got me into all this trouble: kissing someone else!"

"Yeah, but the game's changed now. Right, Jeff?" Barking his agreement, the enormous dog wags his tail. Nathaniel continues. "Hop into the van, gorgeous, and let's plot your revenge on the black knight and his evil new queen."

Laughing, I jump into the passenger side of the van. When he's settled into his captain's chair, behind the steering wheel, Nathaniel adjusts the rearview mirror, peeks up into it and announces. "Wyatt's not smiling down at her anymore. He's looking over here and I bet if I could see his eyes, they'd be filling up with those thunderheads that accumulate when he's pissed off."

"Not good, Nathaniel. I don't want him to be any more pissed off at me than he already is."

"He's getting into his car alone and she's walking away, and she's not swinging her hair and giggling like an idiot anymore, either."

"That's good." I smile. Maybe Nathaniel's silly plot to make Wyatt jealous will work after all. "Let's go drink some cocoa. I'm freezing. I hate when it's really cold, but it doesn't snow. I feel cheated."

"I know, you poor thing. Let's warm you up. We can go to my house. My mother's home. I don't think you've ever met her."

"I'd love to meet your mother."

As the van cruises along, Nathaniel shoots a sideways glance down at my legs. "What's up with the holes in those pants, Annabelle? No wonder you're cold. Can't you afford to buy some new jeans? I'll loan you the money to buy a good pair if you're broke."

"These jeans are brand new and they happen to be very fashion forward."

"I like the look, but still, you must be cold."

"The holes aren't that big, and I'm wearing warm socks and boots, two sweaters and my coat, so I'm fine. I'd just be happier if it snowed."

Nathaniel's cell phone rings and he doesn't answer it.

"Aren't you going to pick up?"

"Nope. I know it's Wyatt and I don't want to talk to him right now. I'll return his call later."

Grabbing his phone, I check the screen and sure enough, the missed call was from Wyatt.

"Promise me you'll tell me everything he says when you call him back." I beg him.

"Better yet. I'll call him as soon as we get to my house and we'll put him on speaker. This might turn out to be fun. There's an evil part of me that loves to cause trouble for people who deserve it."

When we arrive at Nathaniel's house, his mother's home, but she's standing in the hall, about to grab her coat out of the closet. "Lovely to meet you, Annabelle. I wish I could stay and visit but I have to leave for work. Tonight's our night for evening hours."

"I invited Annabelle over to cheer her up. A total douche just broke her heart." Nathaniel embarrasses me.

"I'm no stranger to a broken heart, Annabelle. Maybe Nathaniel's told you that his father disappeared when he was just a baby, and we've never been able to locate him."

Instantly, I like and trust her because she's very direct. I can see so much of Nathaniel in her. They don't look all that much alike, but they have similar mannerisms and expressions. Mrs. Flyte's eyes, like Nathaniel's, dance with humor and fun, even when she's not joking around. How could his dad have ever left?

"He must be an idiot. Look what he gave up!"

"Exactly. He has missed being a part of our family…his loss, not ours." She kisses Nathaniel's cheek and mine, too. Then swings a dark gray woolen coat over her shoulders and slides her arms through the satin-lined sleeves. "Bye, Annabelle, it's been great meeting you. Come over anytime. You're welcome here without an invitation."

And she's gone. Nathaniel wastes no time calling Wyatt back.

"DO YOU KNOW SHE'S NOT EVEN EIGHTEEN YET?" My ex-boyfriend is speaking in all caps

Just like he promised, Nathaniel puts Wyatt on speaker, but it's not necessary. Wyatt's yelling so loud I'd hear him even if Nathaniel's phone was on normal and in the next room. My coconspirator winks and smiles, flashing his white teeth at me as he defends himself against Wyatt's accusation.

With exaggerated patience, Nathaniel answers. "Yes, I know she's not eighteen yet. But she will be in a couple of months."

"NOT FOR THREE MONTHS!"

"Okay, okay. Calm down. And before you remind me, I know how old I am, too. But I need to remind you that Annabelle and I are friends; that's all. So your point is moot."

Wyatt continues to project his voice across great distances without the aid of a megaphone. "YOU KISSED HER ON THE MOUTH! FRIENDS DON'T KISS FRIENDS LIKE THAT!"

"You were spying on me! What the hell, Wyatt!" Nathaniel goes on the offensive.

"I didn't need to spy. You were right out in the open, in the school parking lot."

"I didn't see you. Where were you hiding when you were spying on me?" Nathaniel accuses.

"I wasn't hiding. You had your back to me."

"So you were sneaking up behind me to spy on me."

"I WASN'T SPYING!" Next he again mumbles something about Nathaniel being too old for me. My friend's verbal stunts seem to have discombobulated Wyatt so much, that his voice has quieted down a lot. He repeats. "I wasn't spying and you're too old for her."

"As soon as Annabelle turns eighteen, in March, I'll only be seven years older than she is, plus you're being stupid because we're only friends. And stop spying on me. It's annoying. Goodbye, Wyatt." He smiles and clicks his phone off.

I laugh. "Nathaniel, that was brilliant! I love the way you said 'moot'! Great word!"

"Why thank you. C'mon, my dear. Let's have a cocoa." He wheels over and puts the kettle on the stove top, then empties two packets of cocoa into two mugs.

"Thank you. I'd love some cocoa."

"Mission accomplished. We made him jealous, but we're both perfectly innocent of any wrongdoing. Wait. It's going to get better. I guarantee." He pulls out a drawer and takes out a bag of mini marshmallows, dumps a handful into each cup and throws a handful at Jeff who snatches a few out of midair then nibbles the rest up off of the floor.

Nathaniel pours hot water into the cups, gives each one a quick stir with a teaspoon and I carry the steaming mugs over to the table. We sit down and start sipping our cocoa and reenacting the whole phone conversation together, giggling our dumb asses off the whole time. Afterwards he drives me back to my car. Finally, things are looking up. Wyatt was jealous. He must still care about me.

And for a short while my situation continues to improve. Colleen stops popping up mysteriously in the school corridors, outside my classes and in the girls' room mirror. I still see her now and then, hanging out in the hallways with friends and occasionally with Wyatt, which wounds me, but not mortally anymore. Because thanks to Nathaniel, I know he still has feelings for me. Then, early in the morning, two days after the scene in the parking lot with Nathaniel, I see Colleen as I'm walking out of History class and at first, I don't even recognize her.

She looks like she spent way too long in a tanning booth and she's dyed her hair pitch black so it's shining like a raven's wing. I try not to stare, but it's difficult. For as long as I've known her she's always been a blonde, but now she's extremely brunette. Her hair looks a lot longer, too. How can someone's hair grow eight inches in just a couple of days? It's almost the same length as mine now. Meg's a pretty good amateur hairdresser, maybe she'll know. I'll ask her at lunch. We always sit together in the cafeteria.

Before I can even ask her this question, though, she answers it. "Did you see Colleen Foley's hair extensions? What do you think they cost? They must be the expensive kind because they look real. And the spray tan looks authentic, too; big bucks!"

Jen adds, "How about those green contacts? She used to have blue eyes."

Everyone's talking about her behind her back, not just Meg and Jen. Even her own friends start ridiculing her when she's not with them. This is one advantage I have over her. My friends are loyal. If they think I'm being stupid they tell me to my face. They don't talk about me and laugh at me behind my back. They'd just say something like: "What the hell did you do to your hair? Not a good look for you." Meg would probably volunteer to fix it for me. She's good with hair.

What will Colleen do next? Will she take up long distance running or join the tennis team? It's all kind of flattering in a creepy way.

People start calling her Pocahontas, yelling it out in the hallways and in the cafeteria. It's probably because I'm part Native North American and she's obviously trying her hardest to look more like me. Just in case people don't get it, someone anonymously hangs up two side by side pictures of us, with the caption "Who wore it best? One hundred people were surveyed."

Under my picture it says "Ninety-nine percent" and under Colleen's it says "One percent (Colleen voted for herself.)". I've seen these kinds of pictures before in *Us* magazine. Even when it's celebrities who are used to that paparazzi crap, I think it's cruel. Like, "Who wore it best?" "Katy Perry or Kim Kardashian?" And then the stupid outfit cost about three thousand dollars. Colleen's not my friend and I don't even like her but this was a really malicious thing to do. So I rip the pictures down and toss them in the trash.

The worst thing, though, is that a couple of girls who don't like Colleen start calling her "Ghost Slut." Last year, my friend Meg and I made a movie for a combined English and History project and practically the whole school saw it. It was all about ghost stories and local paranormal legends. Right after we presented our project in History class, Colleen and a few of her friends started calling me "Ghost Girl," in kind of a mean way, but the nickname never really caught on. So, I guess now that she's trying to imitate me, some of the jealous girls at our school are hating on her because they think she deserves a similar nickname, only worse. I start to feel sorry for her.

Then after school, while we're walking out to our cars, Meg tells me about something really stupid that Colleen did. "She went to a graveyard, here in Eastfield, at midnight with her friends. They brought a Ouija board, so they could ask the spirits what to do about Wyatt because he was ignoring her. She must've been really desperate."

"Plus, Wyatt wouldn't be impressed. He'd think that was a dumb thing to do. Bad things can happen when you mess around with the supernatural and you don't know what you're doing. But that explains the ghost slut nickname."

"The ghost part anyway." Meg looks at my face and I crack up. Then she starts laughing, too and we both almost lose it, right there in the school parking lot. I'm still giggling a little when I get into my car.

Three days after her new hair color's debut, Colleen takes out her extensions and dyes it a pretty golden brown with dark blonde highlights. Her spray tan wears off. She takes out the greenish-colored contacts, so she has blue eyes again and people stop making fun of her. She goes back to flipping her hair around and giggling and screaming whenever she sees someone she knows in the halls. I feel less depressed, knowing I'm not the only one who feels humiliated. Nathaniel put Wyatt in his place, and Wyatt's new wannabe girlfriend has embarrassed herself by trying to be more like me and failing. Life is good.

And then it gets better. After lunch, one day at school, I walk up to my English classroom and Wyatt's Uncle Oliver, who's head of the History department, is standing by the door, talking to my English teacher, Ms. Coffman. Wyatt lives with his Uncle, because his dad remarried and moved to California and he doesn't get along with his mother, for a lot of complicated reasons. As I walk by my two favorite teachers, Oliver and Ms. Coffman, I smile at them, and Oliver breaks off his conversation with Ms. Coffman to give me a huge hug and tell me how much he misses me.

Even better, right when all this is happening, Colleen walks by and Oliver ignores her. She makes a big production of screaming at one of her friends "OMG, where did you get those boots? I've been looking for boots that color!" Oliver actually grimaces, and ushers me into Ms. Coffman's classroom with his arm around my shoulder. I couldn't have written a better script.

"Hey," he speaks quietly. "We miss you, Annabelle. Why don't you come over for dinner Saturday? Jackson and Nathaniel are coming. It'll be like old times. We can watch a movie and eat delicious food." About a month ago, we all solved the mystery of Anthony's death together and we haven't hung out since then.

I almost choke on my reply; it hurts so much to say it. "What about Wyatt? He doesn't want to see me."

"I'll give him fair warning that you're coming and he can decide for himself. I'm not giving up our friendship just because my nephew is acting like an idiot."

"You really think he's an idiot?"

"Yes, but he's my idiot and I love him."

I want to say that I love him, too, but my face gets way too hot when I think about saying it, so instead I just thank Oliver and ask him what time I should come over.

"How about around seven?"

"Sounds great. Thanks again."

When I take my seat, in English class, I catch sight of Colleen, who's just outside the door, staring right at me. I think she was listening to everything. She scurries off the second we make eye contact. I don't know what class she has next, but she's going to be late if it's downstairs. No worries, though; probably when you're president of frickin' everything, you never get in trouble.

After school, Meg's waiting at my locker. "We need to talk. Things aren't as hopeless as you think, Annabelle."

"Meet me at my house. We can hang out and do our math homework together."

"Right, I'll bring some really sharp pencils and a calculator." We both crack up. Neither one of us has done any homework in weeks. We're seniors. Meg's already been accepted early action to the culinary program at Johnson and Wales, which is her first choice, so she's all set and has no intention of doing any schoolwork until she starts college next fall. I haven't been accepted anywhere yet. I just have a really bad case of senioritis.

Chapter 4

The Web We're Weaving Grows More Tangled

As soon as Meg gets to my house, we grab some chips, salsa and soda then head down to the basement where we instantly turn on the TV and start streaming the Grinch movie with Jim Carey off Netflix. It was either that or *Toy Story 2*. Nothing like revisiting your childhood, wolfing down a ton of junk food and indulging in some fascinating gossip; it feels good to spend the afternoon with Meg, curled up on the couch together under my old Sponge Bob quilt.

We settle in and I shove a huge chip, dripping with salsa, into my mouth. When I bite into it the chip crumbles and the sloppy mess falls all over my sweatshirt and the quilt. Meg blots at it with a paper towel and we laugh. In between pinching up all the little pieces of chip and swallowing them, I tell Meg about how Oliver invited me to dinner and Colleen heard him.

"Pound it." Meg gives me a fist bump and then she shares her gossip with me. "Ryan says that Colleen chases after Wyatt hardcore and everyone on the soccer team thinks she's a big joke."

"What? I thought every guy in the whole school thought she was hot. I thought they all liked her. She wins every election she runs in."

"Well, yeah, you can't take her hotness away."

"Damn, I wish I could."

"Yeah, me too. But Ryan sees through her. There's that whole strange Ouija board thing; how pathetic was that? She knows you went ghost hunting with me, so then she goes ghost hunting 'cuz she assumes it'll make Wyatt think she's more interesting. Plus, Connor told Wyatt about last spring's prom fiasco."

"Poor Connor. That sucked."

"Big time. Anyway, Wyatt thinks she's a tool and he's really annoyed because she won't leave him alone. Ryan and I think that she feels like she's running in one of her elections and he's the only vote she can't win, so she chases after him. Colleen can't believe there's a guy on this planet who doesn't want to date her. She doesn't even know Wyatt. It's just that he's good-looking and he's a challenge, so she's going for it."

"Are you sure he doesn't like her?"

"Pretty sure. I didn't hear it from him or anything, but Ryan's a good source. He said Wyatt's depressed. He sucked in that playoff game. Soccer's over. You two aren't together anymore. I don't think he's interested in any other girl besides you. Why did you guys break up, anyway? How come you don't talk about it? You always used to tell me everything. Are you hooking up with that hottie in the wheelchair?"

Word travels fast. Someone must have seen Nathaniel kissing me in the school parking lot. Now it's probably all over the whole school. I don't really know why Wyatt broke up with me, which sounds ridiculous so I tell her a half truth. "Wyatt's jealous; I think that's part of why we broke up. But he won't talk to me so I might never find out the real reason."

Wyatt's probably still pissed off because I kissed Anthony. However, I deliberately steer Meg toward thinking that he's jealous about my so-called relationship with Nathaniel. But I can't tell the whole, weird story to anyone. That's one reason I miss Wyatt so much. We're both freaks and we understand each other on that level. No one else I know has experienced anything like what we have. No one my age, that is. Nathaniel's a freak, too, but he's older. It isn't the same because he isn't in high school. I miss Wyatt so much.

I can't tell Meg about kissing Anthony's ghost. So I have to let her think Wyatt might be jealous of Nathaniel. Besides, Nathaniel made sure that Wyatt is jealous of him. Meg doesn't have the right time frame, though. The whole Nathaniel prank happened after Wyatt and I had already broken up. It's not the reason for the break up.

"There's one other thing you should know, Annabelle." Meg's voice drops down like a bomb falling out of a plane.

"What? Is it about Wyatt?"

"Yes. It happened shortly after they lost the soccer game; the same night, in fact. I think you two might have actually broken up shortly afterwards, but you didn't tell me, so I can't be sure."

"We never broke up. Wyatt just stopped calling me and wouldn't return my calls or texts. He texted me right after the soccer game ended and that was the last time I heard from him. What happened that night, after the game?"

"Wyatt got drunk at Liz Dalton's party and hooked up with Colleen. Then he never called her afterwards and she became obsessed with him."

My throat closes up because I'm choking on withheld tears, but I manage to croak out, "Do you really think she's obsessed with him?"

"Yes. He's the one vote she can't win and she feels like the whole election depends on that one, single vote."

I think back and remember that Liz Dalton did have a party on the night of the soccer game. After the game, in the parking lot, I heard some people talking about going.

Meg rests a sisterly arm around me and gives me a half hug. I lean my head on her shoulder and we watch Jim Carey in silence for a few minutes. I'm not thinking about the film, though. I'm beginning to piece together the sequence of events. My thoughts and feelings somersault all over each other, as I picture Wyatt, reeling from the experience with Anthony and then on the same weekend, missing the shot on goal and losing the soccer game.

I imagine him walking into Liz's party without me. Meg and I went over to Jen's and watched movies together that night. If I had gone to the party, would things have turned out differently? Would Wyatt and I still be together? Wyatt never asked me if I wanted to go to the party and I wouldn't have gone on my own. I'm not friends with Liz or any of her friends. Plus Meg wasn't going to the party with

Ryan. Jen and Connor didn't go either. So basically, none of my friends went. None except Wyatt and Ryan, but Ryan didn't cheat on his girlfriend at the party. And Wyatt did.

When the movie's over, Meg leaves and my mom and I eat dinner together. Dad's working late again, hurrying to finish up all of his outdoor building jobs before the first big snowfall.

Spaghetti and meatballs is one of my favorites, but I don't feel very hungry. Maybe because I ate too many chips. Or maybe because I keep thinking about what happened the night of Liz's party. Trying to make some sense out of it all.

After I got home from the chick flick festival at Meg's that night, I stayed up and watched *The Silence of the Lambs* for the hundredth time. When the movie was over, around one in the morning, I went to bed, but not before texting Wyatt, because it's one of his favorite films, too. "I watched *Silence of the Lambs* without you…not fun." Then I paraphrased a quote from the movie. "My life is more interesting when you're in it."

Wyatt never texted me back. At the time, I thought he'd gone to bed early because he was exhausted and depressed about the game, but that isn't what happened at all. Instead, he went to the party and hooked up with Colleen. He didn't even wait and think it over. He raced out, got wasted and made out with her.

The only good news is: he seems to regret it, according to Meg. Colleen's been chasing him constantly and he isn't responding. He responded to seeing me and Nathaniel together, though. So this is the bottom line: I'm jealous of Colleen. She's jealous of me, and Wyatt's jealous of

Nathaniel. It's way too *Midsummer Night's Dream*. We read that play in English class two years ago. And it was funny. But living it isn't very funny. Wyatt and Nathaniel and Colleen and I are kind of like Demetrius, Lysander, Hermia and Helena; except Nathaniel's also playing the part of Puck, manipulating everyone just to cause trouble.

Not fair. Nathaniel's the only one who's having any fun. The very second that I finish thinking this thought, my phone vibrates and it's my buddy, Puck/Nathaniel, the mischievous medium. "Hey, Annabelle, can we talk?"

"Sure, what's up?"

"No, I mean in person, face-to-face. Can you come over here? You don't have to stay very long if you don't want to."

"That's okay. I don't have any plans. I can come over around eight. Is that a good time?"

"See you at eight, then."

When I arrive at Nathaniel's and ring the doorbell, Jeff lets me in. On the front door, instead of a doorknob, there's a lever he can push down with his paw. Jeff's a way better judge of character than any human I know, so Nathaniel trusts him to let in only safe people, no strangers or criminals. The giant mutt greets me with his usual sloppy kiss and I hug him. Then follow him down a hallway into a cozy room with a big flat screen TV, a couch and a couple of recliners.

Nathaniel has created a little heaven on earth for his angelic presence. The fragrant, burning logs in the fireplace cast a warm golden glow over everything. The dim flickering of the TV screen provides the only other light in the room. Nearby, his wheelchair sits empty, and he's lounging on the couch, like any other young guy, watching a basketball game on TV with his feet up on the ottoman, drinking beer out of a long-necked bottle and eating popcorn. Pointing with the bowl of popcorn, he offers, "There's soda and fruit juice in that mini fridge over there if you want anything."

"Thanks." I walk over to the small fridge in the corner of the room and pull out a single serving sized bottle of cranberry/raspberry juice. Then I collapse down on the sofa next to him and grab a handful of popcorn out of the bowl in his lap. "Who're they playing?"

"Knicks. Celts are up by six, but it's been back and forth the whole second half." Just then the Knicks score a three pointer and Nathaniel swears.

Sitting in friendly silence for awhile, we eat popcorn, sip our drinks and watch the game. Finally the Celtics have a ten point lead, close enough to the final buzzer so their victory will be a lock. Nathaniel nudges my side with his elbow and I turn to gaze at his beautiful profile.

Staring straight ahead, he says. "It's not all acting."

"What are you talking about?"

Turning to face me, he takes a deep breath and responds. "My big attraction to you. I'm not just trying to make Wyatt jealous. As a matter of fact, I would prefer that you two not get back together because I want you for myself, Annabelle."

I don't know what to say. I can't make eye contact with him.

"Whoa." I know I sound like a tool, but I need time to think. Clueless about how to respond, I sit there like a dumbass in a speechless trance. When I finally snap out of it, I realize that my mouth's hanging open. Before I can shut it, though, Nathaniel smiles, reaches out and chucks me under the chin, closing it for me. Jeff ambles over from his spot by the fire and licks my hand.

"We're a package deal, Annabelle. You get me and Jeff." The most lovable dog in the world licks my hand again, and then nudges his head underneath it, so I'll scratch him on his favorite place, the flat spot, between his ears.

This is so unfair. I'm so emotionally vulnerable: grieving over Anthony, not even close to rebounding from my break up with Wyatt. And Nathaniel's playing the dog card.

"That's cheap, Nathaniel. You're hitting me when I'm down and using your dog to persuade me."

"I'll do anything, Annabelle. There's no low I won't stoop to."

"But why me? You know lots of women. What about the girl you met when you were out walking Jeff? What did she have, a Chihuahua?"

"She was okay. But Jeff didn't like her dog. Too yippy."

"Didn't Oliver fix you up with the new math teacher last month?"

"We went out twice and that was two times too many. No sense of humor."

"Maybe you're being too picky. You should give her another chance. Take her to see a funny movie. See if she laughs."

"No. Neither one of them was right for me. Nobody's right for me. I'm not gonna lie, Annabelle. I've dated a lot since Holly died."

Four years ago, the love of Nathaniel's life died in the same accident that turned him into a paraplegic.

"It took over a year, but I finally started to entertain myself by dating again. And it has been entertaining, but that's all. I've never felt even a glimmer of emotional connection to any woman until now. When I first met you, you were with Wyatt and I thought it would be hopeless to tell you how I felt because you two were so much in love. But now's my big chance, my window of opportunity. I know it might be a small window, too, so I need to seize the moment. Wyatt might come to his senses any day now. I have to take a big risk and tell you that I'm in love with you."

"No, no, noooo! Can't we just stay friends? You're ruining everything. I can't lose you, too, not over this, Nathaniel. I'm too confused. I can't deal with this right now. But I'd be so lonely without you. It's not fair!"

"Of course we can stay friends. But you have to understand that I want to be more than your friend. Don't worry; I'm willing to take it slow. I know twenty-five seems old to you right now, but it's really only a seven year difference. You're almost eighteen. When you're twenty and I'm twenty-seven, it won't seem like such a big gap. As we get older, it will get less weird."

Through the stunned numbness in my brain it occurs to me that Nathaniel is talking about a relationship that will last years. This realization renders me speechless once again. Finally, the buzzer sounds and the Celtics win, but it's anticlimactic. The drama of the game was long past by the time it ended. The drama in my life is picking up speed at a heart-fluttering pace.

Nathaniel reaches for the remote and clicks off the TV. With one smooth motion, he picks up another remote and clicks on some music. I begin to wonder what "I've dated a lot" means. What exactly are the numbers? For a moment, here in the firelight, everything seems too rehearsed, like he's done it a million times before and it has always worked for him. And I can see why.

His warm coppery eyes radiate sincerity as they stare into mine. The illumination from the brilliant flames reflects off his biceps. He's wearing a short sleeved t-shirt, even though the temperature outside is in the single digits. Is this planned? Is he trying to manipulate me with his physical beauty? Is he using everything to his advantage: my loneliness, his muscular perfection, the fire, and now the music? *Third Eye Blind* sings out from the speakers. "Motorcycle Drive By". Emotional, melodious and passionate, one of my favorite bands, and he knows that.

I stand up, walk over to a recliner and sit down, to put some distance between us, but I don't push back and recline. Instead I pull my legs up and sit cross-legged, perched on the edge of the oversized chair. Jeff plunks down in front of me and rests his head on my knee.

"Annabelle, I loved Holly so much. I never thought I could love anyone, ever again. Then I met you."

"You can't possibly feel for me what you felt for Holly."

"Even Holly didn't have what you have. She wasn't who you are."

What does he mean? Why is he talking to me this way?

"Nothing like that could ever happen to you. I wouldn't lose you like I lost Holly. If we had a child together, this could never happen to him." He points down to his immobile legs.

And then the bomb detonates. I understand. I feel stunned, but incredibly relieved; I finally get it. He doesn't love me. He loves my gift; my ability to heal myself.

Nathaniel has brought up the one thing that will destroy the mood completely. He makes it impossible for me to consider a romantic relationship with him.

I inherited a gift from the ancestors on both sides of my family. My mother is related to the witches of Salem, Massachusetts and my father's the direct descendant of a brave Wampanoag Warrior. The white settlers kept shooting at my Indian ancestor and he kept recovering and coming back at them, even more lethal and violent than before. They thought he was immortal, but he was just harder to kill than most people. And so were the witches. They died, but it was difficult to finish them off.

I have the same genes. Whenever I injure myself, I heal almost immediately. I'm not immortal, but I'm much more difficult to kill than other humans. Only my parents and Nathaniel know. And Nathaniel has decided that this crazy gift is a good reason to fall in love with me.

I can't be angry with him, either, because his life was changed forever by a horrible tragedy. And this miraculous inheritance from my ancestors, the ability to heal myself, shines for him like a brilliant beam of hope. He can risk loving someone again, and that someone is me, because I'm as close to immortal as any human can get. It's unlikely that he would ever lose me in a tragic accident, like he lost Holly. And in the future, any children Nathaniel and I might have together would be likely to inherit this trait. Poor Nathaniel. I know, however, that to show him any pity will be an insult, so I keep my thoughts to myself. As best as I can, I explain that I'll never love him in that way.

"Nathaniel, I can never love anyone who loves me for my paranormal talent. I need to be loved for my ordinary self."

"There will never be anything ordinary about you, Annabelle."

I chug down the rest of the juice, to stall for time because I don't know how to respond. When I move the bottle away from my lips and put it down, I hiccup, like I always do when I drink juice too fast. But I don't stop at one hiccup. Four more come up, in quick succession, and I giggle, which makes it worse. I can't stop. My hiccups are huge and loud and they're rapid fire. There's a frickin' symphony of them. My timing's perfect. What could be more aggravating than a girl who is uncontrollably hiccupping during an intensely romantic conversation? I try to explain how wrong he is and how ordinary I really am, but my stupid-sounding, loud hiccups punctuate every three words, so I can't speak in coherent sentences.

He holds his hands up in surrender. "Okay, you win. You're ordinary! Drink some water or something. Hold your breath. Damn it. That's an annoying sound, Annabelle!"

I answer him by hiccupping loudly six more times in a row.

"Okay, Okay! I give up! You're the most ordinary girl I know! Please don't start belching or worse, farting, just to prove your point!"

Then we both crack up. He turns back into the same old Nathaniel, joking, flirting and a lot less scary. "You can come back over here now. We can be friends like before. Nothing has to change." He pats the spot beside him on the couch.

My hiccups die a gradual and natural death and Jeff and I move back over to the couch, with me in between him and Nathaniel. On my left I have the biggest, warmest, snuggliest animal ever. Jeff is all about cuddling. On my right sits one of the best looking guys I've ever seen, and he's just practically proposed to me.

Then he leans over and kisses me. Soft and long and with a tenderness that brings tears to the corners of my closed eyes. It's a move that's so typically "Nathaniel," I should have seen it coming. I also fail to predict the next series of events that happen. My left hand develops a mind of its own and moves behind his head, to rest on his beautiful, strong neck. Slowly, I start to stroke his warm skin and silky curls. Then he reaches his right arm behind me, curves it around my waist and hitches me up against his side, so close that I'm practically sitting in his lap. Breaking off the kiss for a second, he nuzzles my neck, before he moves his lips lazily back onto mine. That's when I reach both of my arms up and form a circle around his neck, so I can hug him even closer. It feels natural and cozy and sweet to be holding him and making out. For a minute or two I don't feel lonely anymore. I feel like I belong here, kissing Nathaniel in the firelight. Finally, I disconnect my lips from his, pull back an inch and stare into his glittering eyes. I try to find the strength to pull away from him, but it eludes me. I know I'm weak, but giving in feels so good.

"I'll always love you, Annabelle. Maybe not the way you want to be loved, or the way you deserve to be loved, but I'll always love you."

Damn, he's a good kisser. The only problem is that his technique is way too perfect. He's obviously had tons of practice.

"I love you, too, Nathaniel. And I need your friendship more than ever right now." Keeping my arms looped around his gorgeous neck for a few seconds more, I rest my forehead against his. Then finally, I let go before he takes the opportunity to plant another kiss on my all-too cooperative lips.

Laughing, he reaches down to the floor beside the couch and grabs his flannel shirt which has probably been lying there since right after I rang the doorbell. One sleeve at a time, he slowly pulls it on, so I get a last chance to admire his biceps in the firelight, before he covers them. Flashing those big, white teeth at me again, he says, "It's getting cold in here. I guess I better bundle up."

"The fire's kinda low. Want me to put another log on before I leave?" I stand up and stretch.

"Yes. Thanks. I think I'll stay here on the couch a little longer."

The fireplace has a brass, curtain-style screen, and I pull on the metal chain to open it then ease a medium sized log onto the fire. "Is this one big enough or should I add another?"

"It's perfect. Can you pass me that book over there, please? I think I'll read for a while."

The book he gestures toward is lying on a small table near the fireplace. It's an old library edition, with a cloth binding. Lifting it to my face, I open it wide and inhale. The pages have been baked dry and sweet by the centuries; aged to perfection. To my book-loving senses, it smells better than a warm chocolate chip cookie.

There's nothing printed on the front cover and I'm always curious about what people are reading, so I turn the book over in my hand and check out the title. The Gothic style lettering, embossed in still-bright gold on the faded binding, shines up at me.

"*Pride and Prejudice* by Jane Austen," slowly, I pronounce the title of one of my favorite stories, written by one of my favoritest authors ever.

Understanding finally dawns in my dense brain and I laugh out loud. Nathaniel staged the scene perfectly: his ripped biceps glowing in the firelight, slow, romantic music by a band that he knows I love, and he's reading Jane Austen, my favorite author. He starts laughing, too. "You know, Fitzwilliam Darcy was a lot older than Elizabeth Bennett."

"You're thinking of Emma. Knightley was sixteen years older than Emma."

"Wow! See! Our age difference is nothing! Jane Austen would have approved."

"She wouldn't approve of you mixing up which characters are in which of her books."

"She'd forgive me." He flashes the grin that has been working for him since he was born. Women melt in its presence. Jane Austen is probably melting in her grave, right now, just because Nathaniel is talking about her. Then he tells me one of his harmless, charming little lies. "After all, I've read so much Austen, so often, that I get some of her characters mixed up. Sorry. It won't happen again."

"It better not, Flyte. Don't think that I don't know you borrowed those DVDs over there from the library, too, and watched parts of all of them. That's why you have the characters mixed up. I doubt you could sit through the whole film version of even one of her books, never mind actually read several of her books from cover to cover." A sloppy pile of DVDs is lying on the floor, next to the TV, not tucked quite far enough back to be completely concealed. If I lean toward the television, I can even read the titles: *Sense and Sensibility* with Emma Thompson, *Emma* with Gwyneth Paltrow and my favorite, *Pride and Prejudice* with Keira Knightly.

"You couldn't hang in there and watch any of them until the end, and your crash course on Jane Austen just backfired. Maybe you should have hidden the DVDs better."

"And if I drove you home in the van, you'd see that I forgot to take the audio book out of the CD player. It's *Mansfield Park*. Don't ever drive around listening to that. You'll get so caught up in the action you might run a stop sign."

"Very funny, absolutely hilarious."

"Not meant to be funny…meant to make you fall in love with me."

"You're too good at it. And way too obvious."

"You're too smart. It's worked for me many times, but you called me out. I should have realized that any girl who reads this crap is smart enough to see through me."

"Crap!" I pick a pillow up off the chair nearest me and throw it at his face. He's quick, though, and catches it, then flips it back at me, bouncing it off the top of my head. Maybe that's why my mother calls them throw pillows.

"Jane Austen is not crap!"

"No, she's just boring. No violence, no sex. Where's the fun? Give me Nelson DeMille any day."

"I like him, too, but I love Jane Austen."

"And that, my dear Annabelle, is the only boring thing about you."

Nathaniel's transparent attempt to manipulate me has failed, but I appreciate his efforts. At least he's amusing and clever and an amazing kisser. I forgive him because I know the real reason why he's trying to win my love. It's rooted in the tragedy that resides in the center of his heart and his life. He thinks my ability to heal myself will prevent our relationship from ending in disaster. He believes that any children we might have together will be almost indestructible: as close to immortal as is humanly possible, like me. So I put up with his attempt to misrepresent himself as a Jane Austen fan. I tolerate his charm, his physical beauty and highly advanced kissing technique. I guess I should admit to myself that I have more than tolerated him tonight.

Fortunately, we're both a couple of idiots and can make each other laugh with our own stupidity, so we part friends, maybe a little bit more than friends, but not a lot more. There's a definite attraction here; the possibility of romance, but nothing like what I still feel for Wyatt.

At least I haven't broken Nathaniel's heart by turning him down. I've merely disappointed him, ruined his misguided plan, but he'll live. His heart was broken four years ago, when Holly died, and nothing I do will make it any worse or better, no matter what he believes. I'm the only one with a recently broken heart and I'm hoping that it will soon be mended, but it's up to Wyatt and he isn't cooperating, which is stressing me out. Hugely.

Wishing goodnight to my two best buddies, one human and one canine, I head home to get a good night's sleep in order to face another early morning. Tomorrow's only Wednesday. Three more days until the weekend. I almost wish Wyatt wasn't in my first period class. I almost wish he'd move back to New Hampshire.

Chapter 5

Irony

It's Wednesday morning and I've barely managed to make it through another History class without having an emotional breakdown. My friend Kelsey stops me in the hallway and checks around us and behind us to make sure Wyatt isn't nearby, or Colleen, who seems to be alternating between stalking Wyatt, then me, again. That girl needs a life. Isn't being president of everything enough to keep her busy? Evidently not. She has plenty of time to relentlessly pursue Wyatt and creep up on me, too. Anyway, miraculously, she's not within listening distance, so Kelsey can tell me her news.

"Wyatt was staring at you all through History class."

"Thanks, Kels. Good to know."

"Don't worry. Colleen's a douche bag. He'll see through her eventually."

Yes, but when? At least when he stares at me though, it's a positive sign, even if he doesn't sit next to me anymore. He's still interested. This was how our big, hot relationship began. He kept staring at me during History class. Kelsey kept track for me back then, too. Now he's at it again: good!

I walk off to my second period class almost smiling. I can't achieve a truly happy facial expression, however, because I still miss Wyatt too much. We always used to walk to classes together and eat lunch at the same table. If he had the chance, he'd text me during school, too. We were pretty inseparable, but not anymore. We're very separate now. I haven't gotten a text from him in weeks. Suddenly, my phone vibrates, in my right jeans' pocket. A text! I whip it out and check. It's Nathaniel. "Wyatt called me last night after you left. He drove by my house and saw your car. And he's not happy."

So, Colleen isn't the only stalker. Wyatt doesn't live near Nathaniel and there's no reason for him to drive by Nathaniel's house, at night or any other time. Nathaniel and his mother live on a cul-de-sac. I can't figure out if it's good or bad that Wyatt is checking up on me and Nathaniel. I don't know if it's good or bad that he isn't happy about my nighttime visit to the Flyte's house. Life's too complicated. I want some good news, really good news; not confusing news like this.

Instead, I can tell I'm gonna get bad news that can't be interpreted any other way when Meg and Jen meet me in the cafeteria, wearing matching "We need to talk" expressions. The three of us sit down at a table together and huddle in close. Jen looks at Meg and Meg nods at her.

She starts in. "Colleen has been putting her best moves on Wyatt to get him to ask her to the Winter Ball, kind of like she did last spring with Connor and the prom. Except it worked with Connor. It hasn't worked with Wyatt. He hasn't asked her yet."

I exhale with relief. "Whew! You two looked like you were going to deliver really bad news. That's good news. I don't know if I could go to the Winter Ball, if they were going to be there together. And I really want to go. It's our senior year; the last Winter Ball."

I love to dance and whether I have a date or not, I can dance with my friends and have fun. They always have a good DJ at the Winter Ball. My sense of relief lasts less than a minute, though. Meg and Jen exchange a grave look. Oh no, there's more news and it's bad. I can tell.

This time Meg speaks up. "So, finally, I guess Colleen didn't want to leave it up to chance anymore. She didn't want to wait for Wyatt to ask her. She asked him last night. She called him, like around eleven. And he said yes."

I try to hold back the tears and for the most part succeed, but I can feel my face redden with the effort. "He said yes?"

"He did. I don't know what changed his mind. I didn't think he liked her. He told Ryan that she was always bugging him and he wished she'd stop. Maybe he didn't want to hurt her feelings so he said yes." Meg tries to soften the blow.

"That's not the only reason why he said yes." I know the main reason why. I'm sure Wyatt doesn't want to hurt Colleen's feelings; that's probably part of it. He definitely isn't the type of person who goes around deliberately hurting others' feelings; only mine, but evidently, he thinks I deserve it.

I explain to my two best girlfriends. "He said yes to Colleen because he drove by Nathaniel's last night and saw my car parked in front of his house. He agreed to go to the dance with her so he could get back at me for hanging out with Nathaniel." Not only am I in hell right now, it's my own fault that I'm roasting in these torturous flames. I let Nathaniel kiss me. "Thanks, you two. I know it was hard to tell me, but I'm glad I know. I wouldn't want to find out some other way. Whoa! I'm going to be late for English. See you later. Don't worry. It will be okay. I'll think of something."

I spin around to leave the cafeteria and spin right into my other ex-boyfriend, Matt Riley. "Why so serious?"

Can't he think of a more original line? However, he does resemble Heath Ledger, without the Joker make up. He looks more like the young Heath, in *Ten Things I Hate about You*, not the right-before-he-died Heath in *The Dark Knight*.

"Matt, hi."

"You look depressed and you're so much prettier when you smile." Matt can be charming. At this particular moment, I appreciate his lame compliment. Call me superficial. A month ago it would have annoyed the hell out of me, but today, after the news I just got, Matt's silly flattery sounds fine to me.

Then he adds, "You're gorgeous and you look like you need to hear that right now."

"Thanks." I try to smile, but only partly succeed.

"Hey, can I walk you to English?"

"I'm kind of in a hurry." The fact that he seems to know my schedule makes me feel a little creeped out. We broke up almost six months ago. Why does he know that I have English right after lunch?

"That's okay. I can walk fast. What I really wanted to ask you is if you'll go to the Winter Ball with me."

I look up at his face, which I used to find very attractive, last year. This is too much. What the hell am I supposed to say to him? I can't decide now. My life feels hopelessly complicated and I can't deal with it, especially when I'm going to be late for English. I say the first thing that comes into my mind and out my mouth. "Call me later."

Then I dash off, full speed ahead toward the stairs. I'm in no mood to further ruin my day by getting a detention for being late to class, and Coffman will do it, too. She's a hard core hater of tardiness. I increase my pace both to put some distance between Matt and me and to get to English before the bell rings.

I'm taking the stairs in a rush; two at a time, when I hear someone scream my name. "Annabelle!"

I pivot; crash into two guys from the football team and then stumble down the ten or so steps I just ascended a few seconds ago. Steph is standing at the bottom of the stairs, grinning with eyes a sparkle and both "jazz hands" raised high.

"Annabelle!" she shouts again. "I could have texted you last night, but I wanted to tell you in person. I got accepted early admission to Smith and I got a letter from the tennis coach."

I scream and jump into her outstretched arms. This is her college dream come true; her stretch school; her first choice. We hop up and down, hugging, tears in our eyes, tears of joy. Now this is the kind of news I need to hear. This is great news! I'm so amazingly happy for her. I jump up and down two more times and then hug her again.

From a couple of feet behind us, I hear a mean-sounding laugh. Someone is attempting to trample on our high spirits. "Dyke."

Then another voice follows up with, "Fag."

We ignore them.

Unfortunately Steph's used to it. I glance over discreetly to see who's sending homophobic messages in our direction. Five senior girls are standing in a group; Colleen's one of them. She's fake-attempting to hide a nasty giggle behind her professionally manicured hand. Hovering two feet behind this gaggle of gigglers, Wyatt's standing completely still, with his mouth agape. He makes eye contact with me, closes his mouth and stalks off, up the stairs.

Colleen's clique calls themselves the "Juicies". I don't know what they mean by that, maybe like a juicy apple is the best kind of apple. I'm not going to waste any time trying to figure out why they call themselves the "Juicies". It's a stupid-sounding name and I wouldn't want to be called that. But they would never invite me to be a Juicy anyway. I'm too much of a misfit. They are as far away as high school students can possibly get from being misfits. They fit so perfectly into their environment; they define it and rule over it. Most of it. There are probably around twenty girls in the Juicies, altogether, and they're the most popular girls in the school. Colleen is their queen: the juiciest member of the Juicies.

They don't make the rules for weirdoes like Steph and me, though. Fortunately, the group they can't dominate grows in number each year. It's called social progress and I'm happy to take an active part in it.

The Juicies have certain unwritten rules, like if you play a sport; it has to be soccer or basketball. All other sports are too dorky. You have to wear expensive, fur-lined boots and own lots of pairs of them, in every color and style. You have to own the latest smart phone with tons of apps and always be on it and you have to carry a huge designer bag that's bigger than two Juicies' asses lined up side by side. Your parents have to own a second home so they're gone every weekend and you can host parentless parties with lots of alcohol and all of the popular boys. And you need to be tanned year-round. You can only date the hottest guys and you can make fun of people, but no obvious bullying. The Juicies make fun of people mostly to prove their own exclusivity. Hurting people's feelings is just collateral damage.

A Juicy has to be judgmental about anyone who's different than her. And she always has to be aware of others' judgments about her. I almost feel sorry for them sometimes. Their self-consciousness is more burdensome than those huge designer bags they carry everywhere. Oh, and one more important rule, I almost forgot. You can't be a lesbian or have a lesbian friend. If you do have a lesbian friend, you can't hug her in public, especially if the Juicies are watching.

Besides being doubles tennis partners, Steph and I are co-leaders of the Gay Straight Alliance. None of the Juicies are members. Last year, at the first meeting, when the faculty advisor asked the group who wanted to be the leader, only Steph and I raised our hands. So we skipped having an election and agreed to share the responsibility. We've led this organization together for a year and a half now, and will have to hand down our crowns to two deserving sophomores upon graduation this coming spring. Steph is the gay half of our leadership team, and I'm the straight half, not that it's anybody's business.

When I first joined the alliance, I researched the whole issue and found out that in the early nineties, Massachusetts' Governor William Weld signed an executive order, promising to make public schools in our state safe for gay and lesbian youth, who are statistically more likely to face bullying and violent victimization, oftentimes leading to suicidal behavior. Lots of public high schools have gay straight alliances so we can work toward solving the problem. Currently, there are over two hundred Gay Straight Alliances in Massachusetts and over three thousand five hundred nationwide. The Juicies of America and their ilk are not members of any of them.

Maybe Colleen and her friends think that Wyatt will be less likely to get back together with me if someone points out, in a public setting, that I'm a lesbian. Perhaps Colleen thinks that Wyatt doesn't know that I'm "batting for the other team". I'm a "fag." Can girls even be "fags?" Who knows? Who cares? I don't think she realizes how severely she just bit herself on her own skinny ass. Steph and I walk up the stairs together, arm in arm, smiling smugly. She announces to me, "Now all we need is for you to get accepted to River Wind and we can really celebrate. I'm going to college…Woooo Hooooo!"

"Woooo Hooooo!" I echo. She walks me to English to share the good news with Ms. Coffman. I'm late, but when we tell her about Smith and the acceptance letter and the tennis team, Coffman is so thrilled for Steph that she forgives me and doesn't hand me a detention slip. Maybe my life is taking a turn for the better. I'm actually looking forward to the Winter Ball, to seeing Wyatt and Colleen together, hanging out with the other Juicies and their dates. He'll be miserable, squirming and uncomfortable all night. He probably won't even dance with her. It should be a fun evening. I love dancing, and I plan on having an amazing time. The big question now is, "What should I say to Matt Riley?"

I'm different than most high school girls because of my paranormal talents. It's a well kept secret, but people like Colleen and her friends seem to be able to sniff out my weirdness anyway. Probably my history project involving the ghost hunting last year gave them a big hint. Also, one obvious thing about me is that I think for myself, all supernatural talents aside. I'm neither a trend setter, nor a trend follower. I wear what pleases me. I play the sports I enjoy most. I hang out with a handful of people I like, and they're not members of the popular crowd at school.

However, when faced with the decision of going to the ball with Matt or not, I do what any typical mainstream teenage girl would normally do. I don't think for myself. I consult my two closest friends, Meg and Jen. They tell me to go with him, on one condition. Matt and I have to share a limo with them, not with his friends. Good advice, because his friends will be going to the ball with members of the Juicies' entourage. These people won't want me in their limo, and I don't want to be with them, either.

Jen, Meg and I share a laugh over the reaction these elite girls will have when they find out that Matt asked me to the ball. They'll be pissed that he didn't ask one of them. He's really popular and all the girls in our school think he's hot. So, my mind is made up. When Matt calls me after school, I tell him yes. I'll go to the ball with him if we can go with Jen and Connor and Ryan and Meg in their limo. He agrees. I have a date for the ball, one whose identity will annoy both Wyatt and Colleen and her gossipy, ridiculous friends, and I'll have my wingmen there to run interference if Matt decides to put the moves on me. I start to feel a little bit happy for the first time in weeks.

Steph calls me that same night, because she and a group of our friends from the GSA are going to the ball together and want to hire an old fashioned trolley. It will be way cheaper than a limo and fits twenty people, which will make it way more fun. They need more people to fill it, so she asks me if I know anyone who would be interested. I call Jen and Meg and they think it's a great idea, so do Connor and Ryan. Matt will obviously go along with any plans I make as long as I go to the ball with him, so I tell Steph to go ahead and rent the trolley for the night. It will only be twenty-five bucks each, instead of about seventy-five for a limo, plus we'll have a blast with all those people on board.

I text Matt and predictably, he agrees that it's a good idea. He especially likes the twenty-five dollar price tag and seems relieved when I volunteer to pay for my own ticket to the ball and my seat on the trolley. He has an afterschool job and his parents are about as rich as my parents, which is not rich at all. Plus the Riley's have four kids to put through college, so Matt has to pay for a lot of stuff himself. It's one of the few things I still like about him.

My next big, unsolvable problem is that Matt wants to hang out with me, and I don't want to hang out with him. I have no interest in starting up our relationship again. At least this coming weekend I have an excuse. Saturday night I'm having dinner at Oliver's house. And I'm really looking forward to it, even though Wyatt might be there and things could get awkward.

Chapter 6

Family Calls from Far Away

Friday night, as my parents and I are eating an early supper together, my mother tells my dad that Oliver invited them to dinner at his house on Saturday. Dad says he has to work late Saturday, because he's behind schedule on a huge, expensive house he's building for someone and it's supposed to snow this weekend. This suburban palace will have lots of floor-to-ceiling windows, and that's causing some problems because the glass had to be custom ordered and it finally arrived today, so he has to work all day Saturday. He's hoping to get them all installed before the snow starts. "I'll try to get over to Oliver's later on, but we could be working late, and then I'll have to come home and shower first."

"Mom, I'm going over to Oliver's on Saturday, too, so we can go together and meet Dad there if he can actually make it."

"You're going?"

"Yup, I told Oliver that it might be weird because Wyatt and I broke up, but he said I was still an important friend to him and he misses me. I didn't know he invited you."

"He called Wednesday. I asked him if I should bring anything and he said no, so maybe I'll just make him a little gift package with a couple of teas."

"Good idea. He liked the last tea you made him. He's probably almost out of it by now."

"That's what I'll…" My mother doesn't get to finish her sentence because the house phone rings. We always jump when the landline rings. Everyone we know calls our cell phones, and my mother worries when the house phone rings that something might have happened to one of my brothers who are both away at college.

A few seconds after she says hello, Mom plunks back down hard in her chair with the phone still held tight to one ear. She reaches for a napkin with her other hand and starts to cry into it. Dad and I sit there anxiously, fixated on her face, trying to figure out what's wrong. Dad quickly glances at me and we make intense eye contact. Then we both look over at my mother again. From listening to my mother's side of the conversation, I can tell that someone's in the hospital. She pauses to listen for about thirty seconds. Then she speaks again.

"I'll catch a flight tomorrow. Tell her not to worry."

The call's not about Clement or Joe. They both go to college right here in Massachusetts, so Mom wouldn't have to catch a flight if she had to visit either one of them. Plus, I heard my mother say "she". Dad and I continue to listen to her end of the conversation.

"Tell Maeve I'm coming. Right away. I don't want her stressed out. That would be the worst thing for her. Everything's going to be fine. I'm on my way." The call was about her twin sister, Maeve.

She hangs up. Dad and I wait while she dabs at her eyes and blows her nose into the napkin. Finally, my mother composes herself and begins to explain. "Maeve has had a stroke. It was a minor stroke, not horribly serious, but she's scared and she needs me. That was the manager from her bar. She got our home phone number from directory assistance."

We've only gotten together with my Auntie Maeve a handful of times because she lives in Key West and owns a bar there. We only visited her once and I was only three. The other times Maeve came up North to visit us; always in the summer and not even once a year, even though she's my mother's only sister and they're twins. Mom has always been a little disconnected from her family and I recently found out why. They're directly descended from the historically famous Salem witches, and they can trace their genealogy back to King Arthur's day and even before. She kept all of it a secret from me until a couple of months ago, but weird things started to happen in my life and she had to tell me the whole story. I missed out on getting to know Mom's side of the family because of her commitment to secrecy. Maybe she's experiencing some regrets now that Maeve's sick.

My dad bends down to help my mother out of the chair she collapsed into. "Pack your bag, Susannah. I'll go online and get you a plane ticket to Florida for early tomorrow. Don't worry, honey. Maeve'll be fine. She has a strong spirit. And as soon as she sees you, she'll feel better. You know it, babe." He wraps her up in a big hug.

But Mom doesn't look convinced. She still looks worried. "I should call Aleister."

My mother's younger brother is a big shot doctor in one of Boston's most important hospitals.

"Go ahead, Sooz, but make it quick because you should pack and then try to get some sleep." My father looks concerned. Mom hates to be called "Suzie" but she lets my dad call her "Sooz." No one else calls her that; only Dad. And he doesn't do it often.

Whipping out her cell phone, Mom calls her brother and I can tell from listening to her side of the conversation, that he's promising her he'll call the hospital in Florida and find out more. Then my mother gets up out of the chair, hugs my dad again and goes upstairs to pack her bag. Dad runs into his home office, grabs his laptop and finds her a flight to Florida that departs at six in the morning.

"I'll be getting up pretty early tomorrow." He doesn't look pleased.

"What about Auntie Maeve? Will she be all right?"

"Your mother said it's not too serious, but she's young for a stroke. And they've both always been so healthy. They'll feel better once they're together."

"I wish I knew Maeve better."

"She's a character. Even though they're twins, your mother's the opposite of Maeve in a lot of ways."

"What ways?"

"Susannah has always chosen to downplay her supernatural talent and not talk about her ancestors. She doesn't like a lot of attention. She's never exploited her talent in order to make money. Not that Maeve has done that, but I think that's how Susannah sees it sometimes."

"Maeve is rich?" I know that she owns a bar in Key West, called Priestess, but I've never thought of her as rich.

"Yes. Priestess is one of the most popular bars in the Keys. Mostly because it's so unique and the whole concept's so mysterious."

"I was just a little girl when we visited her. I don't remember much about the bar."

"Probably because you kids were young and we kept you out of the bar."

"That makes sense." I laugh.

Dad continues. "Priestess is a huge attraction because Maeve uses her connection to the supernatural community to spice things up. She hires attractive young people who read Tarot cards, crystal balls, palms, tea leaves, you name it. They have real talent and their readings and predictions are spot on."

"Wow!"

"Plus, they serve a drink there called Strange Brew. A cloud of mist drifts out as you sip it. It's served in a tall, novelty glass with a sliver of new moon etched on the side. She charges about fifteen bucks just for one drink, but you get to keep the glass. Someone started a rumor that drinking two of them enhances any supernatural talents you might have. Maeve doesn't endorse this theory, but she doesn't deny it either. She's good at selling the mystery and the money keeps pouring in. Your mother never criticizes her sister for any of it, but it's the opposite of the way she lives her life. And she hasn't made an effort to get down to Key West in almost fifteen years."

"Because Maeve's way down South and we're up North?" As if reminding me, the winter wind rattles our kitchen window with a sudden gust.

"That's part of it. Plus they're so different."

"I get it. Mom keeps all the family secrets well hidden and Maeve puts them out there for strangers to see and charges them admission."

"And there you have the biggest difference between them. Also, because she's the older of the two, by about two minutes, your mother has the candlesticks. Strangely enough, though, Maeve's talents are more powerful."

"Mom has never said anything. What's Auntie Maeve's talent?"

"She's a psychic. She can tell things about people she's just met, things she has no way of knowing. She can't truly read minds, though, not the way you can read a book. She gets impressions of what people are thinking sometimes. And she can predict a vague and changeable version of the future. But the future can shift one way or another because people are able to make choices and change it, so sometimes your aunt's predictions aren't accurate."

"And she's never married."

"No. She's never married or had any children. I think she can tell too much about guys as soon as she meets them. It kills any desire she might feel to get to know them better. Your mother can only detect evil, which is an advantage when you're meeting people you might potentially want to date. Maeve can tell more than that. I guess she always sees everyone's faults right away. Normally, you get to know someone and then if you really care about them, their imperfections aren't always deal-breakers. You're in love, so you learn to live with minor character flaws, like the vows say, 'for better or for worse'. Maeve can never get to that point. She sees the worse part immediately and the 'better' part doesn't have a chance. It's not easy. Some people wouldn't call her talent a gift."

"I know. I appreciate my talent. It saved my life this past fall, and it probably will again, but I don't want people to know about it." I almost tell my dad about Nathaniel and how he thinks he loves me, but really he's infatuated with me because of my ability to heal myself. Then I stop for a second and think and decide against confiding in my dad. He has enough to worry about, and he's my dad. It would be too awkward to talk to him about guys and relationships.

* * * *

Early Saturday morning, he drives Mom to the airport, long before I even wake up, and then he heads off to work on the house with all the glass walls. Before lunch, Nathaniel calls to see if I want a ride over to Oliver's for dinner, but I thank him and say no. He doesn't argue with me, which is good, because I can't explain my reason to him. I don't want Wyatt to see Nathaniel and me arrive together because then Wyatt might think we're more than friends. I don't want him assuming anything; just in case he might be thinking about getting back together with me. At least, at this point, I know Wyatt and Colleen will never be a couple and Wyatt regrets agreeing to go to the Winter Ball with her. He's stuck, though. And he's way too polite to take back his answer. No matter how much he hates the idea, he has to go as her date to the ball now.

I don't want to be alone for the whole day, so I call Jen and Meg and ask them to come over later and help me decide what to wear to Oliver's. I haven't been in the same room, outside of school, with Wyatt in a long time, and I need to look really hot. They'll know what to do, and Meg, especially, will enjoy the challenge. She loves fashion and make up, and if she goes overboard, giving me a makeover, I can tone it down after she leaves.

After an awesome lunch of leftover spaghetti and meatballs, I hop on the elliptical and watch a couple of episodes of *The Office* and then take a shower, but I don't dry my hair. Meg will decide if it should be down, loose and wavy, or straightened, or some other half up/half down thing she's done for me before. She's good at braiding, too. I miss my mother already, even though she only left this morning, but she's hopeless at hair. Her own is always coming loose from whatever non-style she's tried to arrange it into. When I was little, other girls would have French braids in their hair, but I'd always have to settle for a plain old ponytail. I don't really care, though. I hate anyone fussing over my hair. Sitting still for anything aggravates me. Only Meg's allowed to style it.

She and Jen arrive at four thirty and Meg starts on my hair right away while it's still damp. We laugh and talk and the time goes by fast. Meg asks me why my hair always smells so good.

"It's a secret," I answer.

"C'mon. We're your best friends. Share. We wanna have great smelling hair, too."

"My mother makes a rinse for me. But it's for brunettes." Meg has blonde hair.

"I'm a brunette." Jen makes a puppy face. But, the secret hair rinse is one thing I won't share.

"It's for really dark hair. Yours is too light. Besides, my mother won't even tell me what's in it."

"Ask her to make up a rinse for us." Jen begs.

"When she gets home from Florida I will."

Meg finishes drying and straightening my wicked awesome-smelling hair. Mom will probably enjoy making a rinse for them with her herbs and the rainwater she catches in buckets and saves. I thank Meg for doing my hair. "It looks so much better than when I do it myself."

Next it's time for me to get dressed. Jen brought over a really short stretchy black skirt. It's knitted like a sweater and barely covers my ass. She recommends that I wear it with black tights. Then Meg looks through my closet and picks out an army-green sweater to bring out the green in my eyes. After I'm dressed, they do my makeup; brush my shiny hair one more time, and when I look in the mirror I actually look good! I don't need to change anything. My hair hangs straight, swinging free and glossy, down my back and I hardly have any makeup on, so my face looks normal. Meg's a huge fan of the smoky-eye, and sometimes goes overboard with the makeup, but she didn't tonight, so I don't need to clean any of it off. About a half hour later, I'm saying goodnight to my super-helpful, best girlfriends ever and zipping up my black leather boots. Then I hop into my car and head over to Oliver's.

When I arrive, Oliver makes a big, embarrassing production out of hugging me and telling me he misses me. Then Jackson Andrews, fellow ghost hunter and good friend, does the same. Nathaniel greets me and kisses me, on the cheek, thankfully, not the mouth, and Jeff places his huge, adorable furry head under my hand so I'll scratch him there. He refuses to leave my side for the rest of the night: best dog ever. If he were a person he'd be best human ever. All this affection makes it really obvious that the only one in the room who isn't all over me is Wyatt. He doesn't even nod in my direction. I wish I had one of my girlfriends here to check if he looks at me when I'm not looking at him. Kelsey always does that in History class and it's good to know.

"Everyone's here. Annabelle, your dad isn't coming until later, if he can make it at all, so this is it, probably," Oliver announces, and Jackson starts pouring champagne into glasses. He even gives Wyatt and me a glass.

Okay, now I'm wondering what the hell's going on. I know they're all happy to see me, except for Wyatt, and we haven't all hung around together in a long time, but I don't think the occasion of our reunion calls for champagne. I look at Nathaniel, but he just shrugs away the question in my eyes. Evidently, he has no clue, either. Then Jackson clinks his champagne glass with Oliver's and raises it.

"We were going to wait until after dinner, but we're too happy to keep our surprise a secret any longer."

I hold my breath and look straight at Jackson. He can't stop smiling. Finally he speaks. "Oliver and I are getting married."

It's only the five of us, six including Jeff, but the room explodes. I hug Jackson so hard and so enthusiastically that I spill my champagne on his sweater. Oliver picks me up and swings me around. Miraculously, I don't break the champagne flute, but I only have one sip left at the bottom after all the excitement and jumping up and down. Oliver manages to make his voice heard over the noise and the hugging. "Wyatt, we want you to be our best man."

Wyatt's beaming. I've never seen a more beautiful smile. If I wasn't so in love with him already, I'd fall in love with him right now.

"As your best man, I'd like to make the first toast." Wyatt raises his glass and we all stop making noise. Everyone follows his lead as he toasts the happiest engaged couple ever. "To Oliver and Jackson. To being in love. To having it last forever." Then we all take a sip of champagne. Wyatt stares directly into my eyes, with his glass at his lips and smiles. I smile back and we share our first real communication in almost a month.

Jackson walks over to stand beside me and asks. "Annabelle, will you be our maid of honor?"

I hug him, to hide my surprise. I'm not just surprised; I'm totally flabbergasted and speechless. Finally I find my voice. "Of course. It's the best compliment anyone has ever given me in my whole life."

"Great! And I get to dress you in Vera Wang. My treat. You'll look amazing. Every wedding should have Vera

Wang and Oliver and I won't be wearing her. It's up to you, Beautiful. I can't wait to see you in the dress."

"Vera Wang? How can I refuse?" She's such a famous designer that even I've heard of her. "I have to call my mother. She needs to hear good news."

"I already told her. When she called me to tell me about Maeve, I spilled the news, and she agreed to keep it a secret so we could surprise everyone. Right before you all arrived, I called your dad and told him, so he knows, too, and he's coming by later if he can."

Eventually, our happy little party sits down to dinner and Wyatt ignores me for the rest of the night, but I don't care. I'm too happy for Oliver and Jackson, and I have a strong feeling that everything will work out for Wyatt and me. I still feel warm from the smile he sent my way when he was making the toast. Plus, we'll be thrown together at the wedding, which is in early March, a long time to wait when I miss him with every breath I take, but waiting until March is better than waiting forever. And you never know, maybe we'll get back together before then. Even if I have to wait until the wedding, it might not be such a bad thing, especially since I'll be wearing Vera Wang and looking amazing.

Nathaniel sits next to me during dinner and after, too, when we go into the living room to gather around the fireplace and share some more friendship and goodwill. My dad shows up around nine and we all sit around and talk for a while more. Jackson makes a joke about how boring it is without any paranormal mysteries to solve and we laugh. I joke with him.

"I hope whatever ghosts are waiting to make an appearance will wait until my mother gets home from Florida." I'm not completely joking around, though. Her ability to sense and ward off evil helped me stay alive this fall when we solved our first paranormal mystery.

We say our goodnights around midnight and when I head out to my car, it's freezing. The temperature has dropped around fifteen degrees since I arrived and there's a coating of slippery frost on the ground. Muffled by a thick cloud cover, the moon wears a hazy silver halo. When I breathe in deep, the cold stings my throat as if I'd swallowed a huge spoonful of crushed ice. The freezing air stiffens the tiny hairs inside my nostrils and slams me between the eyes, sending a sudden whack of pain straight into my sinuses. Ah, winter! The season that slaps you in the face; stunning and dazzling you at the same time. It feels good in kind of a sick way.

Slipping as I drive over every ice patch on the frost-covered road, my poor little car scoots ahead fast and then rocks sideways and back a few inches every time the wind blows. I don't feel in control. I wish I could be in the truck with my dad. He's right behind me, so if my car slides off the road, he'll be first at the scene. He sticks close until we reach our driveway and finally I feel safe, except my mother's in Florida, so I don't feel completely safe. I keep thinking about how perilous life can be when she isn't home to scare away anything wicked that dares to come my way.

Chapter 7

"In the Startled Ear of Night..."
—*Edgar Allan Poe*

Late the following afternoon, I try to fill my mother's culinary shoes and fail. The macaroni and cheese casserole I put together for dinner looks nothing like hers. Maybe it will taste okay, but probably not. I plunk myself down in her big, overstuffed chair, look out the kitchen window and pout at the view. Heading toward their collective destination with purpose, an unending herd of clouds migrates across the sky like the ghosts of elephants who remember exactly where to go every year. I've never seen so much gray. We won't see the sun again for at least twenty-four hours.

Our backyard has turned into frost-encrusted tundra. Slick ice coats the tall, dried-out sticks that used to be my mother's perennial garden. A renegade downdraft rattles the spindly, frozen twigs. When they clack together they sound like they're made of cheap plastic; a soulless noise. In contrast, my mother's wind chimes sing like crystal wine glasses touching after a toast. I can hear the passing of years and decades in their echoes, the passion, the sorrow and the joy of centuries. She should've brought them inside before she left for Florida, so they won't get wrecked if a nor'easter slams us while she's gone. She loves those wind chimes and so do I.

The dwindling day dims toward twilight, and I can see my foggy reflection in the big window. I start obsessing about my mother and how much I miss her. The funk I'm indulging in right now would piss her off and she'd let me have it, though. I need a good dose of her tough love. I'm letting the weather and a boy get me down. She raised me better than that.

As the wind gains momentum, its gentle moans grow into frightening howls. The leafless trees at the rim of the forest sway and creak. A limb or two might fall victim to the brewing storm, but most of the woods will remain undamaged. The roots of deciduous trees run deep and their leafless boughs offer minor resistance to the wind, so unless this storm turns out to be particularly freakish, the oaks and maples will survive.

The pines that ring the yard look hardy, because they keep their deep green needles through the winter, but their roots are shallow. The evergreens are always the first to go down during a gale force wind. Brushy and full with needles, the boughs will accumulate heavy loads of snow and bow down with the weight of the weather. Some will crack under the pressure. In a town like Eastfield, where the trees edge the roads and sidewalks, dangerously close to the wires that supply us citizens with power, we lose electricity at least twice a winter.

As I'm staring out across the howling, clattering landscape, my dad paces into the kitchen with his cell phone cocked to his right ear. Shoving his left hand through the sleeve of his red and black plaid woolen jacket, he ends the call and drops the phone into his pants pocket with his right. Then he reaches for the keys on the hook near the door. "That jackass, over on Chestnut Terrace, in the new mc-mansion that we didn't want to build him, screamed at me because a tree fell on his house. Crashed in a ton of that custom-ordered glass. His 'solarium' is ruined. Cold air and snow is pouring into the house. I have to head over there with a couple of my guys and close it off with plywood and plastic tarps. Then calm him down before he has a heart attack."

Looks like I'm about to be abandoned during a blizzard. Dad bends down and kisses my cheek. "I really don't want to leave you alone, Annabelle, but you'll be okay for an hour. Nothing bad's supposed to happen until a few hours from now. Then we'll get the worst of it… maybe ten to twelve inches of snow, deeper where it drifts. I'll be home way before then."

"You shouldn't be out driving in it, Dad."

"Don't worry about me, honey. I'll be in the truck, with the plow. Even if the storm starts up before I get back, I'll be safe."

"So you have to leave just because your customer's having a panic attack?"

"Yes. I've been complaining for months because the guy insisted that his house be built in a grove of 'majestic pines.' His words. Not mine. If he had grown up here, in the middle of the forests, he'd know that those pines were dangerous, not just majestic. Now he's miserable. He should've listened to me."

"You tried to tell him, Dad."

"Before we even dug a hole for the basement, I told the idiot that the closest evergreens needed to come down. That house was doomed before we poured the foundation."

"Dumbass."

"Tall pine trees close to a glass-walled room, stupidest idea ever; some people are so ridiculous you can't talk any sense into them until they've lost thousands of dollars over it. I'll only be about an hour, honey. I just need to reassure him that it can be fixed. A couple of guys from my crew are meeting me there. We'll board up the windows and nail up some tarps to keep the cold out. Then we'll finish the repairs as soon as the storm clears."

"You're always right, Dad."

"Yeah but it gives me no satisfaction—just a butt-load of aggravation."

Swearing and muttering, he grabs a bowl out of the kitchen cabinet and piles some of the weird looking mac and cheese into it. When the first spoonful assaults his taste buds a shudder starts in his neck, shakes his broad shoulders and then shimmies down his spine. "This is good, honey, but I don't have time to eat right now. I'll microwave the leftovers when I get home."

His bowl hits the sink with a clatter and then he opens the backdoor and closes it behind him. A second later I hear the hum of our automatic garage door rising and then falling. My dad has entered the domain of the gathering storm.

Soon darkness blots out the view of our landscape and I can see only my own forlorn reflection on the shiny surface of the windowpane. Behind me, in our well-lit kitchen, the time on the microwave says 51:4. That's 4:15 backwards, time for sunset. But there'll be no sunset tonight: too overcast. The weather continues to brew up temporarily contained violence outside the cozy sanctuary my father and his ancestors built. Each generation added its own rooms and wings. Our house was built to last through hundreds of Massachusetts' winters, which it has done. Following a silly design that his client insisted on, my father recently finished building a brand new, super-expensive house, but it's not engineered to withstand the New England weather, which is pissing him off, big time.

Shaking my head as I think about poor Dad's dilemma, I feed all of the mac and cheese to the garbage disposal and make myself a peanut butter and jelly sandwich on whole wheat. Standing up in front of the fridge I shove it all down in five bites and then gulp down a glass of cold milk. After, I head back to my seat by the kitchen window, overlooking our backyard. So I can keep up with my busy schedule of sulking and feeling even more depressed now that my dad's gone and I'm truly alone.

A sense of security, inspired by the thick and ancient walls of the Blake family homestead, lulls me into a bored doze, until a violent gust whips my mother's wind chimes into a frantic chorus. My eyes snap open and I shoot up out of the chair. Cupping my hands around my eyes, I press my pinky fingers against the cold windowpane and peer into the darkness. My mother's favorite wind chime is flung out horizontal to the ground. It flies straight out for ten seconds, clanging an emergency warning. Taking action, I grab my brother Joe's sweatshirt off the peg by the door, where it always hangs, pull it over my head, yank the hood down low and rush out into the storm. First I take a look out back, to assess the situation; then I head for the garage to get a ladder. The damn thing's heavy, but I manage to half drag, half carry it around the side of the house. "Crack!" A loud splitting sound practically deafens my right ear. A ten foot long tree limb hits the frozen ground inches from my right shoulder, causing me to drop the ladder. Determined, I hoist it back up against my hip and forge on toward my destination. Finally, after half dragging and half carrying our tallest ladder for several meters, I make it to the back of the house and lean it up so it's resting against the rain gutter.

Rung by rung I climb, until I'm close enough to reach out and unhook the first wind chime on my right. Next, I extend my other arm to the left and free a second one. After climbing down, I place my mother's treasures carefully on the snow-dusted ground. The pelting snow stings my face so I have to squint as I move the ladder over, climb back up to the top rung and reach out to lift two more sets of wind chimes down. When I get to the top, a cold blast smacks me in the face, sweeping the hood of my sweatshirt all the way off as another gust of vicious wind brings tears to my stinging eyes. The snow blowing into my face feels like confetti made from ground up glass. I can barely see at all. Clutching the chimes protectively to my chest with my right hand, I clasp one rung of the ladder in my left. The next squall swirls around me in an icy tornado, lifting the ladder up off the ground and away from the house. Shivering in my grip, it topples toward the earth. I don't remember anything else, except the freefalling instant when I experienced a flash of common sense and let go of the ladder, so I wouldn't pull it down on top of myself.

When I finally open my eyes, my head is thudding with intense pain and I can barely lift it. Staring up at the dark sky, I shiver and realize that my clothes are soaked through and if I lie here any longer I'll die from hypothermia. My mother's wind chimes will never make it back inside safely before the snowstorm has a chance to do its worst. I roll over onto one side and pick up all of the wind chimes which seem to be remarkably undamaged. Then, cradling my mother's treasures against my roiling stomach, I heave myself up into a crouch and half crawl, half stumble toward the backdoor. Maybe I can get the wind chimes safely packed away in the pantry and the ladder back into the garage before my dad gets home and discovers what an idiot I've been. Nausea and dizziness threaten to send me back down to the frozen earth where I nearly cracked my skull open. Evidently, I have a ridiculously hard head because I manage to stand upright and stagger toward the back door.

Within a few minutes, the throbbing behind my eyes eases a little and then completely vanishes. Until recently, I took my bizarre self-healing talent for granted, but now I'm acutely aware of how valuable it can be. Anyone else who fell like I just fell would still be lying on the ground unconscious, freezing to death. There's no doubt that I have a concussion. But within a half hour, I probably won't even have a headache. I straighten up and face the sharp, icy wind, head on. Blinking away tears, I run into the house, then back out, and accomplish my mission.

Finally, all the wind chimes are packed away and the ladder is back in its place in the garage. Before I put the kettle on for tea, I hang Joe's sweatshirt up and brush the dirt and snow off of the back, then sweep the tiny pile of debris into a dustpan and throw it away. My tracks are now effectively covered.

Satisfied that no evidence of my recklessness remains behind to tattle on me, I settle into the big arm chair near the kitchen's bay window again to hug my mug of hot tea and watch the storm grow more menacing from inside the sanctuary of the old Blake house. Silently, I promise my absent mother I won't leave the safety of this armchair until the last gust of wind dies and the last flake settles. Nathaniel lent me a Jeffery Deaver paperback, something about a woman detective who's an expert reader of body language, and I start in on it. No matter how closely I watch for clues as I read, Deaver sucks me in and fakes me out every time. Soon, I've lost awareness of my surroundings until the storm has grown so loud I can't ignore it any more.

When I look up from my book, the wind has gained its full voice. This storm is the mad child of Father Time and Mother Nature. Wailing away in no predictable rhythm, their monstrous offspring's throwing a hackle-raising temper tantrum. Underscoring the hideous howl, I detect another, quieter sound, a pitiable, weak whimper which has been all but completely drowned out by the epic volume of the screaming wind. With slowly dawning terror, I realize this cowardly voice is my own; escaping through the narrow opening of my barely parted lips. Where's my dad? Why is he taking so long?

The weather ignores my whining questions and continues to whip itself into a raging convulsion. The windows rattle and the wind screams. But the sounds are no longer random.

In the midst of the chaos, the howling begins to form an elongated word. Horrified, I recognize the stretched out syllables of my own name.

"Aaaaannaaaaabelle."

What on earth does it want with me?

"Aaaaannaaaaabelle!"

What the hell does it want with me? Then another terrifying thought occurs to me. What if whatever is howling my name also knocked over the ladder?

Suddenly, the back door bursts open and I curl up into a cowardly ball, burrowing deeper into the chair cushions with both arms curved around my head.

Stomp! Stomp! Uncle Johnny clears the snow from his heavy boots as he blusters into the kitchen. Melting snow drips off the visor of his cop's hat. "Your dad got stuck on his way home from the Kelley's house. The power lines are down over there, and a huge tree's blocking Prospect and Bay at the crossroads. He's really pissed that those jackasses insisted he come out in this storm and you're stuck here by yourself. I'll stay until he gets home, unless they call me out for another emergency. How're you holding up, honey?"

In answer to his innocent question, I jump out of my chair and fling myself into his arms.

"Annabelle, what is it, baby?"

The wind answers his question by crooning out my name from deep in its cavernous throat.

"Aaaaannaaaabelle."

"Holy shit! What was that?"

"I don't know, but it knocked me off a ladder, too."

"We can talk later about why the hell you were up on a ladder during this freak-show of a storm. That thing's not human. Here we go again. Damn it, Annabelle!"

"It's not my fault." My voice is quivering.

Uncle Johnny must hear the tears in my voice because he eases up on me. "Of course it isn't. I'm sorry, honey."

"Aaaaannaaaabelle," it wails, louder this time.

"I wish my mom was here."

"I wish she was, too but we can't call her. She'd make herself sick with worry and there's nothing she can do all the way from Florida."

"What will we do?"

He pauses for a moment, and then says, "I'm calling Nathaniel."

Before I can protest my uncle yanks out his cell. I don't stop him because I don't want to explain why I'm reluctant to ask for Nathaniel's help. It's way too complicated and personal. So Uncle Johnny ends up shouting into his phone at our local, gorgeous paranormal expert who happens to be seriously crushing on me at the moment. My poor, clueless uncle doesn't need to know how complicated my life is. He has no idea how hard I've been trying not to lean on Nathaniel.

"No, don't try to get here. Just tell me something we can do. Some creature from hell knocked Annabelle off a ladder, and now it's out there howling her name." They're on speaker phone, so I can hear Nathaniel's reply.

"It called her name?" he asks.

"Yes. Something really loud and scary is out there and it's screaming her name."

"Tell her not to answer." Nathaniel raises his voice several decibels and yells some more. "Whatever you do, don't answer it, Annabelle! Promise me you won't answer it, honey."

I shout back, "I didn't say one damn word, Nathaniel. I was too scared to talk."

"Good! I can be there in ten minutes. Don't answer that thing, whatever it is, and don't go outside!"

"It's too dangerous to drive. There are trees and power lines down everywhere," Uncle Johnny warns him.

Nathaniel ignores my uncle, the cop, and yells to his wingman. "Jeff, get in the van." The dog barks twice and then there's silence. He's hung up.

When Nathaniel pulls into our driveway, my uncle races out to help him into the house, leaving the door to the breezeway flapping open behind him. A few seconds later, Jeff leads the way into the kitchen, shaking the snow off his coat and snuffling it out of his nostrils. I run to get a towel and start drying him off. While I'm rubbing the dog's wet fur, Nathaniel wheels in, his golden brown curls sparkling with drops of melting snow and his face reddened with cold and the effort of moving himself through the storm and into the house. Uncle Johnny's right behind him. As soon as he slams the door shut, his radio begins to crackle with static.

"Damn, I can't hear a word they're saying. Gotta get this in the cruiser. There's probably been an accident. If I'm closest to the scene, I'll have to respond."

When he comes back in, my uncle is shaking his head. "Some damn fool took his Mercedes SUV out for a joy ride to see how it would perform in a blizzard. He ended up in a ditch off Summer Heights Road. The SUV's lying on its side. I'm the closest to the scene. Sorry, I have to get out there fast. He has two little kids in the car with him."

Uncle Johnny's gone before I can say, "What a dumbass."

Nathaniel and I look at each other. As if our connecting eyes give the horrifying creature strength, it howls again, keening out my name, much louder than before. Glass shatters nearby. I run out the kitchen door, into the breezeway, heading full speed toward the garage, with Jeff and Nathaniel tearing after me.

"Annabelle! Stop!" Nathaniel yells, halting me with the force of his voice.

For once in my life, I do as I'm told.

"Get behind me." I do it. Fast.

I'm that scared: of Nathaniel's anger and also of whatever made the crashing noise. My medium friend sounds like he's really pissed off.

The sound definitely came from the garage. I follow Nathaniel and Jeff across the flagstone floor of the breezeway and over to the door that leads into the garage. Nathaniel, Jeff and I, in that order, stare across the roof of my mother's Subaru at the damage. A tree limb crashed through a window. And landed right where my dad usually parks his truck.

Encased in ice and laden with chunks of snow, a giant limb from a huge oak tree is lying across the front of my mom's car. A powerful downdraft must've hurled the ill-fated bough through the garage window, like a medieval battering ram. The cliché "torn limb from limb" occurs to me as I stare at the damage and breathe in the frigid air.

The area where the branch separated from the trunk is a mass of splinters and the pale and vulnerable flesh of the inner wood is exposed. I hope the tree survives this catastrophe. My mom's windshield is shattered, and the whole front of her car is caved in, but my old Chevy Prizm is safe because it isn't in the garage. It's under a mound of snow in the driveway, next to Nathaniel's van.

"Get back in the house, now, Annabelle." Nathaniel's command and his harsh tone of voice snap me to my senses and again, I don't even think about arguing. Jeff lets out a low, threatening growl, and his owner places a calming hand on the huge hound's head. "Stay with Annabelle, Jeff."

The dog and I rush back to the kitchen together, leaving our brave medium to face my nemesis alone. Nathaniel's back in two minutes. "She's furious and she hates you, Annabelle."

"Thanks. I could have figured that out without your supernatural expertise, Einstein. She crashed a tree into our garage!"

"Seriously, this is no time to be a wise guy."

"I'm serious. Dad's gonna be pissed!"

"Everything can be repaired. Your parents' insurance should cover the damage. My main concern is for your safety."

"I'm scared out of my mind." I admit.

Two seconds later, another wailing whoosh of wind shakes the whole house. I run to the front window just in time to watch a huge maple tree fall over, blocking the driveway. I'll need to get out there with the saw so Dad can drive up to the house when he gets home. Farther away, toward the end of the driveway, a sharp pop like a rifle shot splits the night air and I can see and hear the sizzling, crackling green fire as a crazy wire flies down and dances frantically in the white night. Immediately, our house lights black out and we're left in complete darkness. The hum of the furnace dies with a thump.

Nathaniel tries to call the fire department to report the loose wire, but he can't get through on either his cell or our landline. In an urgent voice, he starts bossing me around again. "Annabelle. Light the candles. Then come over here. Sit across from me and hold both of my hands."

"I gotta get out there and saw apart that limb. It's blocking the driveway. Dad won't be able get up to the house."

"On a cold day in hell. No way are you going out there. See that dangling live wire out by the street? She'll string one of those around your neck. She's just waiting for the opportunity and she's not patient. When she learns patience she'll be even more dangerous."

"It might be exactly that, Nathaniel."

"What do you mean?"

"A cold day in hell. Except it's night. You said she. How can you tell it's a woman?"

"She's definitely not a natural creature of this earth and I'm a medium, remember?" he asks gently, raising his eyebrows. "Come over here. We can figure this out, together, honey. I refuse to let her hurt you."

I use the light from my cell phone to find some matches and light the two tall pillar candles on our kitchen table. Then I pull a chair over and sit down across from Nathaniel. Jeff retreats, through the kitchen door and into a corner of the living room. He hates ghosts, and we're definitely dealing with a ghost, again. While Nathaniel holds my shaking hands in his two, large warm ones, he stares into my eyes. At first he seems to be seeing only me and thinking about me. Then his gaze grows less focused and he speaks. "She's furious with you!" His voice hoarsens with disbelief. "She's murderously jealous!"

Next he directly addresses the dangerous apparition. "Whoever you are, leave her alone. There will be serious consequences if you don't."

The answering wind screams out my name in a pitch that makes us both cringe. In the next room, Jeff howls long and loud; then his voice fades to a rumbling growl. I can barely see him in the dark. But I can tell he's crouched, huge and ready with his teeth bared. Nathaniel flings back his head and the muscles in his neck flex as he hisses at our new enemy. "Leave her the hell alone or I will come after you and send you down to a place where few go and no one ever returns."

The next sound raises my hackles like nothing ever has before. She laughs. Cackling and shrieking, she shakes the house until several slate tiles slide off the roof, down past the kitchen window, and slice into the drifting snow below.

Silently, I stare down at the cuts in the snow and listen to the thundering of my own heartbeat. When I finally look up, I see her for the first time. And the only good news is: she's in retreat. From behind she looks like a huge stingray formed from a thick mist of snow. Billowing, her magnificent presence sweeps across our backyard, toward the forest. Even though it's dark outside, her physical manifestation casts an even darker shadow and it's about a quarter acre wide. She hovers for a moment at the edge of the woods. From this distance, she's barely visible in the swirling madness of the storm, as she cuts an evil swathe between two towering pines. The whole house shakes, from foundation to chimney top when the trembling trees crash to the ground.

"She hath risen." A voice from the past whispers out from between Nathaniel's lips. He sounds like someone from another century. Staring at him, I wait to hear more, but he just sits there silently for a minute, then blinks his eyes and shakes his head. Grabbing both of my hands, he pulls me into his lap. Jeff trots over and lays his big, warm head on my knee.

"What demon from hell have you pissed off now, Annabelle?" Cradling me softly in his arms, Nathaniel tucks my head under his chin and strokes my hair. Jeff licks my hand.

Then my friend the medium continues. "Whoever she was, whatever she is now, her first goal is to harm you. I can't tell yet how much control I have over her, but maybe if I stay close I can protect you. I think I scared her off for now. She knows I won't let her have you without a fight."

Jeff barks, adding his own exclamation point to Nathaniel's statement.

"Whatever you do, Annabelle, when she says your name, don't answer. If you answer, she'll have power over you. And I'm not talking about the power to scare you half to death. Her power over you will be hypnotic. You'll want to do what she tells you to do and she'll tell you to do something dangerous. Her mission here on earth is to hurt you and she will if she has a chance. She might even kill you."

"Why? Who the hell is she? What the hell have I ever done to her?"

"You've got the hell part right. That's definitely where she's from and she wants you to join her there."

"How do you know that?"

"I've read about spirits like hers, but I've never encountered one until now."

"What kind of spirits?"

"In many cultures, people tell traditional stories about evil ghosts who lure victims to their deaths. In India, there's a certain kind of Bhoot, or ghost, called a churail who looks like a young woman and lures young men to their deaths. In the French ballet, Giselle, the Willis are the ghosts of young girls who drive the character of Hilarion to his death. Your ancestors, the Wampanoags, feared the Pukwudgies, troll-like creatures who attack their victims and lure them to their deaths. I think your new enemy is this type of supernatural being. She has risen from the grave for one purpose, to lead you over to the other side."

"The other side?"

"Yes, Annabelle. The dark side, the afterlife."

"But what does she have against me? What did I ever do to her?"

"Probably nothing. This grudge isn't about something done intentionally by anyone she ever knew. In life, she was jealous, vindictive and evil. After death, she's worse."

"I still don't understand."

"That's because you're a good soul. Another good soul, someone who knew her when she was alive, made sure she couldn't return from the grave, but that's over now. Our girl waited a long time to be free so she could destroy a young life again. Somewhere, deep down in her hateful, twisted soul, her actions make sense. I think that recently, someone here in Eastfield deliberately set her free and for some outlandish reason that only makes sense to her, this vengeful spirit thinks you deserve to be punished. We need to find out more so we can stop this evil, destructive creature."

"How will we find out more?"

"We'll do what we did before. We need clues: supernatural clues and clues from this life, too. Someone invited her back into the land of the living where she doesn't belong. I just don't know who would do that. We'll figure it out. Try not to worry."

"But I can tell that you're really worried. So how am *I* supposed to be brave?"

"I can be brave for both of us. You need to focus on staying safe. Like I said before, and I can't emphasize it enough, if she calls your name again, don't answer her. And whatever you do, Annabelle, when she tries to summon you, don't go outside."

"Believe me. I'm not even tempted. I want nothing to do with her." Which is kind of true, but like always, I'm also curious.

"She's new at this. I don't know who made it possible for her to escape from the grave, but somebody here on Earth helped her rise from the dead and it happened recently. Then right away, she found you, Annabelle. She wants to have power over you and hurt you, but she doesn't know how to go about it yet. She's being way too obvious. She doesn't realize that scaring the crap out of you won't work if her goal is to lure you outside and into her supernatural force-field of power. She'll figure it out, though. You'll have to be on your guard. It will eventually occur to her that she has to be sneaky, not forthright. She has to trick you. So watch out. I'm scared for you. I'm scared for us."

If Nathaniel's afraid, it must be bad. It must be downright horrifying. I try to calm down and think straight, but I'm quivering.

Then my cell phone vibrates and it's my dad calling. The reception's terrible but we manage to communicate through the weird echoes and the static by shouting and repeating ourselves.

"I'm fine!" He screams into his phone, "but I still can't get home."

"It's okay. Nathaniel's here with me," I assure him. "I'm all right. But the power's out and there's a tree down across our driveway."

"I'm just a few miles away, outside, with a road crew, sawing at a giant tree that fell over last night. It's blocking the crossroad at Prospect and Bay."

I can hear him as he yells to the guys he's working with. "There's a live wire down in front of my house and a tree blocking the driveway!" Then he turns back to me and says, "They're dispatching a crew over to our house, honey, so sit tight. Help's on the way."

"Good, because it's starting to get really cold and dark and scary in here."

"I probably won't make it home until morning, but try not to…"

I think he said "worry", but right then we lose our connection, so I'm not completely sure.

Nathaniel, Jeff and I are sitting in the kitchen, with the fragrant candles burning beside us on the table. Outside, the wind has died down and the snow's falling in soft, silent flakes, instead of miniature, pelting meteors, like before. Huge white domes and drifts have transformed our backyard into a magnificent, sloping, glistening landscape, silent and untouched by humans, the way it must have looked centuries ago.

The scenery might look peaceful and beautiful right now, with the flakes falling and the mounds of white growing higher by the minute, but our dreamy, idyllic landscape was more like something out of a nightmare a few minutes ago. Shuddering, even in the warmth and safety of Nathaniel's lap, I ask him, "Do you think she'll come back?"

He wraps his arms more tightly around me. "I think her strength comes from the weather and our fear. But mainly, she rides on the wind with a fury born in hell."

"And she hates me?"

"Yes, but I don't know why. I keep getting this feeling that she's jealous."

"She's a raving, jealous, homicidal demon who's recently escaped from hell."

"I didn't want to spell it out like that. You're scared enough already. But yes. That's exactly what she is."

"What do we do now, Nathaniel?"

"For now, you're safe, because the violence of the storm has died down, and because I'm with you. She knows that I have some power over those who don't belong here among the living. As long as you're physically close to me, I don't think she'll get violent again."

Feeling a little safer because of Nathaniel's reassurances, I stand up from his lap and stretch. Now that I'm not scared half to death, I realize how sleepy I am and yawn.

Nathaniel grabs my hand. "C'mon darlin'. Let's snuggle you up so you can get some rest. Jeff and I will protect you."

Too traumatized by the horror of our experience and basically just completely worn out, I don't protest. I follow him and Jeff out of the kitchen so we can all cuddle up and get some sleep.

Chapter 8

The Day After

Sometime during the night, the power must've come back. I can tell because the reading lamp next to the couch is on. But we don't need the light from the lamp. The window shades are up and a bright and beautiful new day dawned while we were sleeping. The sun in the blue sky has resurrected itself as if everything's fine in the world, but my situation is anything but. Last night I fell asleep with my tangle-haired head resting on Nathaniel's chest and right now I'm wedged in between his strong, warm body and the back of the couch. Gently and quietly I lift my cheek off of his shoulder so I can sneak a look at him while he's sleeping. His chest moves up and down in a velvet rhythm and his breath is easing in and out like shallow waves at low tide on a perfect beach day.

Except for maybe Wyatt, Nathaniel is the most beautiful man I've ever seen, but his beauty is more angelic, and Wyatt's more earthbound. If Michelangelo met Nathaniel first, he never would have sculpted David. The man's an artist's vision; inspired by a higher power and set down on Earth to bring mayhem into the lives of as many women as possible.

This last thought occurs to me because I can hear the plow on my father's truck scraping up our snowbound driveway. Hopefully, he'll take another swipe at the long and winding path that leads up to our house, before he comes inside, but I can't take any chances. So I leap out from the cozy niche where I slept for the whole night. The den's my dad's sanctuary. I think I can safely predict that he'll be really pissed off if he finds Nathaniel and me sleeping together on his couch. Before I head upstairs, so it will look like I slept in my own room, I glance back at my gorgeous friend. He blinks sleepily and smiles a lazy smile before his eyes close again. Next to him, down on the rug, Jeff lies snoring quietly, in a huge, curled-up furry pile. His body is wound around in a complete circle, with the end of his tail draped over his nose. Last night was long and stressful for all of us; both my houseguests look exhausted.

I can't afford to drift back to sleep, though. Like most fathers of teenage girls, mine will be enraged if he finds me asleep in the arms of a man, no matter how innocent the situation is. So I race upstairs to ruffle up the covers on my bed, intending to make it look slept-in. When I reach the door to my bedroom, however, I burst out laughing, from pent up hysteria and relief. My bed not only looks like I slept in it. It looks like a very rowdy Girl Scout troop has been camping out in it for a month. The whole room is a disastrous pit of chaos, like it always is. Only *I* can find anything in here. Actually, sometimes even I can't find what I need in this mess. Pivoting, I head back down the stairs to greet my male parent who walks into the kitchen at precisely the same instant I reach the bottom step.

Racing full tilt, I run over and throw myself into my father's arms.

"Whoa, sweetheart, I'm getting old. You're going to knock me over one of these days. Take it easy."

"Dad, I was so worried."

"I'm fine, just tired. I've been up all night helping to move the huge oak tree that was blocking Prospect Street. I've never seen anything like it. You know the giant tree that shades the whole crossroads down at the four corners where Bay meets Prospect?"

"Yes, it's been there for centuries. What happened?"

"The damndest thing…almost gave me a heart attack. I was driving home and just as I got to the crossroads of Prospect and Bay, a giant bolt of lightning lit up the sky like it was noontime on a sunny day. There was one big flaming, split-second flash." With his hands palm up, he stretches his arms out wide. Then he starts frantically waving them in the air. "I've never seen such white light in my life, and I hope I never see anything like it ever again. A huge lightning bolt formed, high in the night sky. Sizzling and crackling like the fires of hell, it shot down and exploded. The tree split in half and crashed across the road. Right in front of my truck." In the middle of this wild speech, Dad reaches up as high as he can reach, with his right hand, to demonstrate the height of the oak and the level of the catastrophe. "I had to back up fast. The whole damn tree was steaming; flames shooting up everywhere. Branches, limbs, the giant trunk: all blocking the road, all of it on fire. There's only a tall, jagged, blackened stump still standing."

Nathaniel appears at this moment, sitting in his gleaming wheelchair, looking like his usually gorgeous self, except a little more rumpled. "Lightning? I've never heard of lightning during a snowstorm."

"Practic'ly scared me to death…damn tree almost fell on my truck."

"Thank god you're all right!" The details of my father's ordeal horrify me. He could have died.

"Yup, I'll admit. It was a close one."

"What happened after the tree fell, Dad?"

"I got on my cell and was able to get through to the fire department. Then, once the fire was out, we had to wait for the snow and the freezing cold air to cool everything off before we could touch it. I stayed and helped saw the damn thing up and get the logs out of there. It took all night, but we did it. I managed to reach Johnny and later I got my phone to work again and called you, but our cell service was in and out all night because of the storm. What happened? Why is Nathaniel here?" Before I can start answering his questions, Jeff ambles into the kitchen and with one quick bark demands to be let out to do his morning business.

Dad laughs and ruffles the fur on Jeff's head. "First things first, I guess. Answering Nature's call can't wait, right, fella? C'mon boy, go out and make some yellow snow. It's a good thing you're long legged. One of those little squirt, ratty dogs couldn't travel through this mess. What do the Chihuahuas do in this weather?" He lets Jeff out into the backyard and waits at the door for him to nose through the powdery white drifts and accomplish his mission. When my dad and Jeff come back into the kitchen, they both look as hungry as I am. I'm sure my stomach's grumbling so loud that at the very least, Jeff, with his super acute canine hearing, can hear the rude noises.

As if he's reading my mind, or maybe listening to my stomach, Nathaniel asks, "What's for breakfast? I'm starving. Our story is too complicated and too scary to tell on an empty stomach."

"Scary?" my dad asks as he fills the teakettle, puts it on the stove and turns on the burner.

"Very scary," I answer from inside the kitchen cabinet where I'm rummaging around, looking for mixing bowls, pots and pans. I'm thinking about how thankful I am that our power got restored and the tree's off the driveway, too. According to my dad, a lot of people in town still have no power and tons of trees came down. We're lucky my dad was working with the town's road crew and they sent someone over here right away.

Everything's working and we can make a hot breakfast, which we all need. I'm grateful that Nathaniel's awake now, too, and can help me explain his own presence in our kitchen at first light.

Chapter 9

We Consult Oliver

I start whipping up a dozen scrambled eggs with a few handfuls of grated sharp cheddar cheese. They're my specialty; one of the only things I can cook without screwing up. Adding a little milk—not water—I use the electric mixer and beat the eggs on high speed. This makes the whole concoction super fluffy. Then I pour it into a pan and sprinkle another handful of cheese onto the top. I also prepare a huge pile of really buttery toast and fry up some breakfast sausages that I found in the freezer. After we sit down to eat, Nathaniel and I explain the situation to my father as well as we can. We don't know very much about the vicious spirit who rose from its grave last night and drew strength from the power of the storm. So our story's kind of short.

Dad has a helpful suggestion. "We need to call Oliver. He might know something about the town's history that fits in with what few facts we have."

So he calls Oliver and puts him on speaker. After a brief exchange of polite storm discussion we get down to business. My father explains that we know the ghost is intimidated by Nathaniel.

"And she hates Annabelle. Nathaniel figured that much out."

I didn't need Nathaniel's expertise as a medium to reach the conclusion that I was the target of the creature's supernatural hostility. "Yeah, I actually figured it out before Nathaniel did. When she knocked me off the ladder and I almost fractured my skull, my first thought was, 'Maybe she hates me. A lot.'"

Simultaneously, Dad's and Nathaniel's heads snap up and Dad demands to know what I was doing up on a ladder during a storm.

Nathaniel echoes, "What the hell were you doing up on a ladder, Annabelle?"

"Mom's wind chimes were blowing around like crazy and I didn't want them to get damaged. So I got the ladder out of the garage and climbed up and took them down."

"Annabelle! You could've been killed!" Dad's eyes are blazing.

"You stupid, dumbass! You're lucky to still be alive!" Nathaniel looks like he wants to jump out of his wheelchair so he can finish the job the ghost started.

Predictably, they're both really pissed off at me.

"She's a jealous, homicidal bitch." Nathaniel offers his professional opinion. "She's not gonna stop until she hurts you, Annabelle. Or kills you. You need to be more careful than you've ever been before in your life if you want to stay alive."

"And that means staying off of ladders during raging blizzards," my dad adds.

Oliver speaks up, saying, "Let's all calm down now. Annabelle's okay and she realizes she did something incredibly stupid."

"Thanks, Oliver."

He laughs. "Anytime. We all need to stay focused now and figure this out. I need more to go on, Nathaniel. I can't just start researching the history of jealous homicidal bitches who hate Annabelle. Can't you guys tell me anything else? There aren't many chapters on that particular subject in Huntington Phelps's History of Eastfield. Tell me how the whole thing started. What was the first sign, sweetie?" He directs his question at me.

"I think maybe the way the wind whirled around the ladder like a tornado. I was at the top and it felt like the legs of the ladder actually rose up off the ground."

Dad cuts in. "If we think back over everything that occurred last night, the situation with the old oak tree could be connected. I couldn't get home to Annabelle because that huge, ancient tree, at the crossroads of Prospect and Bay, almost fell on my truck when I was driving home last night. It was struck by lightning."

"Whoa! Lightning during a snowstorm is very rare, Bill. Did anyone else see any lightning or hear any thunder last night?" Oliver asks.

"We could Google it," my dad suggests.

"Good idea. Jackson's getting right on it." Oliver pauses and then after a minute or two, speaks again. "I'm thinking about the location of the lightning strike. Right near the crossroads where the lightning hit the tree is an old burial ground and the woman who has two graves is buried there."

Oliver certainly knows some interesting and unusual historical facts about our town.

"Why does she have two graves?" I ask.

"No one knows for sure, but there's been some speculation. Her family and her husband's family might have argued about where she should be buried. She was born a Littlefield and she married a Hayward. The Littlefields and the Haywards didn't get along. At the beginning of the nineteenth century the two families were engaged in a full-out feud. They battled over the boundaries of their land constantly. No one was ever killed, but Hastings Littlefield was seriously wounded when Hieronymus Hayward shot him in the shoulder in 1805. Hayward spent a couple of years in prison and after that they cooled it with the violence but still wrangled constantly about who owned which acres near the adjoining border of their farms."

"Tell us more about the woman with the two headstones." Her mysterious graves fascinate me.

"On the Littlefield side of the Prospect Street Burial Ground, she has a grave marker and one on the Hayward's side, too."

"Okay, Oliver, you're in charge of digging up information about the woman who has two graves. What else?" Dad chuckles at his own obnoxious pun and I elbow him in the bicep.

"The spot where that old oak tree grows...I guess I should say grew...is right at the crossroads, a few meters away from the Prospect Street Burial Ground. Rebecca Morse is buried exactly there. At the crossroads, in unhallowed ground. She was a suicide."

"Holy shit!" Nathaniel almost falls out of his wheelchair.

"Take it easy, Nathaniel. We don't need any injuries." My dad's only half-joking.

"Point taken." Nathaniel adjusts himself so he's more firmly seated again and then gets us back on track. "Oliver, is it possible that the two women are connected: the one with two graves and the suicide buried in unhallowed ground?"

"They both lived in Eastfield at the same time. They were born within about ten years of each other, too. Rebecca Morse was born in 1847 and died in 1867. Her husband's descendants still live here in Eastfield. You know them. The Morses: the elderly couple whose land adjoins yours way out toward the back of your property. And, according to the inscription on both of her headstones, Katherine Littlefield Hayward was born in 1837 and died in 1885."

"How did Rebecca die?" I want to know. "She was only a couple of years older than me when she killed herself. Why would she do that? What on earth could have happened to her that made her not want to live anymore?"

Oliver answers me in a solemn voice. "She walked out onto the ice on Deep Water Pond; out back of the Morse's, not too far from your house... Fell through and froze to death. They didn't find her body until the spring thaw."

"Couldn't it have been an accident? We ice skate on Deep Water Pond all the time. If you don't test the ice, if there hasn't been a bunch of freezing cold days in a row, anyone could fall through. There's an underground spring that feeds the pond in the deepest part, near the middle. That's always the last section of the pond to freeze over and the first to start melting, with the exception of a few spots along the edges. If no one was there to help her when she fell through she wouldn't be able to get out."

"She wasn't ice skating; it didn't happen during the daytime or early evening when people might normally be ice skating. Plus it happened in March, when the ice on Deep Water Pond is notoriously thin and it's too dangerous for skating. Everyone knows that now and they knew it back then, too. No, Annabelle, she had no reason to be out on the ice and she should've known that it's not safe during the month of March. Rebecca Morse deliberately walked out onto unsafe ice at about eleven o'clock at night, all by herself. She headed straight for the thinnest ice in the middle, on purpose. There was a witness. But the witness was too far away to help her. Plus, the other person might have been killed, too, if he ventured out onto the thin ice."

"Does anyone know who the witness was?" The story of Rebecca Morse's suicide is unnerving me. I can feel my interest in the incident begin to escalate into obsession. I ice skate on Deep Water Pond every winter. She was only a couple of years older than me when she died. I need to know more. We have to find out everything that happened.

"I don't know who the witness was," Oliver says. "I just remember hearing part of the story from Hazel Vincent one night. We were doing the Eastfield cemetery tour, the week end before Halloween, to raise money for the historical society."

"Maybe we should contact Hazel," Nathaniel suggests.

"Good idea. She's more of an authority than I am on the genealogy of Eastfield's families, especially the ones who're buried in that particular cemetery. Someone from Hazel's mother's family is buried there. Anyway, the Prospect Street Burial Ground was the last stop on our tour that night. I remember how cold and dark it was by the time we arrived at the graveyard. Hazel pointed out the two gravestones of Katherine Hayward and then she mentioned Rebecca's final resting place, outside the graveyard. Hers has no headstone. Originally there was a crude wooden cross formed from two thick sticks marking her grave, but it's long gone. A grave marker like that doesn't last long, not like the stone ones."

"So one woman has two headstones and the other has none. Doesn't seem fair." I'm already beginning to feel sympathetic toward the underdog: Rebecca Morse.

"What did Hazel say about Rebecca's death?" Nathaniel asks.

"Hazel didn't mention the name of the witness when she was telling us the story. If I remember correctly, we all got spooked out there in the dark, talking about suicides and unhallowed ground. It was the last stop of the evening. The corner of Prospect and Bay is pretty remote. There aren't any houses nearby; no streetlights, either. Like I said, it was very dark and cold by the time we got there. Some of the people on the tour wanted to leave. It's a creepy spot, even during the daylight. Hazel probably skipped over some of the details so we could end the tour and go home. I can give her a call, though."

"So it's scary out there, huh, Oliver?"

"Annabelle, don't get any ideas." Nathaniel shoots me a warning glance that could kill, but I already have plenty of ideas. And when I start getting ideas, no one can stop me. I can't even stop myself. My reckless imagination has gotten me into dangerous situations before. And often.

"Oliver," I lean toward my father's cell phone which is lying in the middle of our kitchen table, "we need to talk to Hazel Vincent immediately and I need to go out to the old burial ground."

"No one's going anywhere for a while, Annabelle. Some of the roads haven't even been plowed yet," Oliver answers. "I'll call Hazel as soon as I hang up. If she has any information I'll get back to you right away."

I thank him and we all say goodbye. Dad pockets his cell phone.

Then he points out, "Oliver's right. No one's going anywhere today. It's too snowy and slippery."

"But you have the plow on your truck and brand new tires, with super thick treads, Dad. Please? We have to find out what she wants or she won't leave me alone."

"You're staying right here, Annabelle."

"But this is exactly where she attacked me last night."

"As long as I'm here, Bill, she's safe. Whatever caused all that excitement last night is reluctant to cause trouble while I'm near Annabelle. She'll be okay if I stick close."

"Thanks, Nathaniel. I'm at a loss about what to do with Susannah gone. We can fix up the couch in the den for you."

Great! Things aren't awkward enough between me and Nathaniel. Now he's moving in with us indefinitely and my dad actually invited him! The only good thing is that maybe he can help me find out more about Rebecca Morse. I suggest, "We should have a séance."

"Slow down, Annabelle. Let's see what Oliver comes up with first. You're forgetting how scared you were last night. This spirit, whoever she is, is very powerful and destructive. We need to be careful," Nathaniel warns.

"We need to act fast, before she strikes again. The more we know about her the better off we'll be. We need to take the offensive; be proactive," I answer him.

"Honey, you sound like a damned football coach. Slow down." Dad's not buying into my idea. "Step one, Annabelle, let's clean up breakfast. Step two: we wait for Oliver to call back. Step three: I go over to the Morse's house. I always plow them out first 'cuz they're elderly. Maybe they know something about this woman's suicide."

"The Morses? I'm definitely coming. They're sure to know something about Rebecca Morse. Her husband was related to them."

The phone rings just then but it's not Oliver, yet. It's my mom calling from Florida. She saw footage of the storm on the TV news and wants to make sure everyone's okay. My dad reassures her, telling her that we lost power but it's back and everyone's fine. He puts me on the phone next, holding one finger to his lips to signal me that I shouldn't get her all worried by telling her about the mysterious destructive force that seems to have it in for me. Duh. I would never do that anyway. All of the runways at both Logan and Green are closed and there's no way she'll be able to get a flight back anytime soon. She'd just worry herself sick. And she's already worried enough about her sister.

My mother needs to stay in Key West and take care of Maeve who's doing better and will be released from the hospital soon. But she'll need home care for a while. Mom plans to stay at Maeve's house and take care of her for at least a couple of weeks after her twin sister gets out of the hospital. I would feel better if my mother and her invaluable talent for warding off evil could be here with us, but this is no time to be selfish. And we have Nathaniel, so everything will be okay. I hope.

Then my mother tells us some really exciting news. Auntie Maeve wants our whole family to come down to Key West for Christmas. And Dad agrees. We'll fly down the night before Christmas Eve and back on New Year's Day. I won't have to miss any school, which sucks, but it's going to be an amazing trip. She and Maeve already went online and bought us the tickets. It's the best Christmas present ever and I can't wait. We say goodbye to my mother and I start to feel better about missing her because we'll be together in a couple of weeks.

I'll be safe in Key West and for now I'm safe here, too. I'm actually starting to feel a little too safe. Last night I was terrified, but in the brilliant sunlight with the smell of toast still lingering in our kitchen and both Dad and Nathaniel close by, I start to forget how petrified I was in the middle of it all. Things are getting too boring and predictable in our cozy kitchen. My restlessness is building up again. I haven't even been housebound for twenty-four hours yet and I'm getting cabin fever. I want to be out hunting down information about Rebecca Morse and the woman with two headstones, not sitting around waiting for Oliver to call.

Then I get one of my great ideas. "Dad, before you say no, hear me out."

"I hate it when you say things like that, Annabelle."

"Really, Dad, I have a great idea. I can go over to the Morse's with you right now. You've been up all night so you shouldn't drive over there alone. You can plow out their driveway quickly. While you're doing that, I'll go in, pay a little visit, brew them up some of Mom's tea, whatever. They're old. We should make sure they're okay as soon as possible."

"You're annoying, Annabelle, but you're right. Get your coat. Put on your boots. We'll be home in about an hour, Nathaniel. Hold the fort."

Jeff barks, answering in the affirmative for his master.

Chapter 10

Rebecca Morse

The most direct route to the Morse's is a path through the woods leading to Deep Water Pond. To enter their backyard, you can either follow that path along the shore or row across the pond. They live less than two miles away from my house if you take this short cut. When you drive, though, it's about seven or eight miles. Mr. and Mrs. Morse are both in their mid eighties and aren't going to go jogging through the woods and rowing across the water anytime soon, just to visit us. Once in a while, my mom drives over, the long way, to bring them tea and candles and to chat about this and that. I used to go over with my mother when I was little. Sometimes when I'm running in the woods, I take the trail to their house and pop in to say hello, but I haven't done that in a couple of years at least.

When we arrive at the Morse's, Dad has to plow his way into and up their driveway. As soon as we get near their house, I grab a snow shovel from the truck bed and scoop out a path to the backdoor. Then I bound up the steps and knock. They're thrilled to see Dad and his plow and happy to see me again, too. I feel a little guilty about not visiting them in a while and promise myself that I'll visit more often. They've got a fire going in the woodstove, warming up their cheerful kitchen. Mrs. Morse is knitting baby clothes for her newest great-grandchild and her husband's reading yesterday's paper. She puts the little sweater down to give me a hug and tell me how pretty I am. Mrs. Morse can't say enough about how tall I've grown. I'm five six, but Mrs. Morse is about four foot ten, so I must look gigantic to her.

"My goodness, Annabelle, look how grown-up looking and beautiful you are! Ed, look at her!"

Ed looks at me. "So, Annabelle, movie star or fashion model, what's it gonna be?"

"Time for a new eyeglasses prescription, Mr. Morse." I volunteer to take them both to the eye doctor. We all have a good laugh over that one. Mr. Morse especially loves to share a few giggles.

He finishes chuckling, catches his breath with a wheeze and asks me for serious what my future plans are.

"I applied to River Wind University. I don't know what I'm going to major in yet, but I know it's not acting. And I don't even think models go to college. I hate having to stay still to get my picture taken anyway, so I could never do that. Plus I'm not tall enough."

"Bull feathers! You could be famous and make millions and we could brag to our friends that we know you." Mr. Morse laughs long and loud at his own joke.

"Yup, that's pretty funny, Mr. Morse. Hey, Dad's out plowing your driveway. Is there anything I can do for you while we're here? Do you need anything?"

"No, we keep all the necessities in stock especially in the winter."

"Well, I brought you some of my mom's chamomile tea. It's good for the digestion and if you have a cold, too, it helps."

"If you add enough honey to that crap, it actually tastes decent." Mr. Morse is cracking himself up. He's right, though; the tea only tastes good with a ton of honey in it.

"Ed, stop it. Thank you for the tea, dear. That was very thoughtful."

"I brought you some candles, too."

"Lavender!" Mrs. Morse takes the candles out of my outstretched hand. "My favorite! I feel a little tickle in my throat. I'm sure that your mom's tea will prevent it from developing into a cold. Let's put the kettle on and have a nice cup of tea. There's a jar of Mr. Long's honey on the shelf nearest to the stove, sweetie."

One of our neighbors is a beekeeper and he supplies some of his friends, including my family, with organic honey. Moving around their kitchen, I locate the honey and put the teakettle on. Then we chitchat for a few more minutes while I set everything up. They really are a nice old couple and Mr. Morse is a hoot in his own annoying little way. My grandparents live in Naples, Florida and I miss them. I rarely get to see them more than once a year. The Morses will have to do for now.

The Morses and I sit down to tea and I begin by asking about their living relatives. "How're the grandkids and the great grandkids?"

It takes a full ten minutes for Mrs. Morse to recite their names, ages and accomplishments while Mr. Morse fetches the photo album. Then we all sit down at the table with our tea and I ooh and aah over how handsome, beautiful, cute and adorable all the children are. Finally I get down to business by segueing into what a great gene pool the Morses have. I ask if any of their ancestors were known for beauty or accomplishments.

Bingo!

Mr. Morse starts talking about her right away. Her beauty was renowned. "Rebecca Morse was her name. She was only a Morse by marriage, though, and she and her husband didn't have any children, so we can't claim that our grandkids take after her for looks. Her name was Burns before she married Jonathan Morse. Her family was from up on the north shore, Peabody I think."

"No, Salem, dear. Her folks lived in Salem."

"Hmmm. Guess you're right. Salem it is; it was. Any-hoo, she moved down here to Eastfield. I think she had a sister and three brothers, too, but they stayed up on the north shore with the rest of the Burns' family. Rebecca moved here because she married Jonathan Morse. He joined the Union Army but never returned from the Civil War. Died a hero; killed by General Stonewall Jackson's troops in Virginia; 1862. He and Rebecca hadn't even been married a year. And, like I said, they had no children."

"So she was widowed?"

"Yup, and she was only sixteen. A beautiful young girl, the respectable widow of a war hero, but she kept to herself in that little stone cabin on the edge of Deep Water Pond, out where you kids go skating every winter."

Mrs. Morse seems to know a lot about her.

"She grew wildflowers, herbs and vegetables; very self sufficient. Like your mother, she could heal, too. The townspeople visited her in the little cottage to buy herbal remedies and to get advice about sickness and injuries. People had to come to her, though. After Rebecca's young husband died so tragically, she never left the cabin or the garden much."

Mr. Morse adds the saddest part. "But she died in disgrace and couldn't be buried in the Prospect Street Burial Ground with the rest of the Morse family. She killed herself. In a very unusual way…"

The old guy's voice drifts off and Mrs. Morse completes his thought. "She walked out onto the deepest part of the pond and fell through the ice." Evidently, the Morses have been married so long they finish each other's sentences.

Dad comes in right then and announces that the driveway is clear and the path, too. Neither of the Morses drives anymore, but now friends and relatives can get in and out. And if they have an emergency, they can be rescued. I want to hear more, but Dad needs to get home. He's exhausted. We say our goodbyes and I promise to visit again soon. I can't wait to find out more about Rebecca.

As we drive slowly over the roads made white with packed-down snow, I fill Dad in on what the Morses had to say about the unfortunate Rebecca Burns Morse. When we arrive at our house, Jackson's SUV is in the driveway, next to my father's truck.

Oliver and Jackson are sitting around our kitchen table drinking tea with Nathaniel when Dad and I come chuffing and huffing in out of the cold.

"Hey, you two! How'd you get over here so fast?" Dad greets our friends.

"Oliver's driveway isn't very big, so we were able to clear it with Wyatt's help. Then we just jumped into my SUV and hit the road. Threw a couple of snow shovels into the back in case we got stuck," Jackson answers him.

"School's cancelled until Wednesday at the earliest. I got the call about a half hour ago," Oliver announces.

"Thank you, Mr. Finn, for that information." I'm happy to have some time off.

Oliver continues to fill us in on the latest storm news. "It will take at least that long to clear the parking lots and dig out the buses. A lot of the secondary roads haven't been thoroughly plowed yet, either. Plus a few neighborhoods still don't have power."

Jackson grins. "Oliver couldn't stay home another minute with Wyatt. That kid has been in such a foul mood lately. He mopes around and speaks only in monosyllables. We had to get away." Then he winks at me.

I don't know how to respond, so I smile back at him. I get it; Jackson's hinting that Wyatt's depressed because we're not together anymore. This pleases me, but also raises an important question. Why don't we get back together? He's miserable without me. And I would love to get back together. But we're not here to talk about my nonexistent relationship with Wyatt. We're here to start the new paranormal investigation.

I can't wait to tell Oliver what I discovered over at the Morse's, but first I want to find out if he dug up any additional information. "Did you find out anything more about Rebecca Morse or Katherine Hayward?"

My dad excuses himself. "Hey, it's not that I don't find all this fascinating, but I can barely keep my eyes open. I'm just gonna head to the den and take a quick snooze on my couch for an hour or two."

We all wish him pleasant dreams and then get back to business.

"Yes I did and that's the reason I came over instead of just calling."

Jackson joins in. "He was on the phone with Hazel for almost an hour."

"Fascinating story. We're going to have to research it further, but Hazel knew a lot of details." Oliver waits a moment for me to sit down at the table with everyone before he continues. "The person who witnessed Rebecca's walk out onto the ice was Katherine Littlefield Hayward: the woman with two graves."

"Whoa!"

"Yes, it's a matter of public record. The complete transcript of Katherine's testimony is in one of the old files over at town hall. A few years ago, Hazel read the whole thing from cover to cover. She took a lot of notes, too, and read them to me over the phone."

"So what's the story, Oliver?" I'm literally sitting on the edge of my seat, gripping the sides to stay anchored.

"Hazel says that the night Rebecca died, Katherine couldn't sleep. She suffered from insomnia and it was her habit to take long walks in the fresh air to tire herself out. She was walking out by Deep Water Pond at about eleven o'clock at night and she saw Rebecca rush out onto the ice. The young war widow appeared to be all distraught and upset. Once she got out to the middle of the pond, at the deepest part, the ice cracked. It was early March and they'd had some warm days recently."

"And Rebecca fell through and died?"

Oliver nods his head. "The whole story is in the old files down at the Eastfield Town Hall. Katherine Hayward signed an affidavit. She went on public record saying that she ran to get help, but by the time she returned with her husband and his older brother Robert, Rebecca had sunk completely out of sight, beneath the ice. They couldn't find her. Katherine's husband crept out onto the ice and fell through, but his brother fished him out safely. No one else even tried after that. The three of them just went home."

"Oh my god! How long before they found Rebecca's body?"

"It took a few weeks, but finally the ice melted and they found her. By then, Katherine's official testimony had been written down and signed. Rebecca Burns Morse had to be buried in unconsecrated ground because her death was ruled a suicide."

As the events replay themselves in my mind's eye, like a tragic scene in a film, I start shivering. "So Rebecca ran out onto the ice for no reason? Way out onto the middle of Deep Water Pond?" I find this hard to believe. Why would a twenty year old woman do such a thing?

"According to Katherine, no one was chasing her. There was absolutely no reason for Rebecca to venture out onto the thawing ice."

"Everyone assumed it was suicide?"

"The only witness to the event claims it was. Katherine reported that Rebecca seemed upset and she deliberately ran out onto the dangerously thin ice. Katherine told the authorities that she called out Rebecca's name several times and tried to get her to come off the ice so she'd be safe, but Rebecca refused and kept going until she fell through. She did it all deliberately. As a result, she couldn't be buried in the main part of the cemetery. Her final resting place had to be unhallowed ground and preferably a crossroads, too."

"Why a crossroads?" I ask.

Jackson answers me. "The roads form a cross, a holy symbol for Christians. It was considered to be the next best thing to being buried in sacred ground with your other family members."

"There's another reason, too. Superstitious people believed that the crossroads location prevented the suicide's spirit from walking the earth after her death." Nathaniel seems to be familiar with the old tradition. "Because a cross is a sacred religious symbol, it keeps the evil spirit of the dead person in the grave. They can't walk about, stirring up more evil."

"Evidently that particular theory is flawed. If our visitor from last night was Rebecca Morse, she managed to come back."

I fill Oliver and Jackson in on what happened last night and then I repeat what the Morses told me. We continue to discuss and theorize into the late afternoon, wondering out loud to each other about the ghost who wreaked so much destruction in the midst of the storm.

Finally, Dad wakes up and comes into the kitchen. "I have a lot of plowing to do before I can get any real rest and I'm completely exhausted after dealing with that giant tree all night. The sooner I get going on those driveways, the sooner I can come back home and sleep for about ten hours."

"Is there anything I can do to help, Bill? You look completely done in," Nathaniel asks.

"Nah, just stay here and take care of Annabelle. I'll go over and check on your mother. Make sure the driveway's clear so she can get to work. Children don't stop getting sick just because there's been a snowstorm. The doctors she works with will probably want to open the office for afternoon and evening hours."

"What about the old railway station?" Oliver asks.

My father promises Oliver he'll start to clear that parking lot right after he digs out Nathaniel's mother, but he might not finish the whole thing right away because it's big and he's tired. Eastfield doesn't have any trains coming through town anymore and for about the past ten years, the unused station has served as the headquarters for the Eastfield Historical Society. Their collection of archives and artifacts are all housed there.

Oliver continues, saying, "I want to go over there and start putting together a genealogy of both the Burns and the Hayward families, and maybe start in on the Littlefield's and the Morse's, too."

He can't start soon enough to suit me. I can't wait to find out more about these mysterious families from Eastfield's past.

So Oliver and Jackson say their goodbyes and my father leaves again. I make popcorn with tons of butter and Nathaniel, Jeff and I watch a movie on HBO. *Role Models*, one of my favorites. Even though I've seen it twice before, I want to see it again. We all need to lighten up and for me the movie's even funnier the third time than it was the first and second times. Nathaniel laughs his ass off, too. Jeff, however, sleeps through the whole thing, up on the couch with his big, warm head in my lap. Afterwards I kill Nathaniel at Scrabble and he makes a few lame jokes about how smart I am because I read boring books by Jane Austen.

When my dad finally gets home, he's dragging his butt. Nathaniel builds a fire in the living room fireplace and I heat up some soup for dinner. If my mother's going to be gone much longer, I'll have to start watching some cooking shows on the Food Network. I wish I'd paid more attention to what Mom does in the kitchen. I've always been happy to help eat the meals and kinda willing to help clean up, but I've never done much cooking. My dad isn't any better, and neither is Nathaniel. Dad decides to clear away an area of snow next to the kitchen door so they can get the grill out of the garage and set it up. They're both good at cooking cheeseburgers and I like cheeseburgers, so that's okay by me. We can live on salads, baked potatoes and cheeseburgers. Also, Dad makes a mean grilled salmon. Mom doesn't usually let him eat cheeseburgers because of all the bad cholesterol.

As the sun sets, the wind kicks up again and I start to get scared. The three of us sit around the fire playing rummy and listening to it howl. Nathaniel calls his mother at work and I can hear his side of the conversation.

"Hey, Mom, be careful driving home. This wind could blow your little car into the next lane on Route 138, right into oncoming traffic. Or a tree could fall across the road. I can come pick you up in the van if you want me to."

Holding the phone to his ear, he listens in silence to her response and then says, "I'm gonna put you on speaker phone, Mom, and I want you to say that again."

"There's no wind here, Nathaniel. It's very still outside the doctors' office and we're starting to close up so I'll be leaving in just a few minutes and I'm sure I'll be fine."

Nathaniel shoots me and Dad a meaningful look, says "Goodbye" to his mother and then calls Oliver, who only lives a couple of miles away from us: no wind there, either. The three of us go into the den and turn on the Weather Channel: no significant winds tonight, or tomorrow. Nothing's brewing except at our house. As if on cue, a soft, crooning sound surrounds us inside the room where we're all sitting and, at the same time, it echoes outside, too, quietly vibrating the windowpanes. The fine hairs on the back of my neck rise and dance to its tune.

Dad clicks off the TV and we listen. "Aaaaanabelle...Aaaaanabelle." I can barely hear her eerie voice. Nathaniel reaches over and takes hold of my hand. My father puts his arm around me. They heard it too. The window panes rattle. I turn to look at the black, shiny surface of the nearest window. A splash of heavy snow, mixed with ice, blows off a nearby tree branch and hits the glass with a whomp. We all jump and I scream. Jeff starts barking. Then, just as suddenly, the night grows quiet and still.

"Son of a bitch." Nathaniel breaks the silence.

My dad says, "Damn it, Susannah, I wish you were here."

I'm thinking the same thing. I wish my mother was home right now. Dad gets up, steps over to the window and runs his hand lightly over the pane of glass. "Holy shit. She cracked the damn window. What the hell do we do now, Nathaniel?"

Nathaniel's eyebrows shoot up and he looks at Dad but doesn't answer. I don't think he's ever seen my father this pissed off before.

Dad can be kind of a control freak. It makes him grouchy when he feels like something's beyond his control. He swears and he bitches at people who don't deserve it. But then right afterwards, he apologizes because he knows he can be an ass sometimes. Right now, though, I can tell that Dad hasn't reached the apology stage yet. His right eye is all squinty and the rest of his face looks like it's chiseled onto the side of a large, cold chunk of granite. Just in case Nathaniel wasn't insulted enough by my father's sarcastic tone of voice, Dad adds, "You're the so-called medium. Got any big ideas?"

"No. I don't, Bill. Whoever she is, she has it in for Annabelle and I can't tell why. Not yet. I'm sorry."

Dad's face finally softens and he puts his hand on Nathaniel's shoulder. "Not your fault. I know you're trying, son." Then he turns to me. "Look at this crack in the window, honey, what do you think?"

"I think it's not her style. One thin scratch. She would've blasted this window apart. We'd be standing in a heap of broken glass."

Dad and I put our faces up close to the window and examine the vertical crack on the shiny black windowpane; it's thin, as if a very sharp, pointed fingernail scratched it into the glass. As we stare, the tip of one pale finger stabs at the faint line, from outside. I jump back and gasp. Dad remains steady. Focused. Whoever it is begins to trace along the crack, from top to bottom. Gradually, a woman's stark, white face fades into view. Her mouth is open as if she's trying to speak; her eyes look wide and startled. Long, dark hair billows and floats around her image as if she's underwater. Gawking at her, we watch the strangely peaceful apparition gradually disappear into the night.

"What the hell was that?" Dad whispers.

"You're right, Annabelle, it wasn't her," Nathaniel answers with a distant look in his copper eyes, like he can see for miles, through the window, into the darkness and beyond. "It's someone else. Someone who wants to help, but doesn't know how."

My father's eyes narrow. "We have to figure this out. This is the second window that those dumbass ghosts have broken. And in the winter, too. Pain in the ass. I'm going to get some plywood from the garage. The cold's already starting to seep through."

"This spirit wasn't the same one that crashed a tree through your garage window, Bill. Tonight's apparition wasn't nearly as powerful or as evil. She wants to help."

"Great way to help. Crack the damn window. Thanks a bunch. That was real helpful. I think I have some plywood that'll fit over it until I can replace the glass. If these damn ghosts keep damaging our windows, I'm gonna run out of plywood."

"I don't think there's anything out there right now, Bill, but be careful. I'd come with you, but I need to stay here with Annabelle and I don't want her going outside after dark. If the evil spirit from last night appears, Annabelle can't answer when it calls her name and she can't go outside if that thing is anywhere nearby. Evil and violence seethe off of this demon. I need to figure out how she grew so powerful."

"It might help to find out what she has against Annabelle, too." Dad looks from my face to Nathaniel's.

"I don't know, Dad, but at least she's a little afraid of Nathaniel. That's what you said last night, right?" I look hopefully over at my friend the "so-called medium."

"That's right. I think she respects my experience with the supernatural. She senses my confidence."

"I'd appreciate it if you stayed at least one more night, Nathaniel. The roads are okay now and I'm sure a van the size of yours travels well in the snow, but I think Annabelle would feel safer if you were here. You could sleep on the couch in the den again if it's comfortable enough for you."

"Oh yeah, it was amazingly comfortable. I can't remember when I've ever slept better."

I refuse to look at him. Instead, I bury my face in the fur on Jeff's neck so I won't make eye contact with Nathaniel accidentally. Even though I'm not looking at him, though, I know there's a smart-ass grin spreading across his face and a twinkle dawning in his copper eyes.

"Can Jeff come upstairs and sleep with me in my room?"

"Of course, Annabelle. That way if she comes anywhere near you, we'll know immediately. Jeff will raise the alarm and you can run downstairs and wake me up." Nathaniel's all for it. And then he looks right at me with a wide-eyed, innocent stare and says, "Just like you did that one time last night only not as scary because Jeff will be sleeping right beside you."

I did elbow Nathaniel awake at one point last night, because I thought I heard something. But it was just the wind, clacking some icy tree branches together. He reassured me and I snuggled up a little closer, against his warm, comforting body. Then we both went back to sleep.

Fortunately, my father doesn't pick up on the fact that Nathaniel's teasing me. He's too exhausted. He ruffles his sparse silver hair with both hands, then smooths it back down again. "You picked a fine time to have your stroke, Maeve."

"Daddy?"

"What, Annabelle?"

"I'm afraid to sleep alone in my room tonight, even with Jeff." My admission of fear seems to bring him back to his senses and he morphs back into his usual protective and compassionate self.

"You can put a sleeping bag on the floor of my room, honey. I'm sorry that I'm a little grouchy. I miss your mother."

"I miss her too."

"I know you do, baby. Grab the Scrabble board. We can play until you get sleepy and then we'll go upstairs with Jeff and you two can cozy up on my floor. I'll pump up the air mattress. Then you'll be real comfortable. This problem could take a while to solve unless someone comes up with a brilliant idea soon."

"Thank you."

"You stay put here with Nathaniel and Jeff. I'll only be gone a few minutes. I just have to grab the plywood out of the garage and nail it onto the outside of the window. Be right back."

Dad leaves to take care of the repairs, just as Nathaniel's cell phone chimes. He reaches into his jeans pocket to grab it. "Mom, how was the driving?" He puts her on speaker.

"Not bad at all. Tell Bill thanks for plowing the driveway and shoveling the walk. When will you be home?"

"Not 'til tomorrow sometime. I need to stay another night. We've got a supernatural problem going on here and Bill and Annabelle need my help. Will you be okay?"

"Of course. I'm fine. You stay and do what you need to do. How bad is the ghost situation? Do I need to worry?"

"Actually, Mom, we think the phantom that's plaguing Annabelle might have a connection to a couple of women who are buried up at the Prospect cemetery. One's buried there, anyway. The other's buried at the crossroads; a suicide." Nathaniel explains about Katherine Hayward and her two gravestones. Then he tells his mother about the tree and the lightning and its connection to the final resting place of Rebecca Morse. "Katherine's maiden name was Littlefield and Rebecca's maiden name was Burns. Your family's lived here in town for a few generations. Hayward, Littlefield, Burns, Morse. Do any of these names sound familiar, Mom?"

"Yes, but none of those names are from my side of the family, Nathaniel. Your father's mother, Grandma Flyte, was a Burns before she married Grandpa Flyte and took his name, but she wasn't from around here and Burns is a common name. She died before I married your father so I never met her. But I do know that she grew up on Winter Island, which is part of Salem, up on the north shore."

I interrupt. "Mrs. Flyte, Rebecca Morse's maiden name was Burns and she was from Salem."

"I don't think it's a coincidence." Nathaniel's voice sounds low and serious.

His mother continues. "Wow, Nathaniel, you could be descended from her. Your grandmother's maiden name was Burns. She married James Nathaniel Flyte Jr., who was from Peabody, but they settled down on Winter Island in the house that your Grandma Flyte grew up in, the old Burns' place. They had two sons, your father: James Nathaniel Flyte the third and his younger brother, your Uncle Jeremiah."

"So the name Nathaniel has been in your father's family for generations. Cool."

"That's right, Annabelle." Mrs. Flyte continues her complicated story. "Your grandmother Flyte's maiden name was Sarah Jane Burns. She met your grandfather, James Nathaniel Flyte Jr. on Winter Island. When Grandpa Flyte was orphaned, he was sent to live at the Plummer Home for Boys up on the northeast shore of the island. He and Grandma Flyte met, got married and settled down in the old Burns' House on Winter Island Road. It's the only road on the island, and the Burns' family owns two pretty big houses on it. That's where Nathaniel's father grew up with his brother, Jeremiah. James didn't move to Eastfield until he married me."

Nathaniel's mother is spitting these bits of family history out pretty fast. Nathaniel gestures frantically for a pen and paper and as soon as I hand them to him he starts scribbling everything down, drawing diagrams and slashing lines with arrows to connect everything. Standing behind him, with one hand resting on his shoulder, I try to read and make sense out of everything he's recording. First he sketches out a rough outline of an island with scribbly waves all around it, to represent the ocean. Then he draws two straight slashes and labels the space in between, "Winter Island Road". Next, he sketches out two squares with triangles on top, to represent the Burns' family's houses. Beside one house he lists the names: Grandma Sarah Jane Burns Flyte, Grandpa James Nathaniel Flyte Jr., James Nathaniel Flyte III–my father, Jeremiah Flyte–my uncle. As fast as his mother recounts her in-laws' family history, Nathaniel hustles to record it all on my mother's grocery list pad.

He's a pretty good note taker and I'm paying attention, too, making sure he doesn't miss anything key.

"Whoa!" Nathaniel exclaims. "Back it up, Mom, to where you told me that my father's mother was a Burns. I need you to repeat everything more slowly."

"Yes, dear, his mother's side of the family was named Burns and they lived on Winter Island. Your Grandfather Flyte wasn't from Winter Island. He grew up in Peabody. When his parents both died of tuberculosis, the authorities sent him to the Plummer Home for Boys which is located on the northeast corner of the island."

Up on the top right corner of his sketched out island, Nathaniel adds a broad rectangle and then draws two triangles, side by side on top of it, to represent the roofs on a large institutional style building, and writes Plummer Home/Grandpa Flyte/orphan beside the rectangle.

His mother continues, saying, "Your poor Grandfather, his baby brother died, too, and all their relatives were too poor to take him in, so they sent him to the Boys' Home on the Island, but it turned out well because he met and married your grandmother there. And together they had your father and your Uncle Jeremiah."

"So my Grandmother's maiden name was Burns?" He takes the pen and makes a dark circle around the name Burns on his diagram, right where this very significant name rests, between Grandma Sarah Jane and Flyte.

"Yes, honey, I think I've already explained that a few times. Do you think she was related to the Burns in your ghost story?"

"This can't be a coincidence. Rebecca Burns' family was from Salem, according to Annabelle's neighbors, the Morses. The spirit that's haunting Annabelle is connected to the suicide buried at the crossroads and the woman with two graves."

"How can you be sure?"

"We're not one hundred percent sure quite yet. We still need to do some more research."

"What happened during the storm? Why are you so interested in the Burns' family?"

"Bill Blake couldn't get home because the huge oak tree at the crossroads of Prospect and Bay was felled by lightning. It almost hit his truck. He was unable to get back here and Annabelle was alone. That's when the ghost attacked her."

"Is Annabelle okay?"

"She's fine, but we need to know more in order to keep her safe."

"I'll give your Uncle Jeremiah a call in the morning. See what we can come up with. He still lives on Winter Island and works in Salem. When your grandparents died, he moved in with his aunt, Maggie Burns, in the other Burns' house on Winter Island Road."

Nathaniel picks up the pen again and writes Great Aunt Maggie Burns–Grandma's sister and Uncle Jeremiah Flyte–my father's brother beside the second little square house that he drew on his map of Winter Island. I feel a little sad that he doesn't ever say or write Dad, always my father. Nathaniel never had any relationship with his father that he can remember. He was too young when James Flyte abandoned him and his mom.

Each time the name Burns appears on Nathaniel's diagram/map, he draws a dark circle around it. Now he has two of these circles, one for Sarah Jane Burns Flyte and one for Maggie Burns, her sister.

His mother continues, saying, "Aunt Maggie's gotta be about ninety or so, but she's still really sharp. Winter Island's a pretty small place, only about forty houses, and all of them are on the northern end. Everyone knows each other well. That's one of the reasons your father was happy to leave. Everyone's aware of everyone else's business. I wonder how they weathered the storm up there? I'll give you a jingle tomorrow, as soon as I hang up from talking to Jeremiah."

Nathaniel turns to us, after he clicks his phone off. "I'm positive that I'm related to Rebecca Burns Morse. I can feel it in my bones. My supernatural bones. There are Burnses in my father's family, and they're from Winter Island, which is part of Salem. Rebecca was from Salem, too." His head's spinning; I can tell from the wild look in his eyes. But he stares down at his map for a minute, and that seems to calm him down a little. My dad noisily finishes nailing the plywood over the outside of the cracked windowpane frame and comes back into the den.

Then we all go into the kitchen and spread out a big piece of unlined paper on the table. Dad draws up a family tree based on what Nathaniel's mother told us. He leaves the top branches bare, waiting until we find out about Nathaniel's great grandparents and great aunts and uncles. Maybe we can find out about some great-great grandparents, too. I'm hoping Nathaniel's Uncle Jeremiah and Great Aunt Maggie are well informed about their family history.

Nathaniel has never mentioned either of these relatives to me, so I ask him, "What are Great Aunt Maggie and Jeremiah like?"

"I've only met my great aunt, Maggie Burns, a couple of times and I've never been to Winter Island, but my Uncle Jeremiah visits us every few years. He either comes here to Eastfield or we meet somewhere nearby, for dinner at a restaurant in Boston or Cambridge. A couple of times, probably about ten years ago at least, he brought Great Aunt Maggie with him. He still lives on the island with her. Neither one of them ever married or had any children. He was really helpful, though, to my mother, when my father disappeared. He tried his best to track the bastard down, but never succeeded. Jeremiah helped us out financially a couple of times, too, when I was younger." Nathaniel turns his face away and stares out the window where all you can see is black sky and mounds of white everywhere.

I don't know what to say to my friend. I'm very curious about the Burns' branch of his family, but I care enough about his feelings regarding his missing father to conjure up some self control. So I stifle my urge to fire out tons of insensitive questions and give Nathaniel time to process what he's learned. Just to make sure that I don't blurt out something rude, I busy myself by putting on some water for cocoa and finding a bag of marshmallows. Then we all sit down for a cutthroat game of rummy, the only kind worth playing.

Chapter 11

Judith

Half way through beating me and Nathaniel at rummy for the second time Dad gets a brilliant idea. "As much as I'd love you to move in here, Nathaniel, so I can kill you at rummy on a daily basis, you're going to have to go home eventually. We need to figure out a way to keep Annabelle safe when you're not here."

"I don't know anyone else with Susannah's talent for warding off evil. What about her relatives? Do any of them live close by? Do any of them have the same kind of paranormal gift?"

My dad looks up from his cards and takes out his cell phone. "I know. I can call Aleister. Annabelle, maybe your uncle knows someone who can help and I think he'll agree to keep everything a secret from your mother so she won't worry."

My mother's brother, Aleister Knight, is a very busy, very important doctor at a big Boston hospital, but he gets back to my dad just a few minutes after we leave him a message on his voice mail. Dad answers his cell as soon as it starts vibrating and explains the situation to Aleister. They talk for a while, but I can only hear my father's side of the conversation. After Dad finishes telling Aleister about the ghost and the wind and the damage she did, Aleister does most of the talking and my dad does most of the listening. I watch carefully and try to figure out what Uncle Aleister's saying, but I can't hear much. Finally my father clicks off his phone and turns to me.

"Aleister used to have a student in one of those pre-med biology classes he teaches over at Boston University. She displayed some special talents of the healing variety. He shared some of his own family background with her and they became friendly. They kept in touch even after she transferred out of BU because she decided not to become a doctor; well, not a human doctor, anyway. The young woman became a veterinarian. It turns out that she was very in tune with the evil side of people's natures and it soured her toward helping and healing certain members of the human race."

"So, she can detect evil? Kind of like Mom?"

"Sounds like it from what Aleister told me. She considers animals to be pure of heart and decided to use her healing talents to help them instead of people. Aleister's going to contact her and see if maybe she can get out here to meet us. The roads should be a lot clearer by tomorrow. It's supposed to warm up into the high thirties and according to the forecast the sun will be shining for most of the day. Some of the snow should melt. The young woman's name is Phoebe Walker, Dr. Phoebe Walker. She lives over in Freewater; farm country. I guess she treats the big animals, like cows and horses, too, not just pets. It shouldn't take her more than ten or fifteen minutes to get here once the roads are drivable and she can clear her schedule."

"Dad, someone we don't even know? I don't like it."

Nathaniel adds his opinion. "I don't like it either, Bill, a stranger? What if she finds out about Annabelle's talent? The less people who know about Annabelle, the better off she is."

"Calm down, you two. This is no time to get your undies in a twist. Let's meet her and see. Aleister seems to think very highly of her and I trust him. Give her a chance, Annabelle."

My father has obviously made up his mind, so I have no choice but to give her a chance if she agrees to come and stay with us for a while. I put away the cards and Nathaniel leaves to go home and pack up a few things. He's back within an hour and settles down for the night, on the couch in the den. He'll be staying here with us, at least until my uncle's former student shows up. And that might not happen for a few days. Dad, Jeff and I all go upstairs for the "big camp-out" which is really a "camp-in", in my parents' bedroom. The night passes uneventfully. I sleep like the dead because I'm so exhausted.

As I'm pouring hot water over a store-bought teabag, my dad shares some information with me. Doctor Phoebe Walker called his cell early this morning, before I was awake and told him she was "intrigued" by our situation. She's interested in coming over to meet us and should be able to drive up from Freewater within the next few days.

"You should give her my cell phone number and she should call me instead of you. After all, I'm the one she'll be spending the most time with. If I like her and invite her to stay." Peering through the steam from the hot tea, I dip my mouth down and take a sip.

Ooh.

"Not enough sugar."

As I'm reaching for the sugar bowl and the teaspoon on the kitchen table, Nathaniel wheels in. He looks a little rumpled and sleepy-eyed, but still gorgeous. "What would your mother say, Annabelle? Sugar? And that doesn't look like herb tea in your cup. It looks like Lipton."

"You should know. You're the one who brought this stuff back with you last night." I grin.

He winks at me and then turns toward Dad. "Bill, maybe I should meet with this Phoebe person before she comes over here. I can get an idea about the extent of her supernatural talents and assess whether or not she can be of any help in this particular situation."

Nathaniel's idea sounds like a good one. "Okay by me." I throw in my vote.

But when my dad makes up his mind, there's no changing it. He frowns and says, "Phoebe will be coming over here to meet with all three of us and we'll 'assess this particular situation' together. End of story."

I roll my eyes and add another teaspoon of sugar to my tea. "Okay, Dad. Whatever you say."

"Damn right. I'm heading over to the Eastfield Historical Society's headquarters right now to finish plowing the parking lot, so Oliver can open it up and begin researching Katherine Hayward and Rebecca Morse. Plus I have a few other jobs to attend to. Hold the fort, Nathaniel. You too, boy." He reaches down and ruffles the fur on Jeff's head. Then he grabs his coat and gloves and stalks out.

My father can't clear the historical society's parking lot out fast enough to suit me. I'm anxious to discover everything I can about "this particular situation", as quickly as possible.

* * * *

By ten-thirty in the morning, I know my dad has finished plowing what I consider to be the most important parking lot in town, because Oliver and Jackson stop by with tons of stuff in a box that they found in the historical society's archives. We spread it all out on the kitchen table. At first glance, it looks like most of the items were donated by the Hayward family throughout the years. We call out to Nathaniel, who's been in the den, on the phone, rearranging his busy séance schedule, and he and Jeff join us. Sitting around the kitchen table, we start working on my least favorite part of a paranormal investigation. While the four of us are all reading, looking at old photographs, sorting and taking notes, I hear a car pull up and park in the driveway.

Oliver and Jackson don't even pause for a second; they're too busy poring over all the information they can find about the Hayward family. But I jump up to see what's going on. Running over to the front window, I pull aside the curtain and peek out. It's Judith Curtis, climbing out of her blue Taurus. I have a few seconds to change the shocked expression on my face to a welcoming one before she knocks and I let her in.

Judith's my father's accountant. Unless my mother got a brain transplant, she could never keep track of the financial side of my father's business. She's good at cooking, gardening and herbal remedies and stuff like that, but details concerning quantities of supplies and money are not her thing. My dad's capable of keeping accurate financial records, but he doesn't have time for it, because he's always busy building houses. So, about twenty-five years ago, he hired Judith to be his bookkeeper. He often says how Blake & Sons Construction couldn't function successfully without Judith. Throughout the years, she's become way more than my father's accountant. She's a valuable and much loved family friend. Even though she's kind of formidable, I adore her.

Her lips are perpetually pursed in moderate but never blatant, disapproval. I have never seen her crack a full-fledged smile. Every freakish family like ours needs someone like her. She sits in constant judgment of us and makes us think twice about some of the crazy things we might do. Without her we'd never survive.

I don't know how old she is because she doesn't age. She's been working for my dad since way before I was born and for as far back as I can remember she's always worn the same tortoise-shell glasses, the same short, curly dark brown hairstyle and in winter she always wears the same size six LL Bean corduroy pants, which she owns in several conservative colors. In summer she wears what my mother calls "A-line" skirts that Judith sews herself, using cotton fabric in quiet floral prints and the same sewing pattern she probably bought when she was taking a high school sewing class back in the mid 1960's. She knows what works for her and refuses to change it. Every four years she replaces her old Ford Taurus with a new Ford Taurus, purchased at McDonough Ford over on Turnpike Street. It's always dark blue with a beige leather interior.

Her husband, Earl Curtis, is a lawyer; he also collects stamps and fixes lawn mowers. They have no children, but Judith has formed a special connection with me. I guess opposites attract. She buys me a Christmas present and a birthday present every year. She never gets anything for Clement or Joe, but they don't mind. Her gifts aren't special or exciting. I, however, appreciate them and write her thank you notes. Each year when I write her a note to thank her for the birthday gift, I tuck a wallet-sized copy of my school picture inside. She always says the same thing. "You grow more beautiful every year, Annabelle."

I always think the same thing, but I don't say it. "Maybe I should give you a five by seven next year, because your eyesight's going, Judith. You obviously can no longer see the wallet-size clearly."

She alternates her Christmas gifts to me. One year it's flannel pajamas. The next it's comfortable slippers. For birthdays it used to always be a Nancy Drew book. When I turned fourteen she switched to something from the *New York Times* bestseller list, but never anything too R-rated. She's our rock. She's a gem. She's a peach. She's a treasure. And I love her.

A couple of years ago Clem asked her if he could film one day in her life. He didn't need to say "a typical day" because Judith's days are all typical. That's the way she prefers it. I'll never forget the look on her face when he asked. Her pursed lips turned down an eighth of an inch farther at each corner. I held my breath waiting for her to say no. She seemed to be heading toward a full-fledged frown. But my interpretation of her facial expression was incorrect; she was only thinking. She said yes. When she said the word yes I caught a glimpse of her teeth because she almost smiled. They're white and even. She should show them more often, but that's not her way. And I love her the way she is. I can count on her not to change. It's very reassuring and in my world, feeling reassured and secure is valuable and rare.

It's been three days since my mother left for Florida to take care of her sister Maeve. Judith must have some sort of etiquette book which suggests when to make an unscheduled and unannounced appearance at a friend's house if they might be in need of comfort. She's carrying a basket with a wooden lid which she places on our kitchen counter.

After opening and then reaching into the basket, Judith takes out a lemon meringue pie. Underneath the pie is a thin piece of wood with four little legs and she removes it. On the bottom layer of the basket is a casserole dish. "*Better Homes and Gardens* has the best recipes. When you get married, Annabelle, I'll buy you a subscription for a wedding present." I figure it out right then and there: she gets that same gift for every bride she knows. I don't have to ask.

"Judith, thank you so much. This looks delicious! What's in the casserole?"

"Turkey tetrazzini. It's Earl's favorite. I cooked a big turkey yesterday so I'd have enough left over for two casseroles."

Wrapping my arms around Judith, I give her a huge hug. She pats my back and says, "Don't worry, honey. Your auntie will be just fine and your mom will be home in no time. If you need anything give me a call. I keep the cell phone your dad gave me in my purse." She takes it out of her purse and shows it to me. I take my phone out of my pocket and we program her number into my cell. Dad got her the cell phone a couple of years ago and he makes her carry it with her. Also, he made her switch from the adding machine and the ledger to a laptop a few years ago, too. She kicked up a fuss at first but then she got used to it all. So last year, he got her a tablet. Now she carries it everywhere with her and she's skilled at Excel spread sheets and Google everything: Plus, Drive, Docs, you name it.

I think maybe she's a little bit resistant to change because she made a big change when she was a young bride. She met Earl when he was at University of North Carolina, Chapel Hill. He swept her off her feet, even though she's always worn the most comfortable, most sensible shoes ever on those feet. I bet she wore the same shoes back then, too, when she was only nineteen. She left her family and her native state of North Carolina, married Earl and moved up here to live among us Yankees: a huge transition. I'm glad she did, though. Having her predictable presence standing here in our kitchen makes me miss my mom a little less, even though they're complete opposites. However, they have one important thing in common: they're both really good cooks. She opens our fridge and puts the casserole inside and then walks over to the table to see what we have spread out all over it.

"Oliver, you're researching the Haywards? Earl's momma was a Hayward; tight family and mighty weird, too, which I didn't find out until after I married one of 'em!"

"No way, Judith!" I hug her again and she laughs. It sounds a bit rusty, but it's a definite laugh, not quite a guffaw, but more than a chuckle. I catch another rare glimpse of her beautiful, shiny white teeth.

"Yes way, Annabelle. At least Earl's half Curtis so he's fifty percent normal. The Hayward side's crazy, though. What do you need to know? His momma's still in town. He and his brother Timmy moved her into one of the new independent living senior citizen apartments over near Langwater Pond. We see her all the time. Maybe she knows the answers to some of your questions. Earl and Timmy know a lot about the Hayward branch of the family tree, too. They've all stayed pretty close throughout the years."

"Maybe this weekend we can visit Earl's mom over at Langwater. Do you think she'd mind?"

"She'd love to meet you. I'm sure. Why are you all so curious about the Haywards anyway?"

"Oliver's doing some research for a book about Eastfield's graveyards and the woman with two graves, over at Prospect Street Burial Ground, was a Hayward. I'm helping him with the research for my senior year honors History project." The glib lie floats off my tongue.

Sometimes it's scary to be me. Even I don't always know what I'm going to say or do next. Judith buys it, though, for now anyway.

She warns me. "The Haywards are very superstitious about that graveyard. They never go over there. Someone made up some nonsense about a demon or something. They all think that demon's deadly dangerous. No one's been over there for decades. Earl's family buries their dead over on Route 138 now, in the cemetery the Episcopalians built back in the 1940's. The Haywards haven't buried a family member over on Prospect Street since Jamison Henry Hayward. He was the last one; died during the great blizzard of 1958 when he fell off the roof of the barn trying to clear the snow with a shovel, to keep it from collapsing on top of the cows and horses. He saved the animals but lost his own life. Rest in peace, Jamison; he was the last Hayward to be interred at the old Prospect Street Burial Ground."

If I tell the truth and explain about the ghost who was howling my name and trying to murder me, she'll just roll her eyes and give me a "C'mon now!" It sounds like "Earl's momma" is a believer, though. Maybe I'll learn about some interesting Hayward family traditions when we visit her.

Chapter 12

The Haywards vs. the Littlefields

Oliver and Jackson want to go over to the Langwater Pond Senior Citizen condos with me, but they have some wedding planning to do. And Dad's working, so I'm on my own. I feel tempted to invite Nathaniel, but resist because I don't want him to think I'm changing my mind about his offer to be more than my friend. All alone, I prepare to set out for Mrs. Curtis's home. Flying solo. First, I make a little gift basket with two kinds of teas and some of my mom's famous lavender-scented candles in it. As I'm heading upstairs to take a shower, Judith calls my cell and offers to pick me up around two forty-five, so I'm not on my own after all. This should be interesting.

Mrs. Lavinia Hayward Curtis is expecting us for tea at three. Predictably, Judith and Earl are prompt and we three fit snugly in the cab of his pickup truck, which has a squishy little backseat for extra passengers like me. When we arrive at

Judith's mother-in-law's condo, Judith starts bustling around in the kitchen, which is nothing more than a corner of the main room, lined with cabinets and appliances. It's open to the living and dining sections. Judith starts setting up the tea things on a low table in front of Lavinia's little couch.

Soon Earl's brother Timmy shows up and his mother seems thrilled to see him and to be the center of attention. Judith told me that Lavinia loves to talk about the Haywards' family history. Holding both of my hands in both of hers, my hostess thanks me wholeheartedly for the basket of teas and candles and insists that I call her by her first name. Then she sits down on one side of an antique, brocade loveseat and pats the cushion on the other side, inviting me to join her. But soon someone else knocks on the door and Lavinia hops up to let in a tall, elderly stranger who's holding a cardboard box that used to contain bottles of Pinot Grigio, my mother's favorite kind of wine.

"I invited Abner Littlefield over, too, Annabelle. I hope you don't mind. He lives on the second floor here at Langwater and we play poker together on Friday nights. Last night, after I finished winning twenty-five dollars off him, I mentioned that you were coming over to ask about Katherine Littlefield Hayward and her two gravestones. He volunteered to come by with some old letters and what not. We thought you might be interested."

I rise to shake his hand and then sink back down onto the comfy loveseat. "That's great. I'm happy to meet you, Mr. Littlefield, and anxious to find out more about your family. Wasn't there a feud between the Littlefields and the Haywards, way back when?"

"Oh, yes. It was always about the land with these old New England families. When they weren't busy fighting over the land with the Indians, they fought over it with each other."

The doorbell rings just then and Lavinia goes to the door to buzz someone else in. Less than a minute later, Nathaniel wheels in, with Jeff right behind him. My hostess announces his arrival. "Annabelle, I think you might already know Nathaniel Flyte." It's a good thing I'm sitting down because I would keel over from surprise if I weren't. Nodding my head, I close my mouth which had fallen open at the sight of his gorgeous self. Of course, he scoots his wheelchair right over as close as he can get to the loveseat and invades my personal space in a big way. "Hello, Annabelle. Always a pleasure." And he grabs my arm, pulls me closer and kisses my cheek, lingering three seconds too long, with his warm lips against my skin.

Lavinia's oblivious. She settles back down next to me on the loveseat and explains, "When my sister Muriel died, Nathaniel contacted her for me and we had the loveliest chat about where she hid our mother's cameo brooch and some other jewelry. I didn't want my daughter-in-law to get it. She and Timmy bought Muriel's house, shortly before my sister went into the nursing home. Soon after, my son and that nasty piece of work were in the middle of their divorce proceedings. Now she's his ex-wife. She's always been a sneaky, greedy bitch. Finally Timmy wised up about her."

Timmy shakes his head. "Say what you mean, Mom. Don't hold back or nothin'."

Nathaniel looks like he's trying not to crack up, but breaks into a mile-wide grin despite his efforts.

Lavinia continues. "Nathaniel here was a great help. My sister told him exactly where to look for the jewelry. Timmy gave us his key and Earl and Judith and I went over to his soon-to-be ex-wife's place one day when she wasn't home and packed up a lot of stuff that had belonged to Muriel. We found almost everything of any value and smuggled it out of there. Timmy's ex was fifteen minutes too late, and all that was left of Muriel's belongings was a crappy old TV and a pair of Wedgewood lamps that are worth about a hundred bucks each. Too bad about those lamps, though, my father bought them as a birthday gift for my mother back in the thirties. I'm still hoping Timmy's crazy bitch ex wife will electrocute herself one of these days. The wiring was never quite right in those old lamps."

Nathaniel has to cover his face with both hands and fake a cough to hide his giggling. But I can tell he's laughing, because his shoulders are shaking. The old lady is pretty hilarious. I'm happy that she got her jewelry, especially the brooch. I admire people with determination and she's very cute, too. Her hair is short, dyed a shade of blonde that doesn't exist in nature, and tightly curled. She's not even five feet tall and she keeps jumping up off the loveseat and bustling around the room in a pair of adorable little red ballet-style flats. Adding to her interesting fashion statement, the dark seams on her baggy pantyhose crawl crookedly down the backs of her tiny calves. Extending a quarter inch above the real outline of her upper lip and a quarter inch below the outline of her lower lip, her lipstick matches her shoes: not usually a good look on anyone, but she pulls it off with style.

Now that everyone's here, we all sit around Lavinia's snug living room/dining area to sip tea and munch on delicious homemade cookies. I miss Wyatt. He would love this: a hilarious little old lady who believes in ghosts, a family feud, and wonderful food. It's just his cup of tea.

Then Abner Littlefield asks, "Do you go to Eastfield High School, Annabelle?"

"Yes, sir, I'm a senior."

"My granddaughter's a senior, too. Do you know Colleen Foley?"

Now I'm glad Wyatt isn't present. "I know who she is, but I don't really know her very well." I do not add that she's hell bent and determined to hook up with my ex boyfriend.

"Everyone at the high school knows Colleen; she's practically the mayor. She's president of the Student Council, president of the Honor Society, president of the school spirit club, and a few other organizations, too. A very popular girl, and pretty, too: personality and looks. She'll go far in life. Takes after my daughter, her mother." Abner Littlefield certainly is a very proud grandpa.

I avoid looking over at Nathaniel because I think he'll be grinning sarcastically. But I'm wrong. As soon as Mr. Littlefield looks away from me, Nathaniel reaches over and gives my hand a quick and supportive squeeze. I turn my face in his direction and he winks at me.

Finally the social chitchat ends and we get down to business. Nathaniel tells Lavinia about the ghost knocking down the huge old oak tree at the crossroads and all the excitement at my house on the night of the snowstorm.

Judith's lips turn down in disapproval. She walks over to the kitchen area to put some more of the delicious cookies on the empty platter and brew another pot of tea. Abner, Earl and Timmy all look at Lavinia. Their facial expressions are as electrifying as the lightning my dad witnessed on that fateful night. Something's up and I can't wait to find out what. I only have to wait a few seconds before Abner begins to tell the Littlefields' side of the story.

"The Haywards and the Littlefields owned abutting acres of land over where Prospect and Purchase intersect. They were always arguing over the boundaries and access to the roads. There's an ancient cart path that runs through both families' properties and ends up out on Bay Street and there were a lot of disagreements over that, too. Occasionally a fistfight would break out between members of the families and a couple of times shots were fired. Someone was seriously injured once, but no one was ever killed. Still, it was only a matter of time before a member of one of the families would lose his life because of the feud."

Timmy prompts Abner to get to the point. "Tell Annabelle how the Haywards and the Littlefields solved the problem, Abner."

"They arranged a marriage between Katherine Littlefield and Lieutenant Elias Hayward of the Union Calvary. I actually have their marriage certificate in this here box."

"Wow! The marriage was arranged? I've never heard of such a thing. How does that work?"

"Not well. Elias didn't love her. An arranged marriage means that the couple's parents get to control the deal. It's usually a business deal, too, in which the bride's family pays the groom to marry her. This sum of money was called a dowry. Young Elias married Katherine reluctantly, to solve the problems between their two families. He was considered to be a very eligible and handsome bachelor and an accomplished horseman. He had a lot of friends in Eastfield and some of the surrounding communities. Katherine was the opposite. She kept to herself. She was nervous and introverted; high strung."

"She was a bitch." Lavinia seems to really like that word.

Abner stands up for his family. "Katherine wasn't a typical Littlefield. We're a friendly, humorous bunch. She had no friends and a sour, anxious disposition. But the rest of us aren't like that."

Timmy adds, "She was pretty enough, but not at all the total package. Looks can only take you so far. Men might be attracted to you at first, but you need some personality to keep a guy interested. The only way to marry her off was to offer the Hayward family five acres of land, exclusive and full access to the cart path leading out to Bay Street and the duck pond for fishing and hunting wild fowl and a considerable heap of cash; all in exchange for their son Elias' hand in marriage. Poor Elias didn't have a choice unless he wanted the whole Hayward clan to disown him."

Lavinia points her pinky up and delicately, through her brightly painted lips, takes a tiny but noisy sip of tea. Then she places her china cup back on its matching saucer and says, "He had to marry the miserable bitch." Her short little legs are crossed at the ankles and her dainty feet dangle two inches above the plush carpet. She keeps swinging them back and forth. Majorly adorable. I love her.

Abner shakes his head and goes on with the story. "Elias married Katherine and left to fight in the Civil War almost immediately after the wedding. In the summer of 1863, he came home to a hero's welcome, minus his left arm and his enthusiasm for life. He lost both at the Battle of Chancellorsville. The Haywards sent him over to visit his friend Jonathan Morse's young widow, Rebecca, because she was known for her ability to heal both physical and emotional wounds with her herbs and potions. She still lived in Deep Water Cottage on the Morse's property, which was located about a half mile through the woods from the Hayward's land. Not too far from the southwest corner of the Blake's property, Annabelle. Elias' wife Katherine visited her often to buy a concoction of herbs that did wonders for her insomnia and her nerves. The family was sure that sweet, gentle, talented Rebecca could help poor Elias. After all, he and her husband were close friends before Jonathan died in the war."

Nathaniel takes a guess about the direction in which Abner's story is headed. "And Elias fell in love with Rebecca."

"Yup." Abner confirms Nathaniel's suspicions. "Elias was over there all the time. He recovered his physical health and he was happier than he'd ever been in his whole life. Katherine wasn't happy, though. She'd never been the cheerful sort anyway, but she got worse. She wanted to give

Elias a son, to carry on the family name and she couldn't get pregnant."

Timmy explains the young couple's marital problems for us. "Because Elias wouldn't sleep with her. When they were first married, he told her he didn't want to knock her up and then take off for the war, maybe never to return. Then when he got home from the war his excuse was the world is too violent and horrible. He didn't want to bring a child into such a terrible place; a place where young men who lived in the same country butchered each other on its battlefields."

My new hero, Lavinia, throws her two cents worth into the conversation. "That's baloney. She was a mean and nasty bitch with a horrible disposition and he couldn't bear to touch her."

I ask, "How do you guys know all this?" These are intimate details from someone's marriage. None of this information could be written down in any public records. Could it?

Lavinia solves the mystery for me. "There's a diary. Elias confided in his sister-in-law, Elizabeth, and she wrote everything in her diary. When Nathaniel helped us find the jewelry, we found the diary, too. My sister Muriel had it. Timmy and Earl and I have all read it. I let Abner read it, too. Elizabeth Hayward often wrote about Katherine and she's his ancestor. Everything was all tied up in an old keepsake box. The jewelry and the diary were in there and the box was tied closed with a black satin ribbon."

Nathaniel asks the same question that just jumped into my mind. "Can we see the box?"

"Why, of course, Nathaniel, I'll go and get it. I keep it in my bedroom." Energetic little old Lavinia hops the two inches down to the rug from her perch on the loveseat and hustles off to the bedroom to get her family's treasures. When she returns with the box, which is indeed bound together tightly with its original morbid ribbon, I lean over closer to Nathaniel as she places it in his lap. He tugs at one end of the ribbon and the slippery, soft satin fabric slides off the box. Jeff gives out a howl like a werewolf during a full moon at midnight. The room grows colder. Jeff howls again, vibrating the close atmosphere in the small condo with his loud and mournful voice.

"Earl, will you take him out to the van. I think someone from the next world has dropped by to visit." Nathaniel throws his keys to Earl who swipes them out of midair with his right hand and walks to the door with Jeff. Nathaniel's constant canine companion hates ghosts; it's kind of ironic that he belongs to a medium, but they make it work.

"Don't let anything exciting happen until I get back," Earl calls over his shoulder.

"Then you'd better hurry. Someone's here and he wants to speak. My control over the situation's limited." Nathaniel yells just before the door slams shut behind Earl and Jeff.

I have a feeling about this and my intuition's usually spot-on. "Don't touch the box until Earl gets back, Nathaniel."

Earl returns quickly, before his mother has a chance to settle her butt back in the loveseat and resume swinging her little legs like a first-grader. Everyone pulls their chairs into a tight circle, around Nathaniel, Lavinia and me. The mysterious box rests in his lap. As he lifts off the lid, I hold my breath and shiver. He hands the cover to me and I peek inside the box. Nestled on a bed of pink satin lie several items of old fashioned jewelry, among them a delicate, ivory brooch with a woman's face, neck and shoulders carved on it. An oval of tiny, slightly tarnished silver flowers frames the cameo. Beside the jewelry sits an ancient, leather-bound diary. We all ooh and aah over the Hayward family heirlooms. The room grows colder still.

I feel a chilly hand on my shoulder where it joins my neck and turn to see if Lavinia is touching me, which would be really awkward. Even weirder, though, her hands are folded in her lap as she leans forward to look into the box. I whip my face in the other direction. Both of Nathaniel's hands are on the box and he's staring at me with his mouth open. The hand on my neck moves an inch or two and what feels like an ice cold index finger extends upward to caress my earlobe. I look into Nathaniel's eyes and beg him, "Make it stop."

"Don't be afraid, Annabelle." Nathaniel's lips are moving, but the voice isn't his. It's deeper. "Take the box. Look inside. Look harder than you've ever looked in your whole life, until you see what you need to see." The finger traces down the back of my neck and back up to my hairline. Then the hand opens and the spectral palm presses against the back of my head, urging me forward. I move even closer to Nathaniel, until our knees touch. He puts the box in my lap. One at a time, I pick up each item of jewelry and the ancient diary and hand them to Lavinia. Then I peer into the box. It's deep and I put my face right inside and breathe in the old-fashioned scent of verbena mixed with century-old dust. Scrutinizing the satin lining from one corner to the next, finally my gaze lights on the fourth corner; squinting, I inspect it more closely. Somebody scratched something into the fabric with a needle.

"I see something, but I can't make it out. It's tiny and it looks like it's been etched into the satin with the point of a pin." I look up from the box and my gaze meets Lavinia's.

"Earl, hand me that magnifying glass over there, on the end table, near my book." Earl does as he's told and she hands the magnifying glass to me. "Here, honey, see if this helps."

I close one eye and peer through the magnifying glass with the other. Inside the box, on the corner of the fabric, someone etched three letters. "E.B.H." I read them out loud.

"Elizabeth Burke Hayward, Elias Hayward's sister-in-law," Lavinia announces. "It must have been her box."

Gingerly, I poke at her monogram with the index finger of my right hand. The corner comes loose. The fabric was evidently glued down only around three edges and three corners. Whoever glued it missed the last corner. Or maybe they left it unglued deliberately. Pinching the satin delicately between my forefinger and thumb, I pick it up and peel it back a little. Underneath there's an old sepia photograph. I look over at Lavinia and she nods her permission for me to tear the satin lining loose from the bottom of the box, so we can take out the picture. I do it carefully, so as to avoid damaging the box. The lining comes loose slowly and intact.

Lifting out the photograph, I begin to examine the sepia-tinted portrait of a really handsome man who looks to be in his forties. The hand at the end of his only arm rests affectionately on the shoulder of a beautiful teenage boy who resembles him a little around the eyes and the nose areas. They have the same straight, strong nose and the same arch to their eyebrows. The man and the child are wearing similar facial expressions, as if they're pleased to be spending time together. Behind the adult's close lipped smile, in his eyes and the thinness of his face, I can read worry, though. He looks haggard. The teenager seems more contented; clueless and happy to be a kid. But something weird causes me to sit up straighter. My mouth drops open and I'm not the only one.

Simultaneously, as if we're all connected to puppet strings controlled by the same puppeteer, we all look at the photo and then at each other and then at Nathaniel. The boy in the picture looks exactly like him. He's a younger version of my friend the medium. Lavinia reaches over. She and I each hold onto a corner of the picture. We have the best and closest view. She takes the magnifying glass from me and looks through it. Then I let go of my corner and she turns the portrait over and reads the inscription on the back out loud. "My brother-in-law Elias and his son, Jonathan Elias Hayward."

We carefully pass the picture around the circle. Nathaniel smiles calmly and nods at me as if we share a secret, but the smile isn't his. Neither is the voice that explains: "Now you know. Everyone needs to know, so you can be safe again, Annabelle." As Nathaniel pronounces these last few words, his wild eyes stare at me. Then they roll up, behind his eyelids, and all I can see are the whites. When he rolls his eyes back down again to look into mine, he looks dazed and exhausted. He reaches out, to hold my hand and his feels unnaturally cold. In his own voice he tells me, "That was Elias Hayward. He wants everyone to know that he had a son named Jonathan. They must have named him after Jonathan Morse, Elias' young friend who died in the war."

"Also Rebecca's war hero husband." I hand Nathaniel the antique photograph and he looks at it for the first time with his own eyes.

Then he looks into my eyes and asks me, "What the hell is happening here, Annabelle?"

Lavinia picks up the diary and gives it to our friend, the medium. "Nathaniel, if appearances mean anything, it looks like we might be related. My family always thought Lieutenant Elias Hayward had no direct descendants. There has never been any mention of his son anywhere; not in any documents or photos or records. You need to read Elizabeth's diary. Maybe it will give us some clues."

Nathaniel opens the diary to the first page and reads a few paragraphs silently; then he turns some pages and finally flips carefully to the end. "You can see here, near the binding, where someone cut some pages out. It appears that they used a very sharp knife. I think that the mystery surrounding Lieutenant Elias' son might have been explained in the missing pages."

"That makes sense. There's no record anywhere of Elias and Katherine Hayward having a son. Those must have been the pages that mention him. We need to find the lost pages." Earl seems determined to uncover this important piece of his family's history, which has been missing for almost one hundred and fifty years. "Where should we start looking?"

"I have some more boxes of my sister's things stored in your attic, Earl. There was a lot of junk, but I didn't want to throw anything out before we looked through it carefully. So I packed everything away right after we looked through Muriel's house, figuring I'd sort through it eventually. I think the time has come for us to search through those boxes." Lavinia's ready to finally look through her departed sister's things.

Earl adds, "Even if we don't find the missing pages, maybe we'll at least find a clue about where they could be."

Judith's always practical to a fault. "I hope no one destroyed them."

If the pages have been destroyed we might never find out what we need to know about Lieutenant Elias Hayward, his wife Katherine, Rebecca Burns Morse and the mysterious young boy named Jonathan, who looked just like Nathaniel. I'm not an expert on genetics, but I figure out something important right there on the spot. "If Nathaniel's paternal grandmother's maiden name was Burns and Elias' son looks a lot like Nathaniel, I don't think the boy's mother was Katherine…"

Nathaniel finishes my thought for me. "His mother was Rebecca and his last name was Burns, not Hayward. That's why your family never knew about him, Lavinia."

Earl's beginning to figure some stuff out, too. "That's why we've never heard of him before now."

"What does any of this have to do with me and the demon that's after me?" I ask.

Nathaniel answers, "I don't know, but we need to find out fast before she pays you another visit."

Chapter 13

Phoebe

Three days after our eerie little meeting at Lavinia's condo, I arrive home from school to find my dad taking a late lunch break with Nathaniel, in our kitchen. They're eating baloney and cheese sandwiches and throwing bites Jeff's way now and then. Again, I bring up my fabulous idea about going out to the graveyard so I can do some exciting paranormal research and Dad and Nathaniel immediately start arguing against me.

Nathaniel says, "The next step should be to search through the boxes in Earl's attic."

"But that's a good job for Oliver and Jackson, not for me. I'd rather be outside, hunting down the demon."

My dad weighs in, saying, "The demon who tried to kill you. No way are you going near the Prospect Street Burial Ground or the crossroads. Not without me and Nathaniel."

"Okay, you guys can come. Let's go. Now."

They both refuse to come with me, insisting that we need to know more before we venture out to where Katherine and Rebecca are buried. Dad and Nathaniel and I reach a stalemate in our negotiations.

The doorbell rings just in time. Phoebe's finally here. After scuffing the snow off her boots on the welcome mat by the door, she stands, perfectly balanced, on one foot at a time, with her hands in the pockets of her baggy jeans to pry off her well-worn, sturdy boots by alternately stepping on each heel with her toe. Finally, in her thick wool socks, she smiles and walks into our kitchen. I know she's from New England, but she looks like she just got up off a milking stool on some farm in Nebraska. In the afternoon light coming through our kitchen window, her shoulder-length blonde hair shines like pale honey on a bright morning. Her blonde eyebrows, eyelashes and flower petal pink cheeks complete the Midwestern corn-fed farm-girl look. She's not wearing a jacket, but her sweater's huge, heavy and the same natural shade as sheep's wool. It looks hand-knitted. A few pieces of straw are stuck in the weave, as if someone sheared the sheep in the barn, spun the wool into yarn on the spot and knitted it into a big, warm sweater. Then Phoebe pulled it on, over her head without shaking the hay off first.

She's grassy hilltops overlooking pastures speckled with lambs and cows. She's milking and herding and leaving your boots outside because they're coated with muck and manure. She looks like she's from a ranch in Wyoming. I've never had a sister and the second I look into her morning glory blue eyes surrounded by those colorless lashes, I feel like I have one. I notice that she's not wearing any make-up, not even mascara, and immediately decide never to wear make-up again, either. Everything about her intensifies the fire of my sisterly love. I start wondering where I can get a sweater like hers and how long it will take me to break in my new boots that I'm going to buy with my babysitting money. I want them to look worn in like Phoebe's instead of brand new. Maybe I can find some already broken in, scuffed up ones at a thrift store.

Right off the bat, Nathaniel starts playing his own version of I'm more supernaturally gifted than you are. "So you think you can keep Annabelle safe? How do you plan to do that? Hit the ghost over the head with a bale of hay, farm-girl?"

Phoebe hits one right back at him. "Aleister mentioned that you guys knew a medium who tried to help. But he wasn't very effective. So you called me."

Nathaniel and Phoebe eye each other like boxers stepping out of their corners on the way to the center of the ring. I wonder who's going to win this slugfest. It's love at first fight; the wrangling has started, not even two seconds after Phoebe entered our kitchen. Anyone who's watching Phoebe and Nathaniel together can guess how it will end. You don't need to be a psychic or a medium or a healer or a super duper detector of evil to predict the outcome.

I don't feel jealous at all, which is a relief, because it clarifies my feelings for Nathaniel. The pressure's off. I'm glad that his attention isn't directed toward me anymore. What I felt for Nathaniel was a short and very temporary attraction, mostly because Nathaniel's gorgeous and has good moves and I'm so lonely without Wyatt. Nathaniel and I are destined to be no more than close friends. Phew. I can relax and focus on worrying myself to death over my break up with Wyatt. Even though kissing Nathaniel felt amazing, I'm pleased that he and Phoebe have found each other. Hopefully they won't kill each other before they finally hook up.

My dad steps forward and shakes her hand. "Welcome to Eastfield, Phoebe. I'm glad you could come."

I can't just shake her hand. I go in for the hug and she responds, squeezing me back. Maybe she doesn't have a sister, either. Ever my mother's daughter, I turn to the stove to put the teakettle on. Next, I hear a deep voice coming from the godlike presence in the pimped-out wheelchair. "Hey, Farm-girl, I hope you have some experience with fiends from hell because I think we've got one here."

"Ah, you must be Napoleon. I've heard so much about you."

I want to correct her and tell her that his name is Nathaniel, but I'd have to duck while speaking those words to avoid getting wounded in the crossfire.

Jeff takes sides immediately by loping over and nosing the bottom of Phoebe's sweater, then her hand, which instantly finds the spot where he loves to be scratched. She's a veterinarian and a healer. No contest. Jeff's people instincts are superior to any human's and he sits down handsomely on his huge haunches, as close as he can get to Phoebe, arranging himself with his head against her waist. Then he nudges her hand over, so it's resting on his shoulder.

Hiding my grin, by turning around, I busy myself with tea and honey and mugs, while Nathaniel, Phoebe and the kettle steam away.

My dad pulls out a chair. "Take a load off, Phoebe. Nathaniel, Annabelle and I can fill you in on what's been happening."

She stands next to the chair, but doesn't sit down immediately. Instead our new friend reaches out and strokes one of the silver candleholders that have always decorated our table. "Wow. My mother has a set of candleholders just like these. I can feel the warmth vibrating in them. Can we light the candles? They look like the homemade candles Mom uses."

"My wife makes them herself. She uses the bees' wax from our neighbor's bees and the flowers and herbs from her own garden," Dad explains as he grants Phoebe's request by striking a match and igniting both wicks.

In the glow from the newly-lit candles, I feel awestruck. Then it dawns on me that everything makes sense and I shouldn't feel so surprised. Uncle Aleister knew. That's why he sent her. We *are* sisters, in a way. Her ancestors and mine were part of the original coven of thirteen pagan priestesses who possessed the Holy Grail back in King Arthur's day. Trebuchet, the pagans' smith, melted down the silver, combined it with other precious metals and forged twenty-six candle holders, to be passed down in pairs, from mothers to their daughters throughout the centuries. Some of the original thirteen women fled to Salem, Massachusetts in the seventeenth century to seek freedom from persecution only to be executed as witches.

Both Phoebe's ancestors and mine managed to keep their candleholders secret and in safe hands.

"Mmmmm, orange peel, rosemary and apple-mint." Phoebe caresses one candle, examining the flecks of orange peel, needles from the rosemary plant and leaves of apple-mint embedded beneath the waxy surface. "My mother doesn't do the whole herb garden, holistic healing thing, but she buys candles like this from some woman who sells them at a yearly harvest fair in…" I watch the realization dawn on her wholesome features. Her white teeth flash for an instant when she grins. "A fair in Eastfield. The Eastfield Harvest Fair, every October. My mother has been buying your mother's candles and teas for years."

"Small world." Suddenly, I miss my mom so much that my eyes fill with tears and I have to turn away.

I didn't turn away soon enough, though. Nathaniel doesn't miss any of it. "Nice job, Old MacDonald. Now look what you've done. Annabelle hasn't been through enough. You're supposed to help solve the problem, not upset the poor kid even more by talking about her mom, who's too far away to help her right now."

Within minutes of Phoebe entering our kitchen, my status as the love of Nathaniel's life has sunk to that of some pitiable little kid. This amuses me enough to cheer away my brief flicker of the blues. I sneak a glance over at Dad who shakes his head and winks at me.

Even an old guy like my dad can tell that sparks of passion are flying between Phoebe and Nathaniel. I pour out mugs of tea and put some cookies from a box out on the table. While we sit around the candles, warming our hands around the mugs, I do most of the talking with Nathaniel butting in to make wisecracks here and there. Folding her hands around the warm mug, Phoebe listens calmly, but flushes a little pinker whenever Nathaniel speaks. Jeff's sitting between us two girls and we take turns scratching and petting him. I wouldn't be surprised if Nathaniel referred out loud to his formerly loyal hound as Benedict Arnold. I know he's thinking the word traitor, even though I'm not a telepath. Anyone with a pinch of common sense and a little intuition could figure that out.

We all agree that Nathaniel and Phoebe should both stay the night, to see if she shows up again. That way we can all experience the same phenomena together, first hand, before Phoebe takes over as my guardian angel.

When I suggest to Phoebe that we should go over to the old Prospect Street Burial Ground, she agrees right away. Dad and Nathaniel aren't happy about it, but I need to check out both of Katherine Hayward's headstones and the fallen tree where Rebecca is buried at the nearby crossroads. The term "unhallowed ground" both petrifies and thrills me. If it weren't scary, it wouldn't be so interesting.

Nathaniel's not sure it's safe even in daylight, so he decides to tag along and bring Jeff. I'm not pleased at the thought of having to referee round two of Nathaniel vs. Phoebe, but I don't have a choice. Fortunately, there's still a lot of snow on the ground, so our wheelchair-bound medium will be stuck in the van or near it most of the time anyway. And at least we'll have Jeff following us around the "unhallowed ground". He's a good watchdog when it comes to evil spirits. Right now, of course, the sun's reflecting brilliantly off what's left of the glistening snow and ice, making the possibility of another supernatural disaster seem very unlikely. Later on, as shadows lengthen and the sun begins to set, I might not feel quite so brave.

My dad heads off to join Oliver and Jackson at Earl and Judith Curtis's house where they'll be collecting the boxes from their attic and bringing them back here to look through them for the missing pages from Elizabeth Hayward's diary. At the same time, Nathaniel, Phoebe, Jeff and I will conduct some outdoor research. We'll all be in touch via cell phone; talking, texting and sending pictures back and forth.

Chapter 14

One Woman, Two Graves

During the short ride from our house to the cemetery, the temperature rises quickly into the mid-fifties, unusual for December in New England. A thick fog descends slowly from above and tendrils of vapor swirl up from the snow-covered ground as everything frozen starts to melt. Soon, not only is the sun invisible; the sky is too. We're suspended in a thick, dingy vapor created by melting snow and sunken clouds. And it's growing thicker by the second. As Phoebe, Jeff, and I wander out of Nathaniel's van and into the old Prospect Street graveyard we enter a nightmarish fairytale setting. I can feel the ground under my boots but I can't see it. If I stretch my arm full length out in front of me, I can't see my hand. After stumbling into a pale, spiked obelisk marking the Hayward side of the burial ground, I snap a quick picture even though the visibility's nonexistent. Then I shove the phone back into my pocket.

Phoebe squats to feel the raised letters on the monument's square base. "H, A, Y... Here they are, Annabelle, the Hayward family. Katherine must be nearby."

"If this is the real grave. She might actually be buried over with the Littlefields. Oliver said the two families are at opposite ends of the cemetery."

Prospect Street itself actually divides the graveyard in half. Originally, a path for horses and carts ran through the cemetery, so the deceased could be transported to their final resting places. Sometime in the mid-nineteenth century the citizens of Eastfield widened the path and then eventually paved it and it became Prospect Street.

"Then the Littlefields are across the road, Phoebe. Even after death the families chose to be separated."

"Now that's what I call a grudge."

"Elias' marriage to Katherine was supposed to dissolve that hatred, but I think it got even worse because of her. Otherwise, why the two graves? Did the two families battle over who got to claim her after her death?"

"Maybe it wasn't who got to claim her. Maybe it was more like who *had* to claim her."

"So you think that no one wanted her buried with their family?"

"It's possible. Did both sides want her in their family plot? Or neither?"

The thick, textured soles of our boots stomp down the snow and dirt into a path of barely visible murky footprints as we move from one headstone to another, searching for familiar names: Lieutenant Elias, Elizabeth, Katherine, maybe even Jonathan, Lieutenant Elias Hayward's mysterious and elusive son. We find Elizabeth first. She was Elias' sister-in-law, married to his older brother, Captain Robert Hayward, also a Civil War veteran. The small American flag next to his grave dangles limply on its iron spike.

Evidently, they lost a baby girl named Grace, in the first year of her life, most likely due to one of the childhood illnesses vaccines protect us from now. Her tiny white stone is planted next to her parents', barely tall enough to be visible in the thin layer of crusty snow. Only the baby's name and significant dates are inscribed on it. Elizabeth lies beneath the respectable description, "Devoted mother. Beloved wife. Born 1834—Died 1899." Her husband was ten years older than she was, but lived to bury her. Maybe she and Elias were close because he was nearer to her age than Robert was.

I picture a respectful but distant husband. Captain Robert Hayward loved his wife but didn't understand her, perhaps neglected her. Elizabeth was a lonely, bereft young woman who had recently laid her sweet baby girl to rest in this desolate burial ground. Her husband's younger brother was also miserable because he was imprisoned in a loveless marriage. A close friendship with many shared confidences seems likely between the brother and sister-in-law if you think about it like that.

I can feel the warmth of Phoebe's hand through my windbreaker as she rests it affectionately on my shoulder. The hand of a healer; it's generating more heat than someone else's hand normally would. Her energy glows through my jacket, warming the skin beneath. Jeff's cold wet nose bumps against the back of my dangling right hand and I absently scratch his right ear as we ruminate. I realize that Phoebe's drifting along on the same thought wave when she says, "It's good that Elizabeth had someone to turn to when she was grieving over little Gracie. Elias loved the baby, too."

We look at each other with identical startled eyes and I blurt, "Because he was expecting one of his own. He was very interested in his little niece!"

Phoebe intensifies the physical connection between us by turning to face me and grabbing my other shoulder with her other hand. I step toward her and rest my hands on either side of her ribcage in a loose embrace. The heat between us is from another world, not this one. A swath of fog drifts aside and we can see Nathaniel as he wheels himself out of the van, over to the edge of the road. Surrounded by heavy mist, his dark form seems like a vision from another time, a different century. I know he's wearing a dark blue Red Sox hat and his denim jacket, but in the fogbound distance, his clothing looks like a Union army uniform. Phoebe and I stare into each other's eyes and continue to finish each other's thoughts and sentences.

"Elizabeth and Elias cared for the baby together."

A tear trickles from my right eye. "They struggled to nurse her through the fever, but she didn't make it."

"Elias brought her to Deep Water Cottage by the pond and Rebecca tried her best with the herbs and her healing touch, but nothing helped."

"It was a miracle that Rebecca didn't become ill herself from the fever."

"No, Rebecca was safe. She had mysterious immunities. She rarely even caught a cold. Her unborn child was safe, too, protected by the same magically sturdy constitution that saved his mother's life from the widespread deadly fevers of the nineteenth century."

"Gracie died and both Elias and Elizabeth became ill but survived."

"The poor, helpless infant couldn't fight through the fever but the adults made it. Elias was made stronger by his will to live long enough to witness the birth of his own child."

"His son, Jonathan."

"Named after his friend, Rebecca's fallen war hero husband, Jonathan Morse."

"Elizabeth wanted to succumb to the dreadful illness, but Elias and Rebecca kept her strong. They needed her help and emotional support with their own situation. Elizabeth stayed in the world of the living instead of joining little Gracie, so she could help raise another child who would need her."

"A sturdy, healthy, handsome little boy. Jonathan Elias Hayward, whose parents couldn't be together."

"Even though they loved each other more than Elizabeth and Robert did. More than Elias and Katherine did."

"Katherine and Elias didn't love each other at all. Katherine was obsessed with him. It's different."

"And Elias felt repulsed by her."

"Elias' son isn't buried here."

"Why not?"

"I'm not sure. We need to find out but I don't know how to yet."

The low-pitched rumble of Jeff's growl interrupts Phoebe and me. The scenes we were watching with our minds' eyes fade. And we say goodbye to the beautiful, frail baby girl, the bereaved mother, her concerned but uninvolved husband, the passionate father-to-be, the woman he loves who isn't his wife and their beautiful, perfect baby boy. Their faces and interactions disappear into the fog. We watch Rebecca's herb garden and small, cozy home, reflected in the smooth mirror of the pond's motionless surface grow less focused by the second until we can't see the cottage or the pond at all. Phoebe and I re-enter the twenty-first century. Jeff growls again.

Only one thing could be drawing this hostile sound out of our protective companion: a ghost. Phoebe and I let go of each other and send the vision of the past that we conjured up back where it belongs. Nathaniel shouts, "Be careful! Someone's here."

Phoebe and I both know what he means: someone from another century, someone who doesn't belong among the living. A baby's weak cry drifts in from nowhere. A mother's gentle voice sings one line from an ancient lullaby. Silence follows. Dead silence. Not a branch stirs. No living thing offers up even the quietest murmur. Jeff fills the unnatural void with a hackle-raising howl that could wake the dead, except the dead are already awake. Nathaniel yells again. "Get over here, you two!"

His wheel chair won't move through the mucky mixture of melting snow, storm debris and mud so he's probably ready to explode with frustration. It would be kind of funny if we weren't so scared. But curiosity and bravery win out. Phoebe whacks Jeff's butt and sends him over to his master's side, grabs my hand and we continue our trek through the Hayward side of the graveyard. We haven't found Katherine's true resting place, so there's no way we're leaving yet. It must be nearing four-thirty because the dingy white fog is turning grayer. Dusk. Nathaniel's distant cursing interrupts the otherwise silent dimness. Even if we had a flashlight, it wouldn't help us. The beam would only reflect off the thick, pale mist filling the air in the deserted burial ground. Deserted except for Phoebe and me. Our hearts are the only beating ones present, but we're not alone. She grabs my hand in hers. A supernatural warmth generates between our palms.

I reassure my new best buddy, my adopted sister. "Don't worry. It's Elizabeth. She wants us to know the truth."

"Only the truth can save you from Katherine, Annabelle. That's who's been after you. Katherine Littlefield Hayward." Phoebe speaks these words out loud, but they didn't originate in her own mind. Appearing out of nowhere, weird thoughts continue to enter Phoebe's mind and mine. We keep telling each other everything that occurs to us. Nathaniel yells again for us to leave the cemetery and again we ignore him. My cell phone starts vibrating in my jeans' pocket but I disregard it because I know it's my disgruntled medium friend. Jeff barks a single sharp warning, as if he's begging us to join him by the side of the road with Nathaniel. But we don't acknowledge him, either.

"Look, there she is. It's Katherine's stone." I point to a single large white limestone grave marker with two arcs on the top, one for each soul it commemorates. I click off a couple of pictures with my phone then return it to my pocket. "The flash will probably just reflect off of the fog and we won't see anything much, but you never know. We can look at these pictures later; maybe on a bigger screen something will show up."

"Text them to Oliver."

Quickly, I comply, then pocket my phone again.

Phoebe and I bend to examine the pale, hard surface more closely. On the left side, the engraved letters spell out a stark message: Katherine Littlefield Hayward and underneath her name we see the years 1837 to 1885. But no inscription. The right side of the gravestone offers a little more information about what lies beneath it. "Here lie the remains of Lieutenant Elias Abraham Hayward, born 1835, died 1890. Rest in peace brave soul, but it is not likely." Who would choose such a cryptic and eerie epitaph for a deceased relative? Someone who disliked him? Someone who loved him? Someone who pitied him?

"She's not buried here. That's why there's no inscription, only her name and dates. Let's find the Littlefields' plot."

We leave, to hike through the melting snow and across Prospect Street where Nathaniel sits by the side of the road, fuming on his chrome throne. He grabs Phoebe's wrist as we attempt to pass by him and his furry sidekick. "Do not set foot over there, especially with your new partner in crime."

"Back off, Napoleon. She's safe as long as she stays with me."

"Don't go, Annabelle. Be sensible. Remember what it was like the night of the blizzard."

"I have to go. I'll never be safe until we know the whole story."

"There are other, more sensible ways to find out. Jackson and Oliver are working on it right now over at your house. They just called to tell me they haven't found anything interesting yet, but there are tons of letters, documents and photographs."

"This is important, too. We need both kinds of information: the kind Oliver's coming up with, but also information from out here where they're buried. I need to feel what they felt."

"You two don't know what you're dealing with. You're too new at this."

Phoebe wrestles her arm free from his grasp. But Nathaniel keeps staring at her, as if he'd like to hold onto her forever, but he's too civilized to force her. The part of him that's controlled by a twenty-first century, gentlemanly conscience, voluntarily lets go of her wrist but I can tell by the expression on his face that he's steaming mad. We trudge off, through the soggy snow and mud and Nathaniel attempts to follow us but his wheelchair gets stuck. As we leave him behind, we can hear him sputtering and cursing.

Phoebe and I head over to the far corner of the graveyard where the white mist glowing in the darkness is denser, practically opaque. We spy a row of large, squared-off light gray stones and stop abruptly as we slam into a wall of freezing air. My face is stinging from the pinpoints of icy mist, but the back of my head isn't. I take a step back, so that my toes are lined up with Phoebe's. She reaches out and holds my hand, takes one small step forward, then hops back to join me. "I feel it too. She's here."

With my other hand I dig out my phone and snap four fast pictures before pocketing it again.

Gripping each other's hands, we step forward and tiptoe around seven rocks, the size of irregularly shaped grapefruits. They're scattered randomly in the vicinity of her grave. Together we bend to peer at the inscription on a stone that's practically invisible in the frigid cloud surrounding it. Phoebe reads the bizarre words aloud. "Here lies Katherine Littlefield, 1837 to 1885. Please God may she rest in peace beneath this layer of humble earth."

"It's like someone's begging her to stay here."

"She did enough damage when she was alive. They didn't want her restless soul to move among the living after her death."

"But they didn't get their wish, did they?"

"Let's get out of here. I'm so cold my feet and my hand ache."

I know what Phoebe means. My knees and feet are throbbing as if knives of icy mist are stabbing through them, but only one of my hands feels the unholy cold. The hand Phoebe's holding in hers is warm.

"It's going to take us a few minutes at least to get Nathaniel unstuck."

"Stubborn idiot."

"Yeah, but he's my idiot and I love him." I borrow Oliver's phrase.

Phoebe does a double take and blurts out, "Do you?"

"Not in that way," I reassure her, letting her know with a glance that her secret's safe with me. "Nathaniel and I are just really close friends." No reason to go into detail about how we've been there and done that, but it wasn't the right fit for either of us.

We trudge over to the entrenched wheelchair and its enraged passenger. As Phoebe ducks and pushes her shoulder into the back of Nathaniel's chrome throne and I tug from in front, she complains, "This is going to be a royal pain in the ass."

"Just like him." I laugh, feeling intense affection for Phoebe and Nathaniel and relief that we're away from the razor-sharp frost surrounding Katherine Littlefield's grave. After about five minutes of red-faced pushing and pulling we free him from the muck and snow. Leaving us laughing in the slush, he angrily zooms over to the van and begins the process of moving himself inside.

"Wait, Nathaniel. We want to check out the crossroads!" Phoebe yells.

"The demolished oak tree! The unhallowed ground!" I know I'm adding fuel to his furious fire by hollering out these inflammatory words but I'm amusing myself and Phoebe, who snorts unattractively when she giggles: just one more thing to love about her.

Nathaniel's beside us within seconds. "You sound like one of your patients when you laugh, Doctor." He makes the title "Doctor" sound like an insult and Phoebe and I bubble over into fits of uncontrollable giggling, designed by nature to make nearby males suffer from extreme annoyance. We can't control ourselves. The madder Nathaniel gets, the harder we laugh. But finally, we relent and help him stay with us by dislodging his wheelchair every time it gets bogged down in the slush.

When we arrive at the crossroads, he parks himself next to the huge, imposing remains of the fallen oak and announces, "This is a bad idea, but I'm not letting you two dumbasses go it alone."

On one side, casting soft shadows along the bark's gray crust, a thick gloom surrounds what's left of the gigantic tree. On the other side, the fog thins out and we can see how the lightning's violent attack ripped through the sturdy trunk, scorching the vulnerable pale flesh beneath the bark. A narrow, jagged point of wood stabs up into the night sky like a dark, bone-thin accusing finger. Taking out my phone, I capture some dramatic images of the old oak's corpse.

As I aim and click, my emotions edge slowly up the gradual hills and then zoom down the steep drops of the roller coaster they've been riding on lately. I can tell from the way she keeps grabbing my hand, clutching it tight and then abruptly letting it go, that Phoebe's worse. No wonder, on top of the alternating laughter and fear, she's dealing with an intense attraction for my medium friend who's pissed as a newt. He's actually more gorgeous when he's angry, too. His eyes glitter with intensity and his cheekbones grow more defined as the muscles in his jaw flex and twitch. Suddenly, I realize that he's not himself.

Someone else's anger is invading his perfect face: the fury of a man from the nineteenth century.

Before he turns to face the remains of the ravaged old oak tree again, whoever is inhabiting Nathaniel's body shouts over his shoulder. "Leave them alone. You did too much damage on this earth when you were alive."

The fog clears completely for a moment and Phoebe reaches for my hand once again. I notice that she's holding Nathaniel's with her other. Except he's not Nathaniel right now. We three freeze in place as if we've grown roots that delve deeper into the earth than those of the ruined tree before us. Our physical connection generates both strength and a ring of clear light. Behind what remains of the huge and ancient tree stands a beautiful young woman, wearing a long, white nightgown trimmed with lace at the throat and wrists. She's holding the hand of a little boy. Her voice drifts on the wind that's quietly swirling around us. "Elias."

"Rebecca. Jonathan." The hushed voice doesn't sound like Nathaniel's but the words are issuing forth from his lips. "Don't go."

"She's doing her best to protect you, Annabelle. Katherine has no power over here tonight. Elias and Rebecca joined forces and sent her away when she tried to follow us to the tree," Phoebe explains.

"They've all left, now," I announce. "As suddenly as they arrived." I can tell because the night air is no longer clear, but seething with fog once again. Looking down at Nathaniel, I let go of his hand, reach into my pocket, pull out a tissue and use it to dab at the tears on his cheeks.

Grabbing hold of my wrist, he looks up at me. "Thank you." I know that the tears I wiped from his face aren't his, but those of another man from another century. He blinks and one more tear slides down before Nathaniel stops weeping and a smile warms his copper eyes.

"Annabelle, you're safe here." He shakes his head. "Katherine almost killed your father the night of the blizzard. She tore this old tree apart in a rage, but Rebecca's back now. She returned so she can help us. This is her resting place, but she can't rest again until Katherine goes back where she belongs."

And I know why. "Rebecca appeared not just to protect me. She needs to watch over her lover and her son, the man and the child she sees when she looks at you, Nathaniel."

"You're right. I'm her great, great grandson. Actually, I'm not even sure how many greats. Maybe Oliver can help me figure it out."

"It's not important. Rebecca came back so she could help you."

"And Elias and Jonathan, too."

"They're your ancestors, Nathaniel. They live in you."

"Can they really help protect Annabelle, though?" Phoebe sounds unsure.

An expression of intense concentration darkens Nathaniel's beautiful face. "Not completely, but they're here to try. We have to do the rest. Let's go. I don't think there's anything left to discover out here and I want to find out what Oliver and Jackson unearthed from those old boxes. And you never know. Annabelle might have captured some useful information with the camera on her phone. We need to get a good look at the pictures, on a bigger screen. I'm freezing. Let's leave."

So we climb into Nathaniel's van to hurry back to civilization, light and warmth. I ride in the back with Jeff, so Phoebe and Nathaniel can continue pretending that they hate each other in the front.

Chapter 15

Seven Stones

When we arrive back in my cozy warm kitchen, Oliver, Jackson and my father are sitting around the table. Dad's tipping his chair, so it's balanced on two legs. If my mom were here, she'd yell at him, but she isn't. A couple of sturdy cardboard boxes with their lids removed rest on the floor near the table and Jeff plops his huge, furry body down next to one. After giving it the sniff test, he sneezes an extra large-sized sneeze, because he's an extra large-sized hound. It's a wet one and Oliver grabs a napkin to wipe his pants leg off. "Ugh, Nathaniel. Can't you teach him to cover his face when he does that?"

"Normally he does, but he couldn't reach the tissues." Nathaniel rolls his eyes. "What did you guys find out?"

"Not much, yet." Dad sounds frustrated. He's more like me: not built for reading through tons of old papers. He'd be happier trekking around outside, building something or tearing it down.

Oliver's the opposite, which is good, because during our last investigation, he found tons of relevant and valuable information in some old documents. And he had to read a lot of them before he uncovered the ones that mattered. "Pull up a chair, you guys. We could use three extra pairs of eyes. There's tons of stuff to read through here."

"Drat." Good curse word to use when you're surrounded by adults. Plus it sounds like it's from another century which is appropriate under the circumstances. Instead of "pulling up a chair" and participating in the most boring part of a paranormal investigation, I fill up the kettle and start setting out the mugs for tea. Nathaniel, Phoebe and I just came in from the cold and need some warming up.

Jackson asks, "Hey, Annabelle, do you have anything with caffeine? Not that I don't love your mother's home brews, but I could use a little pick-me-up."

I reach into one of our kitchen cabinets and pull out the box of Lipton tea bags that Nathaniel brought over, and some sugar.

Phoebe speaks up. "I'll have some of the herbal. Is there any chamomile hanging around?"

"Yes, literally." I point into the pantry. Bunches of chamomile flowers are literally hanging around in there. My mother bundles and drapes bouquets of the yellow daisy-shaped flowers upside down from the drying racks my dad built her. When they're ready, she mixes them with other herbs and flowers into teas that can cure almost anything.

Sometimes she pours melted wax over the flowers, rolls the mixture up with a layer of softened beeswax, fits it all into cylinder shaped pewter molds and leaves it to harden into candles.

Standing in her pantry, I turn slowly around and breathe in the scents that surround me: lavender, chamomile, rosemary, thyme, a dozen varieties of mint and more. Suddenly, I feel like my mom's here with me, helping to choose which herbs would be best for the occasion. Smiling, I grab a handful of dried chamomile and some Kentucky spearmint, crush it in my fists and empty the fragrant crumbs into a fat-bellied ceramic teapot. When the water in the kettle starts to boil, I pour some over the mixture and also into the mugs containing the store-bought teabags. While our tea's steeping, I set everything on the table with a box of sugar, a carton of milk, a pot of honey, the tea strainer for the tea in the teapot and some spoons. Finally, I find a box of graham crackers and some peanut butter and put that out, too, with a couple of knives for spreading. Not exactly Martha Stewart, but it will have to do until Dad or I go grocery shopping. The pie that Judith made us is long gone. I wish she'd bring over another.

Oliver stands, walks over to the countertop closest to our sink and picks up a round tin that I didn't even notice. He sets it on the table and opens it. "Oatmeal raisin. I baked them this morning." That man's a keeper. We all sit around, sipping hot tea, eating crackers and delicious cookies, reading through the old letters and journals and looking at the sepia-tinted photographs that were in the boxes from Earl and Judith's house. I jump up after about two minutes of this horrifically boring activity and run to grab my phone. We need to see the pictures I took back at the graveyard. Anything's better than this.

As I click on my smart phone and start swiping through the pictures, Nathaniel's looking over my left shoulder and Oliver's on my right. Dad gets up and stands behind me. The pictures look pretty artistic because they really portray a mood: the mood of a graveyard on a foggy late winter afternoon. Unfortunately, that's it, though: nothing supernatural stands out, no orbs or shadows, like you see in the photographs on those paranormal shows on TV. "Boring," I announce.

Oliver peers over my right shoulder. "Zoom in on that one."

I follow his suggestion.

"Let's see what you have there, Annabelle."

Nathaniel announces, "Not quite as boring as you think."

"What? I don't see anything significant."

Nathaniel takes the phone out of my hand and starts swiping through the pictures. He looks through all of them twice then starts to explain. "You took all of these right around the exact time, late in the afternoon, right, Annabelle?"

"Yup, within about fifteen minutes of each other. We didn't stay long in the graveyard."

"Well, this one here's darker than the others. There's a shadow, but it's so large, it darkened the whole photograph, so you can't see its shape. Do you remember seeing a huge shadow recently?" His question's rhetorical. He knows I'll never forget the gigantic shadow that darkened our whole backyard during the blizzard.

"That's her grave, too: Katherine Littlefield Hayward. On the Littlefield side of the cemetery. That's where she's buried. On the Hayward side there's just the headstone. I wonder why." I'm thinking out loud now.

"The shadow isn't the only alarming thing in this photo." Nathaniel's voice is growing louder and more agitated. I think I hear a tremor of fear in it, too. "Look here, Oliver. Count the stones. There's nothing random about the number."

"There are seven." Oliver looks up solemnly, into Nathaniel's intensely focused eyes. "Someone set her free. Perhaps deliberately."

"What the hell are you two talking about?" Pinpricks of ice scoot up my spine and over my scalp. Every one of the hair follicles on my head stiffens. If I had short hair, it would be standing on end right now. I know who Oliver is talking about.

I know who "her" is and I realize what "Someone set her free," means. Katherine Littlefield Hayward is now free to roam among us.

Out loud I announce, "She's on a death mission and I'm her primary target."

Phoebe grabs my hand and squeezes it. "What was keeping her in her grave? And how did she get loose? What happened?"

Nathaniel explains. "When an evil soul has been buried, there's an old custom."

Oliver continues. "The guardians of her grave place seven heavy stones on top of the earth under which she's buried."

Nathaniel finishes. "To keep her down where she belongs. But someone moved the stones off Katherine's grave."

Phoebe asks hopefully, "Isn't that just an old superstition?"

"Think again, Doctor," Nathaniel snaps back, as is his habit with her, especially when the conversation involves Phoebe's supernatural expertise or lack of. Again, he pronounces the title "Doctor" as if he's saying "Dumbass" instead.

Then he proceeds to explain, in the same insulting tone, "A—Katherine Littlefield Hayward is buried there." He holds one hand palm up and ticks off the first thing on his list by bending back his pinky finger with the index finger of his other hand. Then he moves on and taps his ring finger in the same way as he continues to lecture my new friend. "B—Annabelle has been attacked by an evil supernatural presence. C—It happened right after a tree was struck by lightning in the middle of a blizzard near the site of Katherine's grave. D—Nothing like this has ever happened before. E—The stones have been moved and this act set her evil spirit free."

"Unfortunately, it all fits together." Jackson reaches one arm around me and gives my trembling shoulders a supportive squeeze.

"There's a lot of truth in what some people dismiss as old superstitions and legends." Oliver's right. We learned that during our last paranormal adventure.

Poor Phoebe, her cheeks have turned from flower petal pink to sunset fuchsia. Nathaniel's totally overdoing the whole hostility thing. Oliver shoots Jackson a glance and they share a discreet smile. I don't know who Nathaniel thinks he's fooling. Actually, I *do* know. He's fooling himself and he's fooling Phoebe. Everyone else has it all figured out, even Jeff.

"Maybe we should simply go back over there and move the stones back into position. Will Katherine leave us alone then?" Phoebe risks another question, even though Nathaniel might ridicule her.

"It's not that simple." Nathaniel explains, in a reasonably tolerant voice this time. "Before the stone pile can be effective, she needs to be at rest, in her grave and she's not. Her spirit's still at large. We need to wait for her to finish her mission here among the living and then she'll return to her grave to rest. But we can't let her finish what she started."

"Because her mission is to harm Annabelle." Phoebe's catching on.

"We need to find out who moved the stones off that grave. Who on earth would do such a thing and why?" I can't imagine who would wish me harm. The kind of harm that could get me killed.

"I'll give Abner Littlefield a call. I know him through the Historical Society. He's been an active member for years, since before I took over as president." Oliver volunteers to contact the only Littlefield I know of, besides Katherine. He takes out his cell phone and calls his old friend.

I can hear Abner because like a lot of elderly people who are losing their hearing, he shouts when he's on the phone. Oliver explains the situation and Abner yells his reply, so we're blasted with the information, loud and clear.

"I've been looking after our section of the cemetery since my father died in 1955, but I'm getting too old to go out there during the fall and the winter. The fallen leaves make the ground slippery, and of course, so do the snow and ice. Plus I hate going out in the cold. I don't have very many relatives who live nearby, so I asked my daughter and her husband, Brian Foley. He's been going over there since early November, because the weather's too cold for my old bones. Brian was kind of skeptical about the strange story. Didn't seem to believe me when I explained about the stones and told him they needed to stay precisely where they are. I don't think he has much respect for the legend."

"What is the legend, Abner?" Oliver asks. We all have a pretty good idea, but I think he wants to hear it spelled out by an actual member of the Littlefield family.

"I don't have a lot of details, and Katherine, as you know, has two graves, but we think she's resting on the Littlefield side of the graveyard. We're pretty sure that the Hayward side has only a stone commemorating her death but her actual remains are buried on our side. Under those seven stones."

I nod at Oliver who responds. "Yes, Abner, we figured that part out, just from what's written on the gravestones. What's the legend? I need to know for some historical research I'm doing about Eastfield's graveyards."

"It does sound kind of farfetched when you hear it explained, but it's a tradition that the Littlefield's have never messed with. To tell you the truth, Oliver, I feel a little frightened whenever I'm over by her gravesite. The air always seems colder near those stones."

It was a lot colder near her grave today.

"Why are the stones there, Abner?" Oliver's being patient. And it's making me want to rip the cell phone out of his hands and yell at Abner to get to the point and answer the damn question.

He finally does. "The stones are supposed to weigh down Katherine's evil spirit, so she can't escape the grave and interfere with the living. They've been in place since the family laid her in the ground back in 1885. There. I said it. I told you it sounds silly."

"Someone's moved them. They're scattered around near her headstone. Seven of them."

"Well, then. I guess the whole story's a myth, a superstition made up to scare the young people and keep them from vandalizing the Littlefield graves."

"Not quite, Abner. There might be some truth to the legend." Oliver looks to me for help. How can he get more information out of Abner without telling him the whole story about the vicious demon trying to kill me? I give him a nod, encouraging him to leak at least part of the truth. After all, Abner was at Mrs. Curtis' when we looked into the box and Lieutenant Elias Hayward spoke to us, using Nathaniel's voice. After that experience, he has to be open to the idea of paranormal phenomena.

Oliver begins, hesitantly. "Someone's been bothering Annabelle. Someone who's not from the world of the living."

I like the way Oliver has edited "trying to kill Annabelle" down to "bothering". I send him a nod of approval.

"Do you think it's a ghost?" Abner shouts into his phone.

"We're pretty sure it's a spirit of some kind and we think this spirit might be connected to the love triangle between Elias and Rebecca and Katherine."

"Seriously? How do you know that?"

"Bill Blake was over near the graveyard, at the corner of Bay Road and Prospect Street, on the night of the big blizzard and he saw something strange."

"You mean the old oak? The place where Rebecca's buried?"

"Yes, it's not far from Katherine's resting place."

"Bill was there? People say the tree was struck by lightning. Although I've heard such a thing exists, I've never seen lightning during a snowstorm before, and I've been around a long time."

"Bill saw the lightning and he watched the tree split and fall. It almost hit his truck. The part that fell onto the road blocked his way so he couldn't get home to Annabelle on the night of the blizzard. Shortly after that, Annabelle saw something outside their house and it seemed to be paranormal in nature." Oliver is phrasing everything very diplomatically and keeping it vague. Nathaniel and I both smile at him.

"I'll ask my son-in-law if he's been over there lately. Maybe he knows something about the stones being moved."

"We'd appreciate that, Abner. We need to get to the bottom of this. Whatever got started the night of the blizzard isn't over yet and we have to keep Annabelle safe."

"Keep her safe? Why would anyone want to harm Annabelle?"

"That's what we need to find out. Ask your son-in-law if he knows anything and then please get back to me as soon as possible."

While we're waiting for Abner to call us back, I settle down and start looking through the boxes with the grownups. Every few minutes Dad and I make eye contact and share a nonverbal message about how boring the task is. Then Nathaniel reminds me. "Annabelle, you snapped a couple of pictures when we were near the oak tree but they came out kind of blurry."

"Yes, it was hard to see much of anything because of the fog. Do you want to take another look at them?"

"Humor me. Email them to yourself and let's look at them on a bigger screen. Go get your laptop. Maybe we'll be able to see something when the image is larger."

Sure enough, when I do as Nathaniel suggests and we look at the pictures of the old oak on the laptop screen, I see something I didn't notice on my phone's smaller screen. "Nathaniel." I tip the laptop more in his direction.

"I can see the shadow of the tree through the darkness and fog."

"And it looks whole. It looks like it did before the lightning strike."

Everyone gets up to stare at the computer screen.

"Why do you suppose that is?"

"Someone's trying to send us a message. Maybe Rebecca. She's the one who's buried there."

"What could that message be?"

"We're going to have to go back," I exclaim and jump up from my chair.

"Not tonight. You'll be able to see more during the daylight, anyway. We can go tomorrow. You're not going over there after dark. It's too dangerous." Nathaniel starts bossing me around again. Phoebe's right. He's like Napoleon: short because he's always in the wheelchair and wicked bossy. And I don't like it. But I have no choice because Dad agrees with him. Phoebe's the only one who rose out of her chair when I did, ready to spring into action and return to Rebecca's final resting place immediately. We're outvoted, though, and everyone goes back to digging through the piles of boring old papers.

Finally Jackson lets out a "Voila!"

In one hand he's holding up a thick sheaf of filthy and discolored old papers that look like they've been hacked out of a book with a dull knife. In the other hand, he has two old letters; one's in what appears to be a sealed envelope.

"The missing pages from Elizabeth's journal!" Jackson confirms our hopes. As Oliver moves closer so he can see over his fiancé's shoulder, Jackson breaks the wax seal on the old envelope, carefully extracts the ancient papers, unfolds them and starts reading out loud from the letter. "Upon my death, I have instructed my husband to bury these pages with me, without reading them first. I will have carried these secrets to my grave and beyond. No one can ever know the whole truth. The souls involved in this evil situation must be left to rest in peace."

"Too late for that," Nathaniel interrupts. "Those papers actually look like they were buried in someone's coffin. I wonder who unearthed them and put them in the box?"

"Look at this." Oliver unfolds an official-looking document that's only slightly discolored. "It's the certificate giving Robert Hayward permission to exhume the remains of his wife, three days after they buried her."

Jackson stares down at the papers in his hands, drops them onto the table, stalks over to the kitchen sink and starts scrubbing his hands with soap. Over his shoulder, he yells back to us, "Those pages were lying beneath the earth by the side of Elizabeth Hayward's corpse for three days back in the 1800's." The thick pile of ancient parchment is now lying next to Jackson's tea cup, but no one moves to touch it, even though we need to know what Elizabeth wrote. Finally Nathaniel reaches toward the disgusting heap of old paper.

"Stop!" My father jumps up. "I have some gloves I use when I'm handling harsh chemicals on the job." He rushes out to get his tool chest out of his truck and comes back with a pair of latex gloves that look like the kind they use on every crime show on TV.

"Cool." I can't help myself. I feel like we're on CSI or Bones. Everyone's too grossed out to touch Elizabeth's journal because a long time ago the papers spent three days sitting next to a rotting cadaver, six feet under the ground. Surprisingly, Oliver doesn't move from his seat to examine them. Even he's too squeamish and no one loves reading through old stuff as much as he does.

Nathaniel pulls on the gloves and shuffles the papers, trying to find the first one so we can hear, in chronological order, what happened almost a hundred fifty years ago. Finally, he picks up the top paper on the rearranged pile, sits back and begins to read out loud.

Katherine died today. God forgive me for writing down these feelings, but I am relieved that my brother-in-law, Elias, does not have to endure her presence here on Earth any longer. As she aged she grew more sour and evil. She never saw beauty but that she denounced it in favor of fouling the air with her wretched complaints regarding every person she was acquainted with and his circumstances. Her river of bile flowed endlessly, flooding the house and poisoning the existence of everyone in both the Littlefield and Hayward families.

On the night of Katherine's death, Elias spent what seemed like forever by her bedside, until she completely lost consciousness and could not revile his ears any further with her misery. Ten years ago, his profound sadness after the sudden and disreputable death of his beloved Rebecca began to dominate his life. He could only find joy in the company of his loving son, Jonathan. I need to write it down and look at the words. I am weary from hiding such an obvious truth. I cannot believe that no one has ever suspected. Jonathan is Rebecca's son, not Katherine's.

When Rebecca became pregnant, Elias and I conspired to pad Katherine's clothing so she appeared to be pregnant. Rebecca remained secluded in her small stone cottage by the pond, in order to hide her scandalous condition. When the baby was born, Elias and Katherine raised him as their own so Rebecca would not have to suffer the humiliation of bearing a child out of wedlock: the child of a married man. Elias brought Jonathan over to visit with his real mother often, until Rebecca died suddenly and under mysterious circumstances, when Jonathan was only two years old.

Katherine never formed a close bond with Jonathan, but he has always regarded her as his natural mother and shown her respect and moderate affection. However, the feelings he appears to have for Katherine are nothing like the love he shows his father and me. He's a beautiful, intelligent and passionate child. Unfortunately, Jonathan is the only source of joy in his father's life. Katherine has done her best throughout the years to make Elias more miserable as each one passes.

Since Elias left Katherine's bedside yesterday, he has seemed gloomier than ever. What on earth did that diabolical woman say to him before she passed on?

Nathaniel shuffles the paper he has been reading to the bottom of the creepy pile and begins to read from the page now on top.

Today we buried Katherine in a private ceremony: family only. She has no friends in the community and even her own family, the Littlefields, avoided her. However, they agreed to inter her remains on their side of the burial ground if Elias placed a monument to her on the Hayward side as well, to avoid rumors. Elias and my husband Robert have refused to allow her to be buried with the Haywards. Elias was forced to tolerate her during her life, in exchange for the land included in her dowry. He refuses to be buried by her side for eternity. If she's far enough under the earth, with seven stones piled over the exact spot where she lies, we hope her evil spirit will stay at rest. I pray to God that the poison contaminating the very air that surrounded her during her life will stay with her under the ground. Amen.

Nathaniel looks up from the words he has just read with an expression of sadness and disbelief. "The next page is dated seven years after the one I just read and it's about Elias Hayward's death."

He begins to read again.

Elias lies on his death bed, his chest rattling

with every labored breath. Yesterday, Jonathan spent over two hours in the room with his dying father. At the end of the second hour, my nephew ran out of the sickroom, slammed the door and headed out to the barn. He saddled his huge stallion and left. The horse was so startled by Jonathan's heels digging into his sides that he reared up before he galloped off. The last thing I heard was my nephew's voice thundering through the yard. "God Damn your soul to hell!"

He took nothing with him, and said good bye to no one, not even me. We haven't seen him since.

That child has been everything to me since he was born, twenty-five years ago. He is a loving young man who has always been emotionally close to his father and me. However, he never married. He has certainly had many opportunities to marry and produce children of his own. Every unmarried maiden in the village has tried to make him fall in love with her, but he politely rejected each one. Maybe he feared that he'd duplicate the unhappiness of Elias' union with Katherine. He does not know that she wasn't his true mother. I wonder if he's worried about Katherine's evil nature and thinks that his own children might inherit her malevolent disposition. Someone should tell him the truth. She was not Jonathan's natural mother. What if Elias finally told his son about his real birth mother and Jonathan grew so angry, he left us forever?

Please, God, bring him home safely and soon. I am preparing myself to enter the sickroom now to break the news to Elias. He keeps asking for Jonathan but we have not heard from him since late yesterday, when he tore out of here on horseback, screeching a curse to the dark sky.

The last item in the collection of papers lying on the table in front of Nathaniel is an envelope, yellowed with age and pale brown around the edges. The red blob of sealing wax on the flap is broken. With his gloved index finger and thumb pinched together on one corner, Nathaniel extracts the envelope's contents and begins to read the final document.

Dear Aunt Elizabeth,

It is obvious to me that you have deduced my whereabouts. Upon leaving my father's bedside, nine years ago, I fled Eastfield to seek out my true mother's family. In my enraged condition, after my father finally told me the truth and ended his years of deception, I left his deathbed and headed for Winter Island in hopes that the Burns' family would welcome me there, which they did.

Yesterday, I received your letter informing me of your illness and I am preparing for a hasty departure from my island home as soon as I can get my affairs in order here. I have a wife and three young sons now. We live on Winter Island and I own two small fishing boats. It is a simple and sometimes harsh life, but I love it and prefer it to my former, more luxurious life, which was built on a foundation of lies and evil. My father and stepmother forced me to unknowingly live in the shadow of that hideous deception for twenty-five years. My mother's people took me in and helped me build this life that I love and treasure so dearly.

I should arrive in Eastfield within a couple of days and I pray that God does not take you until after I have had one last chance to hear the kind voice of my beloved aunt once again. I have missed you but I could not return and face the rest of that sinful horde. Of course I forgive you for your small and blameless role in the evil ruse that my father and that creature he was married to carried out and got away with for twenty-five years. I no longer call myself Jonathan Hayward and never will again. I'm known as Jack Burns and I live here on Winter Island, in relative isolation, surrounded by relations from my true mother's side of the family. Upon my unannounced arrival at their door, they embraced me instantly as one of their own. They often mention how much I resemble my mother, Rebecca Burns Morse. God rest her soul. I was so young when she died that I do not remember her and have been forever robbed of the opportunity to know and love her. The demon called Katherine wrenched that entitlement from my innocent,

loving hands and heart forever. May she rot in
Hell. I will never forgive her.
  Be strong, Aunt. I will arrive soon.
  Your loving nephew,
  Jonathan Elias "Jack" Burns

"Jonathan must have arrived too late and begged to see the pages from her journal." Phoebe's voice quivers with emotion.

I reach for her hand. "Robert unearthed the pages from her journal and let Jonathan read them and then he hid them so no one else would find them for a long time."

I can tell by the pleased expression on Oliver's face that he can't believe his good fortune. Smiling, he announces, "I guess today's my lucky day. I get to read through letters and journals that have been hidden from human eyes for over a hundred years. What could be better? Earl said they found most of the items in these boxes behind a loose panel in his Aunt Muriel's attic wall."

Nathaniel, however, has had enough of sitting around, reading and thinking. "I think it's time to go to Winter Island and meet with my father's side of the family. I need to talk to my Burns relatives."

I shoot out of my chair and then realize that if I don't tone it down, I'll seem childish and it'll annoy Nathaniel. Silently, I beg him with my eyes.

"Okay, Annabelle, I won't leave you behind, but don't cause any trouble. No mentioning séances or contacting the dead unless I introduce the topic."

Nathaniel may be gorgeous, smart and talented, but

he's a fascist dictator. I want to yell at him, "You're not the boss of me!" However, that would be immature and probably ruin my chances of going with him to Winter Island. Plus this trip is his. He owns it. He needs to go. I'll be merely a spectator; a major player in the drama here in Eastfield, but not involved yet in what's about to unfold on the shores of Winter Island. I keep my mouth shut which is an uncharacteristically wise and mature decision on my part. Instead of yelling at Nathaniel about his bossiness, I mutely glance at my new partner in crime, Phoebe. She rises slowly and moves two quiet steps to her left, until she's by my side.

Nathaniel grimaces and relents. "Yes, she can come, too, but same rules, Blondie, no hassles. My way or the highway."

Phoebe tolerates being called Blondie and I don't jump to her defense. We both desperately want to accompany the despot in the wheelchair to the home of his ancestors. Discreetly, we share a low fist bump, way down where our hands dangle by our sides. It means, *Road trip. Winter Island. Here we come!*

But first we need to revisit the scene of the lightning strike, where the old oak stood tall and seemed invincible for centuries.

Chapter 16

The Old Oak Tree and Winter Island

My dad wants to come and see the tree stump, too, so he can revisit the site where he was almost killed a few nights ago. He plans to pick up Jackson and Oliver and meet us at the scene of the lightning strike. Phoebe had to work at the animal hospital over in Freewater and can't join us right away, so Nathaniel picks me up at school and we head over to the crossroads to meet up with Jackson, Oliver, my father and eventually, Phoebe. My overprotective medium friend refuses to let me get out of the van until everyone arrives and we're all together, so we can join forces like a paranormal militia. Dad drives up first with Jackson and Oliver riding in the truck with him. I stare out the window of the van for a second and think about how Wyatt and my mother are the only two from our original group who aren't here for this adventure. I don't know which one of them I miss more. It's hard to tell because I miss them in different ways. This is no time to start feeling sorry for myself, though; we have work to do.

Finally, Phoebe drives up in her SUV and everyone exits their vehicles to walk over and stand around what's left of the majestic oak. It's nothing but a scary looking ruin, now. Large areas of bark are charred and the jagged insides are black and crusty, with a little pale wood left here and there. I look down at the slushy ground beneath my feet and think, *I could be standing right over the remains of Rebecca Burns*. There's no marker left. The plain wooden cross that adorned her grave over a century ago is long gone, so we don't know exactly where she's lying.

Phoebe and I walk over close to the tree stump and try to peer inside, but it's too high up. Nathaniel moves his wheelchair next to the base of the tree so I can climb up on one arm of it; he steadies me on one side and Oliver spots me on the other. I have to be careful because the wood is splintered into some deadly sharp points up here where the lightning split the top of the tree away from its base. I don't want to get impaled. Dad hands me up his work gloves and I put them on so I won't get any slivers.

I yell down to the others, "I can see something down in here." Amidst the gnarled remnants of the inner wood lies a small leather pouch. "If you look around on what's left of the trunk, over by where Jackson's standing, I think there's a hollow spot, with a small hole leading to the outside."

"Got it!" Jackson shouts. "My hand's too big, though. It won't fit inside the hole."

Phoebe's the only one besides me who might be able to fit her hand into the hole. All of the guys' hands are too big.

She runs over to Jackson and pokes her hand into the opening of the tiny crevice.

"I can see your hand from up here." I start giving her instructions. "Roll up your sleeves so you can reach in farther. But go slow, so you won't get splinters."

Phoebe's wearing the same thick woolen sweater she had on the day that I met her. She rolls one sleeve up and does what I told her to do. Within seconds, her small, pink hand, wrist and a few inches of her forearm appear inside the charred flesh of the tree. "Move a little to the right and you'll be able to feel the leather of the pouch. Go slow and be careful. I see some sharp looking slivers of wood down there."

Within a few seconds, she closes her fingers around the side of the pouch and pulls it out. Oliver and Nathaniel help me down from the arm of the wheelchair and she hands the pouch to Oliver. He removes the contents and hands the Phoebe back to Phpebe. It's a pretty well preserved, rolled up piece of old paper and I'm standing so close to Oliver that as he unrolls it, I can smell the odor of recently charred oak, but also something much more pleasant: lavender. Phoebe sniffs and then smiles at me. She smells it too. We both look inside the pouch she's still holding. The drawstrings are loosened all the way and when we peer into it, I can see some clippings from a lavender bush. They're dried and old but they still give off the signature fragrance of the beautiful perennial which is supposed to bring people good luck. It didn't bring much luck to Rebecca, though.

But the secret document has remained hidden in a small hollow spot in the oak, well preserved for almost a hundred and fifty years. I guess that's kind of lucky. The fire from the lightning didn't destroy it, so maybe the lavender did bring at least a little good fortune after all. The pouch and its contents could also have been picked apart by nesting squirrels or birds, but it hasn't been. Oliver begins to read aloud.

For my mother, Rebecca Burns Morse, from your loving son.

I walked over to your cottage today and clipped some flowers from your plants. Holding them in one hand, I thought hard about you and dipped my other hand into the deep water, where you drowned, hoping to stir up some memory of you from within my heart. What happened next is difficult to describe, but I'll try. At first, the water felt icy cold, but the cool liquid surrounding my hand soon warmed until my flesh glowed with a pleasant heat. I closed my eyes and my soul felt suffused with the most intense kindness I have ever felt bestowed upon me. I knew it was you; my mother. Squeezing my eyelids together, I tried to conjure up the image of your face, but nothing came to me. All I had left of you at that moment was the glowing warmth of your kindness emanating between us because my hand was immersed in the water where you died. I remember nothing about you but still love you with all of my heart.

While I was here in Eastfield, I used my influence as Elias Hayward's son to gain access to the records at Town Hall, under the pretense that I needed to scrutinize certain sections of the deed to the Hayward family's property. When the clerk left me alone in the documents room for a few minutes, I followed through with my true plan and confiscated my birthday certificate. Soon after I left the building I burned it to ashes because it was a lie. Katherine Littlefield Hayward was not my mother. You are and will always be.

Aunt Elizabeth is gone now and there is no one left of the Haywards who will speak of you, except Uncle Robert, and he only does so reluctantly. So I knocked on the door of the Morse's home and introduced myself to your father-in-law. Yourmother-in-law passed away several years ago, leaving him a widower.

Because I did not want to dishonor the memory of Mr. Morse's son, Jonathan, who was a war hero, I did not tell him my secret: that my mother drowned in Deep Water Pond when I was only two years old and my father told me the truth about her on his death bed, twenty-five years later. I introduced myself as Jonathan Hayward and told him I was visiting and wanted to see what was left of her gardens because my father and aunt had spoken of Rebecca fondly and often. I asked permission to clip some branches from her plants so I could grow healing herbs and flowers in my own garden. He agreed and gave me leave to do so, handing me a small leather pouch in which to place my clippings. Together we walked through the tangled and neglected garden. A lot of the plants are still growing strong, and I felt your presence again, as I walked among the flowers you touched when you were alive. Once more, I felt bathed in the warm glow of your infinite kindness.

Mr. Morse told me how you could heal with your hands and with the herbs and flowers you grew. I wish you were here to heal my heart now because it breaks for you, for myself and for my three children who will never know their grandmother. I miss you and I don't believe that you took your own life. I wish I could stay here longer in Eastfield and attempt to seek out the truth, but I must return to my family on Winter Island. I will always believe that my beloved mother is watching over us. No matter where we are.

Jonathan 'Jack' Burns

With this beautiful letter to his dead mother, Rebecca's son has touched our hearts even though his hasn't beaten for over a century. Everyone in our group is silent until I hear my dad clear his throat, probably trying to mask the choked feeling you sometimes get when you're holding back tears. Quietly, we head for our respective vehicles, leaving the scene of our most recent discovery. Oliver holds onto the pouch and the letter, for safe-keeping. I hope that eventually, after we uncover the whole truth, the antique document will sit in a place of honor at the Eastfield Historical Society Museum.

We decide to wait until the weekend to head over to Winter Island because I have school, Nathaniel has séance clients and Phoebe's scheduled to work at the Freewater Animal Hospital. Finally, early on Saturday morning, we start out for Salem in Nathaniel's van, with the papers from Earl's attic in a briefcase, lying next to Jeff. He keeps sniffing it. I'm back here with him, enjoying the sunshine, the passing scenery and the sense of adventure.

Nathaniel called ahead and his great Aunt Maggie and Uncle Jeremiah are expecting us. It takes about an hour and a half to get there. We drive through to get coffee on the way and I order a vanilla chai which is way better than coffee. It tastes like a tea flavored milk shake, except it's hot. When we reach Salem Harbor, I'm impressed by how beautiful it looks in the winter, even though it's desolate and the freezing cold wind coming off the ocean is rocking the van. There are almost no other cars on the causeway that leads over to the island. Nothing's going on here today. Of course, Winter Island must be more active in the summer. We drive by the lighthouse and head for the only road on the island, Winter Island Road. Nathaniel's Great Aunt Maggie lives in one of the dozen houses that sit here on the north end of the forty-five acre island. I wonder out loud about what she does all day.

"She's almost ninety, but she still gets around a little. There's a lot to do on the mainland. I don't know too much about her because I've only met her twice. Out of the few times that I've seen Jeremiah, he only visited us in Eastfield once. Usually I met him somewhere else for dinner. Great Aunt Maggie accompanied him on two of those occasions. But that was a long time ago and I don't remember a lot about her." Nathaniel seems like he's getting nervous as he parks the van in a driveway paved with crushed shells and we all get out. Phoebe and I help Nathaniel with his portable ramp and our apprehensive little group moves toward his ancestral home.

As soon as we knock on the old wooden door an ancient woman with glittering blue eyes, wearing a hand-woven shawl over her shoulders, opens it and beckons us through a short hallway, into the warm, glowing kitchen. In one corner, the wood stove, with its tiny square window, is responsible for some of the light. But my gaze is pulled, as if by a magnet, to the two pillar candles in the center of the big oak table. Nathaniel, Phoebe and I have found each other. There were thirteen original sets of candles. We have ten families to go.

After Nathaniel introduces Phoebe and me, Jeremiah introduces his aunt. "Phoebe, Annabelle, this is Aunt Maggie. You were very young on the two occasions when she accompanied me to your neck of the woods, Nathaniel. I don't know how much you remember."

"I remember the time we ate at that Italian place in the North End and you put the left over bread in your handbag. It's so nice to see you again, Aunt Maggie."

She laughs. "That was incredible bread, crusty and warm from the oven. I couldn't bear to leave it behind. Welcome to Winter Island, Nathaniel. Please make yourself at home."

"Thank you, Aunt Maggie. I've brought my friends Annabelle and Phoebe with me. Let me get right to the point. We've come to talk about Jonathan Burns and his mother, Rebecca."

"Come in. Sit down, girls. I was wondering when you would come to hear her story, Nathaniel. Jonathan told his family here on Winter Island everything, you know. And the sad tale has been handed down from generation to generation. We know about Rebecca. But no one from Eastfield has ever come here and mentioned her name, before today. It happened well over a hundred years ago and you three are the first. I don't know all of the details because Jonathan, known to the Burns' family as Jack, didn't know everything. Some important secrets died with Rebecca and with Katherine. But I can tell you a lot." Aunt Maggie looks almost old enough to have been there when Jonathan Elias Hayward and his exhausted horse arrived on Winter Island after he fled Eastfield. She holds very still when she pauses; only her shiny blue eyes move.

"I've waited a long time for Nathaniel to come here and ask about his ancestors."

Jeremiah adds, "Aunt Maggie will be ninety this May."

"If I live that long, Jeremiah."

"She hasn't had so much as a cold in ten winters. She'll be here for her ninetieth birthday and probably for her one hundredth, as well."

"Congratulations on your excellent health, Aunt Maggie." I'm wondering if she has the same ability to heal herself that I have.

"Funny how everyone calls me Aunt. I never married or had any children, but I'm everyone's aunt." Then she smiles and the young girl within shines through.

I sense that she has earned the title "Aunt" with her offers of friendship, her willingness to listen to confidences and give advice. Also, like my mother and Phoebe and the other women who still possess the candle sticks, the women we haven't met yet, she's a healer. There are rows of various herbs hanging from racks on one wall of her kitchen and Jeremiah is busy pouring hot water over a pile of fragrant leaves and dried blossoms in the bottom of a ceramic tea pot. I start helping him set out the tea things.

"Jack Burns, the man who was formerly known as Jonathan Hayward, told our family everything he knew. He came galloping onto the island in the middle of the night, riding that huge horse of his and everyone realized who he was immediately. He looked so much like Rebecca. He looked like you." Aunt Maggie points at Nathaniel with a steady finger. "Jeremiah will bring you the candlesticks when I'm gone, Nathaniel. And you must pass them down to your descendants when it's time."

"I don't have any children. I'm not married, not even engaged." Nathaniel smiles.

Aunt Maggie smiles back. "A good-looking boy like you will find someone. And when you do, you'll have children together. And your children will be beautiful and talented like their parents."

"Don't be so sure. I might never settle down."

"Watch what you say, Nathaniel. Show some respect. I can tell a lot. As my eyesight grows weaker and weaker, my second sight grows more acute. When I look at you, I can see all of the souls that you love: those who are still with us on this earth, those who have passed on and those who haven't been born yet."

Gooseflesh prickles up the back of my neck.

Aunt Maggie reaches for my hand. "You need to be careful, child. You miss Anthony but it's not anywhere near time for you to join him yet."

"How do you know about Anthony?"

"The same way you know things. Images and feelings appear in your mind's eye and in your heart. And suddenly you know things without anyone telling you."

"But I can't tell the future."

"No one can tell the future accurately because our fates aren't written in stone. They're written on the wind. And the wind can change directions."

"But you felt the need to warn me about joining Anthony and he's dead. So you must perceive something about my future…something about death. I'm in danger."

"She won't stop until you're dead." The old woman grips my hand so hard it turns numb. She turns from me to Nathaniel again. "You can't let it happen. Nathaniel, be more vigilant than you've ever been in your whole life. Annabelle must never be left alone when this woman's evil spirit is near."

"When who's near, Aunt Maggie?" Nathaniel asks, but he knows the answer and so do I.

"Katherine. One of the Littlefields set her free. A young girl who didn't realize what she was doing. She's jealous of you, Annabelle, but she wasn't wishing for your death. She didn't realize what kind of power she unleashed when she moved those stones."

"Colleen Foley." Nathaniel says her name out loud.

Piecing some of the facts I've collected together, I come up with a theory that's probably close to the truth. "Her friends were making fun of her for going ghost hunting. She must've gone to the graveyard and moved the stones on Katherine's grave. She went to the cemetery because she thought Wyatt would be more interested in her if she had a connection to the supernatural, like the connection I have."

"She wants to be more like you so he'll love her the way he loves you. But that will never happen." Aunt Maggie drops my hand and pats it. "Wyatt still loves you, Annabelle, but you both have a long, treacherous road to travel before you can be together again. So dangerous that you might not survive. If you want to stay alive, you'll have to be careful and it's not in your nature to be cautious. Is it, my dear?"

"No it isn't, but she has me and Phoebe to protect her." Nathaniel sounds determined.

"It might not be enough. Even Annabelle's ability to heal herself might not save her this time. A soul as evil as Katherine's becomes something fearsome after death: a creature that's part ghost and part demon, a destructive and vengeful apparition. When she was alive, she never loved anyone, not even her husband, Elias. She felt jealousy and possessiveness but never love."

Phoebe's face lights up with a beautiful innocence. "What a horrible way to live. It's terrifying to imagine such a soulless creature walking this earth."

Aunt Maggie covers Phoebe's hand with her own. "Yes, my child. Someone like you can't even picture what it's like to never feel love for others. Now that Katherine has passed over, she's worse. Her spirit has had more than a century to steep itself in evil intentions, to dwell on destructive plans for those who love each other. She's malevolent and powerful; her first attacks were impulsive, uncontrolled and obvious. But she learned from them. Now she knows she'll need to use more subtle strategies the next time. Once she figures out how best to manipulate you, Annabelle, she'll be more dangerous. She has a good chance of winning and that means you'll lose."

I've never seen Nathaniel look so worried. "What do you mean, 'she'll win and Annabelle will lose'? What will she lose?"

"She'll lose her life. The demon will kill Annabelle the way she killed Rebecca."

"Rebecca was a suicide."

"Katherine lured her to her death. She used Rebecca's own loving nature to manipulate her. And she wants to do the same to you, Annabelle."

"How did Katherine kill Rebecca?" I beg Aunt Maggie for more information because I need to know if I'm going to effectively defend myself against this terrifying demon.

"No one's completely sure about all the details. Some of Katherine's secrets died with her. But she confessed to Elias on her death bed. She admitted that she was responsible for Rebecca's death. She bragged to Elias about separating him from his beloved Rebecca. Shortly before Elias died, he related these details to his son. However, Katherine left out one important detail. She refused to tell Elias how she got Rebecca to walk out onto the ice that night."

"We need to find out before she tries the same thing on Annabelle."

"And you need to do it fast. You don't have much time. Don't let her lull you into a sense of false security. She's learning to be patient and now she's begun to realize that waiting for exactly the right time to strike will be a key part of an effective plan. She'll wait until she's perfected her scheme and the circumstances are right. So she can strike when you least expect it and you're not prepared."

I don't see what the big deal is. "I won't go near the pond. That shouldn't be too difficult. I like ice skating but I can skip it this winter. Or, if I do go ice skating, I won't go on Deep Water Pond. I'll go someplace else. No problem."

Jeremiah speaks up for the first time since the conversation took this weird turn. "Don't underestimate her. She can find a way and you won't suspect what's happening until it's too late."

"Now let's all have some tea and sandwiches. Jeremiah went into Salem earlier and picked up some food from my favorite deli."

I'm surprised to hear her mention her favorite deli. She seems more likely to sip hot soup brewed in an old iron cauldron than to chow down on a roast beef sandwich.

Aunt Maggie looks at me and laughs out loud. "No, child, I won't be serving any 'eye of newt or toe of frog' this afternoon, only pastrami on marble rye and roast beef with Swiss cheese. I hope no one here's a vegetarian."

Nathaniel makes a joke about Oliver. "No, we left our vegetarian back on the mainland."

"Congratulate Oliver on his upcoming wedding for us." Either Aunt Maggie talked to Nathaniel's mother recently or her paranormal talents are even more powerful and uncanny than I thought.

She pats my hand as I reach for a delicious-looking sandwich. "Yes, honey, I'm really that good. No one told me about Oliver and Jackson. I've never met them, but they're important to you and Nathaniel, so I can feel their presence around you. They're thinking about you and worrying and hoping that you'll find information during this trip that will help to keep you safe. I hope so, too. Let us know how it all turns out. I expect that you'll fill us in on all the important details when you visit again in the early spring, Nathaniel."

"I'd love to visit again, but I haven't made any plans to yet."

"You will. I don't want to ruin too many of the surprises that the future has in store for you. And I don't know everything. I can never be one hundred percent sure. You can redirect your fate because you have free will, which enables you to change your mind and your plans."

During lunch no one mentions supernatural talents or fate or murderous ghosts from Hell. We chat about the weather and the food and other ordinary things. Afterward, Aunt Maggie and Jeremiah look over the documents that we brought and offer a few more insights about what happened between the Haywards, the Littlefields and Rebecca Burns over a century ago. But we don't learn anything more significant than what Aunt Maggie has already told us.

On the drive back to Eastfield, the three of us are quiet. Jeff and I both fall asleep in the back of the van, so even if Nathaniel and Phoebe finally manage to have a friendly conversation, I don't get to hear it.

Chapter 17

Reprieve

Aunt Maggie turns out to be right about the ghost of Katherine. She leaves me alone for a while. I try to think of her as waiting, but it's difficult because I start to feel relaxed and it feels good. I can run again, but everyone insists that I keep off the trails I love because the paths I prefer are pretty isolated. They wind through the woods, around the ponds and across the meadows of Eastfield. I feel safe and sense no danger, but my father and Nathaniel aren't willing to take any chances. Phoebe's reasonably fit but she's not a long distance runner and she can't keep up with me. We tried running together a couple of times, but she struggled and hated it. She said that it ruined the beauty of the landscape for her because she was out of breath and her shins hurt. She prefers long walks.

Finally we reach a compromise: I can run on my beloved trails again, but I'm not allowed to listen to my IPod, because then I won't hear any warning signs if danger is near. And I have to take Jeff with me. I'd rather run with my IPod but I'm willing to give it up if the alternative is not running at all. And I love having Jeff along. Whenever Nathaniel brings him over, I jump into the van with my running gear on. Then we ride to the town forest or to the entrances of one of Eastfield's many conservation areas. The second that Jeff and I spring out of the van together, we hit the trails.

Today, I want to go for a quick two-mile jog to visit the Morses, so Nathaniel brings Jeff over to accompany me. He wheels in with a tray of take-out coffee and some donuts for him and Dad and they sit down to watch a college basketball game on TV.

"Dad, half a donut. Remember your cholesterol. Mom would kill us both if I let you eat donuts. And she'd give you an earful for giving them to him, Nathaniel."

"If she killed me for eating a donut, wouldn't that defeat the whole purpose of making me eat a low cholesterol diet so I'll live longer?"

"You know what I mean, Dad. Only a half."

Nathaniel laughs. "Okay. I get it. Half a donut, Bill. I don't want your wife and your daughter hating all over me."

Dad holds up a donut, waves it around and makes a huge deal out of breaking it in half. Then he eats his half in two bites and feeds the other half to Jeff. "Thanks for ruining my fun, Annabelle."

When I start putting on my running shoes, Jeff goes crazy in the den, which is kind of a small room. The giant dog starts jumping around and wagging his tail so wildly, he whips Nathaniel in the face with it and leaves a red welt across his owner's perfect cheekbone. If Nathaniel had been holding his coffee it would've gone everywhere.

"Annabelle, get that crazy mutt out of here!" Nathaniel fingers the mark on his face.

"He's your crazy mutt, Flyte. To me he's just a canine bodyguard. C'mon, Jeff. Let's go!" We race each other to the door and out onto the path that runs through the woods all the way to the Morse's house. "That's some tail you've got, mister!"

Jeff smiles in response and wags it even harder as we head down the trail.

After sprinting the last quarter mile, we arrive at the Morse's. Mr. and Mrs. Morse are thrilled to see us and when I express my curiosity about the little stone cottage out by Deep Water Pond, Mr. Morse insists on giving me a tour because they've been doing some renovating out there. I can't wait to see inside the house where Rebecca Burns Morse lived when she was just my age.

The path from their house to the cottage is a little slippery, so Mrs. Morse stays inside with Jeff, by the fire, and Mr. Morse holds onto my arm. It's slow going but worth it because I'm really curious about the cottage.

"Oliver Finn asked me if one of his friends could stay here for a month or so. The guy's from out of state and needs a place to live for a few weeks. He's a history buff, like Oliver, and would enjoy the ambience at the cottage and the legends surrounding its past."

"I didn't realize that the cottage was habitable. It's always been locked up whenever my brothers or I have come out here."

"Oh yes, it's habitable. We don't want anyone hanging out in there, though. No offense, Annabelle, but we don't want kids wrecking the place."

"No offense taken. It's understandable that you don't want your beautiful little historical cottage used as a teenage hangout."

Mr. Morse unlocks the padlock on the door and we both walk inside.

Turning slowly so I can soak in the feeling of another century, I exclaim, "It's adorable. I'd love to live here."

"One of my sons and his wife came out and cleaned it up; made sure the chimney and the woodstove are safe and working. Oliver's visitors will be arriving in early March, so they'll need some heat. The woodstove keeps the place nice and cozy. There's no electricity so you have to use the old fashioned oil lamps with the wicks. Just like Rebecca did."

"It's beautiful. Can we light one now?"

"Sure." Mr. Morse pulls a book of matches out of his pocket and lifts the globe off of a nearby table lamp. As the wick ignites, its flame illuminates the main room of the tiny cottage.

Slowly, I rotate around again, checking out my surroundings. Running over to the largest window, I peer out through the thick greenish glass that was glazed over one hundred and fifty years ago. "Look at the view of the pond! It looks like a postcard!"

"Yup. My daughter-in-law made new curtains for this here picture window; they frame the landscape quite nicely."

"Rebecca looked out this same window." I might be standing right where she stood, when she looked out over the pond because she was watching for her lover to arrive on the path that opens up into a field on the east shore. Or maybe she stood here the night that she caught sight of her murderer, sneaking down the same path in the dark, intent on luring her to her death. I shiver.

"It's cold in here now, Annabelle, but once the woodstove's fired up, you won't find a cozier place on earth than this here little cottage."

"I love it! Look, there's an alcove off the kitchen area. Is that where Rebecca dried her herbs?" The hooks are still hanging on the walls, just like in my mother's pantry.

"Yup. There's a tangled old field of chamomile, lavender, yarrow and other wild flowers and herbs right outside the back door. A lot of the same flowers that your mother grows still bloom out there every year. It's Rebecca's legacy."

"Mr. Morse, I don't believe that she killed herself."

The instant I speak these words, the flame within the glass globe of the old oil lamp grows brighter until a brilliant glow illuminates our surroundings. From the next room, we hear a baby's cry.

"Ugh, a bird must've gotten in through the chimney." Mr. Morse's hearing is really gone if he thinks the sound we heard was a bird chirping.

I peek into the smallest bedroom to see if there's a trapped bird fluttering around, but it's still and quiet as a grave in there. The main room in the cabin has stone walls but in the cozy little bedroom, someone installed bead board paneling and painted it pale green. Mr. Morse looks over my shoulder to check for the bird.

"Nothing! Where is that darn thing? I don't want it dying in here and stinking up the place."

The next sound we hear is unmistakable, even for an old man who's losing his hearing. It's the loud cry of a hungry newborn baby. Shortly after, we hear his mother's murmuring as she quiets him.

"Holy crap, Annabelle. What on earth is this?"

"I think it's Rebecca's ghost, Mr. Morse."

"Well I'll be. But she never had any children."

"She might have. We're looking into it; me and some of my ghost hunting friends. Sorry, Mr. Morse. These kinds of things seem to happen to me. I'm luckier than most people I guess."

"I wouldn't call it luck. It's downright creepy, Annabelle. Why would a pretty young girl like you mess around with that crap? I've been in here hundreds of times and nothing like this has ever happened."

"I think my sensitivity to the paranormal is hereditary but it skips a generation or two sometimes."

"My family has known the Blakes for centuries. None of them have ever been weirdoes."

"Thanks, Mr. Morse."

"Sorry, Annabelle. No offense intended. The Blake boys have always been able to move through the forest surefooted and quiet, like wild creatures, like the Indians from these parts used to. Their woodsman's skills are kind of uncanny, but they've never been involved with ghosts."

"Well, there's more to the Blakes than meets the eye and my mother's family's pretty weird, too."

"Uh huh. Your mom's known for her herbs and wild flowers and how she can heal ailments with them, but not for communicating with the dead."

"It's kinda all related. Sorry about that."

"Well, I'm spooked. Let's get out of here. And I'm not coming out here with you again. I'll come with one of my boys, but not you. You are one scary young lady, Miss."

As he blows out the lamp and locks up, I apologize again. Mr. Morse doesn't seem to care too much, though. I suppose that when you get to be as old as he is, it takes a lot to surprise you. With the old guy holding onto my arm, I start down the path back to his house.

When we arrive at his un-haunted home, Mr. Morse opens the door and we enter together. Mrs. Morse welcomes us back and offers me a cup of tea, which I accept. Sitting around the table by their woodstove with Jeff sprawled out on the rug at my feet, a cozy, safe feeling warms me but I can't keep myself from thinking about Rebecca's cottage and the crying of the ghostly infant. "I just loved the little stone house. The couple who will be staying there is so lucky."

Mrs. Morse explains, "It's almost ready for them. In late February we'll just sweep it up and double check everything. And my son's going to move a crib in there because the gentleman's bringing along his wife and baby."

I hope they're not afraid of ghosts. I think this but don't say it out loud. Instead I finish up my tea and wish Mr. and Mrs. Morse a Merry Christmas, which is just a few days away. Then I whistle for Jeff, who eagerly springs into action and we head back through the woods to my house.

Chapter 18

Christmas in Key West

The best Christmas present ever is seeing my mom and knowing that she'll be coming home soon. Auntie Maeve is out of the hospital and doing great. And my mother actually enjoys working in the bar, which is kind of weird because I always figured her for more of a tea house personality. But no, she loves bartending, hostessing, talking to customers and giving random advice to people who want their fortunes told by a genuine descendant of one of Salem's witches. Who is this stranger that I've always called "Mom"? She can read Tarot cards! She refuses to teach me, though. And she's giving it up again as soon as she leaves Florida.

When I ask her about the Tarot she says, "I don't like knowing."

"Knowing what, Mom?" We're sitting at a booth in my Auntie Maeve's bar, Priestess. The golden afternoon sunlight bathes the polished wooden surfaces of the tables and chairs and the bar and the floor in a butterscotch-colored glow. Except for a few people who're browsing in the display case for souvenirs, the place is empty. Nothing like last minute shopping. Christmas Eve's tomorrow.

Over the last few weeks, I've missed my mother so much that it has caused me physical pain sometimes, but now that we're together, I feel like I don't really know her. She's thinner, tanned and she's wearing her hair down. When we caught sight of her in the airport, Dad was in such a hurry to get to her that he almost knocked over an old man using a walker. He hugged her so tightly, her feet left the floor and I swear I saw tears in his eyes. Then he wouldn't let her go so my brothers and I could have a turn.

She's taking a long time to answer my question so I ask it again. "What don't you like knowing, Mom? What is it about the Tarot?"

"I see too much about people when I read their cards. Customers come in here thinking it's a game; a diversion. When I look at their cards I see things like someone's husband is cheating on her."

"That must be awful."

"It is. Some poor woman goes out for a few drinks with her girlfriends and the Tarot lady tells her that her man's not faithful. It can really ruin your evening: mine and hers."

"Do you ever keep news like that to yourself?"

"It's a dilemma. Is she better off knowing or not knowing? Do I have the right to make that decision? I don't know the answers to those questions. But they plague me when I do a reading like that."

I can see now why my mother doesn't show off her paranormal gifts. But when I look around me I can also understand why Auntie Maeve capitalizes on hers. This place is fun and interesting.

My mother's forehead wrinkles up and she continues. "There was this one couple. The wife really wanted to have a baby but her husband wasn't ready. That's pretty personal and they didn't tell me about it. I just knew from looking at their cards. Total strangers sit down, handle the cards, choose a few, lay them out and I can see their secrets. Not just the ones they want me to see, either. The woman and her husband started arguing in front of me. It was so awkward. I end up knowing things about people that they'd like to keep hidden."

I put my elbows up on the table and rest my face in my palms. "Would you read the cards for me?"

"Not a chance. Never. When I leave Key West, I'm leaving the cards behind. I've never liked the Tarot and early on I made it a rule never to read for someone who's close to me."

It's just as well. I don't want my mom knowing all of my secrets anyway. Especially the one about the evil ghost of Katherine Hayward. She'd worry too much and maybe even cut short her visit with Maeve. And Maeve probably needs her to stay at least two more weeks after Dad, Joe, Clement and I leave. Before Mom comes back to New England, she wants to make sure that her twin sister's well on her way to a complete recovery. My mother always thinks like a healer, because she is one. Maeve's talents are more of the psychic variety, so she's really leaning on her twin right now. Dad and I have agreed not to tell my mother about Katherine Hayward until she gets home.

"Do you ever know stuff about people without using the cards?"

"Thankfully, no. I can sense evil and send it away and I can heal, mostly with herbs and somewhat with my touch. But without the Tarot, I can't see the past, the present or the future. And that's the way I like it. I buried my Tarot deck years ago, literally."

"Damn, Mom! You buried them? Like in the ground?"

"Yes, and I'm never digging them up."

"Where did you bury them? In the backyard?"

"I'm not saying. I don't want anyone digging those cards up. Especially not you, Annabelle."

"I'd like to try reading Tarot cards."

She sighs. "That's what I'm afraid of. You're almost eighteen so I can't stop you. But I strongly recommend that you leave the cards alone."

"I know someone who'll teach me. Lorenzo."

"I'd like you to stay away from the cards and from him. He uses his mind reading tricks to charm every woman he meets, and some of the guys, too."

"He knows how to do mind reading tricks?"

"Actually, they're not tricks. He's a genuine and very talented telepath. And he's also a player."

"What do you know about players?"

"Oh, we had players back in the day. We just called them something else."

"What did you call them?"

"Douche bags."

"We still call them that, too. What about man-whores? Did you have those back in the day, too?"

"Oh yes. But we called them womanizers. Some guys used being a hippy as an excuse to whore around. You know; free love. Make love, not war."

"Okay. This is getting too awkward. Sex talk with my mom is not my idea of a fun Christmas."

She laughs. "Oh, Annabelle. I've missed you so much. The thing I've missed the most is the way you can always make me laugh, especially when you're not even trying to be funny. And I've missed your face. I love looking at your beautiful face. I can't wait to come back home so I can look at you every day."

"But you like it here?"

"I love it here. Just not as much as I love you and your dad and your brothers."

"You missed a hell of a storm."

"Your dad told me about the lightning strike that knocked over the big oak tree at the crossroads."

Yes, but he didn't tell her the whole story and we're not telling her until she comes home for good.

"Annabelle, I'm thinking of coming here every winter, just for a few weeks, to help Maeve with her busiest season. She'll be less stressed if I'm here to help."

"*Every* year?"

"Honey, next winter, you'll be at college. I'll have an empty nest. This can be my nest for a few weeks every winter when you're gone."

"What about Dad?"

"How much have you seen of your dad lately?"

"Okay. I see your point. He works a lot. He was rushing to finish the outside of a house before the cold weather and the snow set in. Then he was out plowing. Now he's always busy with the finish work on the insides of his houses."

"He's positively obsessive about the finish work. And that means he's hardly ever home."

"I suppose we could cope without you."

"You ladies look much too serious." We didn't hear Lorenzo walk over to our table. Mostly because he glides around silently, like a cat or a snake.

He's tall, dark, thin and way too handsome, with a careless attitude that says, *I'm so good looking I'm bored with myself.* His messy hair is just a little bit too long, so it looks like he doesn't want to take the time to get a haircut, not like he planned it that way. And I've never seen him clean-shaven. Right now he has at least forty-eight hours' worth of scruff decorating his beautiful face and several colorful beads woven into a lock of hair near his ear. A girl he was seeing strung them in there. He's not seeing her anymore but he hasn't taken the beads out yet.

His faded worn-out t-shirt ends at his narrow hips and when he reaches up even a little, you can see only part of a tattoo, gothic style lettering etched in black onto the skin of his tanned abs, right above his beltless, holey jeans. If he's not barefoot, he wears flip flops. He's a gifted psychic and a total man-whore but I like him, partly because he's a little scary and anything scary interests me. I've been in a long term love-hate relationship with scary for most of my life.

He arches one black brow and suggests, "Susannah, Annabelle, let me get you a couple of Strange Brews, on the house."

"My daughter is under age and I never drink before sunset." My mother gives him a look that would wither a lesser man. But Lorenzo's too cool to wither under anyone's glare, even that of the formidable Susannah Knight Blake.

"Lucky for you the sun sets earlier in the winter. You can really party it up, Susannah."

"Yes, that would be me. Party on, Lorenzo." She twirls her finger in the air. Even my mother finds him entertaining when she's not busy being annoyed by his attitude. "How late are you working?"

"Until closing. Let me get you something. An ice tea? And for the beautiful Annabelle, who is not yet twenty-one, a virgin Strange Brew would be delicious I'm sure."

Raging heat rises into my face. I'm blushing like an idiot and I try to laugh his joke off but it's hard to fool a psychic. When I start blushing it's hard for me to fool anyone.

"There are a million things to do before the evening crowd starts arriving, Lorenzo. Go do them." My mother's not smiling anymore.

Lorenzo's still grinning, though. "Ah, the mama bear shows me her claws." He laughs, swivels around and walks away.

"I don't want to talk about it," I warn her, as soon as he's out of earshot.

"You don't have to. But do you see why I want you to stay away from him?"

"I see. End of discussion. I'm going down to the beach."

I can't believe that it's the day before Christmas Eve and I'm wearing a bikini. Joe drops Clem and me off at the beach in Maeve's VW. He'll pick us up again in a couple of hours. After a quick swim, I lie down on my towel for a nap. We've all been staying up late to help out in the bar and because it's fun. Every night is a party at Priestess.

Right before I doze off on the soft towel in the warm sun, I think about Lorenzo and how I don't like it that he knows stuff about me without anyone telling him. And how I have no choice. A lot of my secrets have been revealed to him whether I want them to be or not. I'm used to being kind of a mystery to my friends back home. I don't confide easily or often. I don't talk about my paranormal talents. My closest friends have no idea. Even Wyatt knows only part of what I'm capable of. But I can keep no secrets from Lorenzo; and this makes me nervous.

After my aunt's sexiest employee graduated from Wesleyan University, in Connecticut two years ago, he put off law school to work at my aunt's bar in Key West. I wonder if he'll ever get serious about life. Maybe he'll work at the bar forever, serving drinks, telling fortunes and entertaining himself with the female customers. I drift off to sleep picturing his all-seeing dark eyes behind my sun-struck eyelids. But I dream of Wyatt and home.

When we get back from the beach I take a shower, wring the excess water out of my hair, yank a comb through it and pull on some ratty, faded denim shorts and a cantaloupe-colored tank top. Then I head for the bar which is within walking distance of Maeve's house. Mom will drive my aunt over later. She's resting now.

As I start taking clean glasses out of the dishwasher and putting them back on the shelves, Lorenzo comes over to help me.

"So you want to learn about the Tarot?"

I don't even ask him how he knows. "I might. My mother doesn't like the idea, though."

"And she's our most talented reader, too. She never reads at home?"

"No, she buried her cards somewhere. She won't tell me where."

"I could probably tell you. If I ask her where, the answer to my question might spring into her mind before she has a chance to hide it behind other mundane thoughts."

"Is that how it works?"

"Kind of. Your mother's good at hiding things from me by thinking about boring stuff when I'm around. Once in a while I can see something interesting when I focus on her, but usually not. She's too good, too controlled. And Maeve helps her. They have this incredible twin connection going on."

"Probably because they're twins, duh."

He chuckles and softly pinches my cheek. "Good point, cara mia. You, however, my Annabelle, are like the open book. You have no skills of the hiding type. If you're going to spend time here in your auntie's bar, you should learn some, pronto. By the way, my tattoo is a quote from Camus. Words to live by for me. You can read the rest of it if you'd like to." He hooks his thumb in a belt loop and starts to inch down his jeans but then laughs and stops.

"Close your beautiful mouth, Annabelle. I can see all of your perfect, white molars. I could also see that you were thinking about my tattoo and my impressive abs."

No sense denying the truth to a freaking mind-reader. "I know what your tattoo says, 'In the depth of winter I finally learned that there was in me an invincible summer.'"

He laughs again. "And I knew that you knew, even though you've been careful not to get caught staring. You waited until you caught enough glimpses to put the first few words together. Then you Googled it. And you love it. You memorized it. You keep repeating it to yourself."

"God, you're annoying!"

"But fascinating. Would you like to learn how to hide your embarrassing thoughts from me?"

Now this sounds like an even more useful skill than Tarot card reading. "I would love to learn how to hide my thoughts from you, Lorenzo."

"I can't believe I'm helping you with this, because it's so much fun knowing what you're thinking. But I like you. You're sweet and pretty and your soul is beautiful: generous, honest and pure. That boy who broke your heart is an idiot and you should not waste anymore time thinking about him."

"Ugh, that's none of your business. You're so obnoxious, Lorenzo."

"Thank you again. It's always nice to get a compliment from a beautiful woman. Here's your first lesson in hiding your thoughts from me. Simply think about something else. Keep Wyatt in your subconscious. In your conscious mind, think about your favorite running trail through the woods or your mother's lasagna."

It's almost dinnertime and I'm starving. My mother's lasagna is one of my favorite dishes and I miss it so much. Lasagna and garlic bread. That's exactly what I was thinking about. "Holy shit!" I don't need to tell Lorenzo that he's right, but I do. "That's exactly what I was thinking about."

"Ha! My turn to say 'duh'. I knew that and you knew that I knew it." We both start laughing.

"Okay. I like this. It's easy for me to think about food because I'm always hungry. I'll train myself to look at your face and see a steaming plateful of roast chicken and garlic mashed potatoes."

"Don't forget the dessert. You should always think of something delicious and sweet when you look at me."

"You're ridiculous!"

"That isn't what all the other women on the island say."

"And you're insufferable."

"You're laughing. You're not suffering at all. You need to laugh, too. Your life has been too serious lately." He shoots me an intense stare and grabs my hand, then brings it up to his lips and kisses it. "My poor baby. Be careful and don't worry. Your secrets are safe with me," he murmurs with his lips against the back of my hand.

Then he drops my hand and cracks up laughing. "Turkey dinner!"

"Yes, because that's what we're having tomorrow for Christmas! You're awesome, but so am I. I'm getting good at this."

"Watch out, though. Soon your stomach will start growling and you'll begin to drool. That would give your thoughts away even if I wasn't a telepath. We'd better get you something to eat soon."

I love this adorable guy. Sometimes.

"I love you, too, Annabelle. Stay safe. Stay away from that damned pond. The water is so deep and so cold." He shivers and pulls me against the warm length of his body. The man with an invincible summer inside of him draws me in like the sweet, sticky nectar of a tropical blossom attracts a hummingbird. Even though my mother has warned me to stay away from Lorenzo, I lean into him, body and soul, placing one hand firmly on each of his shoulders. Wrapping both of his strong, wiry arms around me, he presses his face into my hair. I can feel his lips on my neck, right under my earlobe.

Just then Mom walks in with Maeve and they both yell at the same time. "Back off, Lorenzo!"

He holds up both hands, as if he's surrendering before a regiment of armed troops, and backs away from me. He's laughing again. But when I look at his eyes, they're intensely serious. His smile hasn't reached them. He puckers his lips in an air kiss and I blow one back to him.

"Like Romeo and Juliet, my Annabelle. Our love is forbidden but all the more delicious because of it."

"Romeo ends up dead in the end, so watch it with my niece if you value your life, lover boy. And if you value your job," Auntie Maeve warns him.

"Yes, sir, boss. It's so nice to see you up and around and feeling healthy enough to bitch at me." Lorenzo has a trace of an Italian accent, just enough to make everything he says sound sexier than if he didn't have the accent. Also the way he looks amps up the whole sexiness thing. He rushes over to my aunt and kisses her once on each cheek. Instead of getting fired, he'll probably get a raise.

Christmas Eve and Christmas Day in Key West turn out to be awesome. My family's present to each other is the trip so we only buy little souvenir joke gifts and there are plenty of those to choose from in the shops of Key West. We laugh and eat our way through the holidays and on New Year's Day I fly back with my dad and my brothers. My mom will join us in about two weeks.

Chapter 19

The Winter Ball

We've been back from the tropics for a week now and it seems like we never left. Same old freezing cold weather, same old freezing cold shoulder from Wyatt. At least my tan hasn't completely faded yet. The Winter Ball's tonight and we're meeting at Jen's house for pictures. Dad has to work late again, so I'm the only one who won't have any parents there, snapping away with cameras and smart phones. Phoebe helped me pick out a dress and it's made of incredibly soft, clingy, fawn-colored fabric. There's a little bit of silky fringe on the hemline and bodice and only one thin shoulder strap. A few tiny, clear sequins are scattered on the front. Even though it's winter, I'm wearing matching sandals and no stockings. We'll be inside the trolley and the hotel ballroom all night so I won't be cold. Phoebe had this interesting idea: that I should wear a string-thin headband of shiny satin around my forehead. She tied it in the back and threaded a couple of small, delicate seashells onto the ends, so they dangle down, peeking in and out of my long, dark, straightened hair.

"You look like a real Native North American princess." Phoebe smiles. "I wish I could come with you, but it's my dad's birthday and I want to bake him a cake before he gets home so I better get going. Do you want a ride over to Jen's?"

I say yes because I don't want to drive over by myself; I'm a little bit nervous. Big, important occasions and dressing way up have that effect on me.

During picture taking, Matt keeps putting his arms around me from behind and touching my hips, my waist and whatever part of me his hands are nearest to. Also, he keeps telling me how amazing I look. It's gonna be a long night.

I miss my mother. She takes terrible pictures because she cuts off the tops of tall people's heads and moves the camera whenever she clicks it so every shot comes out blurry. But she loves socializing with the other parents and seeing me dressed up.

When the doorbell rings, Jen's dad runs over to open the door for a late arriving parent. And it's Judith. She bustles in and gives me a big hug. "When your dad told me he was missing the Winter Ball picture-taking session, I let him have it and drove right over here, honey. Now who is this young man?"

I introduce her to Matt and she shakes his hand but frowns, probably because his hair is kinda long. We want to take a picture of Meg, Jen and me together with our dates, so the six of us line up and the parents start aiming their cameras. Before anyone can snap a picture, though, Judith runs up to me and Matt. "You're going to bunch up her dress and loosen the sequins grabbing at her like that. Take it easy, mister." Matt moves his hands.

I don't know whether to die of embarrassment or hug her and thank her. There's only one Judith. Matt's not embarrassed at all. He thinks she's hilarious. And he starts being more careful of my dress and where he puts his hands. Judith was right, too. He had already loosened two sequins but they haven't fallen off yet.

The trolley ride turns out to be bomb-ass. The driver keeps yelling for us to sit down because the music's blasting and everyone keeps standing up to dance and fool around. When we get to the ballroom it's beautiful and elegant. For most of the night, we all dance in a group and I manage to endure the three slow dances I have to dance with Matt. I keep dodging his lips, though, and moving his right hand which creeps onto my left butt cheek from time to time. It's one of the most fun nights of my life and the best thing is that Wyatt looks miserable and doesn't dance with Colleen once. I'm careful not to stare at them, but my loyal friends keep watch for me and report back. Ryan goes over to talk to him and then immediately afterward takes me aside to give me a full report about what was said.

Wyatt: "Tonight sucks. I can't wait for it to be over."

Ryan: "I don't know, Dude. Meg and I are having fun."

Wyatt: "Will I get suspended from school if I punch Matt Riley in the eye?"

Ryan: "Hey, don't risk it, bro. He's not worth it. Annabelle doesn't even like him."

Wyatt: "Then why is she with him?"

Ryan: "Because he asked her and she didn't have a date."

Wyatt: "Shit."

Ryan: "It's your own fault, Silver."

I kiss Ryan's cheek and thank him. Then a great song comes on and a bunch of us start dancing like idiots again.

When the ball's almost over, I run into the ladies' room to pee. It's gorgeous in there. They have couches and tables right where you walk in the door. On one table, there's a beautiful bouquet of fresh cut flowers in a vase: white roses, daisies and baby's breath. The whole place smells like a garden, not like a bathroom, and it looks like some rich person's living room. You have to go through a dark, polished wood doorway, into the next room to find the stalls and use the actual toilets.

After I come out of the immaculately clean stall, I wash my hands and dry them with one of the neatly folded paper towels sitting on the countertop next to the sink. Then I use the delicious smelling hand lotion. In the mirror I look pretty good for someone who's been dancing like a maniac in a fancy dress for two hours. A few sequins are loose, but none have actually come off and my hair and headband are reasonably neat and still in place.

Then I walk into the outer room and there she is, with her skinny ass plunked down on one of the cushy sofas. Colleen Foley. She's blowing her perfect nose into a tissue and her eyes are red and a little swollen. I try to walk by and ignore her. We're not friends, barely even acquaintances. But she stops me by calling out my name loud enough so I can't pretend that I didn't hear.

"Annabelle."

I turn and look down at her sitting there. Her legs are crossed and her dress is so short her ass must be pressed up against the fabric on the sofa. Not very hygienic. She should tug her dress down, but then her boobs might pop out because the top part of her dress is wicked low and it's strapless. For a skinny girl, her boobs are huge. I'm standing over her and I can see a ton of cleavage; almost nipple. I don't know where to look so I try her face. She blows her nose again.

"Annabelle, why doesn't Wyatt like me?"

"You're asking the wrong girl. I don't know. I haven't even talked to him in over a month."

"You went over to his house. I drove by and saw your car, and it was on a Saturday night, too."

Aha. She's stalking him. The Saturday night she's referring to is the one when Oliver and Jackson announced their engagement. "How often do you drive by his house?"

"Maybe once a week."

I raise one eyebrow and smirk at her.

"Okay, at least twice a week. I used to drive by yours, too, but his car's never there, so I stopped. Then there's his Facebook page and yours. They both say you're still in a relationship."

I lie, but it's a little white one. "I'm never on Facebook. I'll have to log in and update my page; if I can remember my password."

"Yeah, he's never on either. Maybe he just hasn't updated his page recently. That's the only explanation. Because you two are obviously not still in a relationship. He has probably forgotten his password, too. That has to be it."

"I'm sure that's it. We never even talk to each other."

"He still cares about you, though. He won't dance with me and he's been staring at you all night."

"He has a weird way of showing that he still cares about me: ignoring me and never speaking to me."

"Well, he looks like he wants to talk to you. He can't take his eyes off you. What do you have that I don't? I keep trying to figure it out."

"Don't. We're just different, you and me."

"I've tried to be the same as you. I'll try anything. I dressed like you. I dyed my hair. But it didn't work out. I just looked like an idiot."

The girl has no pride left. "I don't think acting like me is gonna work, Colleen. He hasn't been paying much attention to me lately, either." Understatement.

She moves her eyes up and down, then back up again. She's obviously checking out my dress and hair. "That's a good look on you. I could never pull it off."

"Pull what off?"

"The headband thingy. It's too ethnic for my looks. What are you, anyway? Mexican? Portuguese? Something way more exotic than Irish and English. That's what I am."

"I'm part Native North American on my father's side."

"But he doesn't look like that."

"No, it skips a generation or two sometimes, I guess."

"Shit. You're lucky. Evidently that's Wyatt's type. Someone from an Indian tribe. I tried, but I'll never look like that."

For a smart girl who gets good grades, she sounds incredibly stupid. I don't know how to respond to such idiocy. My speechlessness fails to deter her, though. She keeps rambling on.

"Plus the ghost thing. I experimented with that, too. Scared myself and my friends shitless."

Now I'm interested. It might help my situation with the demonic spirit if I can find out exactly what happened the night Colleen moved the stones. "Why was it so scary?"

"Well, the first time," she sniffles and blows her nose again, "me and Liz and a couple other girls got together at her house and drank some Jägermeister. Then we walked over to this graveyard that's near her house, next to that lake there, you know, the one with that stupid Indian name."

"Sippiwicket," I happen to know the stupid Indian name, probably because I'm part stupid Indian.

"Yes, that's it. Lake Sippiwicket. The graveyard is right near the water. I had bought a Ouija board and we wanted to try it out. We sat in a circle under an angel statue. After we all placed our fingertips gently on that pointer thing, we asked it some questions about you and Wyatt and if he could ever fall in love with me."

"And did the Ouija board answer your questions?" Your stupid as shit questions. I think this but don't say it out loud.

"It spelled out a weird answer. A whole sentence. 'Leave her alone'."

"And that didn't answer your question."

"No."

"Who do you think you contacted?"

"I asked the Ouija board that same question and the little pointer thingy…"

"The planchette."

"Yeah, the whatever. The planchette got freezing cold. Everyone felt it and we got wicked scared. Then the thing vibrated and moved around fast in circles before it finally pointed to the 'A' and then the 'N' and then it stopped."

Anthony. I think those stupid girls contacted Anthony and he warned them to leave me alone. "What do you think the A and the N stood for?"

"I guess Annabelle. Anyway, after that it refused to move again. So the next time we took it over to my family's plot. My ancestors on the Littlefield side have lived in Eastfield for centuries. Their graves are really old. I thought something might happen there and it did."

Here it comes. She took the Ouija board over to the old cemetery on Prospect Street. "Why did you bring the board to that particular cemetery?"

"Because my grandpa told us a ridiculous story about one of our ancestors. She was so evil that they put seven stones on top of her grave, to keep her spirit buried. So we went to the Prospect Street Burial Ground, over to the area where my Littlefield relatives are all buried and we asked the evil woman to make Wyatt fall in love with me."

"Colleen, do you remember the evil woman's name?"

"Katherine. I had just come home from cruising by Wyatt's house and I was pissed off because your car was there. I called Liz and Katie and Ashley and we went over to the graveyard to ask for Katherine's help. It was unbelievably cold out that night and windy. We almost didn't go. But I begged them."

"What happened at the graveyard?"

"We did a few shots of Fireball and lit some candles but the wind kept blowing them out. Finally we got them to stay lit and sat down in a circle right next to Katherine's grave. We were freezing, but Ashley brought a couple of old quilts so we all sat on one and wrapped the other around us. I put the Ouija board in the middle and we placed our fingertips on the planchette."

Colleen learned a new word tonight and she's pronouncing it correctly and using it appropriately, too. Right now, she actually sounds pretty intelligent for such a stupid ass.

Maybe she'll make a good ghost hunter one day after all. Maybe then Wyatt will like her. She's closer to the truth than she knows. The first time Wyatt saw me he couldn't take his eyes off of me because he saw Anthony's ghost following me everywhere. I'm still not sure if he was more fascinated with Anthony's ghost than he was with me. Maybe for him, our relationship was based only on his attraction to my supernatural talents. Maybe Wyatt never loved the ordinary human part of me at all.

"Then what happened, Colleen?"

She sniffles a couple of times and then stops crying. Looking very serious and scared, she says, "Katherine communicated with us, using the letters on the Ouija board to spell out her answer. She said, 'Move the stones.' It took at least three full minutes for the planchette to finish spelling out her answer. My hands felt like they were going to freeze off. Even my wrists began to feel numb."

"Did you move the stones?"

"We did. We were scared but kinda drunk, too, so we were laughing; you know, like a nervous laughter."

"And after you moved the stones off of her grave, you just left them scattered all around?" I know the answer to this question because Phoebe and I saw the stones and I have a photograph of them.

"We had to. The wind whipped up and we heard a terrifying voice. It spoke your name. A creepy wind blew all around us in a circle and a voice distinctly said 'Annabelle.' It sounded like the hissing sound a cat makes when it's really pissed off, but instead of just random hissing, that creepy voice pronounced your name. Liz thought Ashley was saying it, but I knew it wasn't Ashley, so I grabbed the Ouija board and ran like hell. We needed to get out of there fast. The other girls were right behind me. I'm never going back."

"Thanks, Colleen. What the hell did I ever do to you?" I flip the light switch off on my way out and leave her sitting in the dark.

Matt's waiting for me outside the ladies' room. "Who was in there with you, Annabelle? I heard voices."

"Thanks for spying on me, douche bag."

Matt looks like I just slapped him. Good, now maybe he'll leave me the hell alone. Which he does. We don't even sit together on the trolley ride back. Everyone's partying it up; singing and dancing but I sit this one out. I'm not in the mood to party anymore. I tell Meg, Jen, and Steph that I have a headache. When we arrive back at Jen's house, Steph takes pity on me and gives me a ride home.

She pulls into our driveway and says, "I never liked Matt Riley anyway. Whatever happened to you and Wyatt? He seems more like your type."

"He's exactly my type, but I don't know if we'll ever get back together again. It's a really long and ridiculous story. Thanks for the ride, Steph. Have fun at the after party."

"I wish you felt better. We'll miss you."

"I wouldn't be much fun. I'm tired and I have a headache." A headache named Colleen. She sent a lunatic bitch ghost to attack me! Is she the stupidest girl on the planet? Or does she really hate me that much? My life sucks.

I call the only person who'll understand: Nathaniel. When I tell him about Colleen and the Ouija board, he comes rushing over.

As soon as he wheels into the kitchen he starts ranting. If he could walk, he'd pace furiously back and forth but he can't. Jeff can, though, and he starts wearing a path in our floorboards, sticking his nose into corners and trailing around our kitchen. While Jeff conducts his canine investigation, Nathaniel explains.

"Think of the supernatural world as a fast rising river during a rainstorm. In order to control the flooding, people build sandbag barriers along the banks of that river. If just one sandbag falls away, the others start coming loose, too. Before you know it, the water rushes out over the land and keeps going, destroying cars and houses, drowning animals and people. When you pick up that planchette and put it down on the board, then ask a question, you've dislodged one of those sandbags."

"Seriously?"

He nods his head. "Yes. With a Ouija board, you open the door to the next world and boom! Anything can come through. No one who knows what they're doing would ever use one. Wyatt and I don't need one. I'd never touch one. I can't believe that stupid bitch did this to you!"

I find myself sticking up for Colleen. "She didn't know. She thought if she had the whole ghost thing going on that Wyatt would like her."

"How would she even know that Wyatt's a medium?"

"She doesn't. Last year when Meg and I filmed at Wild Wood for our big History project, some of the mean, popular girls in school started calling me Ghost Girl. Colleen was one of those girls. So, she figured that Wyatt might be attracted to her if she was more like me; if she did some ghost hunting."

"Because even to Colleen, it's obvious that Wyatt's still hung up on you." Nathaniel finishes my explanation.

"Yeah, awhile ago she dyed her hair black and made it longer with those extension thingies. But everyone made fun of her so she changed it back."

"Basically the girl's a total moron."

"Not really. She's president of the Honor Society."

"She's not very honorable."

"I guess not, but she gets good grades."

"And she's obsessed with Wyatt."

"Obviously. Do you want some tea or something?"

"Sure, why not? When's your mom due back?"

I look up at the clock on the wall. "Seven days, ten hours and thirty seven minutes."

"So you miss her, huh?"

"I miss her more than I miss her lasagna."

He laughs. "That much. Wow."

"The only good thing is Katherine's ghost seems to have given up lately. She hasn't been very active since right after the storm."

"I don't trust her. We need to be on guard. Where's the farm girl?"

"Staying in Freewater. It's her dad's birthday. I gave her the night off."

Someone laughs and Nathaniel assumes it's me. "What's so funny?"

"I didn't laugh. That wasn't me."

"You know, it didn't sound like your laugh and it's coming from outside, not in here."

We hear it again but barely because the voice is so soft. Icy prickles creep up my spine to my neck and then tingle across my scalp. Holding my breath, I wait for the feeling to melt away.

"Looks like I'll be staying over. Wake up your dad and tell him so he won't be surprised in the morning when he finds me zonked out on his couch."

"Thank you." I put my hand on Nathaniel's strong shoulder, lean down and kiss his cheek.

We make it through the night without any more excitement. No more ghostly laughter, no breaking windows. No one calls my name. I don't sleep very well, though, because I keep expecting something to happen. In the morning, Phoebe returns and stays for the rest of the week, long enough to meet my mother when she arrives home.

When I finally tell Mom about the homicidal ghost who wants to destroy me, she's predictably horrified. But Katherine leaves us alone for a while and as a result, everyone gets pretty comfortable. Nothing much is going on in my life. I'm looking forward to the wedding at the beginning of March and a few weeks after that, it will be my birthday; on the vernal equinox. I'll be turning eighteen soon; if I can stay alive.

Chapter 20

The Wedding

The wedding ceremony is beautiful, visually and spiritually. Jackson's church was built at the end of the nineteenth century and the architect is famous for his neo gothic creations. The altar and stained glass windows are internationally renowned for their craftsmanship. Looking handsome together in matching classic black tuxedoes, Jackson and Oliver each wear one perfect white rose in a lapel. The woman who officiates over their vows gives a short, simple and heartfelt sermon about love and commitment. Feeling manageably self conscious, I'm standing on one side of Jackson and Oliver, while Wyatt, in his tuxedo, decorates the other side of the happy couple. I keep trying not to look at him, but it's impossible. I never get to see him this close up anymore and he looks incredible. Not only that, his tie matches my dress. Thank you, Jackson.

I feel almost as glamorous in my Vera Wang creation as everyone says I look. Meg pinned my hair up, into a glossy figure eight on the back of my head and my shoulders are bare, so my neck looks about two feet long. The giraffe look must be popular because the wedding guests are all over me with embarrassing compliments; even people I don't know. When we get to the reception Jackson takes me aside to tell me how elegant and beautiful I am. Of course, he chose the dress and is taking even more pleasure in hearing the compliments than I am. I feel kind of awkward and wish that people would stop staring at me and telling me how pretty I look. It seems like every time I turn around, someone's taking my picture with a smart phone. And, of course, the wedding photographer takes quite a few also. There's a videographer, too and I start to feel like I'm being stalked by the paparazzi. It must be getting to Oliver, as well, because he finally tells the professional photographer and videographer to leave. They don't need any more pictures. Maybe I'll be able to relax now.

For their reception, Oliver chose a lovely room in a historic hall, designed by the same architect who did the church. There's a tile floor with big black and white squares arranged in a checkerboard pattern, and a polished hardwood dance floor over by the grand piano. The food on the buffet table looks elegant and tastes really good, too. But for once in my life I'm too nervous to eat. I try to unwind by doing a little people watching. It's interesting and fun to check everyone out. Jackson's and Oliver's guests are all dressed very fashionably.

On the piano, an accomplished musician is tinkling out jazzy renditions of popular songs, past and present, and a few people are dancing. Over near the dance floor, I spy a man and a woman who look perfect together, like they're posing for a magazine cover. But the photogenic couple isn't dancing. They aren't even looking at each other. They're standing silently side by side. Tall and slim, they look like they're made for each other; at least physically. Wyatt walks up to stand beside me and takes my elbow in his warm hand. I stop breathing for about a minute and a half and forget how to talk.

"Aha. Checking out Mr. James Silver and the former Mrs. James Silver, now known as Rowena Finn. What do you think?"

I suppress the urge to yell out "Holy shit!", hold my breath for a second and then answer him. "He looks like he belongs on the cover of GQ, in his new designer suit; very fashion-forward, skillfully tailored just for him." Not like my dad's suit which comes out of the closet for weddings and funerals and then goes back in until the next important occasion pops up. If he gains a little weight or loses it in between special events, it looks a touch baggy or tight on him, depending.

Dad has already loosened his tie, and it will be completely untied soon. He keeps stretching and adjusting the collar of his blue dress shirt, by sticking his index finger in between the collar and his muscular neck and wiggling it around. He looks tanned and fit, like he works outside at a physical job. He also looks like he'd rather be outside now, wearing one of his flannel shirts, not here at this elegant party in a suit and tie. Mr. GQ model, however, is very at ease and at home, even if he doesn't look at all pleased to be standing next to his ex-wife.

I continue my analysis. "Your mother could be a fifty-year old supermodel; tall, slim, and not happy at all to be over fifty. She hasn't had any obvious work done, but she isn't very wrinkled, either, so who knows? She resembles Oliver: silver haired and impeccably and tastefully dressed. In high heels she's almost as tall as your dad, and he's almost as tall as you are." Rowena Finn stares back at me, and not in a warm or friendly way. Finally, like a crack on an otherwise frozen solid pond, what looks like a well-practiced, socially acceptable smile spreads across her chilly face. I can feel the coldness of her gaze in my bones. There's no message of warmth in it. Then James Silver turns my way, to see who Rowena's smiling at. A sly look crosses his handsome face as he stares into my eyes with Wyatt's eyes. They even change color, darkening and intensifying in that uncanny way I know so well.

Wyatt squeezes my elbow, gently as if he might break it if he isn't careful, and whispers, "How would you like to meet my parents?"

"Thanks, but I already have." I grin and point my chin in Jackson's and Oliver's direction. They're standing shoulder to shoulder and both of their heads are thrown back, laughing at something my mother's saying.

"You are the smartest and the most beautiful girl I know." Wyatt bends and tickles my ear with his whisper. It's my pointed, fairy ear, and his lips brush the tip of it when they pucker out to form the "B" in "beautiful". I have mismatched ears. One has a round top, like most human ears and one has a pointed top, like a fairy's. "C'mon. They're both looking over here. My mother looks like she could single-handedly keep the ice sculptures on the buffet tables from melting. And my dad looks like he'd like to make you his next wife."

I crack up. "Tell him to get in line. Everyone keeps saying how pretty I am. It's embarrassing. I hate strapless. I feel like tugging this dress up every five seconds. Jen gave me this two-sided tape, and I'm literally taped inside the dress with about seventy-five pieces of it. So I know it won't fall down. But it still makes me nervous."

Wyatt's face turns red. "I'm not going to even comment on that. Let's get it over with. Move." He nudges the small of my back with one large hand and I attempt to glide forward gracefully in my high heels. I manage pretty well, too.

We cross the few feet of black and white checkered floor together and I extend my hand to be shaken, first to the former Mrs. Silver and then to Mr. James Silver, who holds onto it for several seconds beyond what would be considered polite and insists that I call him by his first name. I squirm and feel my face redden, which is probably what he intends.

"You are obviously a friend of my son's. Now I know why he doesn't want to live with me in California."

I grit my teeth in a rigid smile and seethe. I know why Wyatt doesn't live with his father, because Wyatt told me. His father has never invited him to even visit his new home in California. I don't care how good-looking this guy is, or how charming he thinks he is; he's pissing me off big time.

Wyatt's mother, at least, doesn't attempt to hide her feelings. The frosty witch doesn't want to be in the same room with any of us. She can't wait to leave and will be doing us all a favor when she does.

"Lovely to meet you, Annabelle. I'm afraid I have to be going, though. I have an early appointment to show a house tomorrow." I vaguely remember Wyatt telling me that she's a real estate broker. "I don't want to get back to New Hampshire too late. Excuse me. I'm going to say good bye to Oliver and Jackson." She walks away and I'm happy to see the back of her. Poor Wyatt. It's a miracle that he's turned into the person he is, a miracle wrought by Oliver.

Wyatt speaks up right away, probably because he doesn't want to give his dad a chance to comment on his ex-wife. "Where are you staying, Dad?"

"Oliver arranged for us to stay with the Morses. We have their little cottage, out by Deep Water Pond all to ourselves. It's very private and picturesque, but my wife's nervous about the baby going near the pond."

"She's right. It's very deep in the middle, hence the name of the pond." I'm about to explain about Rebecca Morse's untimely death by drowning right outside Mr. James Silver's new front door when the ringing of his cell phone interrupts us.

Wyatt's father takes the phone out of his pocket and excuses himself. "Sorry, I have to take this. It's my wife calling. The baby was asleep so she couldn't come earlier. I'll probably have to leave and pick them up now." Putting his phone to his ear, he turns and walks away, seeking a quieter place outside in the hallway where he can talk to his second wife.

"You know he's moving back here," Wyatt informs me.

"Yes, Oliver told me. How do you feel about that?"

"How am I supposed to feel? I don't even know. There's no way I'd leave Oliver's house. I thought he and Jackson might want a little privacy because they're a married couple now, but they've begged me to stay with them, repeatedly. They've offered me some serious bribes, too. Which was unnecessary. If they want me, I'm staying." Wyatt smiles.

"Bribes? Like what?"

"Whatever college I choose, paid for, full tuition."

"Do you know where you want to go?"

"I'm waiting to hear from Brown."

I knew that his first choice was Brown University, in Rhode Island, just a forty five minute drive away. No one ever gets into Brown, but if anyone can; it's Wyatt. He's smart, has an amazing transcript and test scores, great extracurriculars and I know his essay will kick ass. It will be original and stand out from the others, because he does.

"Good luck. I hope you get in." I really mean it, too. I'll be at River Wind. He'll be at Brown. It's not even an hour's drive between the two schools. We can see each other all the time, if we ever get back together. At least, for right now, we're talking: the maid of honor and the best man. I think about how much I love Oliver and Jackson and send a huge thought wave of warmth and affection their way. Jackson catches my eye and winks. Wyatt puts his hand on my bare shoulder and leans down to speak into my ear so I'll be able to hear him. The room's getting a little noisy.

"I hope I get into Brown, too. Oliver's retiring after this school year, and Jackson bought him a house, on the Cape, as a wedding present. Jackson's going to semi-retire and teach psychology part time at River Wind. They want me to stay in the Eastfield house and commute to Brown. They even offered to buy me a new car, but I'm emotionally attached to the old Land Rover. Oliver bought it for me when I turned sixteen. It was all rusty and needed new brakes and tires and some other stuff, but a former student of his fixed it up. It's the car I learned to drive in and it still runs great. We've been through a lot together."

"I know." We both grin. The Land Rover has a history for us. "I can't picture you in any other vehicle."

"Me either. Remember that time, parked outside Oliver's house, when I accidentally leaned on the horn?"

"Yes, I remember." A blush of heat burns across my cheeks and I change the subject. "So Oliver's keeping his house in Eastfield?"

"Yes, his roots are here. He'll never give up the historical society and the legendary Eastfield Film Festival. He can work part time, maybe teaching just one elective, like that History of Eastfield course he designed. Jackson has a lot of friends here, too."

"Good, I'd miss them too much if they moved permanently."

"So you're going to school nearby?"

"Yes. I got into River Wind so I guess I'll be bumping into Jackson."

"Beautiful campus."

"Yup, and it's a small enough school so that I got a letter from the track coach. I can run there. Plus, they have club tennis, so I can do that, too."

"And there's the river and the legend, some story about a mountain lion, if I recall. I'm sure that's part of the attraction."

"Well, the campus is inside the Triangle. The river and an entrance into the swamplands are both right there. Then there's the cat that never dies." The university's mascot is a mountain lion and their motto is "The Cat Never Dies." Throughout the years, there have been several sightings of a one-eyed mountain lion, on and around the River Wind campus. People think it's the same cat, even though the legendary feline would be centuries old if the rumor were true.

"Fascinating."

I see the light in Wyatt's eyes and I know he isn't being sarcastic. He is fascinated. Good, I'll have no difficulty luring him over to the campus to spend time with me. We can check out the cat situation together, maybe get to know each other again.

Nathaniel wheels over to us. "You two are looking a lot cozier than you did this winter. Spring is in the air."

I look across the room at Phoebe, who's wearing a vintage dress that looks like it somehow survived the sinking of the *Titanic*, perfectly intact. "Maybe for you, too, Nathaniel. Maybe spring is in the air for you."

He turns his face away from me and looks toward the entrance of the room. "Oh, good, my mother has finally arrived. She had to work today, so she couldn't come to the ceremony. Come on; show her how pretty you look, Annabelle." He turns his wheelchair in the direction of his waving mother and starts toward her.

Wyatt's father has just entered, also, and Nathaniel's mother is standing about two steps behind him. She spies me next to Nathaniel immediately, smiles and waves again. Then she stumbles and screams. Wyatt's father turns and catches her. They both stand there, clutching at each other for support. Their faces look shocked and horrified. We all rush over. Nathaniel tells Wyatt to get his mother a chair and Wyatt grabs the nearest one, so Mrs. Flyte can sit down before she keels over. I run over to the closest tray and grab a clean glass and a pitcher of ice water. Quickly, I pour some water into the glass and carefully hold it up to Mrs. Flyte's lips. Then I aim my eyes across the room and shoot Phoebe a *Get over here* look.

"Mrs. Flyte, do you feel faint? Can I get you some tea?" I look around for my mother, but she hasn't noticed our little drama. She's on the opposite side of the room, still talking and laughing with Oliver, Jackson and my father. Nathaniel's mother opens her mouth to speak, but no words come out, only an audible gasp for air. I put my arm around her. Nathaniel holds her hand in his.

"Mom, what's wrong? Do you feel sick? Are you going to faint?"

Phoebe arrives, takes her other hand and feels her wrist with two fingers, searching for her pulse, while introducing herself. "Hi, Mrs. Flyte. I'm Dr. Phoebe Walker."

Nathaniel's so upset and worried about his mother that he doesn't take the opportunity Phoebe has given him to contradict her and announce that she's a farm animal doctor, not a human doctor. Phoebe brushes Mrs. Flyte's hair off her forehead. Nathaniel's mother looks into Phoebe's eyes and I witness the healing magic at work. My friend has calmed her with just a touch to the wrist and forehead. Some color comes back into Mrs. Flyte's face and she frees her hand from Nathaniel's to grab the glass of ice water and take two big gulps. Her son repeats his question. "What's wrong, Mom?"

Wyatt's father recovers first. "I can tell you what's wrong, Nathaniel. I've neglected and avoided you and your mother for twenty-three years, two months, one week and five days. You probably don't remember me but I'm your father."

No one speaks.

I reach for Wyatt's hand and he holds onto mine firmly, even though he's trembling. Phoebe pulls a chair over and sits down, next to Nathaniel's wheelchair. She wraps both her arms around his shoulders. She looks like she'd probably climb into his lap if we weren't in the middle of a bunch of gaping people. Nathaniel's still gripping his mother's hand. He rubs his cheek against Phoebe's hand which rests on his right shoulder.

As if on cue, because the scene isn't quite ridiculously dramatic enough, an attractive young woman who looks like she's about Nathaniel's age enters from stage right. She's holding onto the hand of a cherub-faced, golden-haired child, who wrestles away from her and runs in little black patent leather shoes, as fast as she can over to Mr. Flyte, or Mr. Silver or whatever the hell his real name is. No one here knows what to call him, but she does.

"Daddy!" She squeals as she scampers.

Wyatt's and Nathaniel's father scoops her up and kisses her dimpled cheek. She giggles and wiggles free. As soon as her tiny shoes hit the floor she's off, heading full speed toward the cake table. No one else is paying attention except me, because they're all riveted in place waiting to watch the next installment of the Flyte/Silver family soap opera. I'm the only one who notices that the toddler has begun rapidly helping herself to large amounts of wedding cake without the benefit of a fork, a plate or a napkin.

What a tangled web Mr. James Flyte-Silver-whatever-the-hell-his-name-is has woven and now he's inextricably caught up in it, along with Nathaniel and his mother, Rowena, Wyatt, James' young wife, who has introduced herself as Amy, and a sweet, mischievous little toddler named Samantha Olivia Silver. But they call her Sammie. Amy Silver explains that Mr. Morse's son dropped by and offered to give her and Samantha a ride over to the wedding reception after Sammie woke up from her nap.

Slipping away from the awestruck group, I tiptoe over to Nathaniel's and Wyatt's small sister and offer to cut her a single serving sized piece of cake, before she helps herself to another fistful. Placing my hand in her tiny one, I introduce myself. "Hi, Sammie. My name is Annabelle."

She attempts to repeat it after me. "Annaboo," the child says, in a small, twinkly voice designed by nature to make everyone who hears it love her and want to hear her speak again.

"What's my name?"

She giggles at my silly question. "I said it already."

"Oh, please, Sammie, say it one more time." I brush some cake crumbs off the ruffles on her pink party dress.

She complies. "Annaboo." I dip the end of a napkin in a glass of water and then open her chubby fists and start cleaning the frosting and smooshed up crumbs off of her hands. As soon as her little fingers have lost some of their stickiness, I go to work gently on her cheeks and her perfect, tiny pink lips. "Annaboo." She laughs again, sticking one chubby finger into her mouth, sucking on it and taking it out again. "Mmmmm. Good cake. More?" she asks, twinkling up at me and shaking her blonde curls.

"Yes, but this time, we're going to use a plate and a fork and a napkin, Sammie." I slice her a huge piece of cake, thinking that we can share it. I've been so busy mooning over Wyatt all day, I've hardly eaten anything and suddenly, I realize I'm wicked hungry. Sammie's right, too; the cake's delicious. We trade bites and take turns and giggle together and the cake tastes like the most awesomest cake ever.

I sneak a glance over at the love/hate festival happening just a few feet away. Poor Mrs. Flyte, the original wife, is sitting weakly and pitifully in the center of it all. Wyatt looks up and meets my stare, then leaves the commotion behind, to join Sammie and me, at the cake table. Pulling a chair up next to mine, he puts one arm across the back of my chair and smiles at me.

"Who are you? Do you want a bite?" Sammie makes it impossible for Wyatt to ignore her and focus on me, which is what he seems to want to do. Also, he can't answer her because she has climbed up onto his lap with a forkful of cake and is stabbing it at his mouth. He can either open his mouth or get a pierced lip, so he chooses the less painful option.

Suddenly, I can't stop laughing. I stop worrying about the strapless dress falling down, about Wyatt's parents not loving him enough, about whether or not he loves me anymore, about whether or not Phoebe and Nathaniel will ever stop trying to wound each other long enough to hook up. I stop worrying about all the new worries: What the hell will happen now that Nathaniel's father, who's been missing for twenty three years, is back? What will Nathaniel and his mom do? What will Rowena Silver do when she finds out? How does Wyatt feel about all this? Has it ruined Oliver and Jackson's most special day of their lives for them? All these thoughts pour out of me, all over the floor and before they can puddle up, I start laughing. I laugh and laugh and laugh.

Little Samantha Silver joins me. She leaves Wyatt's lap and crawls up onto mine and starts bouncing up and down and giggling. Poor Wyatt doesn't know what to do. He was an only child for sixteen years and not only is he meeting his baby sister for the first time, but he found out just minutes ago that he has a brother. His ex girlfriend is behaving like she's out of her mind—which she most definitely is—and his baby sister has decided that this crazy ex girlfriend is a good role model.

My mother brings us all back to earth when she slides up behind me and pulls up my dress. "Annabelle, your boobs are practically out," she hisses.

This makes me laugh even harder, especially when Sammie yells, "Boobs!"

Wyatt's face turns purple. I don't think he knows whether to laugh or not. But I think he might explode if he doesn't.

"Stop it, girls!" my mother hisses again, in her not-to-be disobeyed voice, which even little Samantha recognizes and responds to. She presses her tiny lips together and gives my mother a mature and serious look of pure innocence. My mother scoops the baby up off of my lap and demands, "Pull yourself together, Annabelle."

And I do. I adjust my dress, so that I won't disgrace the Blake family name by displaying my unruly boobs at an elegant and fashionable social event. Wyatt grabs a glass of ice water off of the table we're sitting at and gulps down about seven gulps, wicked fast, which seems to help him a lot.

He takes my hand and says, "Would you like to dance, Annabelle. I think they're playing our song."

The piano player is tinkling away at a jazzy version of the Beatle's "Long and Winding Road." Believe it or not, despite all the excitement and commotion, a handful of people are shuffling around near the piano, slow dancing to the music. After leading me over to this unenthusiastic little group, Wyatt pulls me into his arms. Everyone else on the dance floor is at least twenty years older than us, but I don't complain because Wyatt's arms are around me.

"It's just an excuse to hold you, Annabelle," he whispers into my hair which is coming loose from its arrangement. We stand there wrapped around each other, barely moving our feet, on a dance floor that's speckled with grown-up couples. Wyatt thoughtfully loosens his grip on me every few minutes to adjust my dress so I don't flash my wild and uncontrollable boobs. Today has been traumatic enough. We don't need that to happen.

Chapter 21

Alone at Last

The wedding was three nights ago and Wyatt still hasn't called or texted me. After the way he acted at the wedding, I figured we'd be getting back together soon. Evidently I figured wrong. I check my cell phone for the tenth time today, just in case I didn't feel it vibrate; no calls, no texts. It's after eleven o'clock and I'm usually asleep by now, but tonight I'm not. That's a new thing. I've always fallen asleep easily and early. But since Wyatt and I broke up, if I don't run my ass off and wear myself out during the day, I can't fall asleep. It sucks.

I'm home by myself right now, which never happens anymore. My parents went into Boston and they were due back half an hour ago. They should be coming through the door any second now. Because they seldom go out anymore, I don't want to bug them by calling their cell phones. My mom will worry if she knows I'm home alone and I'm fine so I don't want to upset her. Phoebe was supposed to be here with me, but she left about an hour ago.

At about ten o'clock, she got a phone call and rushed out. Someone's pregnant goat went into labor two weeks early. When I call her cell to see if everything's okay, she doesn't answer and I decide to try again later. I hope the poor little goats are born healthy. Curling up in the comfortable overstuffed chair next to the kitchen window, I open my book to read, wait for my parents and worry about the baby goats. Two chapters into the Dennis Lehane book I picked up at the library last week, I hear a noise that sounds like it's coming from right outside; close by.

First it's a faint giggle. Then suddenly, two small white palms slap the black glass. Gasping, I jolt up out of the chair. The little hands stick to the window for a second, like the pale undersides of two baby starfish. As I stare at them, the tiny hands drop down and I'm looking at my own goggle-eyed reflection on the window's glossy surface. Three seconds later a small white-fleshed face smashes up against the glass and the same two hands slap either side of it, flanking the distorted features. Who could this be? It looks like a little girl. Then I hear her voice.

"Annaboo."

What is Samantha doing outside at eleven o'clock at night? She can't possibly be alone. Her mother or father must have walked through the woods with her. They have to be nearby. When I was a baby, if I was fussing, my dad used to carry me outside to look at the stars and it quieted me. After a little fresh air I'd go right back to sleep. Maybe Sammie's parents brought her outside because she wouldn't settle down and go to sleep. They must be with her. On the other hand, though, what if she somehow got loose and made her way through the woods, from the Morse's stone cottage to our house, alone? I hear her again.

"Annaboo."

That makes up my mind. Samantha's out there. I saw her and I heard her. She seems to be alone and that's dangerous. I decide to go outside, scoop her up and bring her inside. Then I'll call Wyatt's father. I can get his number from Wyatt. It will be a good excuse to call him. I haven't spoken to my ex-boyfriend since the wedding and after the way he held me on the dance floor, I thought he'd call right away. But it's been three days and I haven't heard from him.

Grabbing my brother Joe's sweatshirt off the hook in the kitchen, I yank it over my head and run out the door into the darkness. At the edge of our backyard, I catch sight of a small figure in white, right before she runs away from me. Her yellow curls glitter and bounce in the darkness. They seem to be generating their own golden light as Sammie scampers down the path into the woods. Heading after her, I sprint across the backyard, but she disappears where the path veers to the right. Hurrying around the curve, I spy a glimmer of her long white nightgown far ahead, right before the black night steals her from sight again. *How can a baby run so fast?*

"Annaboo."

She giggles softly. Her voice tinkles like tiny bells inside my head. Something's not right. Her voice sounds very close but she's far away. I stop for a second to listen.

There's an abrupt rustle in the brush to my right. Thoughts of coyotes send adrenaline zipping through my veins and I suddenly wish I'd grabbed a flashlight. And maybe one of Joe's old baseball bats.

"Annaboo." I've lost sight of her again, but her voice is right next to my ear.

Then I hear a quiet sob.

Oh no, she's afraid!

Running full speed, I head toward the spot where I last glimpsed her. "Sammie, stop. I'll bring you to my house and we can have cake!"

As my words echo through the dark forest, I catch sight of a pale, scampering cherub far away, on the path leading to the Morse's house. She's going to break records when she's old enough to join the high school track team. As I stare straight ahead and speed up, she disappears into the black shadows of the tall trees and I hustle down the path after her. But no matter how fast I run, as far as I can see, the path is empty. So I run and run along the trail until the woods open up and I can see the shore of Deep Water Pond. Across the partially frozen surface of the water, on the other side of the pond, the windows of the stone cottage cast a faint, golden illumination on the opposite shore. And there she is, standing still at last, just a few feet away from me, facing the pond. The yellow curls on the back of her head sparkle and glimmer in the starlight. They seem to give off a twinkling light of their own.

Before I have a chance to yell her name, Sammie scampers onto the ice. She starts laughing and twirling around, barefoot in her long, lacy white nightgown, like a child from another century. Her poor little feet must be freezing.

The landscape before me looks like the opening scene of a nightmarish fairytale. The narrow moon slices the indigo sky like a scythe with tiny white stars spattered all around it. For just a moment, I forget to be afraid for Samantha and stand frozen at the edge of the clearing, spellbound by the sight of this beautiful child, dancing on the shimmering ice.

She's humming an unfamiliar, old-fashioned-sounding tune; her voice is so soft I can barely hear it. The whole experience reminds me of watching a play from a front row seat in the audience. Whoa! I shake my head to clear it so I can focus on reality. I'm staring at Deep Water Pond and it's past eleven o'clock at night. I'm not looking at a stage. I'm watching a baby walk onto thin ice.

"Stop, Sammie. Don't you want to play with me?" I keep my voice quiet so I won't scare her. If she goes farther out, she might fall through. "Look, I'm over here, Sammie. I'll give you a piggyback." Instead of coming closer; she tiptoes farther away. So I step onto the edge of the pond. The ice under my feet makes a cracking noise, but holds me. I move fast, to keep from falling through. My feet fly across the ice, barely touching it. If I lose momentum, this fragile surface will never hold my weight. If I stop and stand still, I'll fall through, into the freezing water.

Samantha is standing still as death on the ice in the middle of the pond, at the deepest part where it's thinnest. I speed toward her. The slick, brittle shell groans and creaks beneath my weight. I need to run faster than the ice is cracking. Suddenly, I hit a slick, wet patch and both my feet flip out from under me. I'm airborne. My right shoulder slams down first and breaks through the ice. Headfirst, I plunge into a deep, dark, liquid universe. No sky above my head, no ice beneath my feet. Only pitch black icy water everywhere. Needles of sharp pain stab at my eyeballs but I stretch my eyelids open wider so I can swim toward where I last saw Sammie. I need to figure out which way is up so I can spot her. And then I need to grab her. Fast.

The agonizing cold shoots through me. My right shoulder throbs. As I move down, down, down, in slow motion, I grab at my sneakers. I need to get them off fast, so I'll be more buoyant. Then maybe I can float upwards. But instead, I keep sinking. I reverse direction and start swimming toward what I think is the surface, but the water's horribly cold and it slows me down, numbing my legs, my arms, my thoughts. Razorblades of freezing pain slice into my skin. A single thought blasts into my brain and paralyzes me: this must be how Rebecca felt right before she died. I shake off the paralysis and start kicking again, determined not to die the way she did.

But my saturated clothes pull me down faster than I can stroke toward what I think might be the surface; it's so hard to tell in this impenetrable blackness. As I struggle to make my brain work out a solution to this horrific problem, my body continues to freeze and sink. In my mind, I keep repeating the phrase *"Find Sammie."* It's my only clear thought. Instinct takes over and I try to breathe. Huge mistake. A deadly lethargy seizes me in its treacherous jaws and I don't feel any more pain. After floating limply in thick, seemingly warm fluid for a moment, I feel the numbness crack open. And the icy cold squeezes me in an agonizing spasm. A titanic-sized tremble vibrates through my body and fear blasts through again. It's fight or flight but I can't fight. I can't flee, either; I can't even lift one arm and swim one feeble stroke.

For the first time ever, I give up. I stop fighting and finally, the battle inside of me quiets. It feels foreign, but lovely. A delicious warmth spreads through me, reminding me of home and love. I'm weightless, resting on a cloud pillow. Everywhere I look, I see nothing but soft gray fog. As I stare into the mist, the gray darkens to black and in the shadowy depths below me, Anthony's white face appears, with his black hair floating wildly all around it. I smile and sink toward him.

Huge hands grip my shoulders and someone screams my name to heaven. But I don't answer. I don't open my eyes. I don't breathe. I don't think. I leave. I need to rest for a while, maybe for a long time, maybe forever. It isn't my decision to make, anyway. Someone else is deciding for me. And I let them. For the first time ever, I don't argue or battle to gain control. I don't struggle at all, because for the first time ever, I don't care.

Chapter 22

The Deadly Cold

I'm hovering over a dream world, looking down on a very dramatic scene. A tall man, in soaking wet pajamas is kneeling over a young girl, screaming her name. "Annabelle, Annabelle!" He keeps screaming, but she doesn't answer him, or even open her eyes. A woman and a child are standing in the doorway of an old stone cabin, watching him.

The man turns his face toward the woman in the doorway and yells, "Call 911! I can't feel a pulse. Tell them we need an ambulance!" The mother pulls the little girl into the house with her. The child is wearing fluffy pink footy pajamas. She looks snuggly and warm. I float down lower, so I can see into the stone cottage through a big window; the cozy room is aglow with warm yellow lamplight. With one arm, the woman puts the child in a playpen. In her other hand, she's holding a phone. She's yelling into the phone so loudly, the cords on her neck stand out like tree roots.

Outside, the man bends back over the cold, limp figure that used to be a girl named Annabelle. The woman, who must be his wife, runs to his side and throws a big quilt over his shoulders. Together, they wrap the frozen girl in another blanket and turn her on her side. The tall man starts pounding on her back. "She has water in her lungs. It has to come out." He starts crying. "My God, Amy, she's so cold she doesn't feel real."

His wife whispers into his ear, "Find her and tell her to come back. You know where she is, James. Go find her."

He looks up into the woman's pretty eyes, tears glittering down his face in the darkness, and tells her, "I can't feel her spirit. She's not inside her body right now. I don't know if she *can* come back."

"Do something, James! Make her stay!" The woman begs. "Please! She's so young."

"Annabelle! Don't go!" No one answers him. He turns the limp girl onto her back and starts pushing on her chest and breathing into her mouth with his own. His wife bends over him, her hands on his shoulders as if she can send her strength through him and into the girl who's lying too still on the cold, wet earth.

The baby in the cottage yells loud enough to be heard outside. "Mama! Mama! Annaboo!"

"She knows." The woman hugs the man's shoulders from behind and he keeps working on the girl who doesn't respond.

"She's gone. I can tell. She's given up."

"Don't let her, James!"

The dead girl's skin is white, tinged with gray, like the stone statue of an angel lying on its back. But someone tipped the sculpture over gently, so it fell to the ground intact. No damage, not one crack. She's perfect. I want to pray for her, but don't know any words to recite, or a god who'll listen. Then the words come to me. *Please send her back. Let her live.* I send my desire to save the girl's life down, into a taproot that draws from the pool which lies at the center of everyone's life force, a pool the whole human race shares with its ancestors, where power and healing and knowledge run deep for those who know how to find them. And I know how to find that power.

The strength of my desire to help the dead girl leads me down and down and then the power starts rising up, determined to find its way out of me. At first I feel only a reluctant trickle of hope, but then it grows into a relentless stream. I focus on the man and the woman and the unconscious girl for what seems like forever. And then finally she blinks. Together, the man and his wife and I fight for the girl who continues to lie so still on the earth. We use the strength each of us has been given to us by countless generations, through the ages.

I have to strain to distinguish words within the man's murmur. He pushes up the girl's saturated sweatshirt and presses his face to her chest. "I think I feel a heartbeat, Amy."

I want to spring up and gallop around in manic circles, but I'm afraid to stop focusing on the girl, so I continue to add my strength to his, so we can both pour the life force back into her. He lifts his head up off her chest and turns toward his wife. The man's tears start falling on the unconscious girl's face and I can feel them on mine.

Then I hear an engine, a vehicle, speeding over the nearby field. A white Land Rover is barreling toward us; flying up in the air over every bump, landing roughly and then continuing to jostle and thump forward. When it reaches us, a tall, wild-eyed boy flies out of the driver's side.

The woman yells, "Wyatt!"

"Good," the man says.

"Good." I think, but I don't know why. I don't know who Wyatt is. I just know it must be a good thing he's here because the man says so.

I'm very glad to see this fast-running boy, so glad that my vision grows fuzzy with happiness. Everything starts to fade away and I feel frozen again. Cold clenches me in its jaws and shakes me. I can't stop shaking and rattling. A horrible, freezing fog blinds me. I want to see the tall boy again, but the dark mist tunnels on forever.

When I can finally see again, I'm far away from the scene on the ice. From above, I watch the four figures, dark against the pale landscape. Three are moving, but the girl lying on the ground near the pond is not. Then a helicopter lands, in a field a few feet away from them and two men run out, carrying a stretcher. They lift the silent, stony figure of the young girl and load her onto the stretcher. After she's inside the helicopter they fly away.

The boy called Wyatt throws back his head. As he watches the helicopter climb higher in the dark sky, he yells the dead girl's name. "Annabelle!" Then he runs over to the white Land Rover, jumps into it and speeds off. The man puts his arm around his wife and they walk slowly into the cabin together. He's talking into a cell phone. Their child's waiting inside, wearing pink fuzzy footie pajamas. She's running around and yelling in her playpen, shaking it like a monkey in a cage. A bunch of stuffed animals lie scattered on the floor directly next to her. She must have thrown them out in an effort to get her parents' attention.

Why isn't the baby wearing the old fashioned white nightgown? Why does she have on fuzzy pink pajamas? Why are these questions even occurring to me? I'm exhausted and I decide to rest for a while.

Chapter 23

Life Support

Whoa! The girl in the hospital bed looks dead. Or maybe she was never alive. Maybe she's a statue, not a real girl. In a graveyard somewhere, I know I've seen a stone angel that looks something like her. But instead of standing upright, with her pale gray wings spread, the poor, motionless girl is lying down in a hospital bed and, of course, there are no wings. Her skin, even though it's the same color as granite, isn't the right texture. It's perfectly smooth and shiny, like wax, not stone. She's beautiful, but gray and cold. Maybe this is a wax museum, and she's a famous person in a hospital scene. It's very realistic, too. The machines are beeping and the IV connected to her arm seems real. She's very lifelike, except she looks dead.

Here comes the doctor.

"Annabelle, come back. I know you can do it. Come back."

Annabelle, what a pretty name, but old fashioned. I know I've heard it before but I can't remember where or when. I guess this isn't a wax museum. It's really a hospital room. He's really a doctor. Here comes someone else, a beautiful young woman who looks like she just walked off a farm in Nebraska.

"Dr. Knight, you have to save her."

"I'm doing everything I can. She's still alive but barely. Any normal human would be gone by now. I don't know why she isn't coming back. Maybe she's confused."

The girl in the bed is confused. Now I know why I'm here. I need to watch over her. She's beautiful and lying way too still and she's confused. She needs me here to keep her safe until everything becomes clear for her and then she'll come back and wake up. I can't leave yet. I have to stay here. I think I can help.

"What should I do? I need to do something," the farm-girl asks.

"Talk to her. Convince her to return to us and to stay, Phoebe. She's your friend. Touch her. Maybe she'll feel something coming from you and she'll respond."

"My healing strength is off. I haven't felt well since last night. I don't know what's wrong with me."

"Maybe you're too tired. We're all exhausted. Give it a try, though, Phoebe. It can't hurt."

The doctor leaves the two girls alone and the blonde girl sits in a chair next to the unconscious girl, holding her hand and whispering to her. Soon the doctor returns to see if anything's changed, but it hasn't.

The girl named Phoebe tells him, "I don't know how long she was under the ice. Her life force is seriously diminished. I wish my touch would work on her, but I keep trying and nothing happens. I can't reach her and she looks so alone. I can't help her and normally I'd be able to. It's hard to explain. I feel weak, like I can't focus on her. I can only focus within myself. The power to heal might still be inside of me, but it won't come out. Something has weakened it."

"None of this is your fault, Phoebe."

"Last night, when it happened, I went out. I didn't sense anything wrong so I left. Her parents were due home any minute and everything was quiet. I thought it would be all right. We hadn't experienced any sign of Katherine's ghost for months."

"You had no way of knowing. Don't blame yourself."

"Look at her, Dr. Knight. She's so beautiful but so still."

"I've never seen anything like her before. No one has. Anyone else would be dead."

"James Silver thinks she came back from the dead. He said her heart stopped beating."

"Well, she's definitely alive now, but she's not completely here with us yet."

"If she wakes up, what will she be like? What will happen to her? Even you don't know what to do, do you? Will she stay like this forever?"

"Her breathing is shallow, but at least she can breathe on her own. We should be grateful for that. At this point we have to treat her like any other coma victim. Keep talking to her and touching her, trying to get through to her somehow. Unfortunately, she could stay like this for a long time, caught in a twilight world between life and death."

The doctor rests his hand on the blonde girl's shoulder. "It's time to let her family in now. Maybe they'll be able to connect with her. We can't give up. Ever. Keep hoping, Phoebe."

"I will." She bends low and whispers in the girl's ear, "Annabelle, come back to us, please."

The doctor doesn't look like he's sure about anything, but the girl named Phoebe seems to feel reassured. She's not giving up hope. "Call me later. I'll keep her in my thoughts, but I have to leave. I don't feel very well."

"You never get sick, Phoebe. Let the nurse take your temperature. Maybe you're coming down with the flu."

"If I am, I better get out of here. You don't need someone with the flu walking around the hospital."

The doctor puts his hand gently on the blonde girl's forehead. "You don't feel like you have a fever. Go home and get some rest. You're too stressed out. You've been up all night. I'll call you later." And Phoebe leaves.

An old guy comes in and bends over the cold girl in the bed. He kisses her pale, waxy cheek. It's hard for him to get close enough, because of all the tubes and wires, but he's determined. He's crying, but not making any noise. I can tell he's crying, though, because my face feels wet from his tears. It feels like warm rain.

"Annabelle, honey, can you hear me?"

She can't hear him but I can. She can't feel his tears, but I can. Suddenly I know. He's her father.

"Mom should be here in about an hour. She had to drive out to Amherst to pick up Joe because his car broke down. Then she's going to swing through Boston and get Clem. Uncle Johnny called me when the 911 call came in at the station and I called your Uncle Aleister. He told us to forget about an ambulance and he sent the helicopter. Your mother and I had just gotten home. I jumped back into the truck and sped over here." He's wiping his eyes with the cuff of his flannel shirt as he explains all this to the motionless girl. He always wears those soft flannel shirts, never a sweater or a sweatshirt, always a flannel shirt and he has dozens of them. He smells like sawdust and the woods on a cold day. This man who is Annabelle's father doesn't belong here in the city. He belongs to the forest and the wild untamed meadows.

"Wake up, Annabelle, so I can bring you home. You hate the city. Let me bring you home, honey. The truck's down in the parking garage. You can ride shot gun. Sunrise is in two hours. You love watching the sun rise." He turns his face away from the girl and talks to the doctor. "Aleister, she feels too cold. Can't we warm her up somehow?"

The doctor's first name is Aleister. That's a British name. He doesn't sound like it, though. Maybe his parents were from the U.K., but I can tell he was born here in the U.S because he doesn't have a British accent. He sounds American.

"We're doing everything humanly possible and more, Bill. Keep talking to her. We can't break her connection to this world. If she hears the voice of someone she loves she might respond to it. Right now she's confused because she's in between the world of the living and the world of the dead. We can bring her back, though. I know we can."

"When?"

"Soon I hope. I have to check on some other patients. A nurse will be in to replace the IV bag in a minute. Don't leave the room. Annabelle needs to keep feeling the connection between you. Don't break it. Keep touching her. Keep talking to her. This method has worked before with other coma victims and she's way stronger than most people."

Dr. Aleister walks out. I don't know what he's talking about. She doesn't look very strong lying on the high bed with all those tubes and wires. She looks dead. Two more people come into the small room and shuffle around trying to find places to stand. Who are they? They're calling him Dad, so they must be her brothers. The big one staggers and his father has to help him over to the only chair.

"Sorry, Dad, she looks so still and she's always moving or talking or running. She never walks when she can run."

The smaller brother adds, "It doesn't look like her face because the expression isn't changing every second."

"It's her. She's in a coma. Hypothermia. They got her heart beating again, but she hasn't woken up yet. The doctor says to talk to her and touch her. It's worked with other coma victims before."

"What should I say? I don't know what to say. She doesn't even look like Annabelle. What do I say to her?" The big guy looks pissed off.

"Think, Joe. What would you say to her if she was awake?"

"Get up, dumbass. You're pissing me off."

"Nice start, Joe. That should cure her." The shorter brother rolls his eyes.

"Okay, Clem, you think of something."

"Don't die, Annabelle." He chokes and turns away.

"Mom's parking the car. She'll be up in a minute. She'll think of something." Joe gets up out of the chair, walks over and puts his arm around Clement's shoulder. A tear trickles down his cheek to his jaw line and he makes no attempt to wipe it away.

I hope the dead looking angel-face on the bed wakes up soon. These people are way too sad. She's depressing the crap out of everyone.

The nurse comes in and shoos Annabelle's father and her two brothers out of the room. She takes the bag off of the IV pole, detaches it and fastens another in its place. Then she inspects all of the other equipment. It's boring to watch her. I want the brothers to come back, with her dad. I want to leave this sad place. There's no one worth listening to anymore. I want to be someplace else.

Suddenly, I am someplace else. I look around me and I'm not in the hospital anymore. I'm floating, without moving my arms or kicking my feet, surrounded by nothing but beautiful, warm water, with gentle waves sparkling in the light.

This water is the perfect temperature, better than the nicest bath I've ever taken. I can't see the shore from where I am, even when I tread water, turn in a circle and scan all around me. But I'm not worried. I don't feel at all tired and I know I can go on swimming around and floating in this amazing water forever if I want to. I'll never sink. But I might dive down to see if there are any fish. Before I can dunk my head under, though, I spy someone in the distance, swimming toward me, with strong steady strokes. It's a young boy. As he gets closer I can see his long, dark, tangled hair and his thin, wiry body. I know him.

"Anthony, you're naked." I laugh. Seeing him like this is surprisingly funny and not embarrassing at all.

"Guess what!" He laughs back at me. "You are, too. We all are. But what are you doing here? You shouldn't be here yet. It's not time, Annabelle."

Why does that name sound so familiar? Annabelle? I know I heard that name somewhere recently. I'm so happy to see Anthony; I start to swim toward him.

"No, don't come closer. And don't go under the water. Keep your head up."

"Why?" The water temperature is so comfortable and perfect that I want to dive under and swim over to Anthony. I need to be closer to him and the fastest way to get there is to swim underwater and wiggle through this beautiful ocean like a sleek fish. I take a deep breath, tuck my chin down, put my hands by my sides and point my toes but before I can sink under the water, someone grabs my hand and pulls me up and out, totally out of the beautiful warm liquid. It's cold and I'm shivering. I want to go back where it's warm but the hand holding onto mine keeps pulling me. His grip is so strong that I can't yank my hand away. Looking all around, I try to find my wonderful ocean but I can't. It's gone. All I can see is the hospital room again.

Someone calls out "Annabelle" from far away. I try to pull my hand away again but the person with the big strong grip refuses to let go. The voice that's calling my name is closer now and very excited. "She's trying to pull her hand away from me."

"Don't let go. Hold on tight. Make her stay. Don't let her slip away again."

I don't like this loud, excited voice and this person with the strong grip. I want to hear Anthony speak my name again. I want to listen to his voice forever because I love him and I miss him.

"Annabelle, go back. I'll see you again one day, but not now, not yet." It's Anthony's voice. He's whispering so softly that I can barely hear him.

That loud voice that I hate keeps calling out "Annabelle!" He sounds closer than before, like he's shouting in my ear. Every time he says "Annabelle" he sounds closer and closer and he sounds wicked pissed off. I'd rather go back and swim in the warm ocean with Anthony who says my name so soft and sweet, with a voice full of love.

"Go, Annabelle. Wyatt needs you. You're the only one who can save him." Anthony's voice sounds so far away. I'm losing him but I need to ask him an important question.

"Save him from what?"

"Himself."

"How can I do that?"

"It's not my story to tell. Wyatt did something really stupid. But he has to tell you about it himself. No one else can. Go back."

Then the strong guy squeezes my hand again. I squirm and wriggle and try to make him let go, but he won't. Suddenly no one's holding my hand and I'm up around the ceiling of the hospital room somewhere, floating and looking down at the scene below. The gray-skinned girl is lying there like a beautiful, smooth-as-wax fallen angel; unnaturally pale and cold. A tall kid with messy hair is standing beside her, holding her hand in a death grip. The doctor's in the room and the nurse is explaining something to him. "She flat-lined. I called a code blue. Make him let go of her. Get the family out of here. Where's the team?"

"The team's not coming. Her heart's beating again, look." The doctor is barely moving his lips because his jaw is clenched. He seems really mad. But he's right, the machine's beeping again. The girl's lying very still and she looks kind of dead, but not quite as dead as she did two seconds ago.

The doctor speaks to the nurse again, in a quiet voice that's worse than yelling. Because he's in control of his anger, it seems all the more deadly. I've never heard a voice like his before. There's no human quality in it. He says, "The family just informed me that you told them to leave the room so you could change the IV."

"I always do it that way. There were too many people in here. I can move around more efficiently when no one else is in the room."

"My orders were for someone from her family to be in here at all times. You're job is not to question or change my instructions in any small way. Don't set foot in this room again, or you'll be working at a different hospital."

She appears to know better than to argue with him and leaves. I think she's scared of him.

"Who are you?" the doctor asks the big guy who's still holding onto the girl's hand.

"Wyatt Silver, sir. I'd shake your hand, but I'm not letting go of her. About a minute ago, Annabelle squeezed my hand. Then she tried to pull away. But now she's still again. We had her, though. She tried to come back. I know she did."

"Whoever you are, Wyatt Silver, you're right. And whatever you do, don't let go of her hand. Keep talking to her. It worked."

"Did she really die and then come back?" Wyatt asks.

"She definitely flat-lined. Someone from the nurses' station was monitoring her from there and called me when it happened. Your touch seems to have brought her back, Wyatt. Keep trying."

This Wyatt guy's big and very good-looking and muscular, with messy golden brown hair. His eyes are wild and they keep changing color. He's holding the almost dead girl's left hand in both of his, now, and his whole body's shaking because he's so mad. Through gritted teeth, he spits the unconscious girl's name out. "Annabelle."

No response.

He tries again and his voice seethes with anger. "Annabelle, come back here. I won't let you go. You can't go."

Why's he so mad at her?

Agony invades my body and all my senses, pain like I've never felt before, pain like I've never even imagined. And I'm freezing; I'm so cold my teeth can't chatter because my jaw's locked shut like it's been sealed with superglue. I try to open my eyes but even my eyes hurt. I can feel my eyeballs and all the ganglia that connect back up into my brain and everything's throbbing with freezing cold, horrible pain. The pain evolves into sharp, stabbing, brilliant blue ice picks of agony. My mind searches for numbness. I try to remember a place where everything wasn't so painful, so I can go back there, but I can't remember. I know it exists but I can't find it. So I finally wrench my eyes open and then I see him.

I see Wyatt and he still loves me. I can tell. I want to talk to him. I want to say his name, but my throat aches and I'm so cold I can't unlock my jaw. Finally, through clenched teeth I manage. "Wyatt, I'm cold."

What the hell's going on now? Everyone's talking at once, their voices filled with the most incredible joy, like the most talented, biggest church choir ever, singing the Hallelujah Chorus. Their excitement is like a million champagne corks popping. Everyone's hugging each other, except the big guy with the messy hair. He's bending over her, lifting her shoulders up off the bed so he can wrap both arms around her and bury his face in her tangled hair.

"She's gone again, but she's still alive," he murmurs against her skull. Then he does the most amazing thing. Without even shoving aside any wires or tubes or anything, he climbs onto the bed and wraps all of himself around her; his big, muscular arms, his long legs. He completely surrounds her with his body.

Her brother, Joe, sounds pissed off. "Hey, man, what the hell are you doing?"

Most of the equipment that used to be attached to her isn't anymore. Buzzers are buzzing and something's beeping rapidly, but the doctor doesn't seem to care.

The guy in the bed with her isn't fazed by any of this, either.

He looks over his shoulder for a second and says, "I don't give a damn about the wires and the machines. She's cold! I'm warming her up!"

The brother takes a step toward the bed, but the doctor stops him. "It's okay, Joe. He brought her back. Let him stay with her. I can work around him." Then he moves over to the bed, turns off all the things that are beeping and buzzing and picks up her arm. Dr. Aleister is checking her pulse the old-fashioned way, with his fingers. He looks at his watch and holds onto her wrist with his other hand. "Her pulse is really strong. And her flesh is warmer. She's coming back."

Then Dr. Aleister announces, to everyone in the room, "Don't leave her alone for even a split second. I don't care who comes in here and tells you to leave. Ignore them. Stay with her and stand firm. Call me and only me if anything happens or you have any questions. Don't call anyone else." Then he turns toward her father and says, " Bill, I need to talk to you."

The two of them step outside the room and stand hunched together in the hallway. The doctor looks around as if to make sure no one's nearby. As soon as he's sure they're alone, he whispers, "Bill, she's going to come around any second now and it's going to become evident that she can do what she does."

"What she does? What do you mean, Aleister?"

"Annabelle can heal faster than any other human on Earth. No one in this hospital has ever seen anything like it. We can't allow any other medical professional near her, only me. Even I don't know exactly what will happen, but I know it will be phenomenal. Unless you want her to be front page news, we have to get her out of here."

What the hell is he talking about? I look back into her hospital room and the big guy is still wrapped around her like he's never letting go. She looks alive, now, too. She's not gray or waxy anymore. Both of her brothers are standing in the corner, watching. The feisty one, Joe, is standing on the balls of his feet, ready for action. The other brother rests his hand on Joe's shoulder, as if to keep him in check.

Outside in the hallway all hell's breaking loose. A short, pretty woman, with long curly hair that's coming loose from whatever straggly arrangement she tried to organize it into, comes running up to Annabelle's father. The woman is crying and she flings herself into the father's arms.

"It's okay, Susannah. She's coming around. Wyatt's in there with her and Joe and Clement. She's going to be all right. We have other problems now." He hugs the woman and pats her back.

The doctor explains the situation. "We have to get Annabelle out of the hospital ASAP, because she's coming to and she's going to heal at the speed of light. We don't want to see her on the evening news or have her kidnapped by the CIA to be vivisected by a bunch of government psychos."

The father laughs, but not the way you laugh when you think something's funny. It's one of those spit-out-your-shock and surprise laughs. If he'd had a mouth full of coffee from that cup he's gripping, he would have spewed it out all over everyone. He wipes the shocked expression off his face with one hand and says, "We get the point, Aleister. How should we go about this?"

"First let me quickly explain what's happened, for Susannah's benefit because she just arrived." He turns toward the woman with the tumbling curls. "Annabelle has been hovering between life and death since she was rescued from the pond. I honestly don't know exactly what that's like, and it's not an exact science anyway. I'm basing my theory on what I've read about near death experiences, and my own intuition, which you know is beyond that of a normal human's."

"So what do you think?"

"I definitely know this much: Contact with the people she loves is what's kept her with us so far. I left orders for her not to be left alone in the hospital room. A nurse disregarded my orders and told Bill, Joe and Clement to leave so she could switch the IV bags. Annabelle flat-lined as soon as they left the room. Wyatt rushed in like a crazy man and brought her back, but not only that. When he spoke to her, she started to come out of the coma. He's actually in the bed with her right now, wrapped around her like one of those Mylar emergency blankets. Once she's awake, she'll heal fast and we don't want anyone asking any questions about why she's suddenly one hundred percent fine and healthy."

"Wyatt doesn't know about her self-healing powers and he can't find out. Annabelle doesn't want that."

Wow, the girl in the bed has some kind of weird special powers.

"Who here is strong enough to pry him off of her?" The father's voice sounds sarcastic.

"We have to think of a plan to get him to leave the room. Clement and Joe don't know, either, and even though they're her brothers, the less people who know about Annabelle, the better off we are. That's definitely how she wants it." Susannah keeps looking into the room while she's speaking. "I want to go in there and see her. It's killing me to stay out here."

"When you go in, Susannah, she's going to respond to you." The doctor grips both her shoulders and stares straight into her face. "We need to be ready with a plan, because things are going to happen fast and she'll attract a lot of attention. That nurse is already gossiping about how pissed I got when she kicked everyone out of the room and how Annabelle flat-lined and then came back without being revived by a team with paddles and CPR."

"Okay, but what should we do? How can we keep her self-healing powers a secret?"

"She doesn't need intensive care anymore; I'm going to fill out some very official-looking paper work to make it look like we're moving her to a private clinic closer to Eastfield. The trick will be to keep Clement, Joe and Wyatt out of her hospital room for at least a few minutes. As soon as Annabelle's coherent, we need to make her understand that she has to act a lot sicker and weaker than she feels.

Within the next hour, I want her moved the hell out of here. Bill, you need to be in your truck, with the engine warmed up and ready to go. I can hustle her into the staff elevator and down to the garage. Then she's on her way to Eastfield. She needs to understand that she has to act weak for at least a few days. She's going to want to run a marathon and she'll be eating like a high school football team. It's important that no one knows that but us."

"Okay, Aleister. I get it. Now can I see my baby?"

"Go for it."

The mother with the tangled hair bursts through the door and into the hospital room.

I open my poor, aching eyelids and see Wyatt's neck and his hair all matted and sweaty against it. Shivering, I cuddle in closer to his warmth. He murmurs and sighs and squeezes his arms and legs more tightly around me. I can feel his heart beating and mine beating with it, and it hurts with every thump. The pain starts in my chest and in my head, with my heart and my brain, and then it moves out and down into my shoulders and hips, throbbing and aching and I'm still cold, but not like before. My jaw isn't frozen shut anymore. I can move it, but it hurts like hell. I want to go back to a place I'm trying hard to remember. I can't think where the place is or how to get back there, but I'm going to try because everything hurts and I know it will stop hurting if I leave.

"Annabelle Blake, don't you dare leave." It's my mother.

"Mom." Something warm and wet is on my face. They're my tears. Wyatt starts kissing them away and I can feel the smile on his lips as they gently touch my face.

"She's back, Mrs. B."

My mother touches my hand. "She's so cold."

"She's actually way warmer now. You should have touched her before. When I first got here, she felt like a stone statue on the coldest day of winter."

"Thank you, Wyatt. Thank you for bringing my daughter back. Thank you for saving her life."

"It wasn't a choice. I didn't decide to do it. You would have done the same thing."

"Yes, but I'm her mother."

"I couldn't do anything else except be here with her and bring her back because I am nothing when I'm not with her."

Lifting her hand up from where it's resting on mine, my mother strokes Wyatt's hair. Doesn't anybody have a comb? These two have the messiest hair I've ever seen. Wyatt's is a wreck because he was wearing a hat. He must've been outside in the cold a short while ago. But my mom never wears hats; her hair just always looks like this. She's hopeless, always has been. Their hair is really annoying me and I hate the way I feel. My body's throbbing with pain. "Can't somebody help me? Everything hurts. My bones hurt. My head hurts. All of my muscles are aching and even my skin hurts."

My mother calls out to the hallway. "Aleister, can she have pain medication?"

The doctor walks in. "I don't want her to go back to sleep. Can you hang in there, Annabelle? If you stay awake, you can go home soon."

Nothing anyone has said sounds better than that. Except maybe all that stuff Wyatt said about being nothing without me. Suddenly I want to go home more than I've ever wanted anything. I also want some of my mom's tea, with a ton of honey, because it will taste like home to me. "Mom, can I have some tea?"

"Aleister, get me some hot water and some honey. I have a little chamomile mixture in my bag, sweetheart. We'll get you some tea and we'll get it fast."

Dr. Aleister doesn't look like he's used to following anyone's orders, but he seems to see the wisdom of doing what my mom tells him to and leaves. He's back in about two minutes with a steaming mug of hot water and three plastic containers of honey on a plate. They look like those cute little jelly packets you get in restaurants, but there's honey in them instead. My mother pulls a small paper bag full of dried flowers out of her gigantic purse. She never uses tea bags. After she dumps the flowers into the cup of hot water, I don't have to wait long before I'm sipping from a mug that's filled with mom's tea.

Wyatt loosens his grip on me enough so I can sit up. Then he insists on helping me hold the cup to my lips. Mom adjusts the pillows behind my back and neck. On about the fourth sip of tea, I notice that I'm not cold anymore and I can bear the pain now because it's fading. I smile at my mom and the smile she sends back my way lights up the universe.

"Wyatt, can I be alone with Annabelle for a few minutes?"

"Sure, Mrs. B, but I'll be right outside the door if you need me, if she gets too cold again or anything like that." He kisses my cheek about ten times and then presses his face against mine for about a minute. Finally he gets up out of the bed and it's a lot colder without him, but I can tell my mother has something important to say to me, so I don't complain.

As soon as he steps outside the door of my hospital room, she walks over and closes it gently behind him. Then she sits down on the edge of the bed. Her face is so full of love, she's glowing. "Annabelle, honey, you know you're healing faster now than normal humans heal."

"It hardly hurts at all anymore. I still feel cold, but not nearly as bad as before."

"We need to keep your talent for healing yourself a secret. Right now, only Dad, your uncle Aleister, Phoebe and Nathaniel know. I don't think we need to let anyone else in on our secret, do you?"

I like the way she's asking me, not telling me, not to say anything to Wyatt about my supernatural talent. I don't want him to know, but I'm glad she's letting me decide. I want him to love me for my human qualities, and not because I'm a phenomenon, so I decide not to tell him, not yet, anyway. "Right, I don't want anyone else to know. The less people who know, the better off I'll be."

"Then you need to pretend you're weaker and sicker than you feel. I'm sorry, but you'll have to try or Wyatt will get suspicious."

"The only thing is: I'm super hungry and I want a cheeseburger with ketchup and tons of fries."

My mother starts laughing like she's going to lose it and I shush her, so no one will come running in to see what's so funny.

"Nothing's open yet. It's four in the morning. I can send Wyatt to the hospital cafeteria to get you a bagel or something. Aleister has big plans for sneaking you out of here. Your official discharge papers will say you're going to a private clinic closer to Eastfield, but really you'll be coming home. Then I'll start cooking and you can eat, but you'll have to act sick when anyone's around if you want to keep your secret safe."

"Aleister's a genius. How did he get to be so devious?"

"Years of practice. Remember, my family has had to keep secrets to save their own lives for hundreds of years now."

"You're so good at it. It's scary."

"Let's put our plan in motion. Your only job is to manipulate Wyatt and act weak."

"The first part will be easy. The second part not so much. When can I get up? When can I go home? When can I start running again? When can I play tennis?"

"Cooperate, Annabelle. Don't screw this up."

"Okay, okay. Bring in my audience. I'm ready to perform." I ease my head back down until it rests on the pillows and smile a pathetically weak half smile that barely tweaks my lips up at the corners. Then I add a few anemic moans and bat my eyelashes, just to try and crack my mother up.

"Don't make me laugh. It doesn't fit in with the scenario."

I send an air kiss her way and wink. "Open the curtain. The stage is set. Bring in my audience."

Chapter 24

Home Again

We're able to pull it off because I act much sicker than I feel. Worrying about me has exhausted everyone except Wyatt and they all leave to go home. Finally my Uncle orders Wyatt to go home also, while he's still alert enough to drive safely. Just a few minutes after the boy who brought me back to life walks out the door, my dad sneaks me into his truck and we hit the highway.

I wish I could drive because I'm tired of sitting around, pretending to be sick and injured, but Dad says absolutely not, so I'm stuck watching the scenery and staring at Dad's profile as he chauffeurs me home. He's wearing a baseball cap with "Blake & Sons" embroidered on it. That's his construction company. My brothers usually work for him during breaks from school. Dad isn't a sexist or anything. I could work for him if I wanted to, but I don't because I stink at building stuff and I hate it. I'm clumsy and reckless, a bad combination. "Measure twice and cut once" isn't my motto. Mine is more like, "Forget to measure, cut too much, and screw everything up." So, it's Blake & Sons, not Blake & Sons & Daughter. That wouldn't fit on the hats, anyway.

The lights from the other cars on the South East Expressway flicker across my father's face. Gray and white stubble's sprinkled across his cheeks from not shaving. His gaze is focused on the road, but I guess he can sense that I'm looking at him, contemplating something, because he asks, "What is it, honey? Do you feel all right?"

"I feel amazing. I can't wait to go running tomorrow. I'm just hungry."

"I'm sure your mother will have plenty of food ready when we get home."

"Don't you think she'll be asleep? Everyone seemed so tired."

"Oh, I expect she'll nap a little, but you know her. She'll make something delicious and have it ready for when we get home. No one ever goes hungry at the Blake's house."

I think about how close I came to never going home again and tears spring into my eyes. "Dad?"

"What, sweetheart?"

"How did Mr. Silver know I was in the pond?"

"Wyatt called him."

"How did Wyatt know?"

"Anthony."

"Whoa. Anthony?"

"Yes. Wyatt was sleeping and he dreamed that he was swimming underwater in a very deep pond. Anthony was swimming underwater, too, and they swam up to each other. Then Anthony started speaking and his words appeared inside of these weird speech bubbles, like you'd see in a cartoon."

"What did Anthony say?"

"According to Wyatt, Anthony said that you were in danger because the water was too cold and too deep."

"I think I remember seeing Anthony, too, but it's hard to remember. I have a very clear memory of chasing Sammie through the woods and then falling through the ice, though. But that's the last thing I remember before I woke up in the hospital."

"You chased Sammie?"

"It looked like her. She was wearing an old-fashioned lacy white nightgown and she ran amazingly fast. Way faster than me. She ran out onto the ice and I followed her, to try and save her."

"Annabelle, it couldn't have been her. How could a two-year-old run faster than you?"

"I don't know, but she kept disappearing and then I'd run really fast and catch sight of her again. She called my name; she said 'Annaboo.' That's how she says it; so I knew it was her. It looked like Sammie, except I never saw her face, just her glittery yellow hair and her fast little bare feet."

"Do you remember anything else?"

"No, just following her out onto the ice. And I saw Anthony, but that part's really foggy. I just remember seeing him and talking to him but I can't recall what we said."

"I need to talk to Wyatt's dad and to Nathaniel."

"We now know that he's Nathaniel's dad, too." I smile but there's no humor behind it. "Maybe they can all come over later."

"Much later. You need to rest, whether you want to or not."

"I'm starting to feel a little sleepy."

"Close your eyes. We'll be home in less than a half hour."

My eyes fall closed and when I open them again, we're in the driveway.

Inside the house, Joe and Clem are asleep, but my mom's waiting for us in the kitchen with a pan of lasagna right out of the oven and some cheesy garlic bread. My favorites.

The three of us sit down and eat. Mostly I eat. No one else is in the mood to have lasagna for breakfast. After, I go upstairs, climb into bed and instantly fall asleep. When I wake up, it's almost dark out.

After a quick shower, I go downstairs and Nathaniel's sitting at the kitchen table with my parents. Jeff's nosing around under the table, looking for crumbs.

Mom smiles. "Hey, sleepyhead. Your brothers got tired of waiting for you to wake up and went out to visit friends. They'll be home later. Dad's driving them back to school tomorrow. They'll have to leave early because your father has to get back to work on that new house he's building in Freewater."

Jeff comes right up to me and starts sniffing me all over, like he's making sure I'm alive and okay. Nathaniel holds out his arms and when I step into them, he pulls me into his lap and crushes me in a huge hug. "We almost lost you," he whispers into my hair.

I pull away from him gently and sit down next to him at the table. "I'm here now and I'm fine. I'm better than fine. I'm so happy that it's just us and I don't need to act sick or weak. Mom, is there any leftover lasagna?"

She laughs and walks over to the fridge. "There's plenty. Do you want some, too, Nathaniel? Bill? Is anybody else hungry?"

Nathaniel gets all serious. "No thanks, Susannah. Annabelle, we need to talk about what happened last night."

"I can't believe it was just last night. It seems like a week ago. A year ago. The woods, the pond, the hospital. It almost seems like it never happened, like I was dreaming."

"It was real. It happened and we need to know everything. Start at the beginning and don't leave anything out, even if it doesn't seem significant."

"The first thing I heard was her giggle. I was alone, sitting in the chair over there by the window and the house was quiet. Then I heard a child giggle."

"Where did the sound come from?" Nathaniel covers my hand with his own, as if to make sure I'm still here with him.

"From inside my head but from outside, too. It must have been coming from outside the kitchen window because next I saw her hands."

"Her hands?"

"Yes. She smacked her little palms against the glass and they stuck there for a second." I stand up and walk over to the window. "I saw two tiny white hands; here and here." I point to the two spots low near the windowsill. "Her hands were white and the rest of the window pane was pitch black."

"Were you scared?"

"No, startled at first, by the slap of her hands against the glass, but not scared. I felt puzzled, curious."

"Then what?"

"She backed away from the window and all I could see was my own reflection."

"And?"

"And then she smooshed her face up against the glass. You know how that always looks so scary, when someone smooshes their face up like that?"

"Yes, I know. So then you got scared?"

I nod my head and look into Nathaniel's serious eyes. "I jumped back a step because her face looked grotesque and distorted. Then she said my name and I wasn't afraid anymore because I knew it was Sammie."

"How did you know?"

"It sounded like her voice and she said 'Annaboo'. That's how Sammie pronounces my name."

"And when you thought you were sure it was Samantha out there, what did you do?"

"Then I was afraid, but not for myself. A two-year-old was wandering around in the dark, alone. It was eleven o'clock at night. I was afraid for Samantha. She was in danger. I went out to find her so I could bring her back in here and call her parents."

"But you couldn't find her?"

"I saw her, but she ran away. I couldn't catch up to her. She was wearing an old-fashioned white nightgown and she was barefoot. She ran across the backyard and into the woods. I followed her but she ran too fast."

"Annabelle, you're on the varsity cross-country team. I've seen you run a mile in six minutes. What two-year-old could beat you in a race?"

"I know. It didn't make sense, but I could see her and I could hear her so I ran after her."

"Where did she go?"

"All the way through the woods to Deep Water Pond."

"And she ran out onto the ice?"

"Yes she did and I followed her. I ran as fast as I could across the ice but it cracked and I went under and I saw Anthony's face under the ice, in the freezing cold water."

"Do you realize now that it wasn't Sammie?"

"Then who was it? The baby in the white nightgown looked real and she said 'Annaboo'."

"It was the ghost of Katherine Hayward. And when she was alive, that's how she killed Rebecca."

"Holy shit."

My mother doesn't yell at me for swearing. Her gaze is glued to Nathaniel's face and her mouth is open, just like my father's and just like mine. It's all starting to make sense. Finally we can link the past with the present.

Nathaniel continues to explain. "I didn't figure it out until you were already out of danger. Your dad called me early this morning, right after you fell asleep. He told me about the baby running through the woods. Then it all fell into place. I knew exactly what happened to you and what happened on the night Rebecca died. She didn't commit suicide. Katherine lured her out onto the ice. It was murder.

In March of 1867, at around eleven o'clock at night, Katherine took little Jonathan out of his cradle, carried him through the woods to Deep Water Pond and sent him toddling out onto the ice. Then she yelled loud enough to wake up Rebecca. When Rebecca came outside, the baby started walking across the pond, toward his real mother. Little Jonathan could've died that night, too, along with Rebecca. Katherine didn't care."

"But Rebecca cared and she did the same thing I did when I saw a baby walk out onto the ice. She risked her life trying to save Jonathan."

"Rebecca fell through before she could reach her son. He weighed much less than she did, so he was able to stand safely on the icy surface of the pond."

"But she couldn't. And she died. Like I did. I died out there. Didn't I?"

My mother starts sobbing quietly. Dad walks over and puts his arms around her.

Nathaniel pauses for a moment and then answers my question. "Your heart stopped beating three times. Once near the edge of the pond, but my father brought you back. Then again in the helicopter, on the way to the hospital and the EMTs saved you. The last time happened at the hospital."

"Wyatt saved me."

"Yes, you responded to my brother's voice and his grip on your hand."

It sounds weird to hear Nathaniel say "my brother".

"Then he climbed into your hospital bed and you regained consciousness. Your parents have been telling me all about it."

The rest I remember pretty clearly. "It hurt like hell when I started to wake up and I didn't want to feel all that pain. I wanted to go back to a place where I wasn't in agony but I heard Wyatt's voice and I felt his hand around mine and I came back."

"Do you remember anything about the time when you were gone?"

"Maybe. I think I remember something. At the time, nothing felt real; I felt like I was dreaming. I could see everything that was happening in the hospital. But I wasn't there. No one could see me."

"What did you see, Annabelle?"

I close my eyes so I can focus better on what I saw. "There was a girl in a hospital bed and her family was there in the room with her. She looked dead."

"What else?"

"Then her family left and a nurse came in. That's when the scene in my dream changed. The hospital room disappeared and I was swimming in a beautiful, warm ocean and Anthony was there, but he was far away." I laugh. "He was close enough, however, so I could tell that he was naked."

"Did he talk to you?"

"He told me not to swim any closer to him and not to put my head under the water."

"Did you listen to him or did you go under?"

"I wanted to go under. I took a deep breath, so I could sink down deep and feel the beautiful warm water all around me. But someone grabbed me and yanked me out of the ocean."

"Wyatt."

"He yelled at me and he wouldn't let go of my hand. It hurt like hell, not just my hand, but my whole body. I was freezing but he wouldn't let me go so I could swim in that warm ocean again with Anthony."

"Good boy, Wyatt. You did the right thing." Nathaniel speaks directly to Wyatt even though he's not in room with us.

"He saved my life."

Dad speaks up for the first time. "He had to get in line. First Wyatt's father brought you back. Then the EMTs. Finally Wyatt grabbed you and yanked you out of the coma. Then you really came back to us. You opened your eyes. You spoke."

"You asked for a cheeseburger." My mother's smiling but a tear's trickling down her cheek, too.

"With ketchup and fries. Can I take the car over to Five Guys?"

"No," my dad answers, but he's smiling. "You just ate another giant helping of lasagna."

"With garlic bread, again," my mother adds.

"Okay, I can wait for the cheeseburger, but when can I go running? I hate all this sitting around."

Everyone starts laughing, but I'm not joking.

Mom speaks to me in a voice she might use to explain things to a kindergartner. "You need to wait as long as it would take for a normal person to recuperate from this kind of ordeal. Otherwise, everyone's going to get suspicious. Someone might find out about your supernatural ability to heal yourself. Someone we don't even know. Someone who might want to study you and find out what makes you the way you are."

"Okay, okay. I get it. How long would it take a normal person to come back from this?"

Dad's expression is grave. "Normal people don't come back, Annabelle. There was no supply of oxygen to your brain and your heart stopped beating. Three times. No one else has ever survived an ordeal like this one. Aleister filled out all your charts. He was the only person who examined you closely. There's no official record of exactly what happened to your body. Right now you're a walking, talking miracle but no one knows it except Aleister and the people in this room."

"There's no telling what will happen if anyone finds out." Nathaniel backs my dad up.

Mom sounds worried. "We can't let that happen."

"I agree. One hundred percent. But you still haven't answered my question. When can I start running again?"

"You're relentless."

"Thank you, Nathaniel. Now could someone please answer my question?"

"Aleister says at least a week. Take it slow. Act weaker and more tired than you are and you can run again in a week. We'll tell people you're home from the hospital tomorrow. Your brothers know not to mention that you're here now. Jackson, Oliver and Wyatt think you're sealed up in a private clinic for a special twenty-four-hour observation period with Aleister as your attending physician. They're expecting to be able to visit you when you come home. Tomorrow. And they're expecting to see a weaker, quieter Annabelle than the one they're used to."

"I get it. I'll cooperate. I can do this for a week."

"I've thought of a nice quiet activity for you: keeping up with your schoolwork online. I noticed that you haven't even asked about that."

"Mom, I'm a senior. What schoolwork?"

"Very funny," my mother says, but she isn't laughing. She has no sense of humor when it comes to grades.

"What about Katherine? Am I safe from her?"

"Yes. Someone put the stones back on her grave. Oliver went out to check and they were all in position," Nathaniel answers.

"But if that's all it took, why didn't we put the stones back a long time ago?"

"Because Katherine needed to return to her grave and she wouldn't unless she believed she had accomplished her goal. She needed to think her evil mission here on Earth was over. Then she had to be at rest long enough for the stones to be put back in their places so they could hold her down there; where she belongs."

"Never to rise again." Right after these words come out of my mouth, I pause for a minute, to process all of this. "I think I understand."

"She thought you were dead, Annabelle," Nathaniel continues to explain, "so she went back to her grave and while she was at rest, someone put the stones in place so we could keep her there."

"Nathaniel, she didn't just 'think' I was dead. I *was* dead. I died."

"Technically, yes, but not permanently."

"Obviously, duh." I'm joking, but inside my stomach, the lump of lasagna does a quick somersault.

Nathaniel reassures me, saying, "Anyway, Katherine wanted you to die and she thought you were dead. Someone seized that moment, the moment when your heart stopped beating. Her spirit went back to the grave and an unidentified person put the stones back in their rightful places. She's no longer a threat."

"Wow. I wonder who did it."

"So do we, honey, but we may never know. No one's admitting to it," my dad says.

"We think she'll leave us alone now," Nathaniel reassures me.

"You're sure?"

"Katherine can't return unless someone moves the stones again, but we'll be careful just in case."

"The Littlefields want to build a crypt over the spot, concrete, with no entrance. I volunteered to do the work for free. If I start tomorrow it shouldn't take more than a couple of days."

"Thanks, Dad. That works for me. Can I at least use the elliptical? Until Clem and Joe get home. Then I promise to act sick."

"Go, go. Get out of here. Run your silly little butt off, Annabelle. I'll get no peace until you're up and around doing precisely what you want to do." Dad laughs and shakes his head.

I hop up, run around the table and kiss everyone on the cheek, including Jeff. Except he doesn't really have a cheek, so I kiss his jowl. Then I scoot upstairs, pull on shorts, a t-shirt and sneakers; scoot back down and put *Catching Fire* into the DVD player. But while I'm watching it, I don't think about my latest fictional crush, Finnick Odair. The whole time I'm pumping away on the elliptical, I think about Wyatt and how I'll see him again tomorrow.

Chapter 25

The Truth about That Night

The next day Wyatt arrives at my house a few hours before suppertime.

"I left track practice early, ran home and showered. Got here as soon as I could." He's whispering, with his lips against my neck and his arms wrapped tight around me. He feels big and solid and warm, like holding onto him could save someone's life.

We head out back to take a short, slow walk through the woods, because that's all I'm supposed to be capable of. I'm trying to act all weak and sickly, but it's hard. I want to run and jump because Wyatt's holding my hand and we're together and it's a beautiful, spring-like afternoon, the first really warm day so far this year. In a few weeks, it will be my birthday and I'll be eighteen. I love my birthday. And I love being with Wyatt again. I'm nervous but it's a happy kind of excitement; not anxious, worrying excitement. I have bazillions of those traditional, cliché, fluttery butterflies flapping around inside my stomach so fast, they're creating a wind tunnel. And they're the most colorful, most beautiful insects on the planet. I want to run and dance and skip and sing and hold onto Wyatt's hand the whole time I'm doing it.

Then he starts talking about the night of the soccer game, the night of Liz Dalton's party. Suddenly, the butterflies in my stomach spin little black chrysalises around themselves. I don't have to fake a heavy, slow, miserable feeling. It comes naturally to me. Wyatt turns to face me in the speckled shade of the forest.

"Annabelle, I feel guilty as hell. That's why I never called you back that night."

I don't want to talk about this right now. I want to talk about the gorgeous weather and about getting into college and about my birthday and how much I love presents. I want to talk about anything but this. But he persists. "I owe you the truth, but I feel so guilty about what I did that the words get stuck inside me and they won't come out."

"What did you do? I heard from Meg that you got wasted and hooked up with Colleen, but I figured it was only payback, for me kissing Anthony. I thought we could maybe work past that. Forgive, forget. No?"

"Once you hear the whole story, you probably won't forgive me for a long time and you'll never forget. I know I won't."

"What the hell did you do, Wyatt?" He's scaring me.

"Let me start at the beginning. And remember, I'm not making excuses. There's no good reason for what I did and

I take full responsibility. I own this mistake and I need to explain what happened. I want you to forgive me, but I won't blame you if you can't. Nathaniel and Oliver and Jackson know the whole truth. But don't be mad at them for not telling you. It wasn't their secret to tell. Only I can tell you."

He lets go of my hand and the whole forest grows dark and cold. The chrysalises in my stomach start cracking open, but instead of butterflies, big, black scorpions emerge. Tons of them. They're crawling and hissing around inside me, flexing their stingers. I close my eyes and anticipate the pain that's about to pierce my life and inject a horrible, deadly poison into my world. "Okay, so spit it out. I'll never be ready. Just do it."

"Ryan called Oliver that night, because I got really drunk. I was so messed up. Oliver came to get me. He knew right away that he'd need Nathaniel. He could have used your mother's help, too, but that was out of the question. He couldn't call her because she's your mother and I had betrayed you."

"Oliver couldn't call her because you were with Colleen."

"Right. So Nathaniel rushed over and helped us out. That's one reason why I got so pissed about him putting the moves on you. I was ridiculously jealous, but that wasn't all. He knew what I was going through and used the opportunity to get closer to you. I hated him for that."

"Don't hate him. He saved me from dying of loneliness this winter."

"He could have done that by just being a good friend to you."

"Wyatt, Nathaniel and I can never be more than friends. He knows it and so do I."

"I guess I realize that now. But I was out of my mind with jealousy and missing you. And it was all my fault. If I had listened to Nathaniel and followed his advice, none of this would have happened."

It's time for Wyatt to spill it out and it's time for me to hear it no matter what the outcome will be. "None of *what* would have happened?"

I try to keep my face expressionless. I want to be close to Wyatt again, more than anything I've ever wanted before. But I don't know if that's possible. First I need to hear the truth; the whole story.

Wyatt takes a deep breath. I watch the struggle in his ever-changing eyes and I can tell by the set of his mouth he's gritting his teeth. Finally, he unlocks his rigid jaw and speaks. "After we lost the soccer game, I went home and showered. Ryan called and asked if I wanted to go to a party at Liz Dalton's. Liz's parents were in the Bahamas or someplace. Anyway, I said sure, he could pick me up, but he didn't want to drive because we'd be drinking. His older brother said he'd drop us off and we could call him to pick us up later."

"Thanks a lot, Ryan."

"None of this is his fault. I could've said no. I should've said no. Nathaniel has warned me many times that mediums can't drink alcohol."

"I didn't know that. Why not?"

"It makes sense if you think about Anthony and how I didn't always have control over the channeling. Mediums always have to be in control."

"And alcohol makes you lose control. I never thought of it that way."

"We can have a couple of beers, but we can never get wasted. If we're out-of-control drunk, anyone can take over. Anyone's ghost. It's like having an open house and putting those balloons on the mailbox: an open invitation. Spirits can barge in. Horrible, evil things can happen and we can't stop them from happening."

"So why did you ignore Nathaniel's warning?"

"Because I'm a stupid douche. I was pissed at you, for kissing Anthony. I was pissed at Anthony for kissing you. I missed Anthony like there was a giant hole in my life that could never be filled. I knew he wouldn't be back. Then, during the soccer game I whiffed that shot and we were out of the play offs. That really put me over the edge. So I went out and did something stupid and self-destructive. I couldn't pound down the drinks fast enough."

"Wyatt!" I can't think of anything else to say.

"There are probably deeper and darker reasons for what I did, too. Psychological reasons. Like the whole situation with my parents and my fears about being abandoned by the people I love most. Jackson's trying to help me work through all that shit."

Wyatt's dad left for California when Wyatt was fifteen and never even invited him to visit. Then, last summer, Wyatt's mother was going to have him committed to a psychiatric facility because she thought he was suffering from hallucinations. In reality, though, he was seeing and hearing the spirits of dead people. He's a medium and he can't help it. He communicates with ghosts and they can talk to him, too. Fortunately, instead of getting locked up in a psyche ward, Wyatt moved in with Oliver. Oliver and Jackson love him and believe in him. I still love him and I used to believe in him. I thought that my love and Oliver's love would be enough to help Wyatt stay strong, to ease his loneliness, but I guess it wasn't enough. Not on the night of Liz Dalton's party, anyway.

I'm furious with Wyatt for his self-destructive behavior, but maybe I shouldn't judge him because his parents hurt him so badly and I have the most loving family ever. They've loved me unconditionally since the moment I was born. Oliver loves Wyatt like that, and now Jackson does, too, but the pain caused by his parents' abandonment still obviously runs deep and strong inside of Wyatt sometimes. So I don't hate him. I'll never know what that kind of rejection feels like and I'm thankful for it.

"Wyatt, you could have died!"

"I didn't think about that. I only thought about obliterating the pain and the alcohol was doing a good job. I walked into the party with Ryan and he went over to the cooler and fished out a couple of icy beers. I remember how good it felt rushing cold down my throat and how I started to feel relaxed and not so miserable anymore. Ryan stuck with just having a few beers, but I didn't. Almost as soon as we arrived, Colleen came over to me and she had a water bottle filled with vodka. She was already wasted and she was all over me. I tipped her water bottle up to my lips and started chugging, figuring if I got drunk enough, maybe I could manage a little payback for the time you kissed Anthony. The thought of making out with Colleen didn't appeal to me, but I thought if I was totally trashed I could do it. And if people at the party saw us together and gossiped about it, you'd find out and know how I felt when you kissed Anthony."

"That's not the same at all! It was totally different. I kissed your lips, even if Anthony was controlling the whole thing. Plus Anthony was leaving us, forever. It might have been wrong of me, but the situation was completely different." I turn away from him and start walking back toward my house, fast. I don't care if he notices that I'm strong and well. I feel horrible inside and I don't care about anything except moving farther away from Wyatt as fast as possible.

"Wait, Annabelle! Come back." He runs after me, catches up with me in seconds and grabs my hand. I wrench it out of his grasp. I missed his touch so much when we were apart, but now I don't want him near me.

He doesn't try to hold my hand again, but we keep walking together, side by side, back toward the house. "I know what you did with Anthony was way different. I know it now and I knew it then, too, but that night, I didn't care. I have no good reason or excuse for my behavior. I snapped because I felt angrier than I've ever felt before. And now I'm completely disgusted with myself; sad and miserable down into my bones because I own it. I did it. I got drunk fast and it was the stupidest thing I've ever done. But, Annabelle, I swear I never even kissed Colleen. He did. I've never found her at all attractive anyway, plus, she was so drunk she was drooling on me. By the time I was wasted enough to even imagine kissing her without gagging, he took over."

"Who?"

"Jake Stone."

"Holy shit!" The legend. The ghost story. The guy who died when he drove his car into Lake Sippiwicket. "What the hell!"

"You've got the place right, Hell. That's where he belongs."

In the legend about Jake Stone's ghost, he comes out of the lake where he died and knocks on the doors of the houses nearby. If you answer your door he stands there, dripping wet, and asks to use the phone because he drove his car into the lake. Then he disappears. Wyatt's story isn't making sense to me yet. But I hang in there and keep listening. "Okay, so tell me about Jake Stone."

"We were all inside, partying. Colleen was hanging all over me with her arms around my neck. Ryan yelled at me over the noise of the crowd. He was trying to convince me that we should go home; that I should stop drinking. He tried grabbing my arm and dragging me toward the door. He told me I needed some air and he wanted to go outside to call his brother. He'd tried texting but his brother hadn't texted him back, so he wanted to try calling. Except he couldn't hear well enough to make the call inside. The crowd at the party was too noisy."

"All right. I get that part. So far, so good."

"Just as Ryan grabbed the doorknob, someone knocked on the door. Ryan was still holding onto my arm and Colleen was wrapped around me, slobbering and pawing at me. Ryan turned to look back at us and then we heard the heavy pounding on the door again."

"Did Ryan open the door to see who it was?"

"No. He said he was worried that it was the cops who were knocking. He seemed unsure about whether or not he should open the door. The people around us were oblivious. I don't think they heard anything."

"So Ryan didn't open the door."

"No, he let go of the doorknob. But there was a window right there, and I didn't see any flashing blue lights. I was sick of Colleen hanging all over me. I wanted Ryan to call his brother and get us a ride home. So I reached past him and opened the door. A kid about our age was standing there, dripping wet. There was a puddle of water, spreading all around his feet. He was big and beefy, like a football player. His hooded sweatshirt was hanging on him, soaked through. His hair was longish and dripping into his eyes. He kept blinking. Then he spoke."

Wyatt lowers his voice, to imitate the wet guy's voice. "Hey, man, can I use your phone? I drove my car into the pond, but I managed to climb out before it went under."

Ice zings up my spine and flash-freezes my scalp. Wyatt pauses and takes a deep breath. When he starts speaking again, I'm relieved to hear his normal voice.

"The sound of his voice sobered me up a little, but my thinking was still pretty fuzzy. I stood there paralyzed and Ryan pulled me away from the door, back into the house. I tried to shake Colleen off of me and looked around to see if I could find any of her friends in the crowd, so I could hand her over. I remember pushing her toward Liz who grabbed her, to keep her from falling down. Then Ryan said we should call someone to help the dude who drove his car into the lake. If the cops showed up, though, we'd all get arrested for underage drinking. I wanted to avoid that, but we needed to make sure the guy didn't need an ambulance or anything. So I suggested we should at least check him out."

"Then what happened?"

"I stepped closer to the doorway to get a better look at the dude but no one was on the porch. So I walked all the way out, onto the front steps and looked around. When I looked down, at the spot where the guy had been standing, the floorboards on the porch were completely dry. I opened my mouth to say something to Ryan, but then Colleen came up to me and yanked on my arm. She was trying to pull me back toward the house, into the party. I took a step toward her and staggered into what felt like a huge, solid wall of ice. It literally knocked my soul right out of my body. And that was that. I wasn't inside of my body anymore. Jake Stone was."

"So the guy on the porch wasn't real?"

"Oh, yeah, he was real, all right. He wasn't alive, though. He didn't belong here on Earth with the rest of us."

Tears of fright sting my eyes and I blink. "I've heard the ghost story before but I thought it was just a legend. You know, one person says something and then everyone who repeats it exaggerates."

"They weren't exaggerating. It really happened. One night a few years ago, Jake Stone got drunk and drove his car into the lake near Liz's house. He drowned. Ever since then, some nights people who live near the lake hear him knocking on their doors. If someone opens the door, they always see a big guy, dripping wet. He tells them he drove his car into the lake and he needs to make a phone call. Usually, that's where the stories about Jake Stone's ghost end. But this time, when he knocked on the door, a medium answered. Me. And I was out of control drunk, so Jake got his big opportunity to stick around a little longer than usual."

Raising my hand to my throat, I whisper, "Oh no!"

"Oh yes, Annabelle. When he was alive, Jake Stone was a big, strong, mean kid, who had a reputation for getting wasted and finding girls who were really drunk and hooking up with them. And I unwittingly gave him a golden opportunity to do exactly what he liked to do, what he had always done when he was alive. So that's what he did."

"He could take over your body easily because you were so drunk."

"Yes, it happened exactly like Nathaniel warned me it would. I was so wasted that I didn't care about anything anymore. Jake busted his way in and I couldn't stop him. I issued a special invitation to him to do what he did best when he was alive."

"What was that?"

"Annabelle, don't be naïve."

"With Colleen?"

"She was just his type that night: drunk and sloppy."

I feel like I should be crying right now, but the tears don't come. "Wyatt!"

"I know! You couldn't be more disappointed in me than I am in myself. It was revolting. It was repulsive. I hate to even think about it or talk about it. I feel sick all over again. But you need to know the truth."

"So tell me the truth, Wyatt. What happened that night?"

"Don't try to imagine it. The reality is worse than anything you can dream up. The worst part is, as soon as Jake took over my drunken body, I sobered up. It was torture. I knew what was happening and I couldn't get control back. I couldn't stop him. He did something truly despicable and he was inside my body the whole time he was doing it. He grabbed Colleen's hand and pulled her up the stairs, to Liz's room. Then, when they got inside the room, Colleen turned and smiled up at him. Jake closed the door and locked it."

"No one did anything to stop them?"

"Annabelle, it was a party. No parents were there. Everyone was wasted. Ryan banged on the door a few minutes after Jake locked it, but it was already too late."

"What about Colleen's friends? She was drunk. Wasn't anybody watching out for her? Didn't anybody care? You two weren't even going out together and she went into Liz's room with you, or at least she thought it was you and then you locked the door. If it was Meg or Jen, I would have tried to do something to stop them."

"Her friends aren't like that. They thought it was funny. All the Juicies were wasted, too. No one cared if Colleen did something she'd regret later."

"And she did something she'd regret later?"

"Yes, and I did something I'll regret for the rest of my life. It wasn't the first time Colleen got drunk and ended up with someone. Maybe it was the first time she did it with someone she wasn't in a relationship with. But it wasn't her first time ever."

"Maybe you should get tested." I can't believe I'm suggesting this to Wyatt, but somebody has to.

"I know. That's what Oliver said. But I had condoms with me."

"You *what*?"

"I always keep a couple in my wallet. Oliver gave them to me. A lot of guys' parents do. Just in case."

"Just in case of what?"

"'In case the opportunity presents itself.' That's how Oliver explained it. I always hoped that the 'opportunity would present itself' with you, Annabelle. Remember that night on the couch at my house? Oliver and Jackson went out. We had a fire going in the fireplace. I asked you to go up to my room with me?"

"I remember."

"You said no. But if you ever said yes, I wanted to be ready."

"Okay. So you just happened to be ready when the 'opportunity presented itself' with Colleen. I get it. I hate it. But I get it."

Wyatt continues his horrifying story. "Jake was too drunk to think about condoms; either that or he didn't care. She wasn't his girlfriend. It wasn't his body. He wasn't going to get a disease or have to pay child support if anything happened. That would be my job."

"Because it was your body."

"I don't need to be reminded of that, Annabelle." Wyatt looks, at this moment, as if he might cry. Then he sucks it up and continues. "Fortunately, even though Colleen was really drunk, she thought to ask Jake if he had a condom and he looked in my wallet and found one. She knew that we needed to be careful. We needed protection."

"Because it wasn't her first time."

"No, but it was mine. Except it wasn't me. It was Jake Stone."

I want to wrap my arms around him, but a double-edged emotional sword, razor sharp, lethal and silent, is lying between Wyatt Silver and me right now. We're both afraid to move because if one of us speaks or reaches out for the other one, the blade will cause a permanent injury. One of us will be maimed forever, or worse. The only way to avoid horrible and inevitable pain is to distance myself from Wyatt; to move as far away from him as I can, as fast as possible. I turn to flee but then spin back around a second later and face him.

"You told Oliver everything?"

"Yes. I told Oliver everything. Like I always have, as far back as I can remember."

"Wyatt, you always tell Oliver everything?" I'm thinking about some very private moments that Wyatt and I have shared.

He reassures me. "Well, not every single little detail about everything, but definitely everything major that happens in my life."

"And this was major."

"Life-changing major, life-threatening major. I feel sick whenever I think about it; like I've never felt sick before, my stomach, my head, but worse, my soul. When Jake grabbed possession of my body, it was nothing like when Anthony took over. Jake Stone's soul is horrible and dark. It's like his very existence was corrupted by a deadly, foul, highly contagious virus. And that virus is called Evil. I don't want to ever feel like that again. I can never forgive myself, so I know you can never forgive me."

"And Nathaniel knew and didn't tell me?"

"Oliver called him over that night to make sure Jake wouldn't make a return appearance. And to help us understand what had happened."

"And Nathaniel didn't tell me."

"It wasn't his story to tell. I had to tell you myself."

I cover my face with both of my hands, as if I could shield myself from the truth. "I want to go back in time; to before you started to tell me. I wish I had never heard any of this. I don't want to know."

"We can't be together unless you know, and we have to be together. You have to know everything that happened. We can't travel backwards in time, Annabelle. I don't expect you to forgive me right now, but maybe eventually. Please try to understand."

I've missed Wyatt horribly. And his only intentional action was to get completely drunk in a reckless and ridiculous way, after Nathaniel warned him not to. I've been reckless before, out of boredom, out of frustration. Wyatt did what a lot of people have done before. He felt pain and he tried to numb it with alcohol. The rest of what occurred the night of Liz Dalton's party happened without his consent. He wasn't controlling his own body.

I try to wrap my mind around the fact that Jake Stone, whoever the hell he was, did the rest. I start to feel sorry for Colleen, because she's also Jake's victim, and the other girls, too: the young women that he preyed on when he was still alive. If there is a hell, I hope Jake Stone burns in it forever.

Wyatt starts to fill in some more details. "Jake made a fast exit as soon as he had accomplished what he wanted to accomplish. Then Ryan started banging on the door. He yelled to me that we needed to go home, that he was going to call Oliver. He was afraid I'd blacked out. Colleen got up, unlocked the door and opened it and then Ryan came in and dragged me out of there. I barely remember that part because by then, I was inside my own body again and I was still really drunk. When Oliver came to pick us up, Ryan had to help me out to the car. I could barely walk. He opened the door, shoved me in and jumped in after me. I remember hearing Ryan say that he hoped I hadn't ruined everything for myself."

On the path in the forest, Wyatt and I stand and face each other silently, with a few feet in between our bodies. I concentrate really hard, so my mind and my emotions can absorb the enormity of what he did. I close my eyes because I can't even look at him right now and I tell him, "Ryan was right. You did ruin everything."

"Annabelle, please listen to me. It was torturous. When Jake was with Colleen, I could see it. Not with my eyes, because, in those few horrible moments, he lived behind my eyes. But I envisioned the whole experience and I couldn't shut it out. I couldn't close my eyes. Only Jake could. Annabelle, I promise; I didn't feel anything. Physically. I don't know what it felt like to be with Colleen. Jake knew. I only knew what it felt like not to be able to stop him."

The horror of that whole night is descending on me faster than I can make sense of it. I can't listen to Wyatt anymore. I can't even look at him right now. "I need time, Wyatt. Time to think."

"Annabelle, I don't want to give you any more time. I've lost enough time with you already. You almost died. I could have lost you forever. I know I did something horrifically stupid and immoral, but I can't pay for my mistake by losing you. If I could live that night over again, like I wish for, every second of every day, it would never have happened, but I can't. I can't go back and change it."

"I wish we could go back, too. I feel so sad and angry. I can't decide anything right now. It's too complicated."

"This fall, when I saw you for the first time, in history class, I fell in love with you, but it wasn't love at first sight. I recognized you. Even though I'd never met you before, I knew you, in my heart, with my whole body, my mind, my soul. I knew you."

"I was in denial then, but I felt it too."

He smiles. "Remember how you'd sworn off boys?"

"Cuz of Matt Riley. He broke my heart."

"You barely even spoke to me, no matter how hard I tried to start up a conversation."

"I liked you though. I felt a really strong attraction to you, right from the start. You were hard to ignore."

"See, we're meant to be together, Annabelle. We both felt it, even in the very beginning."

"Maybe it's just because we both have a sixth sense. Maybe we mistook a deep, life-changing supernatural bond for love. Maybe we don't love each other; we connected on a paranormal level, instantly, and it felt like we thought love would feel."

"Stop over-analyzing, Annabelle, and just feel it. I love you. I'm sure of it. Nothing and no one will ever change that for me. I promise you I will never take a chance with our love again. I want only you and I want you forever."

Wyatt doesn't ask if he can kiss me. If he did, I'd say no. He cups my shoulders with his big hands and tries to ease me toward him. I put my hands on his chest and push, but he's way bigger and stronger than me. He pulls me forward until our faces are within an inch of each other and he kisses my mouth with the lightest, faintest touch of his lips. His kiss is like a whispered question. *"Do you still love me?"*

And I answer him without words, without thinking. I shove him away.

Turning my back on him, I walk away from Wyatt, in the middle of the first warm, sunny, spring-like afternoon of the year. I want to forget about the winter and the cold and the nightmare of being without him. I want to love him. But no matter what he says, I'm not sure he loves me. I might never feel sure that he loves me again.

What if he loses control and Colleen's right there, all over again, waiting for her opportunity? And I'm not? What if it's not Colleen, but some other girl? I can't be with Wyatt all the time to watch over him. I need to be able to trust him. It's not only these thoughts that plague me, either. Something else has always given me doubts, even before this. What if Wyatt only connects with me on a paranormal level? What if he only loves me because I'm different? He doesn't love the ordinary girl, the girl who sobs so loud during every sad movie that the other people in the theatre laugh at her. He doesn't love the girl who doubts herself every time she ties on her running shoes or picks up her tennis racket. What if he yells at me when I start with the hiccups that won't stop? What if he hates that I slurp when I eat ice cream or lasagna or any other incredible tasting food that's even a little bit messy? What if he doesn't love the awkward girl with a long nose, a neck like a llama's and a flat chest? What if he doesn't love the ordinary me that's inextricably connected to my extraordinary and timeless soul?

I turn around and Wyatt's right behind me. Hope springs into his eyes.

"Go away! Leave me alone!" I start running and I don't care if he knows how strong I am. I don't care how suspicious he might get. I sprint as fast as I can until I get to my house. As soon as I'm inside, I slam the door as hard as I've just slammed the door to my heart and I lock it, leaving Wyatt outside. So he can go home and ask himself his own questions that have no answers.

As quickly as it appeared, all my furious energy fades and I trudge up to my room.

Now it's my turn not to return his ridiculously persistent calls; to read his pleading texts and not answer them.

* * * *

Wyatt's pursuit of me is organized and relentless. He texts me at least fifteen times a day, starting at nine o'clock in the morning and ending at ten o'clock at night. He also calls ten times a day and leaves me messages that I refuse to listen to. Meticulously, at the end of every day, right before I go to bed, I erase all of his voicemail messages. Without ever listening to even one of them.

Chapter 26

Phoebe's News

The lion part of March comes in the middle of the month, about a week after the last time I saw and spoke to Wyatt. The cold wind stings my face and the snow flurries don't seem pretty anymore, only annoying. During the freezing cold nights, we have to turn the heat on, even though it's almost March 21st, the vernal equinox, the first official calendar day of spring, also my birthday. After that, the days should start to get warmer, seeing as April will be right around the corner. The weather isn't spring-like yet, though, regardless of what the stupid groundhog did on February second.

I make my second cup of chamomile tea, to stave off the cold which has taken up permanent residence in my bones and in my heart. Not even the four-mile run I just got back from could warm me up. I take a deep sip of the tea, breathing in flower-scented steam. Someone knocks timidly on the backdoor. I get up from the kitchen table and go over to see who's there.

Phoebe's standing on the doorstep, shivering in the cold. Her eyes and nose look red, like she's been crying. I say the first thing that pops into my mind and out of my mouth. "Phoebe, why aren't you wearing your coat? It's freezing out."

She sobs and blurts out, "Annabelle, I'm pregnant."

Grabbing her arm, I drag her into the house. I wanted a sister, along with sisterly confidences, but I'm not sure I'm ready for this. I wish my mother was home, but maybe Phoebe wouldn't want her to know. My first impulse is to ask who the father is, but I don't want to pry. What the hell, though. She just told me something hugely personal. I can ask. "Who did this to you?"

Then she starts crying so hard she can't answer and I realize I should have phrased my question more carefully.

So I put my arm around her and coax her into the comfortable, overstuffed chair by the window. After I put the kettle on again, I grab a box of tissues and pull a chair over near hers, so we're sitting face-to-face. Except she's leaning back into the cushions, sniffling away and I'm perched on the edge of a hard wooden chair like I'm on the starting block, ready to run a race.

She blows her nose, looks up at me with glittering, red-rimmed eyes and says, "Nathaniel."

"My Nathaniel?"

Crap!

Wrong way to say it. Again. I'm the worst idiot ever. "I'm sorry. That came out wrong. I just meant that we're really close friends, that I introduced you two."

She laughs through her tears and reaches for another tissue. Another huge honk comes out of her perfect nose. Some of the implications that will arise out of this situation start to occur to me. She's a healer. He's a medium. What will their child be like? Holy shit! Probably like me, but worse. My mother has supernatural talent, but my father only has the ancestry, and look at me. I'm a freak of nature. Their kid will be way worse. Plus, they didn't seem like they even liked each other. Evidently, my impressions were wrong. I knew there was some kind of weird, intense attraction, but Phoebe and Nathaniel always acted like they were mad at each other.

"How did this happen?" As soon as the words leave my mouth I realize how stupid I sound. Again. The only good thing is it makes Phoebe laugh. I'm actually glad she finds my idiocy entertaining. I love this girl like a sister and I'll do anything to dry up those tears. "I didn't mean it that way. I know how it happens. But why didn't you two..." How can I put it? There's nothing to do but blurt it out. "Why didn't you use birth control?"

"Annabelle, sometimes even responsible, intelligent people surprise each other. We started kissing and we reached the point of no return so fast that we didn't think about birth control."

"There's a point of no return?"

"You've never been there?"

"No, I've been able to return from every point I've ever arrived at."

"So you've never?"

"Nope."

"Not even with Wyatt?"

"It was hard for us to find time to be alone together. It's a long, complicated story." I'm not about to explain to Phoebe that Anthony was always with us when we were together. Besides, this isn't about me and Wyatt. It's about Phoebe and Nathaniel.

"What did Nathaniel say when you told him about the baby?"

"He doesn't know."

"You haven't told him?" I can't believe it. This is bad. Phoebe can't keep this a secret from him. It's his baby, too.

"I don't know what to say to him. We're not really even in a relationship. It just kinda happened. He called me, a few days after the wedding. He was upset about his father. He needed someone to talk to and he chose me. Like a dumbass, I went running right over to his house."

"It was Nathaniel on the phone that night? The night that Katherine's ghost lured me out to the pond?"

"I know. I'm sorry. I told you I had to deliver the baby goats and I left you alone. You almost died."

"I really thought you rushed out because the mother goat went into labor early."

"No. Nathaniel called me. He asked me not to tell anyone. He was all alone and really upset so he called me and I went over to his house. We started talking. I sat down next to him on the couch, to put my arm around him. I thought he could use a hug. I was trying to comfort him, that's all, but what happened when we touched surprised us both. We felt the same uncontrollable feeling. Instantly; we were all over each other. He kissed me and whoa."

"What do you mean, 'whoa'?"

"Everything happened fast. I didn't think. I couldn't talk. The same thing happened to him."

I think about the first time Wyatt and I kissed. We were lying on a lounge chair in Carolyn Allen's backyard. We rolled off of it onto the wet grass and I didn't even notice. "I do know what that's like. It happened to Wyatt and me when we kissed for the first time. But we stopped. We didn't…"

"Well, Nathaniel and I did. No one else was home. He had a fire going in the fireplace. He wasn't sitting in his wheelchair. He was sitting on the couch, with his feet up."

"Yes, I can picture that." I have the sudden urge to drive over to Nathaniel's house and punch him in the eye.

Phoebe's oblivious, though; she keeps telling me what happened that night, while I was busy drowning in Deep Water Pond. "First we couldn't stop kissing. We were wrapped around each other and couldn't let go. And then we…"

"I get it. I know what you did. After all, you just told me you're pregnant. I may be an idiot but I'm not completely clueless."

"When I got up afterwards to leave, I had to look all over the room for my clothes. If there had been a chandelier in the room, my underwear probably would have been hanging from it."

This is way too much information, even coming from someone that I think of as a sister. Despite how hard I'm trying not to picture all of this, though, I'm intensely curious about kissing that gets completely out of control, underwear being flung up high and this point of no return that seems to exist at the center of it all.

Phoebe's face is all pink and red and she starts sniffling and crying again. "I think we were both really attracted to each other and had been holding back for a long time. A lot of pressure had built up."

Ya think? Duh!

Everyone who's ever seen Phoebe and Nathaniel together had that one figured out. I'm kind of relieved to find out that the two of them are even more stupid than I am. "What are you going to do, Phoebe?"

"There are no options except to have my baby. I already love him so much."

"Him? You know it's a boy?"

"Annabelle, I have abnormally amazing intuition. It's grown even more powerful because I'm pregnant. It's weird, though; my healing powers have pretty much disappeared. Being pregnant seems to have amped up my intuition but the baby is draining my healing powers."

I don't say it out loud but I'm thinking that the world doesn't need another super good-looking guy from the same gene pool as Wyatt, Nathaniel and their dad. It's like the three of them were put here on earth to wreak havoc with women's hearts. Now there'll be a fourth one and he'll be just like his father, his uncle and his grandfather. "I suppose adoption is out of the question."

"The baby needs to be raised by parents who'll understand his talents."

"Exactly, the baby needs to be raised by both of his parents, whether you two get together, or not. He'll need both of you. Let's go find Nathaniel so you can tell him about his son. He needs to know."

"Will you come with me? I don't want to face him alone. You've known him longer than I have." If she only knew the whole story. But I'll never tell her. There's no reason for Phoebe to know about my night at Nathaniel's with the fire and the soft couch and the even softer kiss. She'd only be hurt and Nathaniel's attraction to me evidently fled shortly after he acted on it for the first time. Good to know that I'm so easy to get over.

I make a calm and sensible suggestion. "Call his cell phone. Make sure he's home."

"I tried. He's not answering."

I want to say that he always answers, but I stop myself.

"Get in the car. We're going over there."

* * * *

Nathaniel's van is in the driveway when we pull up, so I know he's home. When we ring the bell, his mother opens the door. Jeff's standing right behind her, wagging his tail, happy to see Phoebe and me.

"Come on in, girls."

"We need to talk to Nathaniel." I get right to the point.

"He's not home. I don't expect him back for a while. Can I make you some tea?"

We walk inside and say no to the tea, but thank her. I ask, "Where did he go without Jeff? He never goes anywhere without him."

Nathaniel's mother bursts into tears. "I don't know. I can't really talk about it. I promised him. He just needs time to think."

Everyone's falling apart here. He doesn't even know about the baby yet. Why does he need time to think? It must be because of his father, James Flyte or James Silver, or whatever the hell he's decided to call himself.

"Mrs. Flyte, we need to find him. It's very important."

"Annabelle, you know I'd tell you if I could. I promised him I wouldn't tell anyone where he went. He just took off."

"He can't just take off without his van. How did he get away? You must have some idea. Did someone come and pick him up?"

Mrs. Flyte doesn't answer me. Instead she bursts into a fresh deluge of tears, accompanied by heaving sobs. I place a gentle and I hope comforting hand on her shoulder and shoot Phoebe a look that's supposed to mean *do something*.

Phoebe responds by walking over to the stove and putting the kettle on for tea. I open a couple of cabinets and find mugs and tea bags. Mrs. Flyte sits down, clutching a crumpled-up tissue in one hand and stares straight ahead, like a person who's been hypnotized.

Jeff starts whining.

"I've never heard him make that noise before."

"He's never made it before. He started after Nathaniel left, a week ago."

"He's been gone a week?" I can't believe it. He must have left shortly after I got out of the hospital. A lot has happened since then. I've been so preoccupied with the drama and madness between Wyatt and me, that I never even realized I hadn't heard from Nathaniel in at least a week. Usually we talk or text or get together pretty often.

"He left last Tuesday."

So it was a little over a week. Someone has to tell someone else the truth here. Phoebe doesn't seem to be in any hurry to confide in Nathaniel's mother, but we need to tell her, because maybe then she'll feel compelled to reveal Nathaniel's whereabouts. Unfortunately, it isn't my secret to tell.

After the water in the kettle starts to boil, Phoebe makes tea and we sit around the kitchen table and drink it. Everyone's silent for a few minutes. Finally Phoebe takes a large gulp of tea, swallows it and then speaks. "Mrs. Flyte, I'm pregnant with Nathaniel's child."

Mrs. Flyte jumps up and gives Phoebe a hug. "A baby! Honey, don't worry. It will all work out fine. We just have to find him so you can tell him." Poor Mrs. Flyte has had enough surprises to deal with recently, but she takes this one well. The woman's a champ.

Now we just have to find him. That's all. I thought his mother knew, but she doesn't seem entirely sure. Where the hell can he be? Why would he leave Jeff behind and how is he traveling if he doesn't have his van? Did someone come and get him? Is he alone?

"Do you have any idea where he went or who he's with? We tried his cell phone but it went right to voice mail."

"I know. I think he's off the grid."

"Off the grid!" Pregnancy must release a calming-down hormone in your body or something because I'm the one yelling and freaking out, not Phoebe.

She places a calming hand on my arm, signaling me to chill out. "Annabelle, it's all right. It's going to work out. Mrs. Flyte, where would he be if he's off the grid?"

"You should start looking for him at Winter Island."

I should have known. It makes sense. "C'mon, Phoebe. We're heading out there now."

"Jeremiah came to pick him up last week and I haven't heard from them since. Nathaniel told me he needed time; that he'd call me when he was ready to talk about everything that's been happening lately." Nathaniel's mom dashes out an address on a piece of paper and hands it to Phoebe. "Here, it'll probably take you over an hour to get out there. This is Aunt Maggie's address. She might know where he's headed."

"Thanks." Phoebe takes the paper from Mrs. Flyte's hand. "I've been there before, but Nathaniel drove, so the address isn't in my GPS."

Jeff starts whining again. Phoebe and I look at each other and then over at Nathaniel's mom.

"Go ahead, girls. Take the hound with you. If I opened the front door and set him free, he'd probably run all the way to Winter Island and find Nathaniel himself. If anyone can find him, it's Jeff."

Phoebe, Jeff and I go back to my house to get her SUV, which is parked in my driveway. The Prizm is old and we don't need a breakdown when we're heading north, even though I do have Triple A. I call my parents to tell them that Phoebe and I are going to check out Winter Island because I feel like visiting Salem. My mother sounds puzzled but she's used to me being impulsive and wanting to go on adventures. She warns me to be careful because we've had more than enough excitement lately, and we leave with Phoebe driving, me riding shotgun and Jeff in the back. We have the GPS plus Mrs. Flyte gave us pretty detailed directions. No one's leaving anything to chance.

For a pregnant lady, Phoebe sure speeds right along and we get there in an hour and ten minutes, even though we hit a little traffic along the way. When we stop at Aunt Maggie's house, she tells us that Nathaniel's at the campground, which is easy to find because the island's so small.

Campground? It's been freezing out lately! This is getting crazier by the second. Why the hell is a paraplegic, or anyone for that matter, camping out in this cold? The father of Phoebe's precious child must be completely insane.

When we get to the campground, huge surprise, nobody's there. The nights are very cold this time of year and especially windy because we're near the ocean, on the north shore. All of the campsites look empty.

Finally, we find a campsite with a Harley parked right outside what looks like a brand new tent. A few feet away from us, there's a guy who's bent over, picking up sticks so he can start his fire. There's a bunch of big logs resting next to the fire pit, but he probably needs something smaller to get the blaze going in the beginning.

Grabbing my arm so hard, she constricts the circulation; Phoebe suddenly goes all nervous on me. "Annabelle, ask that guy if he's seen Nathaniel. My knees are literally shaking. I'm so anxious. I can't walk even two steps."

I do the right thing and hop out of the car. Jeff's whining up a storm, so I figure he has to pee and I let him out to do his business. Barking his head off, he bolts over to the guy who's rummaging in the bushes for kindling. When the stranger straightens up, the crazy hound jumps up and puts his paws on the man's shoulders, practically knocking him over.

I run toward them, to try and control the dog. "Jeff! Stop! I'm sorry, sir."

The stranger turns to face me and it's Nathaniel. He's hugging Jeff and Jeff's licking his face all over and I just stand there like a complete fool. After a few seconds, the dog puts all four paws back on the ground, and Nathaniel strolls over to me as if he's been doing it for years. "Hi, Annabelle, what are you doing here?"

Phoebe then decides that now's a good time to get out of the car. She takes a few steps toward us. As soon as she's close enough to recognize Nathaniel, she runs into his arms, yelling, "You dumbass, why didn't you tell me?"

Nathaniel starts kissing her and won't stop, so she has no choice but to shut up.

Once again, I stand there like a complete tool. I feel weird watching them, but there's nothing else to do out here in the deserted campground. So I walk over to the car, lean against it, zip my coat up to my chin and try to keep from shivering too hard. Jeff joins me and I start scratching his head without looking at him. I'm unable to take my eyes away from the dramatic scene that's playing out just a few feet away from us. They keep kissing each other for what seems like an hour. Then Phoebe pushes Nathaniel away from her for a second. I can tell that she just broke the news about the baby because he picks her up in a giant bear hug and twirls her around. Evidently, Nathaniel's thrilled out of his mind that they're going to be a family.

Why am I here? I have no idea how to ride a motorcycle, but I need to leave these two alone. I can't take the SUV, because Phoebe can't ride home on the back of a Harley. She has to think about the baby and his safety. Plus, what about Jeff? He's obviously not going to leave Nathaniel's side without a fight and I'm not up to it. There's no way to fit a pregnant lady and a large dog on a motorcycle, even a big-ass Harley like Nathaniel's.

I decide to call the only person who I know will hop into his car and drive at top speed to come and get me. "Hi, Wyatt. It's Annabelle."

"I know. You haven't picked up any of my calls since the last time we talked. You haven't answered any of my texts. I've waited a long time for this. What changed your mind?"

"I need you."

"I need you, too, Annabelle."

"Please come get me."

"Where the hell are you?"

"Winter Island."

"Where the hell is that? And what the hell are you doing there?"

"Remember Phoebe? I think you met her at the wedding."

"Yes. The blonde girl."

"Well, I'm here at this campground with her and Nathaniel and I need a ride home. Now. As soon as possible."

"What are the three of you doing at a campground? It's freezing out."

"I know. It's a long story and I'd rather tell it to you in person. Put this into your GPS." I give him the name of the campground. "It's the only campground on a really small island near Salem. I'm standing here beside campsite number seven. Can you please leave now?"

"I can be there in less than an hour. Hang on."

"Don't speed. I can wait." I really can't wait, but I don't want him to get in an accident or get a ticket or something. He hangs up and Nathaniel and Phoebe walk over to me with their arms around each other. Apparently, they don't want to break physical contact for one second. They even have to move together. I can see it in their faces and read it in their body language. Plus I have super-duper intuition.

"Wyatt's coming to get me. So you two lovebirds can have some alone time."

Nathaniel smiles. He can't seem to stop smiling. "Good. You and Wyatt should be together. It's time to put the whole mess behind you, Annabelle. You can't stay mad at him forever."

"I wasn't just mad. I was really confused, too. Wyatt told me what happened that night, at the party. I can't believe you knew and wouldn't tell me."

"It wasn't my story to tell. Wyatt had to tell you himself."

"When he finally told me, I was furious. I still am."

"I know. I get it. But it's over. He loves you. He'll always love you. Nothing like that night will ever happen again."

"How can I be sure?"

"You can't. You're just going to have to take my word for it. And you're going to have to trust Wyatt. It will be worth it. I promise." He smiles down at Phoebe.

She just stands there, with both of her arms wrapped around his waist and his strong right arm over her shoulders. Ugh. These two are never going to let go of each other. Where the hell's Wyatt? I'm starting to wish that I didn't tell him not to speed.

"I guess there are benefits to making a baby with someone who's a healer." Nathaniel grins.

Phoebe's face reddens. "I had no idea. I can't believe this happened."

"No one knows except my mother. And of course, Aunt Maggie and Jeremiah," Nathaniel tells us.

"I had no idea," Phoebe repeats. She looks dazed but she's smiling.

"It explains why your healing powers are drained. You poured them all into me when you gave me your heart."

And her body.

I think this but don't say it out loud.

Nathaniel takes his arm off of her shoulder, pries her arms away from his waist and grabs her hand. Then he takes my hand in his other hand and pulls us both toward the fire circle. Jeff follows us. "Let's make a fire and sit down and talk until Wyatt gets here. Inside the tent I have some instant cocoa and a few pots and pans and some old tin mugs from Aunt Maggie's house."

The thought of sipping a sweet, hot drink by a warm fire improves my mood and having to wait around for Wyatt doesn't seem like such a terrible idea after all. Phoebe and I help Nathaniel pile up logs and sticks and we drag over a couple of big logs to sit on, so we can all be close to the fire, once we get it going. Nathaniel pours some bottled water into a pot and places it on the edge of the fast-growing fire so it will heat up.

After the cocoa is made, we stare into the now blazing logs and I love the feeling of having a warm toasty front and a chilly behind. Phoebe's cheeks are flushed pink with happiness and the heat from the fire. Nathaniel looks like he's stuck in the best dream ever and never wants to wake up from it. Finally he breaks out of his trance and makes an announcement.

"Annabelle, I went to the graveyard while you were in the helicopter, on your way to the hospital. I put the rocks back on her grave."

"So it was you?"

"Yes, when Phoebe left my house, I realized immediately that I could walk but I needed to think things over before I told anyone, even her. My father and Wyatt both called me late that night to tell me what had happened to you, Annabelle. So I knew your heart had stopped beating at least once. I was hoping that Katherine's evil spirit would think you were dead and she'd return to her final resting place because her work here on Earth was finished."

I'm very grateful that in the middle of his own incredible drama, Nathaniel went out to the graveyard to deal with my enemy. "And you knew that if she was at rest in her grave and you put the rocks back where they belonged, she'd have to stay."

"Yes. I drove over to Prospect Street in the van. It was very late at night, so I figured no one could see me. I got out of the van and walked quickly to the Littlefield's side of the cemetery. I knew Katherine would never return to her grave unless she thought you were dead. She had to think her mission here on Earth had been accomplished. I was hoping and praying you'd live, but while everything was touch-and-go, I rushed over there and piled the rocks back onto her grave. She was inside it, too. I could tell. She had returned to her grave because she thought her work was finished. She thought you were dead. If no one moves the rocks, her soul will stay buried under them forever."

My words are simple, but their meaning is profound. "Thank you."

"It's the least I could do. After all, you needed my help the night Katherine lured you out to Deep Water and I wasn't there for you."

"You couldn't have known. It's okay. Besides, if it all hadn't gone down the way it did, Katherine might still be at large right now."

"And instead, it's all behind us. Katherine can never come after you again."

"Yes, it's really over. With the Littlefield's permission, my dad built a small, concrete crypt over Katherine's grave and the stones."

"She'll never rise again."

"Colleen…"

Nathaniel interrupts before I can curse her. "She didn't know. She thought the Ouija board was a harmless game. She thought it was like telling the Bloody Mary story in front of a mirror. She didn't think anything would really happen. Colleen went out to the graveyard right before the blizzard, because she was desperate for Wyatt's attention."

"I think I'm desperate to punch her lights out." Phoebe sounds pissed.

Nathaniel continues to explain. "She and her friends were drinking and telling ghost stories. She knew a good one about her own family, so she told her girlfriends about the stones that kept Katherine's spirit buried. Then they decided to go out and move the rocks to see if anything would happen. They took the Ouija board with them and contacted Katherine. Colleen asked for Katherine's help with the whole Wyatt situation."

It's the same crazy story that I told Nathaniel, after Colleen told it to me in the bathroom at the Winter Ball.

Phoebe adds her opinion, "Holy shit. What a story!"

"That's how Katherine's murderous mission began. She did the same thing to Annabelle that she did to Rebecca. Katherine found a way to manipulate Annabelle into going out onto the ice and falling through. She used a child in distress. Except the night she killed Rebecca, she used a real child, Rebecca's son, Jonathan. The night she tried to kill Annabelle, she assumed the form and the voice of a child. Annabelle, Katherine Hayward used your own kind and caring nature to orchestrate your death. She made herself look and sound like little Samantha Silver and she lured you out onto Deep Water Pond."

Phoebe's pissed. I can tell by the way her cheeks turn even pinker than usual when she says, "Does Colleen realize what she did?"

"Nope. I contacted her, to tell her Annabelle was in the hospital. She still didn't say she was sorry or ask if Annabelle had fully recovered. She just wanted to know if Wyatt and Annabelle were together again. Her only regret seemed to be that her efforts failed to make Wyatt fall in love with her."

"Bitch." Phoebe says what I'm thinking. Colleen will never be on my list of people I'd like to be friends with. On the other hand, though, I feel sorry for her because she ended up becoming one of Jake Stone's victims. Even if she still probably thinks she was with Wyatt. No one deserves that.

Nathaniel continues to explain. "The rocks are only symbols. It was Colleen's selfish intentions that really freed Katherine Hayward's evil soul. Whether the rocks were in place or not doesn't matter all that much."

"But it's better to have them there, on top of Katherine's grave. Isn't it? I feel safer knowing they're there."

"Then it's best that they're kept in place, yes. But the real reason Katherine was able to rise from the dead and come after you is that Colleen unintentionally resurrected the same cast of characters from Katherine's original murder."

"I'm confused."

"Colleen's a Littlefield, like Katherine was. And she was not motivated by true love, but by jealousy and possessiveness, just like Katherine. Wyatt's descended from both Rebecca Burns and Lieutenant Elias Hayward. The time of year was the same, the location was the same."

I'm finally starting to get it. "Even the baby she conjured up. I thought the phantom child I was saving was Samantha and she's descended from Jonathan Burns. And he was the baby Katherine used to lure Rebecca out onto the ice, almost a hundred and fifty years ago."

"It's like the perfect supernatural storm."

"Except I survived it and Rebecca didn't."

"In a way she did survive the second time around. Her spirit survived because now we all know she didn't commit suicide and she was the real mother of Elias Hayward's son Jonathan."

"Also known as Jack Burns," I add.

"Buried here on Winter Island, in the Burns' family plot."

"Not in Eastfield with the Haywards." No matter how many different ways Nathaniel explains it, the story's preposterous. But I'm getting used to preposterous. Nathaniel and Phoebe have lived with the knowledge of their own paranormal gifts longer than I have so the whole story seems more logical to them.

"That's right. I'm directly descended from Jack Burns. I visited his grave yesterday."

"Now they can all rest in peace because everyone knows the truth," Phoebe adds and we all smile.

"Nathaniel, let me get this straight. From the night I was rushed to the hospital, up until you left for Winter Island, you pretended to still need the wheelchair." I know what it's like to try to pretend that you're more disabled than you truly are, but not like Nathaniel. His experience is extreme.

He turns to look at Phoebe. "Sorry. I didn't know what to do or how to feel. I needed time to think. I'm so sorry, Pheebs."

"It's okay. You can make it up to me."

"I'll be working on that project forever, for the rest of my life and loving every second of it." They're sitting side-by-side on the same log and Nathaniel has his arm around her. He gives her a one-armed hug. She grins and moves her gaze away from the fire for a moment, so she can stare into his eyes.

Okay, Wyatt better get here soon.

I'm starting to feel like the odd man out, again, because I am.

Thankfully, he arrives in record time. When he sees Nathaniel stand up to greet him, Wyatt looks from me, to Phoebe and then back at his brother again. "What the hell?"

As delicately as possible, Phoebe begins the story by explaining her healing talents. Nathaniel chimes in part way through. "Phoebe and I did something irresponsible one night. We were alone together and everything progressed faster than we'd planned." He pauses to rub his face with both hands, as if he could rub away the embarrassment he's feeling because he's explaining something intensely private and personal. "It turns out that she's an even more powerful healer than she thought. Than anyone thought. It's a miracle."

"So you two?" Wyatt points from Phoebe to Nathaniel and lets out a short, loud burst of laughter.

"Yup." Nathaniel smiles, puts his arm around Phoebe's waist and pulls her up against his side.

"And now you can walk?" He stares, wide-eyed, at his brother.

"I know, it's hard to believe. I didn't tell Phoebe or anyone that I could walk. I pretended to still need the wheelchair. Only my mother knew. I needed time to adjust."

"But his time's up now, because we're going to have a baby." Phoebe's face is ten shades pinker than usual, from the cold and maybe from embarrassment, too. After all, the four of us are standing around the fire discussing hers and Nathaniel's sex-life, basically.

Wyatt turns to face Nathaniel, throws his arms around him, and hugs him so hard that his brother's feet lift six inches off the ground.

Finally, Wyatt puts Nathaniel down and I can't stop staring at them. It's an incredibly beautiful sight; the two of them standing side-by-side. Wyatt looks a little like their father, but more like Oliver and the Finn side of the family. Nathaniel looks a little like his mother and more like their Burns' ancestors from Winter Island. And yet, now that I know the connection exists, when they're together I can see a strong resemblance between them. Their smiles are similar and their faces are different but equally beautiful. Wyatt's two inches taller than Nathaniel who's around six feet. I never realized how tall Nathaniel was before, because he was always sitting down.

"So I recently found out I have a brother and tonight I've discovered I'm going to be an uncle. Wow." Wyatt hugs Phoebe, but a lot more gently than he hugged Nathaniel. After all, she's pregnant. We need to be careful of her.

Then he hugs Nathaniel again. "Congratulations! I know you'll make a much better father than ours."

Nathaniel laughs. "Not a tough contest to win, bro. Dear old dad and I had a long talk, right before I left for Winter Island. He told me how he left my mother and me because he couldn't deal with his supernatural talents. He's a medium, too, Wyatt. We inherited it from him."

"Son of a gun." Wyatt shakes his head.

"He felt confused and because he's basically a selfish douche, he left his wife and young son, changed his name and then met your mother. He was attracted to her because she's so skeptical. She'd never admit that our supernatural talents could even exist. He thought he could ignore that side of his nature because your mother didn't believe in it. At the time, he felt like Rowena Finn was perfect for him."

Wyatt adds, "Then my supernatural talents began to emerge and it freaked him out so he left again."

"He's an ass. But I think his running and hiding days are over."

"So he's going to stay in Eastfield?"

"He wants to raise Samantha here, with her brothers close by. He's growing more comfortable with his gift and the fact that both of his sons have inherited it. He wants to stick around and try to establish a relationship with us. I think I'll give him a chance. I want my baby to know his grandfather."

"And now he'll have a grandchild who's only a couple of years younger than his daughter." Wyatt laughs.

"Hey, families are complicated. I figure if my mother can forgive him maybe I can. Maybe you can, too, Wyatt. One day you might have a decent relationship with him."

"Okay, but I doubt it."

"Give him a chance. He helped save Annabelle's life. He was the first responder."

"Then I guess he can't be all bad." Wyatt grabs my hand and squeezes it.

Wyatt and I only stay for another half hour or so, because Nathaniel and Phoebe obviously want to be alone.

On the ride home, Wyatt brings up the subject first. "I'm hoping we can get back together now, Annabelle."

"I think we should try being friends for a while."

"Okay, if that's what you really want." Wyatt's holding the steering wheel firmly in the three o'clock position and staring straight ahead, at the road in front of us. "Maybe we can go for a run together, or do something else friends do, like watch TV. Or play Scrabble."

He pauses. There's something in the set of his shoulders that I can't quite interpret: disappointment maybe.

Then Wyatt looks away from the road for a second, glances at me and adds, "Or we could bake cookies. That might be fun."

Baking cookies would be fun, but Wyatt's voice doesn't sound happy. This puzzles me. I keep staring at his profile, trying to figure out why his voice sounds so weird.

Then he whips his head around and viciously aims another idea my way, like he's one of those dinosaurs who spits venom. "A slumber party."

And finally I get it. He's mad. And he's done with struggling for self-control.

"A pillow fight. That might be a fun activity for a couple of friends like us." He sounds like he'd like to smother me with a pillow, not participate in a playful scuffle.

He's furious! I can see why people say "white-knuckled" because his hands have turned as red as his face and in contrast, the white skin stretched tight across his knuckles is very pronounced. He's gripping the steering wheel hard, like he wants to rip it from the column and whack me over the head with it.

I try to lighten the mood by laughing; as if he's making a joke. But even to me, my laughter sounds really fake.

This seems to make him even madder. He swerves so fast that the tires squeal as he whips the car into a deserted rest area and pulls up right next to three Porta Potties. Good thing the windows are closed, so we can't smell them. Nothing worse than the odor of rest area portable latrines.

Wyatt's not thinking about the Porta Potties, though. He jerks the car into park, fumbles with the seatbelt and barks out a swear. When he finally frees himself from its restraint, he whips his body sideways and faces me. Thunder and lightning roll into his ever-changing eyes.

"It's not funny! You're torturing me, Annabelle." He leans in closer, staring me down, like he's daring me to laugh again.

I smirk at him, give his shoulder a push and scrunch my back up against the door. Balancing his right arm against the back of my seat, he frees my seat belt with his left. This time there's no fumbling. It clanks open in an instant. Then he lunges at me, shoving his face down close to mine. His lips are hovering inches above my gaping mouth. I battle the urge to cower, scrunch my eyes closed and cringe away from him. Instead I stare him down, teeth clenched, chin up, gaze fierce. If he were a bull, steam would be flooding out of his nostrils and his ears. But he's not a raging animal, he's just a man and sometimes still a boy.

Collapsing back against his own seat, he exhales forcefully and the air goes out of his anger. With nothing but my brave little face, I have deflated a six-foot-three, rabid monster.

"Okay. I know, Annabelle. I've earned every bit of torture you can dish out and more. I was stupid and weak and I let my self-control slip, only that one night, but that was enough. Enough to ruin everything between us."

"It *is* ruined, Wyatt. I can never trust you again"

"But the thing is, Annabelle, you *can* trust me. Because I belong to you and only you. Body and soul. Forever."

"Strong words. And, you have a weird way of proving it. By cheating on me."

"I know. I know. I know," he says, shaking his head back and forth every time he sorrowfully repeats this phrase. Then he closes his eyes and slams his head back against the padding of the seat. "I'm sorry. I've never been more sorry about anything in my whole life. God, I wish I could take back my stupid actions! Travel backwards in time and stop myself."

"But you can't. We both have to live with the consequences of your actions, Wyatt."

"I can't live like this. I've been trying to, Annabelle. And I can't. I need to win you back. I need to prove that I deserve your love. Even though I truly believe that my actions that night have made me…" He pauses as if the words are stuck in his throat. Then he looks at me with a deep blue reservoir of humility in his eyes and finishes, "unworthy of you."

It sounds so medieval when he phrases it like that. I offer up a weak smile, no sarcasm, no humor at all, only a hint of pure forgiveness. My face feels foreign, like I don't own it. Why am I giving in? I swore to myself I never would. I promised. I vowed. I lay awake on more nights than I can count. Sentencing myself to a life of eternal loneliness. Embracing regret like a rock climber embraces the cliff face.

He continues. "I promised myself I'd stay away from you because you should be with someone who isn't like me. Someone who won't be plagued by dead people throughout his whole life. I thought you'd be better off with someone ordinary. I wanted to spare you. To deliver you from all the weirdness, sorrow and fear I have to live with everyday. I've been through hell trying to keep that promise. And I can't do it. I know I broke your heart. But let me put the pieces back together again. Please give me a chance."

I'm not fully convinced yet, but I'm softening. When I look at the tortured posture of Wyatt's powerful body, now slumped over in defeat, I realize I can't hold out much longer.

"Over the past few months, two spirits have stolen possession of my body. First Anthony and then Jake Stone. It's terrifying. But when you and I are together, I can bear it."

"Wyatt, it terrifies me, too."

"I'll never learn to control it if I don't have you. Annabelle, there is a forever part of me. And whether it's inhabiting my body or not, it belongs to you. It always has, since before either of us was born into this world. And it always will, long after our physical bodies have turned to ashes. You're mine and I'm yours. Completely. I can never truly belong to anyone else and neither can you."

Then he pulls me into his arms and kisses me like he's suffocating to death and somewhere inside of me he'll find the oxygen he needs to stay alive. Climbing onto the passenger's seat, he pins my body beneath him and crushes his lips against mine. I wrench my mouth away from his to gasp for air. And he shifts sideways, mumbling a wordless apology. I answer him by fastening my mouth onto his and wrapping myself around him until we're one body with four arms and four legs, all coiled and intertwined together. He responds by unleashing all the adrenaline he's been fighting to hold in check for the past few minutes. I can feel it in the strength of his arms around me and the hardness of his thigh muscles against mine.

Wyatt's kiss invades my soul and shows me what he had so passionately explained moments before: He needs to be with me forever, just like he said, body and soul. And, as I press myself against him, he finally understands what I've been hiding for months now: I think about him every second of every day. I have since the first time I ever saw him. And I'll never stop.

As we writhe together in this confined space, I can feel his life force pushing against mine, striving to enter those private places where no one has ever been before. And for the first time, I touch him. There. Where I've never touched a boy before. I have to squish my hand down in between us to do it, but I manage. And even through several layers of clothing, I can feel the urgency of his desire. He groans and starts tugging blindly at the waist of my jeans. The flat of my other hand slides up, under the back of his shirt. The friction from this stroke further ignites his blazing flesh beneath my palm. And now I know what it's like to reach the point of no return.

Thank god it's so cold outside. If it were summer and we had less clothing to rip off each other, we'd probably be naked and oblivious to our surroundings right now. But as soon as we start reaching for zippers and buttons in order to remove the first of multiple layers, I look out the window and realize I'm in the front seat of a Land Rover parked next to a Porta Potty. The reality of losing it here in this vehicle, parked where it is hits me. And I stop. Wyatt stops, too. With his lips still only an inch away from mine he breaks the silence of this crazy moment. "Friends, my ass, Annabelle."

Then we catch our breath for a minute and get back to it, but now it's more like affection, all sweet and gentle and romantic. Or as romantic as you can get anyway, when you're three feet away from a portable outhouse. We're still making out. And holding each other. But in between kisses we're talking, too.

"I suppose driving to the nearest motel and getting a room is out of the question?" Wyatt bumps his forehead against mine and smiles.

"I need more time. Everything got away from me for a minute there."

"When do you think 'everything will get away from'

you again? Because I don't think I'm going to be very good at waiting for that special moment."

"I don't know, Wyatt. But it's inevitable. Does that help?"

He adjusts the waist of his jeans with his free hand, the one that isn't caressing my shoulder. "Only if inevitable means that within the next few seconds you're going to jump on me again."

"I didn't jump on you! *You* jumped on me!"

Laughing out loud, he pulls his arm out from around me and throws himself back into his own seat, giggling like a fool. He's losing it. So much so that he can barely speak but he manages to squeeze out, through his hysteria, "You're right."

"Thank you." I don't see what's so funny, but he can't stop laughing.

He swipes a tear off his cheek and sputters, "You didn't jump on me. You grabbed me."

If we weren't almost fifty miles away from Eastfield, I would leap right out of the car and start walking home. I feel that mortified. But Wyatt saves the day by regaining some of his composure.

"I'm sorry, Annabelle, but that move was so out of character. You're just so innocent. And I want you more than I've ever wanted anything before in my life. I can either laugh about it or explode. I'll let you decide."

I'm still too embarrassed to answer him.

"It was such a bold move. Especially coming from you."

Finally I find my voice. "Can we not talk about it,

please."

"Yes, my lady, I will honor your request."

"Thank you."

"As long as you promise to let me know when you're ready to talk about it. Like, the very second you're ready to discuss it. You'll call me. No matter where you are. Please."

"I promise."

"Then my lips are sealed."

"Good. Let's leave. Those latrines are freaking me out."

"What latrines?" And he starts laughing again, but not so hysterically this time.

I punch him in the arm and he chuckles and starts the car.

On the drive home, we talk about Phoebe and Nathaniel and the baby. About his father and his little sister, and how we both think she's the cutest, funniest little thing ever. When we get to my house, he walks me to the door and kisses me quickly, once on the forehead and once on the lips, while he holds my shoulders in his big, gentle hands. Then we whisper our goodbyes and he walks away.

Later, curled up in my bed, under the covers, I fall asleep thinking about how I could feel the shape of a smile on his lips when he kissed me goodnight.

Chapter 27

The Last Chapter

Wyatt and I have visited a place that most people will never see because they don't even know it exists. We're members of a very select, exclusive group of people. We live with one foot in this world and one in the next; seeing and hearing things most people can only imagine. Phenomena that can't be sensed with the ordinary five senses. These marvels can only be discerned with a sixth sense and not everyone has it. But Wyatt and I do.

Today we're sitting side-by-side, close together, on a bench Wyatt and Nathaniel and their father built, with my dad's help. The bench is on the shore of Deep Water Pond; near the spot where I stood right before I ran onto the ice to save the baby I thought was Samantha. Close to where Rebecca probably stood the night she ran out of her cabin and onto the fragile ice over a hundred and fifty years ago. We now know that she didn't intend to kill herself. She was trying to save her son.

On the back of the bench, Nathaniel painted these words:

In memory of Rebecca Burns Morse, beloved wife, devoted mother, gifted healer. Rest in Peace, Sweet Angel.1847-1867

The colors they painted the bench blend in with the perennial herb garden flourishing behind it. The huge field of beautiful flowers is in full bloom. My mother and Nathaniel's mother restored what was left of Rebecca's perennials and planted some new flowers and herbs, too. They transplanted a lot of stuff from my mom's garden. And I helped them with the weeding and digging. I wasn't allowed to help paint the bench, though, because I'm too impulsive and sloppy. Gardening requires a lot less precision.

James Silver, his wife and his baby have moved out of the cottage and into a condominium on the Eastfield, Freewater border. They plan to spend summers here, though, after Samantha learns to swim. But they're too paranoid about drowning right now. And that's a good thing. Sammie's excited about becoming an aunt. That's sarcasm. She's only two and has no idea. But her oldest brother is twenty-five and he's really excited about becoming a dad.

Nathaniel married Phoebe. They eloped right after they returned from their impromptu camping trip on Winter Island and for now they're living with Nathaniel's mother.

She'll help with daycare after the baby's born, so Nathaniel can go back and finish college and Phoebe can continue with her job as a veterinarian. Because her healing powers haven't returned yet, she's just like any other vet. She poured all of her incredible desire to heal into Nathaniel's body on that fateful night when they passed the point of no return together.

Nathaniel's going back to school in the fall, to complete his EMT training. The official story about his recovery is that a colleague of Dr. Aleister Knight's, big shot Boston physician, performed some kind of controversial, cutting-edge surgery and it worked. Obviously, duh. Nathaniel supposedly underwent the surgery and recuperation at a very exclusive, private, South American clinic owned by Dr. Knight. All this reputedly happened during the time when Nathaniel was really camping out in the wilds of Winter Island.

He often accompanies me on my runs now and it's a challenge for me to keep up with him. Recently, he beat me to the top of a hill and struck the Rocky pose, like Sylvester Stallone did in the movie, when he got to the top of all those stairs in Philadelphia. Both fists raised high in triumph. Even though we laughed, because it was a funny moment for Nathaniel and me, I cried a little, too.

The baby's due in early December. They're going to name him Jonathan Walker Flyte and call him "Jack" for short.

Wyatt is looking forward to meeting his nephew. Both of us have been spending a lot of time with his little sister, Samantha, and we adore her. After years and years of tragedies and loneliness, the Hayward/Burns/Flyte/Silver family is finally together. Wyatt and I talk about all of this often, but only when we're alone or with family. Never when we're with our friends, because this incredible story is better off kept secret.

It's now two o'clock in the afternoon on the first day of summer vacation. Wyatt and I are rarely alone together because I decided we should put the brakes on our physical relationship after what almost happened in the front seat of Wyatt's car that time. I'm not ready to travel past the point of no return. Not yet. It's an important step in any relationship and I need to feel more emotionally close to Wyatt. We both need to act more mature and learn to trust each other. And that will take some time. There's been way too much drama in our lives and Wyatt and I need to recover from all the hurt and the danger and the outright weirdness surrounding everything that's happened to us over the past few months. We need to grow up together and do ordinary stuff like sit on a bench and talk about our lives and our future, surrounded by beautiful, fragrant wildflowers on an incredible just-right, warm sunny day.

Wyatt lowers his face until he's staring into my eyes and then kisses me with a deepness I can feel in the other world where we both go sometimes. I wrap my arms around his neck. When he moves his lips away from mine, he stays nose to nose with me and whispers, "Promise me we'll never break up again."

I promise him that and more.